THE SWEETHEART DEAL

Books by Robert Rosenblum

THE MUSHROOM CAVE
GOOD THIEF
THE SWEETHEART DEAL

The Sweetheart Deal

by Robert Rosenblum

G. P. Putnam's Sons
New York

All rights reserved. This book, or parts thereof, must not
be reproduced in any form without permission.
Published simultaneously in Canada
by Longman Canada Limited, Toronto.

SBN: 399-11727-X

Library of Congress Cataloging in Publication Data

Rosenblum, Robert J
  The sweetheart deal.
  I. Title.
PZ4.R8116Sw   [PS3568.0795]   813'.5'4   75-34329

PRINTED IN THE UNITED STATES OF AMERICA

*To Philip Solomon,
a believer*

ONE

If Wyatt Earp could only see this, Lindell mused as he entered the Washington headquarters of the U.S. Marshal Service. The domain of two-fisted lawmen had come a long way from their shoe-box lockups in the wide-open towns of the wild west. Carpeted floors, chrome furniture, muted lighting, and the pert brunette receptionist in the Paris copy, guarding Marshal Gabriel Konecki's outer office. Her smile asked all the questions.

"Lou Lindell," he announced. "An appointment was made for me by—"

"I know, Mr. Lindell, go right in. The marshal is waiting for you."

The marshal. That much of the old flavor remained anyway: a word.

The men hadn't changed either, Lindell thought as he came into the office. Konecki had the sort of craggy face that could have been molded in the rough-and-tumble of constant saloon brawls. Even the shock of graying brown hair dangling over his forehead might have been jarred out of place only moments ago by a badman's punch. The broad shoulders and barrel chest projecting above the desktop suggested that Marshal Konecki would not have been unequal to the rigors of law-keeping in the fabled West of Tombstone and Dodge City and showdowns with Billy the Kid.

But it was all a fantasy. This was the twentieth century, a whole new unbrave world of good and bad. There were no quick-draw duels. Men could get shot in the back from half a mile away; or from right up close—when they drew out their hands, empty, for no more than innocent handshake.

And the marshals? They wore business suits and dark ties

and fought crime with a Dictaphone. How much, Lindell thought hopelessly, could Marshal Gabriel Konecki do against the new breed of desperadoes?

"Take a seat, Lindell," Konecki said, gesturing across his desk without looking up from the sheet of paper in his hands. He finished reading. Then, raising his brown eyes to fix Lindell in a hard, penetrating stare, he pushed the paper over to Lindell. "Memo from the AG. You'd better read it, too."

The manner and tone of Konecki's reception, cool and challenging, irritated Lindell. The memo was being presented to him as if it were a bill of indictment against which he must defend himself. He picked it up slowly, and read:

OFFICE OF THE ATTORNEY GENERAL OF THE UNITED STATES

To: Marshal G. Konecki,
Controller Federal Witness Security Program.

Re: Louis R. Lindell

At the personal recommendation of Senator Thomas Ryle, Lindell has approached this office for advice and assistance in a matter that may be of the highest importance in our efforts to combat organized crime on the national level. As a former counsel to the Senate committee which investigated aspects of that subject under the chairmanship of Senator Ryle, Lindell deserves our fullest attention. Initial discussion with him has indicated that the Witness Security Program must now be brought into the picture if we are to proceed further with Lindell on the basis that his information would suggest.

However, it must be emphasized that pending your assessment of Lindell's information and personal motives, no further steps can or should be taken.

Lindell lingered over the final directive. It was a challenge, after all. He would have to prove himself before they would lift a finger to help. Until then he would be under suspicion, his own motives in question.

A momentary surge of rebellious anger crackled through him. He had volunteered to give information which had come to him unsolicited, and to offer his services as a concerned citizen—and right away they had to look for fleas on *his* hide. Still in wearying shock from the corruption it had found within itself, the government seemed to have succumbed to a kind of paranoia. Nothing, no one, was trusted. Once again, as he had been several times in the past few days, Lindell was tempted to walk out and leave them to stew in their paralyzing suspicion.

But he fought down the impulse. Could he fault them for their caution? In his days with the Senate committee he had learned that the underworld organization could get its hooks into any man who came too close. Any man. And he had certainly been close, even if he had stayed on the other side of the fence.

He tossed down the memo. "All right, what do you want me to do? Take a polygraph? They used to be very popular around here."

Konecki chuckled amicably. He leaned back in his chair and put one foot up on the edge of the desk: no boot, no spur, just a plain brown oxford. "You never know; we might come to that. But let's start out the plain old-fashioned way. You talk, and I'll see if any red lights flash in my head."

"I've given all the details to the AG," Lindell protested. "Didn't you get a report along with that memo?"

"Sure did. But suppose you tell it again."

Again. What was this, the fifth time?

Lindell gave a forbearing sigh and began: "As far as facts go, there's not all that much to tell. Since leaving my government post, I've been a partner in a good New York law firm, Beller, Rudge, Cabell, and Parkes. Twelve days ago I was in my office and the phone rang. The man on the line said he was calling me because of the work I'd done with the Ryle committee; he figured that had prepared me to appreciate the offer he wanted to make. He went on to describe himself as a member of a crime family active in every department of the rackets: numbers, sharking, stock fraud, drug importing, the whole candy store. He didn't give any names, but he said I'd have no trouble recognizing his or the family's. Obvious-

9

ly, he was no rank-and-file hood, but a holder of some power. I asked him if he had appeared before the committee, but he denied it. I'm sure that was a lie, to keep me from thinking too hard about who he was. We had most of the big ones, and when this guy got to the main reason for his call to me, it was clear that he's very big. He said that his position had allowed him to accumulate a huge amount of information that would be invaluable to federal law enforcement agencies. To use his words: '. . . enough to put half of the biggest men away for as long as twenty years.' I remember that exactly because it was such an astounding claim it stuck in my mind. Then he gave me a sketchy idea of what he wanted in exchange. A big price—as big as the delivery deserved, he said, but he wouldn't define it in numbers. The purpose of the first call was only to let the government know that someone like him existed, and send someone—me—to sound out its general interest on meeting his terms: the money, lifetime protection, and a guarantee of immunity. He said he'd give me a month to get the feedback, then he'd call again for a report." Lindell turned up his hands. "That's the story."

Konecki rocked in his chair. "Uh-huh," he commented lackadaisically, "so you're here to hand us the biggest breakthrough in crime control this country has ever seen."

"Could be," Lindell agreed, trying to ignore Konecki's mocking tone. "And it's taken me twelve fucking days to get a decent hearing—that's assuming this qualifies."

Konecki squinted critically at Lindell in a way that made him feel like a target at the end of a Colt Peacemaker. "Twelve days," Konecki muttered. "Today's the twenty-second of the month. So you're saying the call came into your office on the tenth."

"Right."

The marshal's eyes snapped open as if he had fired off a shot, a bull's-eye. "The tenth was a Sunday, Lindell. What were you doing at the office on a Sunday?"

Lindell nodded approvingly. No one had caught him on that point before, but it was not without its significance. "I had a court appearance on Monday. I wanted to use the office files to do a last-minute polish on my brief."

"Which means, unfortunately, that you were alone there.

10

The call didn't come through the switchboard. So there were no witnesses to your end of the conversation."

"And none at the other," Lindell amended. "The call came from a booth."

"How would you know that?"

"Mr. X stayed on the phone long enough for me to hear a couple of extra coins getting popped into the slot."

"Sounds like you had a lot to say to each other," Konecki remarked. "But what you've told me so far doesn't add up to nearly a dime's worth."

Lindell gave a tired shrug. "I guess I have taken to giving facts in shorthand. Frankly, I'm pretty fed up with telling the story. For almost two weeks I've been shuffling around this goddamn town looking for a sympathetic ear. Right after the call I tried contacting my old boss, Tom Ryle. He was off on some senatorial fact-finding spree in Thailand, so I had to settle for telling his executive aide, Dick Jenner. Jenner kindly passed me over to some junior boy scout at Justice, who boosted me half a rung up the ladder to another assistant bottle-washer. By then I was ready to drop the whole thing. I've had a bellyful of crime-fighting, if you want to know the truth. When I was here in Washington, on the committee, it was such a pitiful farce. We couldn't make a move without having it counteracted—you know by who." Lindell pointed up. "Sure, we made a little headway here and there, got the Organized Crime Act on the books. But it was token stuff. We were always bucking the current. We'd be looking into Mob connections to labor; then I'd pick up my paper in the morning and discover that Hoffa had been let out of jail on a deal, or some mobbo the Justice boys had sweated for years to drag through the courts and put in the slam had received similar presidential favors. It was soul-destroying to be playing those games, working your guts out and then being undermined from the top."

"Overmined, you might say." Konecki's gentle jibe seemed intended to establish his sympathy with Lindell, a hint of shared experience.

"Call it whatever you want," Lindell snapped, still tense, reliving the frustration. Then he paused to let the fires burn down. Why go over it? Why even take up the crusade again?

11

Would it be any better this time? He resumed quietly: "I was hoping things had changed in the last year. But getting kicked around like a football the past few days has given me a different picture. I don't know why I'm still here, butting my head against the wall. Everyone's learned to live so happily with the Mob, why should I break up the marriage? I was all set to leave town, as a matter of fact, when Tom Ryle got back. It seemed to call for one last try. It was only by going to him and putting this on a personal basis that I finally got to the AG."

"That's the way it works around here, all right. Scratch a pal's back or you'll sit around and scratch your ass forever."

And it would never change, Lindell reflected on Konecki's axiom. Perhaps there were better reasons for pulling the strings this year than there had been for a long time, but influence was still the name of the game. How much you got done depended entirely on who your friends were, how many and how high up. It was a basic corruption that could never be rooted out of the system; there were just too many problems clamoring for the attention of too few effective people.

"The trouble is," Lindell went on, "having used a little juice to get myself heard in the right places, I'm reduced to being just one more lobbyist. Everybody wonders what my stake is, what's my piece of the action, why should I be trying so hard?"

"Which hurts your feelings," Konecki put in, "since you're simply an upright concerned citizen."

"Believe it or not, the species is not extinct." Lindell's words came slowly, ticks in the time fuse of his temper.

Konecki cocked his head, lining up his sights once more from a new angle. Then he lowered his foot and sat forward. "Okay, Lindell, simmer down. I think you've got a story worth hearing, and without any shortcuts. But you can't blame us for going slowly. There are some very unusual features to this situation. We've had informers before, but never anyone who offered a cash-and-carry cleanup of the whole Mob."

"He only promised half," Lindell reminded the marshal.

"Half the top men. I heard you the first time. But that's

12

enough, potentially, to throw the whole organization into chaos. Wherever a top spot falls vacant, they'll start fighting for it. And don't forget any one of the men that Mr. X hands over might also start pleading for immunity, squealing on his brothers. You see, Lindell, we've got a metaphysical proposition here, where a half might actually turn into a whole."

Konecki had pulled open the drawer in front of him. He reached in and pulled out a couple of pages stapled together. He flipped through them in less than ten seconds and set them down. On the top sheet Lindy saw the Attorney General's engraved seal of office.

"Not much in there you haven't covered," Konecki said. "So what the hell did keep you tied up on the phone with this stoolie?"

"Well, he didn't just give me a set speech," Lindell said offhandedly. "There was a certain amount of back and forth. I did what I could to satisfy myself he was genuine. I asked questions. You know, plenty of these guys came up before me at the hearings. I'm not without experience at drawing them out."

"You certainly drew this one out brilliantly. He didn't give you a single name or fact. Didn't give the least hint about the nature of his information. Didn't tell you how much money he wants." Konecki shook his head in mock admiration. "What more could he give you—except the Fifth Amendment."

This time Lindell didn't take offense. He was getting used to Konecki's sarcasm. Perhaps it was this ability to make light of circumstances, to take himself and the vaunted "war against crime" with a grain of salt, that had enabled Konecki to go on working at it long after others had given up in despair. He might have lasted longer himself, Lindell thought, if he had been less of an idealist. For fifty years the government had been trying to bring crime under control and it had only become more virulent, more lucrative, better organized, and more damaging to the national welfare. How could you go on thinking there was hope, unless you had a sense of humor, a healthy cynicism?

Lindell laughed. "I guess I didn't get too much out of him at that." He hesitated. "I'll tell you why we talked for so long:

13

I spent most of the time trying to argue the guy out of involving me."

"Good Citizen Lindell!" Konecki cracked.

"I had an intuition about the kind of ball-busting reception I'd get down here. I explained to him, too, how it would be impossible to get any guarantees on the nothing stuff he was handing out. I kept telling him to go to the FBI, leave me out of it. But he wouldn't, he didn't want the Bureau involved at, all. They could use the information, of course, but he didn't want any contact with them."

"Why not?'

"Why do you think? He's a bigot—prejudiced against the hounds that have snapped at his ass all his life. Or maybe he's afraid of a leak. He will be going way out on a limb, after all."

"A leak in the Bureau?" Konecki murmured, more to himself.

"I'm not saying he knows any particular soft spot. He's just not taking any chances. It was a specific condition of his offer that I'd continue to be the intermediary, and involve as few people as possible."

"And what's the secret of your charm?"

"Just what Mr. X said in his intro. My work on the committee familiarized me with his potential value, and left me with some good contacts in Washington. I'm sure this hood figured I'd head straight for my old boss, and Ryle would fall over for the deal. Old Tom's touring road show may have been five years ago, but the Mob still thinks of him as their biggest congressional nemesis, the third in the holy trinity of Kefauver and Bobby K."

"One thing's for sure, anyway," said Konecki. "Giving you the nod was no spur-of-the-moment decision. Our man has been keeping a watch, looking for a chance to catch you when there were no extra ears around; otherwise, he couldn't have known to call you at the office on a Sunday. You," Konecki added pointedly, "are evidently the one man he trusts in a very hostile world."

There was a pause. Konecki leaned back and eyed Lindell expectantly.

"Sure," Lindell said at last, "I know how it looks. I'm the mouthpiece. I'm down here on a cute little fishing expedi-

14

tion, fronting a setup to use the feds to settle some internal Mob vendetta, maybe earn a few bucks into the bargain. Does that about sum it up? Isn't that why nobody jumps to shake my hand when I walk in?"

Konecki looked like a pitcher trying to decide between a fast ball and a curve. He chose a combination of the two. "It could be something like that. Some of them might even be aware that the hotshot law firm which now provides your daily cake once handled a deportation appeal for a certain Mr. Costello."

Stay cool, Lindell advised himself, as he would any client. He was the witness in this courtroom; losing his temper would only alienate the jury.

"That was long before my time," he replied. "It so happens they specialize in certain kinds of appeals, and that's one of them. But they're not Mob-connected. And"—Lindy's voice rose in spite of his self-admonition—"I haven't been reached. You hear me, Konecki?"

The big man smiled. "Call me Gabe."

"And what if I had been?" Lindell hammered on. "For Christ's sake, if you can get a few heavyweights out of circulation, why do you have to be so dainty about it? You've had informers before. Some of them have been paid damn well, too."

Konecki said nothing. He rose from his chair and moved to the window. He was even bigger than Lindell had judged initially, and admirably solid for a man who administered the law from a desk and not a saddle. As he scanned the view of smog and monuments, Konecki said:

"Do you know why this has been passed to me, Lindell? Why the hot potato has to land in my lap?"

"I read the title on your door," Lindell responded. "Witness Security Program. Obviously our pigeon isn't coming in unless he's sure of staying alive. Protecting him will be your job. If he's genuine that'll be quite an operation. An army of mobbos will be looking for a chance to pay him back before he can get into court. It'll take a lot of men and money to neutralize that—all on top of what you'll have to pay for the dope. You've got to decide if it's going to be worth the heartache."

15

Konecki bobbed his head like a schoolmaster satisfied with a pupil's reply. "Now tell me how much you know about the program."

Lindell bridled at Konecki's patronizing, tutorial approach. "Listen, I was still working down the block in 1970. The hearings had wound up, but I was here when they passed the act that put this show of yours officially on the books. So you can spare me your two-dollar lecture on the wonderful work you do."

Konecki turned away from the window. "Sorry, Lindell. Of course it was partly because of you—the work of the committee—that we finally got official sanction and funding. But you never did get the benefit of it, not as it's presently constituted. In five years we've developed our scope. I don't think it would hurt if I told you how we function, the role we play."

Lindell was assuaged by the evident sincerity in Konecki's approach. "My feelings are still a little tender from the runaround I've had till now. Forget I sounded off. I'm sure I can use the lesson."

Konecki grinned. "I think maybe you deserve the three-dollar lecture." He began to pace slowly past the window. "Any lawyer knows the root of the problem: it takes witnesses to bring in convictions, and nowhere more than in Mob cases, where tangible evidence can be flimsy or nonexistent. But until recent years, it's been impossible to line up those witnesses. Before we could break open any man who constituted a weak link, he'd be hit. The few rats we did get our hands on were generally loyal to the code of silence—*omertà*, as the Cosa Nostra calls it. Or maybe 'loyal' isn't the word. Let's say they were bound by terror. Even in the custody of police or prison officials a pigeon hasn't been safe from retaliation. Anyone might be on the take. Abe Reles—remember him on the Murder, Inc., squeal?—he flew out a window in a hotel that was surrounded by cops; for thirty years afterward no one really believed the good guys could offer any foolproof guarantees. Even Valachi probably didn't believe it. He talked because he had nothing to lose; he was already in prison when he decided to turn, and he'd already been given the kiss of death. And that gave us our chance to prove that we could keep a fink alive. He was prepared to remain locked

16

up, so when he did turn to us we were able to isolate and shield him with comparative ease. Nothing to it. All we had to do was keep him in a hermetically-sealed, glass-walled observation cell under round-the-clock twin guards for the rest of his miserable life. And *that* almost wasn't enough. Twice there was poison found in his food. Once it was salted in by a kitchen worker; the other time it came in through the walls, already inside a package of frozen spinach from a reputable name-brand company. Joe's enemies would have happily poisoned a whole prisonful of people just to get him, to prove their vengeance was absolute, unavoidable."

"I didn't know they'd come so close," Lindell admitted.

"No. We never told Joe either. Though he didn't have to be told. He never got over his fear of being poisoned. And for what? People forget now that nobody actually went to jail on Valachi's squeal. All he told us was that the Mafia *did* exist—until then most people still thought it was a myth—and then he threw in some of the folklore, a glossary of C.N. language. But that was bad enough. In the end I doubt Joe believed it was the cancer that got him." Konecki stopped pacing and looked squarely at Lindell. "The point is that other men did believe it, finally accepted that we could live up to a guarantee to keep them alive. Faced with a choice between suffering or being killed for the sake of some faded Sicilian tradition and taking an offer of lighter sentences or immunity, the ones we could collar started to open up. And each fink we kept alive was another advertisement, selling the benefits of cooperation to the next hood who got picked up on charges, or heard some grapevine buzz that a contract was out on him because he'd displeased his *capo*."

Konecki settled on a corner of the desk. "What it adds up to is that protecting witnesses, doing it well, has become the cornerstone of any hope we have to control and ultimately break the back of organized crime. That may sound self-evident now. The amazing thing, though, is that it took us so long to come up with this program. For years guarding witnesses remained a half-assed, uncoordinated, shoestring operation. Rent a hotel room and keep the pigeon under wraps. Buy him a ticket to Hoboken and send him out of town until the trial. Put an extra guard on a cell block. It

17

wasn't enough. We've only begun to make real inroads by putting this virtually on a war footing. We have a fat budget, sufficient to maintain 'safe houses,' isolated compounds guarded by large teams of marshals. We've been given waivers, so we don't have to yield to the jurisdiction of state or city police, bodies whose diversified interests make them more prone to corruption. We can call on the National Guard if we have the need for specialized backup forces. We're empowered to provide our informers with legitimate new identities, complete with valid birth certificates, licenses, and passports. We have a special liaison with other departments like State, so we can arrange discreet asylum in foreign countries, if desirable. In other words, we have a highly specialized operation backed by laws and lucre and geared to one strategic objective: keeping a man alive, not just between the time he checks in with us and the time when he steps out of the witness box, but all the way . . . until he falls to the Big Hit Man Up There."

Through the ironic glint in Konecki's eyes as he glanced at the ceiling, Lindell saw for the first time the spark of missionary zeal. Hiding behind the casual jibes, there *was* a deep commitment.

Konecki concluded his spiel with a question. "Now, given the progress we've made in the past few years, wouldn't you say it's about time the Mob launched a specific counteroffensive, made some effort to discredit this program?"

It took Lindell a moment to work out the reason for Konecki's query. When it came, he threw up his hands. Despite the liking he had developed for Gabe Konecki, Lindell now had an exasperated realization that this was only one more deskbound bureaucrat, afraid to take any step that might compromise and imperil his own little fief.

"Oh c'mon," Lindell moaned. "You're not saying this is the beginning of some devious effort to cripple your operation?"

"No, I'm not," Konecki said flatly. "Nor am I ruling it out. Suppose we put a fortune into protecting this star informer, pay him a fat fee; and then he turns out to be a dud and his information worthless. We'd come in for a hell of a rough ride in the press if it were known—and leaks to the media could be deliberately arranged. Or try this scenario. After we

18

put all our blood, sweat, and cash into the witness, he finally gets up on the stand and has nothing to say, clams up tight after all the ballyhoo. That could make it look as though someone inside the program had delivered a message. We'd rip ourselves up looking for the bad apple—who might not really exist. See what I mean? And just one more hypothesis while we're at it: suppose that all the time we're making our pigeon feel at home, he's studying our operation, taking mental notes on the mechanics, and putting out feelers for soft spots, trying from the inside to reach someone who could tell what happened to the other men we're shielding. If the new identities we've given our past informers were stripped away—if Itkin, or Slater, or Big Vinnie Teresa were finally hit—the Mob would have shown its vengeance to be inescapable, after all. *Omertà* would be back in force. It might be another thirty years before we could land our next valuable witness."

"You're giving the pretzel too many twists," Lindell objected. "Why not take this at face value? I never heard of a Cosa Nostra family named Machiavelli."

Konecki appeared to enjoy the joke. When his smile faded, he said quietly, "It would be nice, very nice if the offer you got is as simple as it appears on the surface. Somewhere over the rainbow a pigeon waits. He's ready to pull the plug on a busload of bastards we've been trying to put away since before God created Hoover—and all we have to do is pay him well and keep him safe. But something tells me it isn't so cut-and-dried."

"Why not?" Lindell demanded. "You've had other men make the same offer."

"As I said, nothing ever quite this good. And who were they, anyway? Men on the run, men we'd collared, men in jail. Men with a grievance—like Teresa, who got mad because while he was inside, standing up for the bosses, they failed to provide for his family. But this one"—Konecki shook his head—"this one is something different. He comes to us out of the clear blue, wants us to believe it's only a business deal."

"And why the hell is that so hard to swallow?"

"You said that the way he talked convinced you he was

19

near the top of the family tree. If that were so, he wouldn't need money."

Lindell took it in. Then he shrugged. "Maybe that's secondary. He's feeling shaky; a move is shaping up against him on the inside and he wants to strike the first blow."

"As you told it he didn't sound shaky," Konecki countered. "He put the offer pretty much on a take-it-or-leave-it basis. He was ready to deal through you, but not exactly crying for help. Moreover, he gave you a month to set things up; and even before he made the first contact he was moving slowly, waiting for the perfect moment to give you a call."

Lindell could make no sharp rebuttal to Konecki's logic. But talking to his anonymous caller had given him the conviction—perhaps not communicable—that the man's offer was genuine, and would be a bonanza. If Lindell failed to win an ally now, the chance would slip away. How many million more deaths might it mean in drug overdoses? How much more of the nation's capital would be drained off to benefit a few unscrupulous men? The waste of this opportunity to stem the tide would be nothing less than a tragedy.

"I don't know," Lindell declared hotly. "I don't know what his motive is. But I know it was real. Now I'll give a scenario: this may just be the ultimate accolade for your precious program, the pinnacle of your success. You've convinced one top man that the whole structure of the organization is crumbling, existing on borrowed time. And he wants to be the one to cash in at the finish line. He's come up with the racket to end all rackets: selling all the rest of them out. And you're too dumb, or too goddamn cautious to see it for what it is."

Konecki was stone-still, silent. He nodded grimly in a way that seemed to signal the end of the argument, of the interview.

Lindell got up and walked to the door. "Jesus," he said, pulling it open. "This is one hell of a town."

"Close that door," Konecki commanded.

Lindell hesitated.

"You heard me, Lindell! Get your ass back in here!"

"Why should I?" Lindell continued to look out at the pretty receptionist. She had turned to stare at the door. Her expression, an amiable brand of horror, somehow told Lindell

20

that likeable Gabe Konecki was not unknown for having a fearsome temper.

"Because, you stubborn son of a bitch, we've got to discuss your future."

Slowly, Lindell closed the door. He went back to his chair and sat down.

"By the way, Gabe," he said, "my friends call me Lindy."

TWO

"Christ, they're clever bastards," Dom Francini rasped in his rough bass voice as his yellowish bloodshot eyes swept the ocean. "If y'ask me, fish are the cleverest damn bastards on this whole fucking planet."

Francini had reason to think so. For all the hundreds of hours he had spent with his grotesquely obese body strapped into the fighting chair on the afterdeck of his sixty-eight-foot fishing cruiser, he hadn't made more than ten catches. Considering what he had paid for the boat, it had cost Dom Francini more than thirty thousand dollars for each of those fish. Though if you measured the value of the boat by the deals that had been made aboard it and by the ease with which those deals could be discussed without fear of being bugged, the fish would have been cheap at a hundred times the price.

"Always amazes me," Dom went on, "the way they can have that hook planted right down in their gut and then wriggle off somehow, even tear themselves up to do it." He laughed. "Sure, I know. If I wasn't so lousy at handling my end, I'd bring 'em in more often. But so what? The way they fling themselves up, spinning, flying—that's enough, you know. Christ, seeing 'em toss the hook is a bigger charge than making a catch." He gave another rumbling laugh and glanced at the lean, handsome man who sat in the second fighting chair, alongside Dom's. "Lucky thing a man can't do that, eh? Or we'd be out of business."

Dom's monologues on fishing were legendary. From the time the boat left the dock at his bayside home until it had traveled well out to sea, he would sit in the chair ineffectively trolling a line and treating his guest of honor—whoever had been summoned to sit in the second chair—to his rambling

22

discourse. Dom's ruminations on the nature of man, his philosophy justifying crime, his threats, would be couched in the language of a devoted, if highly perverse, sportsman. The habit was responsible, in part, for Dom's mob sobriquet: "the Fisherman." But there were other, darker origins. A numbers banker who had held out a chunk of the takings had been forced to swallow a fishhook before being thrown overboard. A drug dealer who was suspected of informing had been tied up with deep-sea tackle and trolled through the water one summer's night, a vein in his leg cut open to draw the sharks.

Today's lecture on the sport was given to Bart Vereste, Dom's own *consigliere*. A very basic message. The hook is in, our hook. No matter how it hurts, no matter how you wish you could toss it, you can't. Don't fight against your fate, or you'll tear yourself up. End of sermon.

Dom reeled in his line and bellowed, "Giorgio, get me out of here!"

The young soldier who usually drove the boat for Dom came on the run to unstrap the fat man and take the fishing rod. Francini went toward the cabin. Bart Vereste rose and followed.

In the plush salon, watching a tennis match on television, there were five more men. They all glanced toward the door as Dom entered.

"Hey, Fisherman," said one, a dark thin man in brightly colored sports clothes. "Catch anything?"

The men laughed and turned back to the screen. Dom waddled closer to the television set and stood watching the match. The server double-faulted and the announcer gave the score: love—thirty.

"Love?" Dom said. "That means nothing, right?"

A couple of the others murmured assent.

"Hear that, nephew?" Dom looked to Bart Vereste, who had remained standing by the door of the cabin. "Love means nothing." Then he reached down and snapped off the set. "*Uomini*, it's time to talk."

An oversized chair specially made for Dom had been left vacant. He plopped into it with a grunt and the other men pulled their chairs around to flank his. Vereste stayed by the door, waiting until they called him forward. He must give them the familiar signals of respect, he knew, if he were to survive the tribunal.

Arranged in a line, the seated men stared silently at Vereste, the *incolpato*.

To the extreme left was the thin man in colored silks, Frank Gardia.

Next to him was Phil Ricavole, a wizened, sharp-faced man in his mid-sixties. His head was slightly sunken between hunched shoulders and his skin had a sallow, unhealthy cast. Rumor had it that Ricavole was very sick, dying. But no one could be sure. He had always appeared less robust than other men. Perhaps now he was capitalizing on his natural pallor: the rumors were part of his fight to escape conviction in a federal tax case the government was trying to bring against him. Ricavole would not be the first boss to publicize a weak heart or a cancerous liver as a means of delaying prosecution.

At Ricavole's right was Steve Drapetto. Unlike the others, who were casually attired for the nautical outing, Drapetto wore a dark gray suit set off by a tie of silvery shantung. The right sleeve of his suit was pinned up. Drapetto had lost the arm in the landing at Omaha Beach on D Day. It seemed to have made little difference in his life. He had trained himself to function entirely with his left hand. He worked out daily in a gym at his home, so that his one arm had twice the strength in any average man's. He could shinny up a twenty-foot rope to the ceiling of his gym, and raise a barbell with eighty-pound weights on each end. The perfectly knotted silver tie seemed an emblem to remind any prospective enemy that, despite his handicap, there was nothing Drapetto could not do, whether the task required brute force or finesse and dexterity.

At the hub of the two flanks sat Dom Francini. As Bart Vereste's *capo*, it fell to him to preside over the dispute.

Then, placed at Dom's left because he was the party who had brought a grievance for settlement, was Rocco Gesolo. Ironically, though he and Bart Vereste were the bitter contestants at this court, in some ways they had the most in common. They both held the position of *consigliere*, advisers to the *capos* of their respective families; and both were in their early forties, relatively young members of the Mob hierarchy, though Gesolo appeared somewhat older because of his prematurely grey hair. In one other respect Gesolo was sharply different from Vereste. He had come to his position neither by blood relationship nor by marrying up to it as Vereste had done; he had done it purely on merit, by long and loyal service. Gesolo was a "made" man, a man who had killed—not for pay, but as a proof of his fealty—when the task was demanded of him.

The man who had made those demands was here today as sponsor of Rocco's petition and accordingly sat at his right: Don Valerio Ligazza. Aged seventy-nine, Ligazza was the oldest of all the bosses. He had been among the original planners of the Organization which had descended to the present. In the thirties he had helped to engineer the Night of the Sicilian Vespers, that mass elimination of uncooperative elements which had smoothed the way for marking out sensible family jurisdictions while creating a durable formula for settling disputes and for agreeing upon new ventures which might require a degree of national coordination. Now Ligazza was the last survivor of the engineers. He had even outlived his two sons, both victims of gang wars, which accounted for his de facto adoption of Rocco. Those who judged Ligazza by his age and history alone might have thought to catalogue him among the doggedly traditional Moustache Petes. But even though Ligazza had retained a deep respect for the traditions, he had long ago seen the wisdom of combining this with an appreciation of certain new ideas. He had been among the first to disseminate racket moneys into legitimate interests. He was usually the most fervent supporter of the imaginative suggestions for diversification submitted to the *Commissione* by Bart Vereste. Erect, bright-eyed, with a leonine mane of snow-white hair, Ligazza possessed mental acuity and physical stamina which were exceptional for a man of his years. He was not only the richest of them all, but the shrewdest, the most determined, the best equipped to withstand the challenges posed internally by jealous plotting and externally by the law. More than seniority had elevated Ligazza to become *capo di capi rei*, the boss of bosses.

Signaling the start of proceedings, Dom Francini lifted one

of his huge fat paws from the arm of his chair and waved Bart Vereste forward.

"Sit with us, Bartolomeo."

So it was to be like that, thought Vereste. Ceremonial, mired in the old ways, Sicilian names for all. A charade for mummies. What else could it be, though? The issue they were here to discuss was itself a hangover of an antiquated feudal code that took no account of modern realities. The organization were now using machines to count their money, but they were still stuck in the past in too many ways. Vereste noted the smile on Dom Francini's meaty lips. Privately, he knew, the fat man disdained the traditions. But with Don Valerio present, Dom would play the old ritual bullshit to the hilt.

Vereste pulled a chair from beside one of the cabin windows and positioned it to face the line of his judges. Because he was a *consigliere*, he was being allowed to sit, rather than kept standing before them like a naughty schoolboy.

"Don Valerio," Dom Francini boomed abruptly, turning to Ligazza. "You have informed me of a violation committed by one of my men against one of yours. We have brought these men here to face each other, to hear the complaint and the defense. We have agreed, in the interest of reaching fair judgment, to have present a majority of voting parties with no involvement on either side. If grounds for punishment are thought to exist, I hereby guarantee that such punishment will be carried out. If the claim that brings us together is judged to be unfounded, you shall guarantee that the matter is peacefully closed as from today."

"I accept the terms, Don Domenico," said Ligazza in his soft, whispery voice. Then he turned to Rocco and nodded.

Rocco Gesolo hesitated, face lowered, chin pressed down on his chest. Finally he lifted his head and spoke, gazing straight at Vereste.

"This man has dishonored my daughter, my only child. She is a girl of seventeen years, a girl that my wife and I have taken pains to raise by the highest standards. Seven months ago, on the occasion of the birthday party for Don Valerio, my daughter Marianna was introduced to the *consigliere* Vereste. Since then she has met him again many times, in secret.

26

Now"—Gesolo swept a glance down the line—"she has confessed to her mother that she loves this man, *un uomo sposato,* as old as her own father. And while she denies it, we believe it is because of him that she is no longer *intatto*. Her virtue has been spoiled, stolen, by this *adultero*. I ask for the right to punish him for this. The right, under our law, to exact vengeance without bringing on full vendetta between our two families."

There was no visible reaction from the other men when Rocco had finished his statement. They had all come to the meeting fully aware of its agenda. The opening accusation was only a formality.

Dom Francini nodded his heavy head toward Bart. "I invite your answer, *consigliere*."

Verteste replied in a steady voice without hesitation.

"I know the girl, it is true. I have met her on several occasions, it is true. As the *consigliere* Gesolo knows, but omits to mention, we met publicly not only at Don Valerio's birthday celebration, but at the wedding of Don Stefano's brother"— Vereste glanced to Drapetto—"and in Florida during the Easter holiday, when both *consigliere* Gesolo's family and my own were staying at a hotel owned by Don Valerio." Vereste allowed his voice to rise slightly. "As for the rest, it is untrue. I have never met the girl in secret, much less could I have touched her in the way of which I am accused." He eased his tone again. "I do not say that the *consigliere* is lying, that he means to defame me unjustly. But I do say that he has been misled by coincidence. The natural, sometimes passionate concerns of the parent have pushed him to false conclusions, blinded and deafened him to the facts." Vereste was finished with his initial rebuttal.

Gesolo sat forward, the muscles hinging his jaw flexing tightly, sending tremors across his tanned cheeks.

Ligazza reached out and laid a hand gently on his *consigliere's* arm. Gesolo settled back in his chair.

Dom Francini looked to his right, soliciting comment from any of the impartial onlookers. They remained passive and Dom turned back to Gesolo.

"You have told us your grievance, *consigliere*. On what facts is it based?"

27

"The first I have already told you, Don Domenico, the confession made by the girl herself: that she loves this man, that she knows he wishes to marry her. When Marianna told this to her mother and myself, of course it aroused our suspicions and we forced her to undergo a medical examination. It was proven that she is no longer a virgin. As to how and when the violation occurred, I must admit the evidence is circumstantial. But could it be anything else? You cannot expect me to produce witnesses to their meetings in bed! It is established, however, that Marianna has lied several times to account for her whereabouts."

"What is the proof of these lies?" Drapetto spoke up. Gesolo was at last speaking of details the jury had not heard. All the men were paying sharp attention.

"My daughter is a first-year student at a parochial college, Don Stefano. She boards at the school and there is dormitory supervision. But she is allowed weekend and occasional overnight absences at her discretion. The only proviso is that she record her destination in a book left at the dormitory for that purpose. Marianna always claimed to be visiting the homes of one or another of her classmates. But we have checked and found this to be untrue. Even in cases where she accompanied friends to their homes, she did not remain there to sleep."

"But you do not know where she went?" Ricavole said tentatively.

"Yes, I do. To meet him." Gesolo glared fiercely at Bart Vereste.

"We are aware of your contention," Ricavole said. He did seem to have the weary impatience of a man who knew his future was short. "But where did they meet? This surely is a crucial point."

Gesolo paused. "I don't know."

"Why didn't you put on a tail?" Frank Gardia asked, a refreshing relief from the stilted declarative style the others had adopted as accompaniment to the feudal ritual.

"By the time we knew she was lying, it was too late. It was only after she confessed the infatuation that we checked the sign-out book. Of course, as soon as she realized I was ready to cut the balls off her lover, Marianna stopped spending time away from the school."

28

"So much for your crucial point, Don Filippo," Vereste interjected sharply, rupturing the decorum. "The where, the how, they exist nowhere but in his head. The madman not only doesn't know where, but couldn't, as there never were any—"

"Enough!" Dom Francini broke in fiercely. "We are here to settle this without the useless insult that leads to bloodshed. You are given your chances to speak, Bartolomeo. But you will not be allowed to seize them, *senza rispetto.*"

"Pardon my outburst, *Zio,*" Vereste muttered after a moment, pandering to the overripe ceremonial mood. By Sicilian tradition, the word for "uncle" was a term of ultimate respect, used by peasants when addressing Mafia dons. Applied by Bart it had an extra twist, since Dom Francini was, in fact, the uncle of Bart's wife.

Turning quickly to Rocco, Dom said: "You had the report of a doctor on your daughter's condition. How did she explain it? If she denies it was done by my *consigliere,* who then did she name as the responsible party?'

"She named no other man, Don Domenico."

"But then how could she deny that her lover is—was—Bartolomeo Vereste?"

Gesolo said nothing. He stared at Vereste, trembling, hating him now it seemed as much for the indignity of having to appear and recount these intimacies as for the violation itself.

"These are difficult things for a father to speak about," Ligazza intervened. "We understand, Roccino. Take any time you need."

Despite Dom's nominal authority in the proceeding, he knew that Ligazza's word must be venerated. He waited now until Gesolo found his words.

"She would not admit to having sexual contact with any man," Gesolo said at last. "She wanted us to believe . . . she said she had done it herself. With . . ." He faltered, and the men waited patiently. With a visible effort of will, his hands clenching into tightly impacted, quivering fists, Gesolo finished. "With a soda bottle, she said. . . ."

A hushing sound escaped Gardia's lips. Ricavole shook his head pityingly.

After a pause, Francini went on. "In all respect, *consigliere,*

29

such things are. . . ." Dom shrugged his elephantine shoulders. "No one can be sure—"

"I know, Don Domenico," Gesolo said. "Except it is not an object she tells us she has fallen in love with."

With his one hand, Steve Drapetto brought out a new pack of cigarettes from a pocket. With deft fingers he opened the cellophane and wrapping and extracted one tightly wedged cigarette from the others, a veritable feat of prestidigitation for a one-handed man. Drapetto had supplied an intermission, a temporary release of the tension. Only when Drapetto had the cigarette in his mouth, lit, did Francini continue:

"Bartolomeo, what can you add to your defense?"

Vereste scanned the line of accusing faces. What could be said to win them over to his contention of innocence? Were any of them ignorant of his failed marriage to Ginetta Francini? All were from families operating in either the same state or one nearby. The social congress bred by proximity, even more the frequent intermarriages among the neighboring clans, inspired a free exchange of the most intimate gossip. Whether or not proof could be given of any contact between Bart and Marianna Gesolo, the situation which had driven Bart to seek extramarital sex in other times and places was certainly common knowledge. If he survived today's inquisition, it would be only out of Rocco Gesolo's failure to provide any incontrovertible evidence.

"*Uomini,*" Vereste began, "you know, all of you, that the girl of whom we speak is uncommonly beautiful, that many of our most powerful and respected men have sought her as a bride for their sons. I have not touched her, but how do I make you believe it? Yes, she is desirable, and I cannot deny that any man would find her attractive. Yes, if the *consigliere* Gesolo has said she has feelings for me, then it must be true—true that she *said* it. There is, perhaps, only one conclusion you can draw from what you have heard. What is left for me, then? Should I beg you to take my truth instead of another man's? Should I simply get on my knees and plead for my life? Perhaps that in itself would be the proof of my innocence: if I whined for mercy, showed myself to be a coward, without *calzone,* no man at all."

Ricavole responded to the manhood pitch, Vereste noted,

pulling himself up in his chair, trying to appear less puny and shriveled.

"But I will not beg," Vereste continued, "not for your mercy, not even for your trust. I have been shamed too much already—accused of dishonoring the house of a man I once called a friend and despoiling a girl younger than my own daughter. And there is not only my shame to consider, but also the *consigliere* Gesolo's, in having to come here, to be made to speak of these things. I am sure it hurts him no less than me to—"

"*Bugiardo!*" Gesolo exploded. "*Ipocrita!*" His eyes were ablaze with rage. He clawed at the arms of his chair as if trying to retain a hold on a narrow ledge from which he might fall into an abyss.

Again Ligazza acted to restrain him. He did not touch Gesolo at all this time, merely reached out, his old hand poised steady and upright in front of Gesolo's chest; a Moses who could physically turn back the murderous tides in another man's heart.

Gesolo stiffened. His hands ceased their pawing motion. But he did not sit back; he remained balanced on the edge of his chair.

"Why," Vereste resumed earnestly, avoiding Gesolo's gaze, "why should I not sympathize? Like him I am humiliated by the need to speak openly of the most private matters. You will weigh what you know of my personal life into your decision, so I must deal with it. You know my marriage is bad, that there have been violent quarrels and long separations. I admit that I have gone to other beds than my wife's to satisfy the needs of a man. Yet, I swear to you, my wife has my respect. I know that I am bound to her, and would not dishonor her by the affair which has been suggested."

Ricavole bobbed his head approvingly.

Vereste went into his planned finale. "I say again that I believe the *consigliere* Gesolo meant no deliberate harm. I know him to be an intelligent and fair-minded man. But he is also the father of a girl with extraordinary beauty and high spirits. This girl has reached the age where she begins to test her powers as a woman, while the powers may exceed the maturity she needs to understand and control them. She may at once be overwhelmed by them, and resent that others are not." Bart permitted himself a glance at Gesolo; even he had settled back to listen. "The *consigliere* admits that what he knows of the affair comes from his daughter's lips. Perhaps without being fully aware of it, he also acknowledges her ideas of love spring from fantasy as much as truth. What was it she told him? In his own words: 'She confessed her infatuation.' So he and I are not in complete disagreement. I would also say that she is infatuated, victim of one-sided longings that lead her to concoct dreams. And if that is true, it follows that she might . . . touch herself, feel the need to satisfy her cravings for . . . someone."

Vereste hesitated.

"No," Gesolo murmured, "it cannot be." But he did not stir. He was apparently unaware that he had spoken aloud.

"If I am the someone in her fantasy," Vereste said quietly, "then maybe I am not without guilt. For what? For knowing this lovely creature, for enjoying her company in the presence of both our families, for dancing with her in a hotel nightclub—as her father has done with my own daughter. Or even for recognizing her charm and beauty. For knowing that, as a young man, before I had taken the marriage vows, before I was prohibited by the laws of our religion, our heritage, and our brotherhood, I did want such a girl. But now it is beyond wanting. There are tabus I must respect. Like a father, for that matter, who may take pride in the attractions of his daughter, but is forbidden to go beyond a certain point."

Ligazza made a slight sudden move forward. The shrewd old man half suspected what was coming, Vereste thought, but couldn't decide whether to interrupt.

Vereste hurried to the end. "Though respecting the tabus may not be so easy. Even a father may lose his objectivity, look for release from unwilling impulses by ascribing them to other men, accuse them of the desire he can't repress in himself."

It was done. If Ligazza would have stopped him, it was too late. He could only stare at his *consigliere,* waiting for his reaction.

Strangely, it took longest to penetrate Gesolo's comprehension. For a minute his face registered uncertainty more

32

than anger. Then he whispered, *"Sudiciume."* Filth. And as if hearing his own voice had jolted him out of suspension, suddenly he was on his feet roaring a stream of abuse, lunging at Vereste.

The quickest reflexes were Drapetto's. Almost instantly he was behind Gesolo, one arm braced across the attacking man's shoulders to drag him backward. But Gesolo had his hands at Vereste's throat and he clung on, his fingers digging into the neck.

Within seconds, however, he had been overmatched by Drapetto's strength. Vereste pried open the strangling grip and Gesolo was pulled away. Expended, Gesolo staggered back limply against Drapetto, who continued to support him with his massive encircling arm.

At last, preliminary to releasing his hold, Drapetto said:

"All right now, Roc?"

Gesolo did not reply.

Dom Francini looked to Ligazza.

"You need some air, Roccino," said the old man. "Take a walk around the deck, listen to the gulls. Your business is finished here." He motioned to Drapetto. "Stefano, release him."

Drapetto lowered his arm and returned to his seat. Gesolo tucked a stray shirttail inside his trousers and went to a side door of the cabin leading to the deck. There he turned back.

"I will have justice," he said flatly. "One way or another, I will have justice." Then he went out.

The other men watched through the windows as Gesolo went forward and leaned against the railing in the bow, staring down at the plumed water.

Dom made no effort to reassert his presidency. It was Ligazza who spoke harshly to Vereste.

"That was clever, Bartolomeo, very clever."

"It was not to be clever, Don Valerio. It was to explain."

"To explain yourself you must cry *incesto* against your accuser?"

"I was talking only about a state of mind. I wish to make it understood that even though I myself believe the girl and her father are not lying with intent, what she says, what he believes, have no basis in truth."

33

"Fair enough," Frank Gardia put in. "We can't deny Bart the right to say what he thinks. He's had to sit still while Rocco calls him *adultero, seduttore.* And what Bart's sayin' ain't impossible. There's no telling how a guy can get his head fucked up because of his cock."

"Maybe we should get a headshrinker in here to help us decide," Dom suggested sarcastically. "Anyone got one on the payroll?"

"Jesus," Ricavole sighed, hunched again, gazing into his lap, "let's just put the goddamn thing to a vote. We've heard both sides."

"Yes, the vote," Ligazza said, "but first I will add some words." He searched the faces of the others to be certain they were giving him full attention. Then, as if to indicate that his words were not to be taken as the idle ruminations of a failing old man, he rose from his chair and walked to a window at the forward end of the cabin, displaying his straight back and firm step. From the window, he looked out at the lonely figure standing in the bow before turning back. The other men had swiveled in their chairs to face him.

"Among many of our brotherhood there has been criticism of Rocco Gesolo and myself for insisting, in the absence of any clear proof, that this charge be taken up formally. Even if there were some truth, I have heard it said, are we still to treat this as a violation of our law? How many young daughters of our sons are no longer obedient to the traditional virtues? In this day, they spread their legs and offer themselves as the mood strikes them; they swallow a pill and take new lovers daily and never speak of it. Are we to care?" Ligazza laid a hand dramatically over his chest. "Ah, yes, Don Valerio may care because he is old, because he remembers when a man would have his throat cut for no less than a disrespectful glance at a girl like Marianna Gesolo. But the rest of us? We are too wise, too modern, to bother with such things, eh? We are Americans now, not *Siciliani* or *Castellammarese.*" Ligazza cast an eye toward Steve Drapetto, who had given an arm to defend his family's new country, not the old.

"But I tell you, *amici,*" Ligazza continued, "some of what is old-fashioned must not change or we are doomed. The code of our Honored Society must not be raped and weakened by progress, must itself remain *intatto,* or our power shall crumble. That is what is at stake here. Not the life of Bartolomeo Vereste, but the code. *Omertà!* The oath we take to suffer anything before turning against our own kind, dishonoring our friends. It is *omertà* in all its facets that has made us strong, kept us strong. It is *omertà* that for years allowed thousands of us to conduct our affairs without the world being able to detect more than our shadows. If that code is rooted in the past, then so be it!"

Ligazza moved to stand behind his chair, his large hands firmly grasping the back. "That is the real importance of convening here, of treating an affair of honor according to law that some call feudal and ridiculously outmoded. It reaffirms the hold of *omertà* at a time when the Honored Society is under dangerous pressures. It is a warning to all doubters that the brotherhood is not softened by time like the mind and body of a mere mortal. A declaration that our law, as it has been upheld by our fathers and their fathers before them, is still respected, *intatto.*" The old man paused, waiting until he received nods of comprehension from the younger men, Gardia and Drapetto.

Finally, as he came around to take his seat, he added: "But with it, I caution you that our judgment must be pure, untainted by any petty jealousy or private suspicion. It must be seen that our law is truly just and evenhanded. We have, I think, depended too much on fear of our wrath, rather than respect for justice; so that when the fear is removed, our code is dead. It is respect we must instill again. On that, we can stand forever."

Ligazza sat down and folded his hands in his lap. It was clear that the vote could now be taken.

Vereste studied the old man. Which way had he meant to move them? Was he saying a kill would be justified, that it would serve more important ends than satisfying Rocco Gesolo's hunger for revenge? Or was he reminding them that, as in any court, there must be no conviction without proof?

For the first time, Vereste was gripped by fear. The muscles across his stomach became taut, and it was difficult to breathe. He struggled to remember the careful analysis

35

which had allowed him to head into the meeting coolly un-afraid, so sure of which way the men would be pushed by their prejudices. If he had been wrong . . .

Dom Francini, exercising one tiny prerogative, flipped a finger toward Frank Gardia, calling for the first vote. Bart was not expected to leave while the vote was taken. Tradition demanded that he be present, yet harbor no ill feeling against those who had voted against him if the vote went in his favor and he survived.

Gardia glanced thoughtfully at Vereste. "I say no," he announced then. "No kill."

It was up to Ricavole now. Without looking up he answered softly, "Yes. *Farlo fuori.*"

Drapetto took a puff on his cigarette. "No."

Dom Francini's thick lips twitched. He could barely repress the smile, Vereste thought.

"Yes," Dom said.

So far it was all as predicted. Because there was a tie, the sponsor of the petition would be allowed to cast a vote. But which way would it break?

Ligazza turned to look out the window at Rocco Gesolo, waiting for the decision. Whichever way the old man voted loyalties would be strained. Still facing away, Ligazza shook his head vigorously.

"No," he said, then fixed his determined gaze on the others. "There will be no killing."

Vereste's pulse continued to race, but with excitement now, not panic. He had called it perfectly. Ligazza had cast himself with the younger men.

The stolid ceremonial atmosphere dissolved immediately. Except for Bart Vereste, the men were all on their feet. Drapetto at the bar, pouring himself a drink. Gardia in front of the television, catching up on the tennis match. Ricavole and Dom Francini together in a corner of the cabin, muttering to each other. Ligazza on his way out of the cabin, to break the word to Rocco Gesolo. No congratulations were offered to the acquitted *incolpato.*

When Bart stood and started toward the bar, Dom came over to him.

"I called it like I saw it," Dom said, "same as the rest."

36

"Sure, no hard feelings. I'm clear, that's good enough for me." He shifted his eyes from Dom's puffy face to take in the tennis match. "And the judges' decision is final, isn't that right? I know the conditions. I mustn't ever be caught near the girl. As long as I'm not, if anyone hits me, it's all right to hit back. Rocco moves on me, my friends can even call down his guarantor, Don Valerio—*obligato.*"

Dom tilted his head back so that the folds between his several chins were smoothed away. "I don't know about that anymore. Not after the way you mouthed off in here. Rocco's got a whole other case after the insult you gave him. And that's a separate issue for which Don Valerio gave no guarantees." He dropped his chin again, and the obscene drapery of flesh reappeared. "I think you may have to watch out for Rocco for some little time to come. Know what I mean? He's in the bow, you stay in the stern. Give him a cooling-off period."

"Maybe I'll take a trip, me and Ginnie and the kids," Bart said. "Assuming you can manage without me."

Dom laughed. The way things were between them, he fully perceived Bart's irony.

Across the cabin, Steve Drapetto held up a bottle, offering a drink to Bart. All was forgiven. Relations had returned to normal.

THREE

Lindell had been keeping to a strict, monkish schedule, specifically designed to provide ample opportunity for the second contact to be made when he was alone. He would linger at the office each evening after everyone else had left, then head straight back to his apartment, cook his own supper, settle down with some work or a book, watch a movie on television. And wait for the call.

He enjoyed the solitude. It had come at a good time, a welcome relief from his customary, much more sociable habits. Lindell was bored with the cocktail parties and business dinners, irritated by the predictable conversations about the problems of the country, the mediocrity of the leadership, the apathy of the people, the decline of respect for law, love, life. The plays and musicals he had once enjoyed were no longer worth the cost of the watery orange drink sold at intermissions, much less the price of a ticket. Recently, too, he had realized that there was no future for him in either of the two women he had been dating most steadily for the past few months, an actress and an advertising copywriter. The intimate at-home dinners cooked by the copywriter had lately consisted too often of exactly the same "favorite" recipe from the Sunday *Times Magazine*. And while he had to admit that it might be because he was behind the times, a male chauvinist pig, not with it—whatever the hell she wanted to say about him—he didn't feel like coping with the actress's bisexuality anymore, not this year.

So he had found it easy to keep his own company. He had even gone into the office on Sundays, though there was no particularly pressing work.

But there had been no second call.

38

He had begun to regret ignoring Gabe Konecki's advice. Konecki had said there was no point in setting up opportunities. Going to the office on Sundays, re-creating the conditions of the original contact, was especially self-defeating. No Mafioso worth his salt would do anything the same way twice in a row. It was a law of survival to be unpredictable, to shun routine. Any man who left his house after breakfast at the same time every morning, who visited his mistress at the same time every night, who always had his hair cut on the same day of the week by the same barber, was leaving himself wide open to a hit.

"Just maintain your normal schedule," Konecki had said. "If our pigeon is still alive, he'll find his own time and place to reach out."

Lindell had done it his own way, nevertheless. Familiar with bureaucratic patterns, he was still vaguely distrustful of Konecki's motives. For all the cooperation that was now promised, if and when it was needed, the marshal might still be hoping the mysterious caller would sink without a trace. If Mr. X did come in, if he was as big a catch as he had boasted, he was going to take an awful lot of protecting. More than any man who had ever come in before. If that protection lapsed for a split second and the witness did get shot down, it would be a stunning public failure for Konecki's precious security program. Enough to make a lot of congressmen think hard about all the money that had gone into it.

The law of survival in Washington, Lindell well knew, was not to be too ambitious. Sensational achievements risked sensational failures. Better to accomplish a little, just enough to keep the program on its feet. Never bite off more than you could swallow without chewing. It wasn't impossible that Gabe Konecki had been infected by these attitudes. So Lindell disregarded his advice, inconvenienced himself, made the opportunities.

Now, more than a month had elapsed since the first contact. Lindell wondered if he had been taken in by a joker. Or, assuming the approach had been genuine, if the man behind it was still in this world.

As he lingered in the deserted office this Tuesday evening at seven-fifteen, Lindell decided to make at least a small departure from his stern routine. He wasn't tempted to restore open lines to either the actress or the copywriter, but he felt the need for some bright feminine company to take his mind off the silent telephones.

He wondered if Ciel Jemasse was still in her office. She would provide exactly the kind of distraction he wanted. An attractive, charming, intelligent companion with all the pitfalls ruled out from the start.

He made the call and Ciel answered. He said a simple hello, leaving her to guess the name that went with the voice.

"Lindy?" she said after a pause.

"Give the little lady a cigar."

"You know, I swear not ten minutes ago I thought of calling you. But I didn't think you'd be in your office this late."

"Not like you dedicated women."

"As they say in the car-rental ads, baby, we're number two, we try harder."

In Ciel's case, the self-deprecating humor had a double edge. Technically, Ciel Jemasse was black. A slave master had brought her great-grandmother to one of the Carolinas from French Guyana, and this French heritage was preserved in her name. When introducing herself, she always explained that Ciel should be pronounced as in the French word for "sky."

Before taking her accountancy courses, Lindy knew, Ciel had gone off for a stint with the Peace Corps in Nigeria, had returned to become one of the first black models photographed for the glossy fashion magazines, had married and quickly divorced Buck Gracey, the black football star. She also had an arthritic mother, a junkie sister, and a mulatto father who dropped in every two or three years for a few hundred drinks and a handout. Four years ago, Ciel had come to work for a plush firm of accountants that Lindy's law firm retained to assist on cases which involved complicated fiscal matters. Last year one of the senior accountants had died and Ciel had been made a partner—"a show negro in spades," as she had put it. That was only part of it. Ciel was generally acknowledged to be an asset to her company. Not only was she good to look at and fun to be with, but she was smart as a whip with figures. Yet it was not surprising that

40

she picked the lowest common denominator as the reason for her promotion. No trouble spotting Ciel's identity crisis. A mingling of white blood—going back, long before her father, to the usual rapes by slave captains and plantation owners—had given Ciel a light coloring. And although this had helped her career, made her more "acceptable," it had in the long run made her success less than satisfying to her, and in some ways distasteful. Although she had earned a lot of money for as long as Lindy had known her, Ciel had continued to live in Harlem with her mother.

"Why were you going to call me?" Lindy asked.

"You lead off, you spent the dime."

"I wondered if you were free tonight."

"What's the proposition?"

"How's this for glamor—an intimate rendezvous with some hot numbers? A client of mine invested a bundle with a manufacturer who declared bankruptcy. My client's beef is that a lot of his money was salted away in a Swiss bank for the personal benefit of the bankrupt. I've gotten hold of a pile of company accounts and I was going to take them home tonight—"

"And you'd like me to sit in," Ciel supplied, "and see where some of them zeros might've shrunk down to decimals and versa vice."

"Something like that."

"Lover," she purred sexily, "what girl could resist an offer like that?"

"You'll also be able to tell me your business. And if there's any time left over," Lindy added, "we can take in a flick." He offered to buy sandwiches and bring them back to his apartment; Ciel could come over whenever she had finished her office work. She said she'd probably be at his door in an hour, and they hung up.

Ciel arrived at nine. She was wearing a trim dark suit of a type she might have worn to the office, but there was no mark of a long working day on her. She was satiny smooth, perfectly coiffed, and smelled deliciously of perfume. Lindy wondered if she had taken the time to go home and change, just for this working evening. Did she think he had an ulterior motive in asking her to his apartment?

As he filled her request for a bloody mary, he asked again

41

what had coincidentally given her the idea to call him this evening. And for a second time, Ciel deferred giving the answer. Since she wasn't hungry yet, she suggested they get into Lindy's file. Later they could have sandwiches and talk.

While Lindy looked on, Ciel worked diligently through the company books and bank statements Lindy had laid out on the coffee table. At the end of almost two hours, she had ferreted out several large entries and cash transfers of a dubious nature. From here it would be up to an investigator, someone Lindy would hire to follow the trail of the money and ascertain if it had been diverted and laundered.

Lindy went to the kitchen to get the sandwiches. As he was arranging them on plates, Ciel leaned in through the portal.

"Ready for my problem?"

Lindy saw that she had made herself another bloody mary, a pale specimen, with lots of vodka and only a sprinkle of tomato juice. It must be something heavy, he thought.

"Shoot."

"I was also interested in your professional services."

"You got troubles with the law?"

"In a way." She smiled wanly and took a swig of her drink. "Or maybe I ought to say the law's got trouble with me."

Lindy carried the plates into the dining alcove and Ciel followed. They sat down facing each other across the table. After one small nibble of a turkey sandwich, Ciel continued:

"You remember Avril, my younger sister. You gave me that help on her probation petition."

"You don't think I could forget. Sorry that didn't work out."

"Nobody could've done more than you did. Anyway, she is coming out at last. By official definitions, she's cured."

"Great." Lindy tried to sound encouraging.

Ciel smiled sadly. "Let's hope. But you know it, babe: the odds are she'll be back on junk in a few weeks, no matter what anyone does, or says. The psychiatric social workers come around and talk a lot of jive about how she needs to get back her self-respect. So they've put her out on a 'conditional.' She can live at home and take care of mama. It's not supposed to matter that home happens to be set down in a neighborhood where there's a pusher in every doorway, and two outside every schoolyard. But what's the alternative? It's no problem for me to set her up in her own place somewhere else, buy her nice furniture, find her a job. Sure, I can give her all the trimmings of self-respect. Except that I did it after the last cure. She never showed up for the job. Within a week she'd sold off all the furniture for a few fixes. And when the bread ran out she was hooking johns off the street, bringing them up to the pad for a quick twenty-dollar fuck on the bare floor."

Ciel had put down her sandwich. Obviously she had never had an appetite, Lindy realized. Now he had lost his. He stopped eating, sat back and listened.

"Of course, there's the happy medium," Ciel went on. "Big sister parcels out the pennies, assigns little chores like emptying mama's bedpan, holds evening seminars on How I Became a Success in the Big Bad World. All that should do wonders for Avril's self-respect." Her voice broke and her eyes flooded with tears. She grabbed up a napkin, blotted the tears, then looked at the napkin and laughed. "Man . . . I'd forgotten I had those."

Lindy reached across the table and took her hand. "Hey, count on me. Whatever it is."

"I know, man, I know."

But in a moment she retracted her hand, as if embarrassed by the contact.

"The thing is," she sighed, "I don't want to rip myself up over this anymore. Hell, I'll do what I can for my folks. But I can't go on apologizing for being the lucky one. Avril's going to be there with mama now. The arthritis is worse and it takes quite some looking after. I can always get her a nurse; but if this self-respect gig has anything in it, maybe it's best I do leave them alone." She paused, looking into her plate. "You can't imagine it, Lindy, what a hell it is uptown. I went back there after I split with Buck because I thought it would help me find out who the hell I was. Divorce does funny things to people and that's what mine did to me." She glanced up. "But you know that thing someone once said: 'I've been rich and I've been poor, and rich is better.' Well, baby, I've been black and I've been white; and I've got to admit it: in this goddamn lousy world, white is still better."

More than anything else, it saddened Lindy to hear her talk this way. For all her jokes, he knew she had a streak of pride a mile wide. But it was a very down time for her; he had to let out the words and tears she'd been holding back for so long.

"And where does the law come in?" he said.

"I'm moving downtown. I want to start spending some money on myself, lease a place or buy a nice co-op. Two or three bedrooms, so Sis can visit if she stays straight. I could use your help on the purchase."

"Have you run into discrimination?"

Ciel shook her head. "Haven't made my move yet. But when I do, it could happen. It's not the first time I've gone hunting. When I was with Buck we looked for an apartment together. Some places will let you in, some won't. You don't even bother looking on Park or Fifth, of course. Any ole body will say it's fine in principle, they know the law; but if they don't want you, it's easy enough to get the message delivered. Contracts get stalled, places that they were ready to give away suddenly get taken off the market. You know."

"Okay," Lindy said firmly, "if it happens this time, we'll fight it."

"No," Ciel said. "That's not the trick, not at all. I don't want to fight, don't want to prove anything. I just want to be left out of all that crap." She paused. "I was going to ask if you'd front for me. If I find a nice place I'll deal blind, through you, and ease in with no hassles."

Lindy hesitated. It wasn't Ciel's style to sneak in, or his to be an accomplice. Later they might both reproach themselves, and each other, and wish they had taken the braver route.

"However you want it," Lindy said finally. "But my advice is to go into it openly. There are a lot of first-class places where the bars are down. And where they creep into view, they can be knocked down. There are laws on the books for that purpose, have been for a long time. They need to be used, tested. Now, I happen to know there's a penthouse right in this building available on a lease. We could start there."

"I like you too much to drive down *your* property values."

"For Christ's sake," Lindy erupted, "will you cut out that stupid self-denigrating bullshit!"

44

Ciel shied back, shocked. Then she laughed softly. "Denigrating, eh? Now where do you think they got that word?"

They laughed, the tension broke.

"I'm sorry, Lindy. I've had a real bad week."

He was about to pick up his pitch on making an open bid for the penthouse when the phone rang. As Lindy answered, his eyes were still on Ciel, his thoughts on her problem; she was dabbing at her eyes again with the napkin.

"I'm calling for my answer, Lindell," said the voice on the phone.

He recognized it instantly, and turned from Ciel to muffle the conversation. A cassette recorder was on the table beside the telephone, attached by a conducting microphone—a rubber suction cup pressed on the receiver. Lindy didn't want to be doubted again because there were no witnesses. Easing down the "RECORD" button on the cassette machine, Lindy said:

"The answer is yes, naturally. Bring in the goods and you can practically write your own terms."

"Why did you lower your voice?" the caller asked quickly. "Got somebody with you?"

Lindy thought back to the first contact, Sunday in the office. If he had been watched then, why not now? The question could be a test.

"Yes," he admitted. "A friend, that's all."

There was a silence. Lindell held his breath.

"I'll hold on," the caller said finally. "Clear the hall."

Lindy looked at Ciel. She had pulled herself together, was even gnawing at her sandwich. He hated to bustle her out.

But you didn't tell Mr. X to call back at a more convenient moment.

Lindy set the receiver aside and went to Ciel. "Listen, hon, this is a big call, a blockbuster. And my client won't talk unless I'm alone in the house."

She raised her eyebrows, but rose and quickly started gathering her things. "I understand," she said. "Professional confidence and all that."

"Hey, take the sandwiches, too," he said, moving to the phone. "And call me tomorrow, okay, about the apartment thing?"

45

She had reached the door, opened it. A scat wave and she was gone.

Lindy spoke into the receiver. "I'm alone."

He was asked to start at the beginning, give a detailed account of his trip to Washington, everyone he had seen, what had been said, and the degree of interest shown at each turn. He told it chronologically, not concealing the runaround he had been given at first. When Lindy came to recount his meeting with Tom Ryle, the caller interjected, "That's more like it." And for having gained the ear of the Attorney General, Lindy was rewarded with, "Now we're cooking."

Summing up his conversation with Konecki, however, Lindy omitted any mention of the marshal's reservations and suspicions. He said only that the Witness Security Program was pledged to provide the ironclad protection which would undoubtedly be necessary.

"Tell me more about this protection," the caller demanded. "How much do city or state police come into it?"

"They don't. You surrender to federals, and they'll stick with you from there on."

"I told you no FBI."

"Your guard will be federal marshals, round the clock. They're a separate shop from the Bureau."

"And how many do I get?"

"That depends on the situation. While you're under cover and before you give testimony, there would be a couple of dozen. When you go to court, there might even be more. Later, when you're set up with a new identity, the guard would be scaled down. If you seem to be settling into your new life, it could go down to one or two. But only after they're sure you're safe."

"I'm not worried about then," the caller said. "The hot times will be now, as soon as I walk in. Two dozen guys to watch me may not be enough. The organization will send out an army if they ever find out where I'm being kept."

"They won't find out," Lindy said strongly.

"I want to be totally isolated in a *casa privata*, understand."

"You'll have to translate."

"A safe house. Away from everything, a fortress."

"You'll have it."

46

"I have a family. The mob could get at me through them unless they're with me—my wife, son, and daughter."

"You can bring your own barber, if you want."

"Forget the jokes, Lindell. This is my life we're talking about. Now tell me the situation on identities. You'll set all that up, too, for the four of us."

"Including passports," Lindy replied, "in new names."

"I'll want a facial—plastic surgery. Will you arrange it?"

"Family plan, if you want."

"That's up to them," said Mr. X. "I'm assuming there was no objection to giving me a blanket immunity."

"Correct."

There was a thoughtful silence.

"Sounds good," the voice said at last. "That leaves one more thing: the money."

"The government has no objection to paying informers," Lindy replied. "You ought to know that. But the demands do have to be within reason."

"I don't see how mine could be called unreasonable. They've already been set by the government."

"I don't follow," Lindy said. "There's no standard inform-er's fee."

"Oh, but there is," argued Mr. X. "Now get this: my infor-mation may help you lock away the guys on several different grounds. Illegal gambling activities, loan-sharking and extor-tion, some interstate commerce abuses, and stock fraud. But your best weapon—the way you'll get a claw on the big drug financiers, the cream of the gambling skimmers—is going to be something else: the same rap it took to bring down Capone and Costello. Tax fraud. Find the money that's been siphoned off and washed and you get the best and the richest. And I know enough about that end to give the Revenue boys some beautiful days in court. It's their stan-dard rate I want, the regular cut IRS gives any other tax in-former."

"Ten percent against the government's net," Lindy said.

"Ten percent," echoed the caller.

"I guess they can't object." Lindy heard a rumbling laugh over the line.

"Oh, can't they? I imagine in your position, Lindell, you

47

can remember the statistics President Johnson's commission gathered, the last time anything like an official audit was done on the total annual takings of organized crime. The figure they came up with was seven billion dollars, and I can tell you that was on the low side—even then, before inflation. Naturally, that includes every nickel and dime that's taken in at the bottom, and a lot of it gets siphoned off in percentages as the money gets passed up the ladder. But what gets to the top is still nothing to be sneezed at. Last year, for example, all the big mob guys put together took in only slightly less than a billion dollars. And you know the average declared income for each of them? Between ten and fifteen thousand. That leaves a hell of a lot of laundry to be done, doesn't it? I'm not pretending I can tap the whole nut. But I might be able to nail down between one and two hundred million in tax claims. So can you figure what my share would be? Or should I give you some help?"

Lindell was speechless. He could figure it, all right. As much as twenty million dollars. Government-certified payment to a confessed criminal, a felon, perhaps a murderer, a man equally culpable of any of the crimes of which he would accuse others. Lindy could see the shock waves ahead. There was no way to give carte blanche approval on this one.

"Well, Lindell. Don't you think it's reasonable—just the usual tax fink's piece of cheese?"

"Damn it, you know this is different. They can't—"

"That's up to them," the caller cut in coldly. "I'll call once more, in a couple of weeks. If they go for my terms, I'll walk in and sing my head off. Otherwise, we just wipe the slate."

"Look," Lindy pleaded. "You could take a fraction of a tenth and it would still be a fortune. Surely you can see the government won't—"

"Then they don't. I've told you: that's up to them. If they go, it's no bargain basement sale. And when you lay it out for your friends in Washington, Lindell," Mr. X concluded, "make sure to remind them: I didn't really set the terms, they did."

The line went dead.

Lindy cradled the receiver. He sat down at the end of the sofa beside the table, rewound the cassette, and played back the conversation. Twice. He came to some conclusions from listening to the anonymous caller, the tone of his voice. He was no mug; there was a touch of cultivation, an odd hesitation whenever he used any words that bordered on Mob jargon, as though they had been deliberately peppered in to make Lindell think he was dealing with a cruder type than was the fact. Oh, yes, this was a shrewd, cold son of a bitch. He would take it or leave it, play a cool hand to the last, never be outbluffed.

And he wanted twenty million dollars, or thereabouts, give or take a million.

A crusher. They would never go for it. Never.

Lindell suddenly felt lonely, terribly isolated. Now that the call had come, the weeks of solitude took their toll. He wanted a woman, wanted to forget the hopeless crusades. He found himself thinking of Ciel, wishing he had not been forced to drive her away.

Then he realized it was she he wanted, not any woman. But perhaps only because she was haunted by similar confusions about the proper balance between right and wrong, caring and not caring.

He laughed at himself. That would be one hell of a cure for confusion, a love affair with a black woman.

He wished he could do something for her, though. She had a heavy time ahead with her sister back on the streets.

Lindy's thoughts circled back to the caller. The man with the secrets, who could tell where the money came from to finance seventy-five percent of the heroin imports, and where it went after it was sucked out of the pockets of the ghetto poor into drugs, numbers, to pay the "vig" to the loan sharks. Uptown they suffered most.

Twenty million dollars?

If it really bought the means to back the Mob into a corner, twenty million would be a steal. Mr. X knew it; his price was already a bargain, there was no reason to go lower. But would they realize it in Washington?

He had to *make* them realize it, Lindy thought.

And Ciel? He would have liked to help with her battles, too. But how many causes could a man fight for at one time?

FOUR

Tom Ryle finished his second brandy and leaned back in the banquette. Spotting a senatorial colleague just leaving another table, Ryle waved across the elegant smoke-filled elegant recesses of the Sans Souci. The other man waved back, but Ryle was disappointed when he walked out without stopping to talk.

"Another brandy?" Lindy offered.

"No thanks," Ryle replied. "Two drinks is the limit these days before they accuse you of selling favors."

"How about a cigar, then—just a thin, short one?"

Ryle laughed. "I've given them up, any kind of cigar. Make me look too much like a politician."

Lindy fumed inwardly. Did Ryle think he was going to get away without giving an answer? Throughout the meal he had repeatedly diverted the conversation away from Lindy's obvious concern. Ryle had talked of current legislation he was sponsoring, avidly pumped Lindy for his reactions to being a "civilian" again, sought an exchange of views on the presidential prospects of one man or another. Any damn thing to avoid talking about the cassette which Lindell had copied from his original and sent to the Senator's office along with an eleven-page letter.

"Well, looky here," Ryle said, feigning sudden distraction with the scene in a far corner. "Isn't that Abe Oringer's secretary with that Post guy, what's his name? Oringer's moving up on Ways and Means, you know."

Now there would be the detour into the gossip that marked Washington, for all its pretensions, as merely another American small town. Peyton Place in red, white, and blue. The gossip could easily take up the rest of the afternoon.

"Goddamn it, Tom," Lindy burst out, "how long do you think you can keep up this evasive bullshit?"

"Endlessly, boy," Ryle said, rolling it out in his mellowest tones, "endlessly. This is what they call the freeloader's filibuster."

Lindy pushed aside his own brandy glass and hunched over the table. "Look, Tom, I'll admit it. I invited you to lunch to buy favors. But you know who the favors are for: the half-million ghetto kids who'll start popping junk this year, and the same number next year and the year after that. Then there's another few million ordinary suckers who'll get taken in one racket or another. The whole country, for that matter, every last citizen who ends up footing the bill for dying cities, for Mob-controlled labor, for counterfeit tax stamps, for the hundreds of millions of dollars skimmed off gambling receipts. Jesus, you name it! Think of all the legitimate businesses that were forced to turn to loan sharks in the cash squeeze, and now may be—"

"No need for an oration," Ryle said mildly. "We're not in the committee room now."

Lindell sat back disgusted. "What's happened to you, Tom? You were the man who wanted to pass the torch to guys like me."

"I don't mind having it passed back, either. But hell, son, that's different from having a red-hot poker rammed up my ass."

Lindell winced at Ryle's vivid crudity. A good thing he could keep his tongue under control when the television camera was pointing his way. Or were there any illusions left to protect? "Expletive deleted" hadn't simply passed permanently into the American language; it had damn near been written into the Constitution.

"Come on, Lindy," Ryle went on in an appeasing paternal tone, "what did you really expect I could do? You remember what they said about ten million going on a few home improvements for a president. What do you think would happen to me if I nursemaid government compliance with a scheme to put anything up to twice that much in the pockets of a crook—I mean a self-confessed crook?"

"A tax informer," Lindy remarked. "He'd only be getting the same bite Revenue has paid before. On an unprecedented scale, maybe. But only if he delivered ten times as much out of which to pay the bill."

"Don't pettifog me, boy. You know damn well what the media boys would make out of this. Not to mention my congressional opponents, or that goddamn fertilizer salesman who wants to run against me next year down home. There's enough political hay in it to feed a whole fucking cavalry of my enemies. They'll have a banquet at Old Tom's expense." He shook his head sadly as though over his own grave.

Lindell had to smile at the wily tricks. Ryle invariably referred to himself as "Old Tom" when looking for the support and sympathy of younger men. It was a ploy so blatant as to be charming, quaint. Old Tom's hair might have turned to silver to match his oratory on the floor, but he came within hardly a decade of looking his sixty-two years.

"Sure I know," Lindy said, "you'll have to defend your position—the government position. You can't take the high ground without going uphill. But don't tell me there isn't a case to be made, and a vote-getter at that. People are fed up with the way we order our priorities, Tom. We'll spend hundreds of millions of dollars on some cockeyed scheme for the CIA because they tell us it's vital to the national security. But what kind of security have we got while we're being nibbled away from inside? Who knows better than you that billions are being milked out of the economy by organized crime? Forget all the invisible losses and just consider the rising cost of law enforcement. Narcs, Treasury, Customs cops, not to mention ordinary police forces where, statistically, it's gotten so you have to employ a hundred cops to make sure you get nine and one-fourth men who'll do the job right. What would the savings be there, countrywide, if we really succeeded in destroying the Organization? You know what I think, Tom? Twenty million bucks—even assuming it went that high—doesn't amount to more than one half of one percent of the money we'd gain back in *one year*. And if enough permanent damage was done to the Mob, we'd get the benefits for another five, ten years to come." Lindy threw his hands across the table in a pleading gesture. "Tom, whatever this pigeon is asking, you can balance it off a thousand ways and come out ahead each time. He's giving us a bargain."

Ryle nodded placidly. "No need to run it all down, Lindy. I read the tract you sent along with that tape. It's all solid thinking, no denying it. You always could write a hell of a good brief. But sometimes the simple logic of a thing isn't enough. Plain facts may say that the shortest way to get to China is to dig a hole right under this table. But that wouldn't get you appropriations to build a tunnel."

Lindy stared sullenly at his former mentor. What a damn fool mistake it had been to consult Ryle. Gabe Konecki had been ready to proceed without any legislative support.

"Tell the pigeon anything," had been Gabe's advice, "get him in the nest and we'll have him at our mercy. Then we can adjust the terms."

But that was a shortsighted policy, Lindy had argued. Mr. X might come in and give information on credit, but he was going to want his money and guarantees in hand before getting up to testify. The man was too shrewd, Lindy guessed, to put himself in a position where the government could squeeze him. A lot of thought had obviously gone into his plan; some form of insurance would have to be included, the simplest being to withhold testimony in the crunch. If there were any hitches or broken promises, he would allow the government to fail in court, deny prior statements, fudge the truth. And once again, as so many times in the past, the vice lords would go free.

So it was better to make an agreement and stick to it, and that would be easier to do with support up front from the senate's leading spokesman on crime-fighting. Lindy had known Ryle would offer some resistance; but he had bet on the likelihood that Ryle would finally rise to the challenge.

It had been a bad bet. Tom Ryle had lost his appetite for challenges. But perhaps, Lindy consoled himself, it wouldn't matter. The fallback position could still be used: do as Gabe had suggested, bring in Mr. X and try to work him around.

Lindy signaled a waiter to bring the check.

"Listen, son," Ryle said, stern but not unaffectionate, "you've been off this scene for a while. A few years ago you smelled the garbage floating downstream and you upped and left, one of the first to resign. You got out with your principles intact, and I admire you for it. But that doesn't

53

give you the right to come back here so goddamn cocksure that the only way to polish up this tarnished republic again is on your spit."

Ryle interrupted himself to wave and flash a smile of election-eve brilliance in the direction of the entrance. Lindy saw that the recipient had been Mack Sunderland, the muckraking journalist. A stooped, oversized man, Sunderland waved back and mimed with his large paws that he would telephone Ryle. Then he proceeded to a rear table.

"Imagine what that hound dog would make out of it," Ryle continued, turning back to Lindy. "My boy, have you stopped for a good think about exactly why you were picked to carry the word to the citadel?"

"It's self-evident, Tom. Mr. X is shooting for the moon. He knows what his information is worth, and by that reckoning what he's asking isn't necessarily unrealistic. But he also knows he needs support from people who fully understand the value of what he's offering—and there could be no better supporter than you. He picked me as the means through which you might be approached, without being as compromised as you would be if he'd contacted you directly."

"So far that tallies with my reckoning," Ryle said. "Where we differ is on what happens next. There's any number of ways I could be made to look bad if I get mixed up in this; and that would be the end of me as chairman of the Organized Crime Committee, maybe the end of the committee itself. As I see it, the Mob may be angling for that very thing. This is all a dodge to set up the anti-crime program for a big fall."

That sounded familiar, but Lindy repressed his anger and contempt. "Okay, Tom. Forget I raised it. Keep right on fighting them your way. Keep those big TV spectaculars. Keep kidding yourself that they make any difference."

"We've made people *aware*," Ryle said, banging a coffee spoon on the table as if to silence a rowdy demonstrator in his committee room. "That's plenty. Why, nobody even believed the kind of rats we had in the cellar until Kefauver shone some light down there twenty-five years ago. As long as we continue the education, the public will help us make the laws we need to complete the extermination."

"The process is too slow," Lindy grumbled. But he stopped

himself from arguing further. The main thing now was not to irritate Ryle so that he not only refused support but threatened active opposition. Anxious to leave, Lindy looked around impatiently for the bill; their waiter was nowhere in sight.

"It's not only the process that's slow," Ryle reflected. "It's the whole system—cumbersome, inefficient, falling all over its checks and balances. But it's the best I've seen around. And the funny thing is, the way it gets screwed up easiest is by trying to whip it along faster than it was meant to go. The past few years, Lindy, we've had too much of doing things the fast way. Too many fast-talking, fast-shuffling, loose-lipped bastards who thought they knew how to get things done overnight. There are no fast solutions to make the nightmares go away. It's time to steer the ship slow and steady." Ryle paused, gazing into his empty brandy glass, nodding in agreement with some interior voice. "I'll tell you what else, son. If you try to go ahead with this, I'll fight it with everything I've got."

Lindy was stunned. "For God's sake, Tom. All right, keep your name out of it. But at least let things take their course. This man who reached out may be under tremendous heat. If we play the hand right, the money demand might come way down, or even be eliminated. In the end he may be happy to settle for immunity and a place to hide."

"Immunities, clemencies, pardons," Ryle muttered disdainfully. "There's been too damn much of that shit. Now, to top it all off, we're supposed to start making 'sweetheart deals' with Mafiosi. It can't be done, boy! No more. We're ripping the heart out of the law, not giving it a transfusion."

"And what's your cockeyed answer?" Lindy said hotly. "For the sake of protecting the law we should keep the criminals on the street?"

Ryle hesitated, then broke into his hoarse folksy chuckle. "It does sound kinda crazy at that. But damned if it isn't the truth. Leastwise we mustn't resort to desperate measures to haul them in. That wouldn't hurt only the Mob, Lindy; it would hurt us all."

The bill arrived. Lindy took out his wallet and flicked two twenty-dollar bills onto the plate, all the more enraged by hearing Ryle mumble to himself, "Yep, keeping them on the street may protect the law," and then continue chuckling.

Waiting for the change, Lindy shunned conversation, averting his eyes from Ryle to study the other legislators and Washington bigwigs who filled the restaurant. Sans Souci, he thought, what a perfect name for the politicians' favorite meeting place: "without care."

"That was always your trouble," Ryle observed quietly. "Too much of an idealist. Couldn't accept the basic absurdity in this government business. Hell, there's no way it makes sense. They want us to keep the world free without fighting wars. Keep the motors running without using oil. Keep the streets clean without paying for new brooms. Craziest of all, they want us to sit here, year after year in Wonderland, D.C., up to the eyeballs in their shit and still come up smelling of roses. Nonsensical, son. It's downright insane. But it'd be crazier still if everybody left town." He left unsaid the words that Lindy knew he was thinking: *like you did.*

"I'm back now," Lindy declared, implying his determination not to drop the issue.

A plate was set in front of him, jangling with change from the bill. He sorted out the tip and pocketed the difference.

"That was a fine lunch," Ryle said graciously. "I do appreciate it."

Lindy pushed back his chair.

"In fact," Ryle added quickly, "I'd feel bad if I didn't do you some favor in return."

Lindy glanced at him, hopeful.

"Just a piece of advice, son," Ryle explained as he took a tape cassette out of his pocket and tossed it on the table. "Destroy that, and any others like it. You remember all the godawful whoop-de-doo we had around here last time some tapes were left sitting on the shelf."

At six o'clock that evening, Lindy repacked his overnight bag and phoned down to the Statler desk that he would be checking out

"We'll have to charge for the day, anyway," the desk clerk informed him apologetically.

"I know," Lindy said. How many hotels in the city would be broke if they didn't charge for afternoons only? Some things might have changed, but there would always be plenty

56

of traffic for the brief entertainments provided by one lobby-ist or another, a roll in the sack with Miss Mayonnaise or the Mogodona County Muscatel Festival queen.

In the past couple of hours Lindy had become more embit-tered by his own failure of will than by Tom Ryle's. He had left their lunch determined to outplay Ryle, line up the sup-port that might be necessary to strike an effective bargain with Mr. X. Returning to his hotel room—booked in an-ticipation of the days of briefings Ryle would arrange to share the imminent break-through with other legislators, cabinet officers, miscellaneous nabobs from Justice—Lindell had hit the telephone with call after call. To no avail. Most of the people he tried to reach, the young executive assistants and committee counsels who had been in his Washington coterie, were no longer around. Few were victims of the ad-ministration changeover. They had left before the upheaval. Like Lindell, they had given up hope early, had returned to positions in private life. A few had stayed, but were unavaila-ble for this or that reason, according to their secretaries. Lindy suspected that Ryle had gotten to them first, and used his considerable leverage to ensure that Lindy was frozen out.

In other cases, Lindy discovered that Ryle's opposition was effective even though it had not been made explicit. When he succeeded in reaching people who knew him and his work with the committee, it was immediately apparent to them that their support was being sought only because Lindy had failed to enlist Ryle's. And if Ryle didn't like the smell of something, why should anybody else? He was the expert.

Lindy had not wanted to contact Gabe Konecki without first undoing some of the damage, but finally there was no one else on his list. Gabe was not in a position to set policy, unfortunately, only to follow it. As a courtesy, though, Lindy could not leave town without telling Gabe why the brakes were being slammed on.

"I'm sorry, Mr. Lindell," Konecki's secretary told him when Lindy called, "the marshal has left for the day. Is it im-portant?"

"Not very. Just tell him it was nice knowing him, and to look me up if he ever gets to New York."

"Oh. I know he would like to hear from you directly about how your lunch went with Senator Ryle."

"That *is* how it went."

"Well, if you think you might be interested in talking to the marshal, you can catch him at the national sheriffs' convention. They're meeting over at the Statler."

Lindell hung up with a laugh. He'd wondered about the men in Stetsons standing around in the lobby. Oilmen, he had thought, in town to hassle over their precious depletion allowances.

After settling his bill and parking his bag at the desk, Lindy found his way to the grand ballroom, center of the convention activities at the cocktail hour. It was being used as an exhibition hall. In the foyer outside the main entrance, a busty bikini-clad model paraded in a bulletproof vest crisscrossed with a silk sash bearing the name of the manufacturer. Passing through, Lindy overhead the visiting sheriffs at the sidelines making ribald comments about the undoubted merits of the vest had it not been dented by "those cannons."

Inside the ballroom, the floor space was taken up with rows of display stands piled with all the latest developments in sophisticated crime-fighting gadgetry, riot control equipment, armament, and police communications. Lindy pushed up and down the crowded aisles searching for Gabe Konecki. He located Konecki at last near a booth displaying pyramids of aerosol smoke screens and riot-dispersing gases. Deep in conversation with the manufacturer's representative, Konecki was oblivious to Lindy's arrival.

Lindy lifted an aerosol can off the counter. "Draw, marshal," he challenged, pointing the can playfully in Konecki's direction.

Konecki turned with a startled look. Seeing Lindy, he gave a snort of relief. "Buddy, you're lucky I didn't draw. Got to be on a hair trigger in this place. You never know what kind of nuts might wander in."

Lindy twirled the can and set it back on the counter. "Is that what you use for your showdowns nowadays?"

"All of it," Konecki replied seriously, his gesture taking in the room.

"And a lot of good it does," Lindy said tartly. "I stopped in to say goodbye, Gabe."

Konecki excused himself from the salesman and pulled Lindy away from the stand. "What's the beef?"

"I came up zero with Ryle. Worse. He didn't just refuse to help; he swore to block any move we make. He doesn't think we should have profit-sharing arrangements with a hood, no matter what's at stake. A 'sweetheart deal,' he called it."

Konecki steered them out of the crowd to a quiet corner. "So what were you going to do? Toss in the towel?"

"Is there a choice?"

"No problem."

"Wake up, Gabe. Do you know how hard it would be to buck Ryle on any crime-fighting issue? This is his baby. His career's built on it. He's got all the legislative support, and as far as the public is concerned he's Kefauver, Dick Tracy, and Jesus Christ all rolled into one, the Great White Hope of victory over vice. I may not see eye to eye with him on this case, but even I have to admit he's one hundred percent honest and sincere. With Ryle's support we could have made a pretty unsavory proposition seem marginally palatable. To balance his opposition, we'd have to line up fifty good men on the other side. Do you know the fifty, Gabe? Fifty decent elected officials who'll publicly justify this kind of pay-off?"

Konecki thought. Then he said:

"How long before Mr. X makes the next contact?"

"When we spoke five days ago he said the final call would come in two weeks. That leaves only another nine or ten days, assuming he sticks to the schedule."

"Between the original call and the second," Konecki observed, "there was a longer interval. A speedup in the timetable could mean that our man is starting to feel some heat at his back. He may be more susceptible to bargaining than he's let on."

"And what if he does bargain? Gabe, this guy could drop his price by ninety percent and he still would stand to get up to two million. Ryle would still block that."

Konecki pondered another moment. "Suppose we don't pay the pigeon anything? Ryle wouldn't mind that, would he?"

"You'll never get Mr. X for free," Lindy said. "I've talked to this man, Gabe, and I've begun to know him. He's really cool, ready to take it or leave it on his own terms. I don't think he is under pressure."

"Whether or not," Konecki persisted, "we can still own him for nothing. Of course, we promise him all the balloons, whatever it takes to bring him in. Once we have him it's another story; he's at our mercy."

Lindy hesitated. "If that's how you want it, then I can't be the middleman. When Mr. X calls again"—Lindy started away—"I'll give him your home number."

Konecki grabbed Lindy and pulled him back roughly. "Why? What the hell are you so worried about? Breaking your word to a fucking hood!"

Lindy shook off Konecki's grip. "Keeping our word is the only way we can win. I've told you: this is no ordinary squeal and no ordinary man dreamed it up. He'll make us live up to our guarantees. If we don't, he won't take the stand."

"Even if we threaten to toss him back on the street, unprotected?"

"If you did deliver him back to the Mob," Lindy asked pointedly, "would you ever get another pigeon asking asylum with the Witness Security Program? Promises have to be kept, Gabe, otherwise we ruin ourselves. That's why I won't cooperate with a double-cross."

"You win," Konecki conceded. "We'll keep our promises."

"Not without Ryle's help."

"Leave Ryle to me."

"What can you do?"

"Reason with him," Konecki replied quietly.

"I've tried that."

A slim, pretty brunette was suddenly beside them. She was wearing a very sexy adaptation of cowboy vest and chaps and had a tray harnessed around her neck.

"Free samples?" she said with a provocative smile.

Lindy glanced into the tray and saw it was filled with boxes of bullets. "No, thanks."

The girl started to move away, but Konecki reached out and tapped her. "What kind are they?"

"Bennington's new long-range .38 soft-nose," she purred by rote, "with impact fragmentation."

Konecki helped himself to a box. "Thanks," he said with a wink.

Lindy watched the girl pass down the aisle, dispensing her lethal charity to willing conventioneers.

"What does that mean?" he asked. "Impact fragmentation?"

"Dumdums, to put it simply. They're getting to be standard equipment with a lot of enforcement agencies. The hard-nose type passes through the body too easily. A holdup man can conceivably take three shots and still stay on his feet for a getaway. Soft-head fraggers don't pass through. They bring a man right down."

"I know how they work," Lindy said. "They're brutal. In fact, they were outlawed by the Geneva convention, along with poison gas. We wouldn't be allowed to use them in a foreign war."

There was a silence as Gabe Konecki pocketed his free sample. "I'm sorry for you, Lindy," Konecki said at last. "You really hate swimming in these waters; I can see it. You want to see the law work, but you don't have any stomach for the nitty-gritty that it takes. And here you are, caught in the middle, because Mr. X pegged you as his messenger boy. Who knows? Maybe it's because he reads you so well, remembers you from the committee as such a pure white knight, that he trusts you to negotiate an absolutely straight contract with no hidden clauses. So you're stuck with it. But remember this, pal: you can't sit on the fence forever, it hurts your balls. If you want to go ahead, if you'll tell the informer to come in, okay, I'll do my best to back up any promise you make. You can't be on both sides, though. You've got to be with us or with him. And don't kid yourself, we may have to fight very dirty to protect Mr. X once we've got him."

"I understand," Lindy said. "I'm with you, of course."

"Good. Now go home, sit by the telephone, tell our man he's on. Bargain if you can, but wherever he sticks, I'll see that he collects."

"You'll need Ryle," Lindy insisted.

"I'll deliver."

Lindy lingered for a moment. Konecki's words echoed in his mind—a promise. Then the wave of noise in the busy hall washed out his inner voice. Lindy pushed his way quickly through the babbling crowd toward the exit, leaving Konecki and the sheriffs and the happy hawkers of dumdums and tear gas to enjoy their party.

61

FIVE

Bart Vereste sat in the living room of his home. The lights were out, but a dull bluish glow shone through the sliding glass panels to the flagstone patio, emanating from the flood-lit swimming pool beyond. Over the stereo came the voice of Billy Eckstein, crooning a rechanneled collection of his hits from the forties and fifties. At the moment Mr. B was warning his foolish heart about the dangerous line between love and fascination. It was Bart's favorite song.

The two weeks were up. Lindell was also at home tonight, Bart knew. A few fifty-dollar bills passed out among the doormen in Lindell's apartment building, and among the elevator starters in the office building where he had his law offices, brought regular phone tips on the lawyer's movements in and out of both places. The call could be made tonight. But not yet.

Long before he had made the first approach to Lindell, Vereste had begin laying the foundations for his defection. It had been necessary to clear the idea first with his son, Marco. If Marco did not agree, it would be impossible to go any further. But there had been little doubt about which way the boy would decide. He and Bart had always been very close.

Next, Bart had tested his wife to see what her loyalties would dictate. Concealing his own designs at first, he had introduced the general subject of Mafia defections into their occasional conversations, putting down the betrayals of past informers to see whether Ginnie would join in decrying them, or show any sympathy. Her reaction had confirmed Bart's hopes. She could comprehend the desire of those who wanted to be out from under the tyranny of Mob life. Finally,

62

when Bart had dared to reveal his wish to inform, she had cried with relief.

Had Bart and Ginnie Vereste been ordinary people, their marriage would have ended more than a decade ago. During all this time it had been at best a lie and at worst a torture. But the code of the brotherhood bound them together. The ruling members of the hierarchy had very strong feelings against divorce. It was enough for some that their religion forbade it; still that was far from the strongest deterrent. There were also the deep-rooted reverence for traditional promises and an almost superstitious fear of tampering with the classic structure of the family. Overall, there was a keen awareness of the dangers inherent in women scorned, or aging men who lost their senses over pretty and mindless young girls and began to share too much with them. There had been divorces, of course. But where they involved men of consequence, they did not occur without the approval of a *capo;* and if a *capo* himself were the petitioner, or a man very close to him, it became a matter for the Commission. Lately, with the Organization coming under greater attack as the government sharpened the methods by which it encouraged disloyalty, the Commission was steadily less inclined to loosen the reins. Where they had granted men permission to separate, even from mutually consenting wives, trouble had too often ensued. The women would find themselves strapped for cash and try blackmailing their former husbands with threats of revelation. The men, having made one marital change, might be encouraged to try others; and as soon as they wearied of their new wives, they might abandon them, thus creating still more hostile witnesses. Despite the customary reluctance to hit women, it had been necessary to contract against them in several cases where resentments arose from divorce, or the attempt to get one. A messy business. The Commission preferred to tighten the rules.

Bart and Ginnie had understood this and accepted the status quo. Their marriage was over, but they slept under the same roof, received their mail at the same address, and took family vacations together. In other ways, however, they pursued separate lives. On either side there had been dead-end affairs, rarely spoken about, but known and tolerated by both. Bart had the television starlets and ambitious cabaret singers who made themselves easily available to men who could help them up in their careers, and get them a spot in Vegas or a featured role in a film. Meanwhile, over the years, Ginnie —in search of "real relationships"—had given herself to one of the children's high-school teachers, to a gynecologist, to a tennis pro at the club near their home in Silver Hills, and to an architect whom she met when he stopped to help her change a flat tire at the local shopping center. The architect, also drifting in an equivocal marriage, lived not far from the Verestes, so Ginnie's affair with him was periodically revived and then put back on the shelf. Year after year, Bart and Ginnie had maintained their arrangement, unable to think of an alternative. Indeed, since lasting togetherness seemed inevitable, they both clung to the hope that someday there might be a return of the feelings that had brought them together at the start.

They had met while both were attending New York University. Recently discharged from the army after the Korean armistice, Bart had resumed the law studies which had been interrupted by the draft, the GI bill paying his way. Ginnie was being sent through college by an uneducated father who was determined to give her opportunities he had lacked; she was one of the first Mafia daughters given the comparative freedom of attending college classes.

In their first chance encounter at a Greenwich Village coffee house near the school's Washington Square campus, Bart thought of Ginetta Francini only as a lively and pretty coed whose name indicated a background not unlike his own, a potential date for the rare evenings he could spare away from his studies. He did not know that for her to appear by herself in the bohemian rendezvous represented a rebellion against her father's strictures; to be there she had slyly eluded two armed bodyguards who guided her, every morning and every evening, directly from the buildings to the door of a limousine with an armor-plated body and bulletproof windows.

When Ginnie refused his request for a date, Bart thought she simply wasn't interested.

He was surprised to be stopped by her several days later in

a corridor. And when he responded to her hints and asked her out for a second time, she agreed, on the condition that their date would not be in the evening, but in the morning or on the afternoon of a school day. With the heavy schedule he was carrying, this was not an easy condition for Bart to meet. But he was more intrigued than put off. He cut a day's classes to take Ginetta Francini to the Bronx Zoo. She was delighted; at the age of twenty, she had never been to a zoo before, and had never seen a live elephant or lion.

They spent many more weekday afternoons walking in the city, or picnicking in the park, or making love in the bedrooms of a small hotel across Washington Square from the university, before Bart came to comprehend fully the nature of Ginnie's commitment and his own. He had learned early enough that Ginnie's father was Joe Francini, whose name had been brought into the Kefauver hearings. But in those dark ages the Mafia was still a unicorn in the garden of crime, a mythological beast. The wealth that had come to Joe Francini might have been earned in part from "the rackets." But what, in fact, were they? In those days the term "racketeer" still carried the romantic associations instilled by postwar movies. Racketeers were men who wore tuxedos every night and owned nightclubs lavishly decorated in shades of white. They were men like Bugsy Siegel, whom the movie stars who played the stereotyped imitations were proud to call a friend. If some of them, like Bugsy, got their eyes punched out by bullets, still the public watching such events in the newsreels made little distinction between the stuff crusted on Bugsy's face and the prop blood in the "coming attractions." And if the Kefauver Committee had exposed Joe Francini as a man with shady connections, it had also proven that there was plenty of good company in the shade: mayors, congressmen, judges, labor leaders. Oddly, this had enhanced rather than dimmed the reputations of the men who had been mentioned or subpoenaed by the committee. They had been elevated to the status of power brokers, rather than demoted to being common criminals After all, most of them had gone unpunished—as if there were nothing punishable—long after the hearings had finished.

Thus it was possible for Bart Vereste to court Ginnetta

Francini without realizing how wide a gulf he had crossed—
into another world. Whatever Joe Francini might be, Bart
thought, however possessive and overprotective he was as a
father, ultimately Ginnie must be allowed to live her own life.

When he raised the subject of marriage, he perceived her
deep anxiety about what her father's reaction would be. But
whether this was because of her youth, or because Bart was
poor and wanted to make his living from the law—the very
thing which Joe Francini earned his bread by breaking—Bart
did not know. Ginnie never explained the real cause of her
fear. She listened in melancholy silence whenever Bart proclaimed his ability to love, honor, protect, and provide as
long as they both might live. Then one day, without any discussion, she agreed to tell her father about Bart and force an
introduction.

Even then, when Bart received a call from Ginnie to say
that the limousine would collect him the next Saturday for
the ride to the Francini estate, she did not tell him that the
two men riding in the front seat would be carrying guns, or
that the car was armor-plated, its windows bulletproof.

Ginnie was nowhere in evidence when Bart arrived at the
estate. Later he learned that on the day after she phoned him
to set the interview with her father, Ginnie and her twin sister had been sent to Bermuda for a month with their mother.
Only the youngest Francini daughter, Rina, had been left behind. Mentally retarded, Rina required the constant atten-
tions of special nurses and tutors.

Bart was greeted cordially enough by Joe Francini; his
hand was shaken warmly at the door. He was taken into the
biggest, plushest living room he had ever seen and offered a
drink, his preference for a neat whiskey met with a Baccarat
crystal tumbler containing a twenty-two-year-old private
bond that Joe Francini boasted was his best.

"Some men," Francini said as he handed over the tumbler,
"have died for a taste of whiskey like that."

Finally they had settled down for a discussion that started
out like any interview between a girl's father and his prospective son-in-law:

"My daughter tells me you want to marry her."

"That's right, sir."

"She says she loves you. What's the story on your side?"

"Of course I love her."

"How much?"

"How high is up?"

Francini smiled. Bart would always remember the exact tilt of that goddamn guileless smile.

"Maybe later you'll tell me how high," Francini had said. "We'll come back to it. Meantime, tell me about yourself, your background."

Bart obliged comprehensively. His upbringing in the small Connecticut town where his father owned a filling station; winning the scholarship to a state college; service in Korea. And his ambition to be a lawyer; the hard study that had won him a place on the *Review;* his hopes of clerking for a top judge after taking his bar exams.

Francini nodded through the recitation, attentive and approving.

"You seem to be what they call a fine young man," he said when Bart had finished. "Now tell me this: What do you know about me?"

Bart answered absolutely straight. He knew about the Kefauver hearings, had even taken the transcripts out of the law library to get the details. That was it. As an aspiring lawyer, he said, he had to subscribe to the doctrine that a man was innocent until proven guilty; and nothing had been proven against Joe Francini except that he had a lot of friends, in the lowest places and the highest. Everything else Bart had heard was from Ginnie: he knew that the Francini interests included hotels, wholesale produce, vending machine franchises, and importing, all of which had made Joe a very wealthy man.

Nervousness parched Bart's throat. He had gone quickly through his drink to relieve the dryness rather than because of any appetite for rare whiskey. But Francini poured a refill of the special bond as liberally as if it were plain club soda.

"That brings us to the big question," Francini said then. "How do they go together?"

"I don't understand, sir."

"Your life—the things you want to do with it—and mine." The innocent smile again. "How do you fit one into the other?"

"I haven't thought about that," Bart had admitted. "I don't

see that I have to fit my plans into yours. It's your daughter I want to marry, not your way of life."

"The American dream, eh?" Francini laughed. "The pursuit of happiness. Everybody free."

"It's worked for a lot of people."

It was then that Francini explained to Bart about the limousine and the bodyguards. "You think I need that because there's such hot competition in wholesale produce? You really imagine I need a steel-jacket limo with windows an inch thick and two mugs riding shotgun because I'm afraid somebody's gonna get mad at me for selling them a bad lettuce? C'mon, kid, think! Didn't Ginnie ever tell you she used to have a brother, and two years ago he was shot down from a passing car while he was waiting on a corner to cross the street?"

Bart could only shake his head wordlessly.

"I thought she might've held back," Francini continued. "Now maybe you'd like to have another try at answering those questions: How much you love Ginnie, and how your dreams are going to mix with mine?"

"I still want to marry her," Bart said shakily. "And I still don't see that we have to mix, except in a harmless way, like any family, on Christmas or Thanksgiving."

"That's nice, Bart."

The familial camaraderie of a nickname, softly spoken. For a moment, Francini had seemed to capitulate. "You know, I love Ginnie a lot. She's one of a pair of twins and to look at them you almost couldn't tell them apart. But she's special to me, my favorite. There's something between us I can't put into words. Even if she was married, I'd want to see a lot of her. I'd want her to live close by."

"Okay with me," Bart said. "The city's a good place to practice law."

Francini moved from the chair opposite Bart to sit on the sofa beside him. His voice had grown even gentler, the voice of the sympathetic counselor.

"I'd have bet on it, you know—given odds—that you'd be like this. A straight, good-looking, levelheaded, hardworking guy. My daughter can spot class. You could be going places, Bart. Around this neck of the woods, who knows—to put it in your words—how high is up? Corporation law, some big

Wall Street shop, from there into politics. Ten, fifteen years you could be sitting on the bench yourself, in congress. Hell, why shouldn't a lawyer become president? And wouldn't I love to have the president for a son-in-law!" Francini had guffawed, then paused to read Bart's expression. "Don't look so shocked, kid. I'm not making a proposition. I want you to see what I see: It doesn't work. We can't stay in the same territory and work different sides of the street. If you're related to me, no matter how straight you play it, people will say you're crooked. Could you take that?"

Bart's silence was the answer.

"No, I didn't think you could. So what's the way out? You go somewhere else, maybe, somewhere the connection won't be made? No good. I want Ginnie around me, like I told you. I want her to marry, have kids, have a good life. But not so I lose her. Like they say, I've got to gain a son."

Francini stood, signaling that the interview was nearing its conclusion.

"I won't give Ginnie up," Bart declared.

"I know, kid. Your feelings are real. So are Ginnie's. You love each other. If I didn't believe that, I would've painted a different picture. I would've talked about power and money, about the difference between suckers and smart guys. I would have done everything I could to turn you around, now or later. But whether I could or not, Ginnie would hate me for trying. She'd hate me a lot worse than if I bust you two apart. At least that way she'll know you got the kind of life you want. And that'll make her forgetting easier."

Francini opened the door and called in one of the bodyguards. This time Bart was acutely conscious of the bulge beneath the man's jacket at the breast pocket.

"You see how it's got to be, kid."

Bart walked out, not defeated, merely numbed by the combined effect of whiskey and evil.

Then in the foyer he called her name, roared it to the top of the grossly extravagant marble staircase.

The noise brought the retarded girl running to peek owlishly over the balustrade.

"She won't answer," Francini said to Bart. "Ginnie won't see you ever again."

She did not reappear on the campus. Twice during the

69

weeks following his interview with Joe Francini, Bart found his way back to the suburban estate, lingered outside the gates in the hope of somehow catching Ginnie alone. The first time he waited a day and half the night before going away. The second time he was rousted after twenty minutes by the bodyguards who forced him into a car and drove him back to the city.

The Francini phone number was listed in the suburban directory and Bart called, but without getting through to Ginnie. Male voices—sometimes, Bart thought, it was Joe—always answered and told him politely not to call again. There were never any threats.

At last, as he got into cramming for the bar exams, Bart ceased trying. He didn't know if he could forget Ginnie, but doing something about the ache would have to wait.

She had come to him.

Answering the knock on the door of his cheap rented room that midsummer dawn, seeing her, he discovered then that his need for her had been quietly growing, not diminishing, during the empty months. Hungry for her, he tried to pull her inside, clawed at her clothing. But she resisted him, would not even cross his threshold. The seconds were so precious, she explained. When they found her missing, they would know where to look. The plan she had made would have to be followed without delay, without deviation, if there was to be any hope of staying together. A trip upstate, blood tests by a country doctor, a marriage license from a county clerk, a ceremony performed by a justice of the peace. And then consummation, as much concentrated intercourse as they could manage, to give the maximum chances for conception to occur. She had purposely waited for her fertile period before coming to his door.

Even with all the contacts Francini was able to call upon among county politicians and state police, Bart and Ginnie had been in the upstate cabin colony for six days before they were located. On that occasion, the limousine carried a complement of five men. Two of them grabbed Ginnie straight off the bed, wrapped her naked body in a blanket, and wrestled her shrieking into the car. They sat with her and restrained her while Bart was taken out behind the cabins by

70

the other three men and beaten unconscious. The car then drove off, leaving Bart to crawl for help to the reception office.

Yet it was not the beating itself so much as the aftermath that clarified for Bart the power and determination of men like Joe Francini. During the week he was hospitalized, Bart told his story to several high-ranking officers of the state police and made a deposition to the county attorney. But nothing happened. Nothing, except that when the county license office was checked, there was found to be no record of a license issued to Bartolomeo Vereste for a marriage with Ginetta Francini. The justice of the peace whom Bart had named as having performed the ceremony was also unavailable. In fact, the state police captain pointed out, that absence was denial in itself, since the JP was known to have been away in Canada for many weeks, way up north where the muskie fishing was real good.

Bart returned to the city. He could not guess what Joe Francini's next move would be, he only knew that it would come. Joe had given Bart too good an education to waste it.

On a balmy September evening, Bart returned from buying groceries to see the limousine parked at the curb outside his rooming house. He climbed straight into the back seat, and stoically obeyed the grim thug across from him—one of the three men who had beaten him bloody—who said to dump the bag of groceries in the street.

Ever the gentleman, Joe Francini started with an apology: "Sorry it took so long to get in touch, Bart, but I had a lot of thinking to do. I thought maybe you would, too. And naturally I wanted to wait and see what happened with Ginnie." The famous smile again. "I'm afraid you didn't make it, kid. I'm not going to be a grandfather this time."

"That's lucky," Bart had dared. "Because the way you fixed things the child would've been born a bastard."

"You mean because we scrubbed the marriage license? Shit, don't worry about that. The same old hick who pulled it out of the file will be glad to put it back for another two hundred bucks. I can get you married or unmarried anytime. It just depends on what you want."

"You know damn well what I want!"

"No, I don't. I explained the choices last time, but you never made one. Remember, I said you could have either Ginnie or your bright and shiny, nice clean American dream, but not both. Well, it seems that you still want both. And you still can't have them. So now it's time to decide one way or the other."

Joe went on to elaborate the difficulties Bart would have if he refused to make the decision. Try taking Ginnie away, so he could pursue his career elsewhere, and they would be tracked and found again. The organization could find any one, anywhere. And the next time, Bart and Ginnie would be separated permanently. If by that time there were children, they would be claimed for the dynasty; Bart would never see them.

If Bart were prepared to cooperate—to "compromise," as Joe put it—the future need not be so unpleasant. First there would be another wedding. It would have to be done right, though: a family affair, a priest to give the sacraments. Then Bart and Ginnie would move into a house nearby; Joe had already made inquiries with real estate agents and found one or two nice properties in the area. If Bart wanted to develop a career outside the sphere of the Francini interests, he would be permitted a degree of freedom, although it would have to be understood that he could go only so far, rise only so high, lest he create "conflicts of interest." Where such conflicts occurred, Bart would have to act in accord with the family's wants and needs, not his own.

It could be seen as a gesture of conciliation, Bart thought, that Joe did not demand some oath of loyalty, force him to undergo some ritual of initiation. Bart had overdramatized, imagined the terms would be harsher.

It was hours later before he realized that Ginnie had actually set the terms.

In the excitement of their reunion, she had assumed that Bart already knew all the news. So not until they were making love—until she had discouraged his deep-plunging assertions with a lovingly whispered "Hey, go easy. You know . . ."—did Bart learn that Ginnie was pregnant.

Much later he realized that the act which had been meant to insure a happy ending for them both had instead sown the

72

seed of his corruption. And with that, the seeds of contempt for themselves and for each other which eventually strangled their love.

The birth of their son, Marco, began a new phase in Joe Francini's efforts to draw Bart more contentedly into the family circle, heal the wounds of the past. The importance Joe attached to his first grandson was all the more inflated by the desertion of Ginnie's twin, Giulietta. Frightened by what she knew of the circumstances attending Ginnie's efforts to take her chosen husband, Giulietta left home soon after the lavish wedding. Whether her decision was connected with a romance of her own, no one knew, not even Ginnie. Giulietta simply disappeared without a trace. When she had not been found and had not voluntarily resurfaced by the day of Marco's christening, Joe decreed that henceforth no mention of Giulietta's name was to be made in his presence. He regarded her as dead.

Daily, Bart was given new lessons in the meaning of the choice he had made. On his own, aided by his fine record at law school and his exceptional set of bar exams, he came near to attaining a position as clerk to a distinguished judge on the appellate circuit. But when the judge was informed of Bart's marital affiliations, the opportunity vanished. There were other judges who would have regarded the same information as a reason to take Bart into their chambers, but he did not want any part of the patronage due Joe Francini. He settled for a job as a junior associate with a respectable, if not particularly distinguished law firm on Madison Avenue.

Bart's first associations with Joe were innocent ones, revolving mainly around his son. The grandfather doted on Marco at their regular Sunday dinners, and the parties on Christmas and Easter and the boy's birthday. Nevertheless it was this attachment that nurtured Bart's deeper involvement with the family's business. By allowing Bart to overhear certain telephone conversations, and to be present when delicate questions were raised with other men who came to the Sunday dinners, Joe had steadily expanded Bart's knowledge of the full range of his operations. However vaguely Bart might understand them, he knew beyond doubt that there was a correlation between things he heard Joe say and

73

newspaper reports days afterward about a favorable political decision or a gangland killing. Bart was not able to go on pretending that he was uncorrupted simply because he refused Joe's favors. He had to accept the fact that, in a sense, he had begun to break the law. Being a lawyer, he could not pretend otherwise when he was forced day after day to make tacit decisions to withhold evidence.

Finally, mired in an unexciting and unrewarding job, his head full of dark secrets he could not share with anyone outside the family, Bart had to acknowledge that Joe had been right from the beginning. There was only one way his life could go. The choice had been made when he had taken Ginnie.

On the Sunday afternoon after the family lunch at which Ginnie announced her second pregnancy, Bart did not resist Joe's invitation to a quiet man-to-man chat beside the swimming pool. He had guessed what was coming, and was reconciled to it, had begun to want it: a law firm of his own to handle family transactions.

"You don't have to be a mouthpiece," Joe hastened to explain. "We've got plenty of shysters who'll run down with the bail when a man's in trouble. I want an office that works for us across the board. There may be some criminal defense, but that's not the half of it. We're into more and more legitimate angles that need mothering. Real estate and stock deals, corporate takeovers, hotel and office building construction. This would have to be a class outfit, you know, to handle our business: two or three floors in one of those new glass *gratticieli* on Park or Fifth. There'd be plenty of trade that would come your way from other families, too, if you wanted it."

He wanted all of it. And having struck his bargain with the devil, he applied himself as thoroughly as if it had been his original ambition. Many of the corporate mazes and international exchange systems through which Mob money traveled from city gutters to legitimate bank accounts were devised by Bart. His expertise drew *capi* from around the nation to consult him and entrust him with their "laundry."

Then, one Easter during the customary children's party at which Joe doled out the candy, Bart was given his piece. He

74

had been sitting alone with Joe on the patio, watching the kids hunt for colored eggs in the hedges around the lawn.

"Kids," Joe murmured. "What's so bad about being a kid?"

The remark puzzled Bart, but he let it go by.

After a silence, his gaze still fixed on the quiet chaos of the egg hunt, Joe rambled on: "I was having these . . these blank spaces. I'd go for something in my memory, something important, and I wouldn't be able to dig it out. Like those kids with the eggs, I'd know this thing was right there in front of me, but I wouldn't be able to find it. . . . Or at breakfast, I'd be sitting at the table with a glass of juice in my hand, and then I'd close my eyes for a second and when I opened them the glass would be gone and I'd be holding a cup of coffee, like I'd gone to sleep and finished eating while I was out. . . ."

He told Bart about the disease then, the confirmed diagnosis of half a dozen specialists: advanced arteriosclerosis. In two or three years he'd be down there hunting eggs with the kids and believing in the Easter Bunny. Two more and he'd be wearing diapers. Going backwards all the way to infancy. It scared him. If the Mob knew he was going senile, losing control, they would carve up everything, and hit him to make sure he didn't start babbling at the wrong time and place. There had been plenty of talk about doing it to Capone when the syphillis had gotten bad, and they had actually carried through against Moretti when his brain went soft. Joe's childless brother Dom, his under-boss, might fire the shots. It usually came from right up close.

Joe begged: whatever had happened between them in the past, he wanted Bart to become his *consigliere,* wanted to go into his second childhood knowing that he had gained a son.

Bart delegated the office to concentrate on running the family. Standing at Joe's side, issuing orders to an empire in the name of a Caesar who could no longer even tie his own shoes, Bart had grown to love the power.

So it was a bitter blow when the Commission arbitrating the claims to succession after Joe's death named Dom to be the next *capo.* The disappointment left an open wound in Bart's pride. Any chance of reconciling himself to the situation exploded when Bart learned through the grapevine that in the diminishing lucidity of his last years, Joe had still found moments to express his clear wish on the succession to other members of the Commission: he wanted Dom to take over. Bart would always be an outsider.

The song ended. Bart's reverie of the fifties evaporated. He looked impatiently at his watch: almost two-thirty. Where the hell was she?

Although he had told his wife and son about his plan to defect months ago, Bart had waited to the last moment to cue in his daughter, Fabrizia. If she was allowed to harbor the secret, her rebellious nature might incline her to do something which would wreck the plan. If forced to move quickly, however, she would follow Ginnie's lead.

Until he had devised his scheme, Bart would not have minded if his daughter's rebellion had found some decisive expression. He had wanted her to cut the ties. But a combination of factors had dulled her will. First there had been her abrupt expulsion from the exclusive New England girl's college, midway through her sophomore year. Though the college administration had been tolerant of her family background, electing to accept Fabrizia on her scholastic merits, certain brahmin families had been aghast at the revelations of their daughters, who spoke with such admiration about beautiful "Bits" Vereste, who even thought of inviting the girl to their homes. The brahmins, who regularly gave fat pledges to the college endowment fund, had made known to the administration their displeasure at having the daughter of a gangster mixing with their own privileged progeny.

In the wake of her expulsion, Bits had seemed to resign herself to the stigma. She had returned to live at home while continuing her studies at a community college. Recently, therefore, she had seen more of her mother, grown more sympathetic to her binding isolation. Their mutual understanding was strengthened by the similarity in the patterns of their lives. Bits seemed to become steadily more reluctant to desert her mother.

Now, in his own way, Bart hoped to help them both break out of their trap.

76

But he couldn't call Lindell without knowing where Bits was. Bart looked at his watch again. Another ten minutes had elapsed. Goddamn it, what form was her rebellion taking tonight? Tonight, of all times, had she suddenly decided to disappear forever?

Why not? One of old Joe's girls had done it.

Or had Bits eloped, as Ginnie had done in her time? Bart knew there was a boy Bits had been seeing seriously, a student from an ivy league college whom she had met while away in New England. The boy's parents had objected to the romance, but he had defied their threats of disinheritance; he had his own car and made frequent overnight drives to rendezvous with Bits.

Bart rose and reset the needle of the stereo to the record's first track. He had waited too long for this night to believe it could be undone by an unexpected caprice.

As he was returning to his chair, Bart was startled by the slam of the front door. He saw a shadow flit across the living room portal.

"Bits?"

There was no answer, but he heard her footsteps lighten as they continued toward the stairs.

"Fabrizia!"

In a moment, her shapely silhouette appeared in the doorway.

"Where have you been?" he demanded.

"If you're worried about the company I keep," she replied, "you'd want me to spend less time at home, not more."

He had failed to curb her insults and rebukes, he guessed, because they were perversely welcome; they spoke for that vestige of himself that was sometimes repelled by what he had become. Yet, having resigned himself to his choice, he had tried to help Bits understand it. He had told her the full history of his courtship with Ginnie. He let himself be drawn into arguments with her about the family business, defended it to her: the organization did not spring from the malice and venality of one group with a desire to subvert society; it supplied a demand, was subsidized by the basic corruption of the system and every man in it. In these attempts to justify himself, Bart had shared a great deal with his daughter. Bits

77

knew more than most of her generation about the operations of the brotherhood. This had done nothing to diminish her scorn.

"Please," Bart said quietly, "turn on the lights and sit down with me."

She obeyed, aware that a grave matter must be occupying him if he did not snap at the bait of her insolence.

"Is mother all right?" she asked.

"Fine. She's asleep."

Bits relaxed in her chair. Bart hovered before her awkwardly. He wished it were possible to express his pride in her openly. But for years she had disdained any commendation from him. At her high school graduation he had rewarded her with diamond earrings. Taking them she had remarked cruelly: "Not hot, are they? I wouldn't want to be arrested before the graduation dance tonight." Later, from Ginnie, Bart learned that the earrings had been sold and the money sent anonymously to a charitable organization for the rehabilitation of drug addicts.

A minute had passed. Bits shifted restlessly in her chair. "Look, I'm tired. If this can wait—"

"It can't wait!" Bart roared, then cursed himself. He mustn't drive her away now. "I'm sorry," he went on quickly. "Listen, there's something I want to tell you, something very important. But first I need to know about you—about this guy you've been seeing."

Bits brushed her long black hair away from her face, as if to expand the scope of her vision. "I've been seeing a few guys."

"But one special, whenever he makes the trip. Your mother told me about him. Is he the one you were with tonight?"

She remained silent, studying Bart with her dark eyes. She heard the real concern in his voice, but she also knew the family history, had always feared the cycle of events would someday wreck the hopes of her heart.

"Tell me," Bart persisted. "Where do you want it to go?"

"Don't worry," she retorted bitterly. "I wouldn't make mother's mistake and try to hook him in. I'm on the pill—in case you didn't get that out of mother in your cozy family conferences."

"Listen, baby. I want you to have things your way. But I need to know what you want before I can fix it."

"Why?" she cried, anguished. "What's brought all this on? Sitting here in the dark listening to nostalgic songs, wishing you had it to do all over again? Maybe that would have helped me: if you hadn't sold yourself."

Bart had ceased hearing the music. He turned off the phonograph and then sat down in front of Bits.

"You can cut loose, that's what I'm telling you."

"Oh Christ," she muttered brokenly. "Just what do you think cutting loose is? Maybe mother could have done it, twenty years ago. She didn't have to know all the shit about *nonno* Joe—have the world know it all—the way I do about you. The books everywhere, movies, newspaper stories. How do I cut loose from that? It isn't only what other people know that bothers me. It's what *I* know. I can't kid myself about what you are, and what that makes me."

"There is a way you can be free," Bart assured her again. "But you'll have to trust me. To make it work I need your cooperation—and it won't be easy to give. But if you do, you can have a new life."

The strength of his conviction was apparent to Bits. She sat up, listening with new interest.

"Tell me, then," Bart continued, "where are things at with your college boy?"

"He wants to marry me," she replied.

"And you love him?"

A final pause. She was still worried about history's repeating itself. Then the tears flooded her eyes. She bowed her head as she nodded and the drops rained on her clenched hands.

"Suppose you two were separated . . ."

Bits sucked in her breath and glanced up, terrified.

"For a while," Bart added emphatically, "a few weeks, maybe a couple of months. Suppose you had to go away without telling him where or why. Would he wait?"

"Oh, God, what do you want?" she pleaded. "What is this about?"

Bart breathed deeply. "I'm going to become a government witness."

79

It was a second before the full impact hit her. Then she jolted forward, her hands clutching his, nails gouging him painfully in the straining, frightened grip.

"Daddy, you can't."

"There's nothing to worry about," he soothed, "if we do it together."

"Mother, Markie?"

"All of us. We have to be under government protection. If I went in alone, any one of you might be killed or kidnapped, used against me."

She released her grip and pushed his hands away. "Don't do it. If it's me you're worried about, it isn't worth it. I'll work something out on my own."

"It isn't just for you, baby, not by a long shot. We can all get something we want out of it."

"How can we? We'll be killed in the end. We can't live in a cage forever, but as soon as we leave it we'll be hunted down, wherever we go." She was trembling, Bart saw, and a hysterical edge had crept into her voice.

He went to the bar and poured two whiskeys. When he brought the glass to Bits, she grabbed it and drank automatically.

When she was calm again, he told her as much as he knew about the Witness Security Program, its impressive successes in protecting others who had turned on the Organization. He told her about the new identity she could have, fully documented so that no one would ever know she had been a Vereste, the granddaughter of the Francinis. He told her everything but his own motives.

"I thought about it once a couple of years ago," she said when he had finished. "Some other guy had turned himself in and made the news and I thought, Why couldn't it be you?" She studied Bart. "But I never imagined you really would. All the time you've been getting in deeper. It always seemed to me that you wanted it. Oh, not at the start; maybe you couldn't help it then. But from the time *nonno* Joe was sick and you helped him. It never seemed as if you had any regrets."

Her gaze, probing, accusing, made Bart uncomfortable. He stood up and moved away.

80

"I can make the call right now," he said, "and tell them I'm coming in. But you have to be ready to go with me. I'd surrender tomorrow."

She hesitated. "If I could just tell Danny, my guy . . ."

"You know it's better if you don't. The more he knows, the more danger he's in."

She nodded. Then she put her glass aside and got up. "All right," she said. "I'll take the chance."

"If he really loves you," Bart said, "you'll make it back to him in time."

"Well," she sighed, "I'd better get some sleep. Tomorrow's going to be a busy day." She went out.

Bart turned to the telephone. He wondered once more if he was daring too much, making another bad choice.

Then he picked up the receiver and began to dial the number.

SIX

Lindy leaned against the gargantuan orange—somebody's brilliant idea for a fruit juice stand—and searched the faces cascading toward him from a vanishing point far beyond the rainbows of plastic. Tired but satisfied faces of men and women, bright enchanted faces of children being led by the hand from the Tomorrow Train monorail to the African Safari boat ride. Vereste had certainly picked a dandy spot for the meeting.

Lindy set his empty cup down on the counter built into the mammoth hollow fruit.

"Another?" asked the counterman, laboriously and inexpertly squeezing the "Fresh Florida Citrus" ballyhooed by the stand.

Lindy shook his head.

"Take another," the counterman commanded. "It makes a better impression." The drink was poured out. Lindy picked it up and turned to scan the crowd again. Within the immediate vicinity he estimated there were no less than a couple of hundred children. Farther from the specified rendezvous point, gathered on the other thoroughfares of Wonderworld, there would be thousands more. The potential for carnage would be breathtaking if, against all odds, against the minimal conventions of decency generally observed by contract killers, an attempt were made here to hit Vereste and abort his squeal. A bug on a phone, a leak from somewhere, a careless move by Vereste—if by any such means his defection had been discovered, what wouldn't be done to stop it?

Perhaps, Lindell reflected now, he should have refused to meet Vereste under these conditions. But the call last night had woken him from a deep sleep. At first he had been too groggy to realize the complications of the point chosen for surrender. And then, when the long-anonymous voice had finally spoken its name, Lindy had been shaken out of his stupor, but had been too excited to think of arguing over any of the terms.

Bart Vereste. No common torpedo by any means.

Lindy recalled the research he had done on Vereste before his appearance at the Ryle committee hearings. Good conduct medal from Korean service, honors student at law school, son-in-law to the late Joe Francini, reputed *consigliere* to Joe and his successor, Dom. It had been known prior to the hearings that Bart Vereste was responsible for the deft handling of financial yields from the Francini interests. Investigation and questioning during the hearings indicated that Vereste's abilities had attracted the business of other families as well. His name had surfaced in suspicious linkages to corporate investment, massive foreign exchange transactions, huge institutional stock portfolios, and one large contribution to the '72 Nixon campaign. Yet he had never put a foot wrong. No clear evidence had been unearthed that these transactions were founded on illicit receipts.

Also fresh in Lindy's mind were recollections of his clashes with Vereste at the public hearings. Unlike other witnesses, Vereste had the legal training to understand the limits of the committee's power. More hardened, less educated men could sometimes be rattled by the effect of high-sounding phrases echoing down from a rostrum in the corridors of the Capitol; their ingrained respect for authority could be turned against itself. But Vereste had remained cool, imperturbable. Improper questions were turned aside; the proper questions were given minimal, valueless replies. Voluminous records had been willingly produced, all attesting to the absolute propriety of his activities. Rarely had Vereste had to resort to the cheap way out of uncomfortable probing, the convenient lapse of memory.

Though he had kept Vereste on the stand for two complete sessions, Lindy had achieved only petty victories. His best consolation had arisen from a stray reference to Vereste's inside nickname:

"Isn't it true," Bart had asked, "that you have been so heavily involved in the handling of illicit moneys, concentrated so much of your talent on doing the 'laundry'—I believe that's the term your associates would use—that you are commonly known among your peers as 'the Chinaman'?"

For some reason that odd morsel gleaned from an FBI wiretape had touched a nerve. Vereste had visibly reddened on the color TV monitors.

"That's an asinine joke," he had snapped. "I wouldn't consider anyone who called me that to be my peer. But if it amuses you, Mr. Lindell, then go right ahead."

Lindy had been struck by Vereste's need to dissociate himself in this trivial way from Mob customs. Thereafter he had been able to gain a few more points by shagging in references to Vereste as the Chinaman. Nevertheless, he could not deny that Vereste had carried the day.

It was on the basis of that performance that Lindy had been so astonished to learn the identity of his caller. He had picked Vereste as a man who would continue to dominate the underworld scene, whose talents were so perfectly suited to the requirements of the Organization in the computer age that he might conceivably attain the pinnacle of power. Lindy had sensed that Vereste, too, had pegged himself to reach the highest rungs on the ladder. If a man like this was ready to give himself up, Lindy thought, then the structure of organized crime was truly on the brink of collapse. With Vereste's help, surely the economic base could be blown out from under the Mob. If he said he could reclaim a couple of hundred million dollars it was no exaggeration. It might well be an understatement.

A faint parroty squawk burst suddenly from the inner recesses of the orange:

"Lindell? Is Lindell there?"

The counterman backed away to a pile of orange crates and lifted a palm-sized two-way radio from the top.

"Right here, Gabe. On his fifth cup of juice."

"Let me talk to him before he floats away."

Lindell huddled over the counter and took the radio. "I'm on."

"Where's your man?" Konecki asked irritably. "He did say exactly fifteen minutes past the hour, didn't he?"

84

"No, he didn't say 'exactly' fifteen minutes past," Lindy corrected. "He said 'precisely' fifteen minutes."

"Whatever he said," Konecki broke in, "right now he's precisely twenty-one minutes late. We'd better try a little change of plan. He may have decided to hang back in a corner, and wait until he spots you first. Move yourself out in the open more; go stand by the hot spot."

To minimize any conspicuous signs of a rendezvous, Vereste had instructed Lindell not to linger at the meeting place, and to approach only after Vereste himself had appeared. Waiting at the hot spot, in front of the ticket booth for the Safari canoe ride, might anger Vereste since it contravened his instructions. But Lindy did not argue with Konecki. With fourteen federal marshals posted near the hot spot, he could hardly believe that it was not already conspicuous. Though they might go unnoticed by the crowd, who saw them only as balloon sellers, ticket takers, Safari guides, and orange squeezers, every one of them loomed large in Lindy's view. The only one he could not see was Gabe, positioned with a pair of binoculars in the space capsule atop the quarter-scale Saturn rocket which gave some overview of Wonderworld's acres of "Fun for All the Family."

Handing the radio back to the counterman, Lindy moved across the midway toward the appointed meeting place. Mingling with the throng of innocent pleasure-seekers, he shuddered again at the thought of violence erupting. God forbid that there had been a leak. It was far from impossible. Before flying up from Washington this afternoon, Konecki had held a briefing with almost fifty men; a couple of dozen other marshals in the security program, a team from the FBI, a number of investigative specialists from Justice, a personal representative from the Attorney General's office, and two liaisons from Treasury. A dangerous number of people. If just one of them had Mob connections . . . But Konecki had said the briefing was essential. Sticking to the timetable Vereste had prescribed left no time for individual instructions decentralizing the operation so that the left hand wouldn't know what the right was doing. Movements had to be quickly coordinated; everyone essential had to be told the schedule as quickly as possible.

Everyone essential, Lindy mused, hadn't included Tom

85

Ryle. He hadn't even been told the operation was on. Lindy had warned Konecki again in their four A.M. phone call that the thing would blow up in their faces if Ryle came out against them after they had gone too far. Gabe's only reply had been a passive repetition of his promise to deliver.

Well, maybe he would. He had delivered the strategic necessities so far. A platoon of men to surround Vereste as soon as he showed his face. And—an even greater achievement—he had convinced the Bureau's people to accept Vereste's refusal to deal directly with them, and not to try horning in on the Wonderworld meet. The prize for their cooperation would be to get the lion's share of the credit in the weeks to come. All of Vereste's information would be fed to the Bureau and they would process it, make the arrests, and prosecute the cases in conjunction with Justice.

Reaching the hot spot, Lindy took up a position against the railing that separated the midway from the edge of a canal which, for the purposes of the Safari canoe ride, represented an African river. The canal charted a winding course around an islet of simulated jungle. Plying the waterway were dugout canoes steered by "natives" in drip-dry loincloths. The passengers were treated to the thrill of mechanical hippos popping out of the water close off the bows of their canoes and the sight of live zebra, water buffalo, and other African animal refugees that were safely marooned on the jungle island.

Lindy watched three full canoes go by.

No one tapped him on the shoulder.

When he glanced around the next time, he caught sight of the counterman inside the orange motioning to him.

"Another twelve minutes," Konecki said when Lindy picked up the radio. "You're our resident expert on Vereste. How do you read it?"

"He'll come," Lindy said. "What else can we do but wait?"

"We could pick up the wife and kiddies," Konecki said.

Vereste had specified a separate pickup for his family so that they would not be exposed with him at the moment of surrender. As soon as he was in custody, a team of marshals standing by near the Vereste home would be immediately notified to move in. Until they had the Verestes under their protection, the house itself was expected to provide protection enough, since by Mafia convention a man's home was off limits to reprisals.

In fact, everything Vereste had specified for the operation indicated a definite fear that his movements were under surveillance. He had probably chosen Wonderworld for the meet because the new amusement park was the most crowded place within easy distance of his suburban home. The crowds would help him evade unwanted watchers, or lose any of his own bodyguards who might have tailed loyally along despite Bart's giving them an afternoon off.

"Wait," Lindy repeated to Konecki. "We've got to handle everything the way he wants it."

"Okay, pal," Konecki answered. "I just hope you know what you're doing."

"Shit, Gabe," Lindy said. "You *know* I don't."

He was about to hand the radio back to the counterman when Konecki's voice came back on with an excited yell:

"Hey, there he is! I've got him in my glasses, just walking through the main gate from the parking lot. Puts him about a five-minute walk from you, Lindy . . . no, maybe more, the way he's going. He's not in any hurry, strolling along like there was nothing on his mind. . . . The two guys I posted down there are falling in behind him. . . . Don't see anyone else who looks like a tail. . . . Vereste sure doesn't seem worried about a scalping party . . . he's walking straight down the middle. . . . Stay with me, Lindy, I'll talk him all the way in."

"I'm with you," Lindy replied quickly, though Konecki could not hear while he continued to transmit.

"Okay . . . there's a third one of our guys joining the caravan. Vereste is still pokin' along. . . . Well, well, he's buying an ice cream." Konecki chuckled. "We make a little back on this deal, anyway. The vendor is one of our men. . . . Now he's moving on, unwrapping the ice cream. Litterbug. . . . Boy, if they were going to hit him here, he'd have had it by now. . . . He's passing the fairy castle, Lindy, coming up to the Atom Smasher. . . ."

Lindy tensed. The Atom Smasher was a ride in the promenade that intersected the midway on which Lindy was waiting.

"You'll have him in a minute," Konecki said. "Uh-oh, that

87

could be his ulcer acting up—he's stopped, looking this way and that. . . . Funny time to get nervous. . . . Okay, he's satisfied; he's walking ahead, faster though . . . finally seems a bit anxious to see your ugly face, Lindy. ; . . He's about to turn the corner. . . . Ooooh-KAY!" Konecki shouted. "You should be seeing him any second. Let me hear as soon as you've spotted. I'll give the call to pick up the other Verestes and then climb down from this tin can."

Lindy sorted through the faces on the midway, a box of colored buttons, meaningless.

And then he recognized Vereste.

"Got him! Moving up fast." Lindy thrust the radio into the counterman's sticky hands and turned away from the huge plastic orange. Suddenly his heart began to pound. A bubble of acid rose from the overloaded reservoir of juice in his stomach, making a horrible taste at the back of his throat. He was scared, plain scared. He was a lawyer, for Christ's sake, not a lawman. What the hell was he doing here? Why had Vereste singled him out?

Vereste had reached the ticket booth ten paces ahead. He paused to look for the contact just as Lindy came up. Recognizing him instantly, Vereste gave Lindell a thin smile.

Lindy was lost for words, trying to catch his breath.

Vereste broke the silence. "I'm warning you now," he said, raising a stiff, pointing finger. "Don't ever call me Chinaman." Then he changed to a more urgent, demanding tone. "Come on, let's move. Where've you got the cars? Has the word gone out to take my family?"

Lindy nodded. "We're all set. The cars are at a side entrance. We'll go straight from here to the safe house. You'll meet up with your wife and children en route." Lindy signaled with his right hand to the nearest marshal, who had been working as the ticket taker for the Safari ride. Hooking his other hand around Vereste's right elbow, Lindy steered him toward where the cars were waiting. A man wearing a red jacket with a lapel badge marked "Information" fell in at Vereste's other side. A man in a gaudy sport shirt who had seemed to be a parent waiting for a child to emerge from one of the rides moved over to walk directly ahead. The balloon seller quickly thrust a free bunch of his wares into the hands of a delighted little boy and took up the rear position. Other disguised marshals loitering alone the sidelines closed in to form a vanguard. Passersby turned curiously as the tight formation took shape and moved up the midway.

Vereste glanced around him and smiled. "Nice," he said. "Very nice."

The first shot came at that moment, the punctuation to Vereste's pleased comment. The man in the red jacket on Vereste's left flank pitched to the ground. A woman who had been leading a small girl in the opposite direction narrowly escaped being knocked over as the man fell. She paused, shocked, looking down at him. It took a moment before she registered that the man's head had been blown open and blood and brain were spattered down one side of her child's dress. She screamed. Then the second shot came. The women threw the child to the ground and fell on top.

Vereste was already down. He had hit the ground faster than anyone else, his reflexes tuned by the perennial expectation of a hit.

But Lindy was still on his feet as the balloon vendor took the second bullet straight through the neck.

The screams of the first woman were joined by others, hundreds, like the cry of a whole rocky island of gulls stirred to flight. People crouched, crawled, ran in circles crying the names of children from whom they had been separated in the pandemonium. A third report cracked through the cacophony, but without taking any apparent toll.

"Over *there!*" cried the marshal who had been handling the tickets for the Safari. He was huddled beside the ticket booth; the high-velocity rifle which had seemed a useless prop in his "white hunter" costume was in his hands, aimed across the canal.

The other marshals scuttled to put shelter between themselves and the line of fire from the jungle island.

Lindy stooped beside Vereste, prodded his motionless figure.

"You can't lie out here, for Christ's sake. Get under cover."

Vereste lay still and gave no immediate response to Lindy's order. Then at last, without lifting his head, he replied in a hoarse whisper:

"The bastard's just waiting for me to put my nose up. I don't think he's got a line on me while I'm down flat."

Since the first fusillade half a minute had passed. The gunman hidden in the artificial jungle, safely removed from any assault on his position by the thirty-foot width of the canal, had picked a perfect vantage point for his sniping. If he wasn't waiting to draw a fresh bead on Vereste, he might already be beating his retreat, unseen, toward the far side of the island.

But the marshals could not be sure. They held back, unable to know where to direct their fire, unwilling to leave cover and risk being fired upon.

Most of the crowd had found refuge. Shrill screams had died to whimpers. In the lull a child could be heard asking: "Is it part of the show, Mommy?" The score of people who had done belly-flops onto the open concrete of the midway were inching themselves toward cover.

From somewhere in the background came a blaring voice that Lindy recognized as Gabe Konecki's. "Move up, goddamn it! Tarbel, Finch, Resser! What the hell are you waiting for? Close in and flush that murdering bastard out of there!"

Lindy looked over his shoulder. Konecki, pistol drawn, was edging his way along the booths and stalls at the side of the midway. Then Konecki caught sight of him.

"Lindy, you idiot! Get that son of a bitch into the shade!"

This time Lindy did not prod Vereste gently, but gave him a hard jab in the ribs. "You heard the man."

"Go fuck yourself, Lindell. I'm not moving."

But, slowly, Vereste raised his head to look toward the jungle. As he did, one of the dugout canoes, which had been making its tour of the winding waterway, came around one side of the island and headed toward the landing dock. Having been out of sight since the drama began, and perhaps confusing any shots and screams with the sound track of authentic jungle noises which was being played over a stereo system on the canoe, the passengers were oblivious to the danger. Realizing this, several of the marshals began trying to attract the attention of the young man who was controlling the boat. Shouting, signaling with their hands, they directed him to reverse his course. Their combined efforts only con-

90

fused the helmsman, and he kept steering toward the dock. The passengers stared curiously at the deserted midway, sufficiently distracted that not one of them screamed when a mechanical hippopotamus came snorting out of the water.

Vereste had watched the drama intently. As the canoe glided forward, he drew his legs under him, preparing to leap up. He would make his run for cover when the boatload of passengers came into the line of fire, shielding him from the gunman's sights.

Lindy perceived Vereste's intention and saw that if another fusillade came from the jungle as Vereste was running some passengers in the boat would probably be hit. Despite Konecki's instructions and his own attempts to get the valuable witness to take cover, now Lindy reached to hold Vereste down.

But the boat had come far enough. In the same instant that Lindy put out a staying hand, Vereste sprang to his feet and sprinted for the juice stand, the nearest protective structure.

A burst of shots was fired as the gunman tracked the moving target.

But Vereste made it safely around the back of the gigantic orange, and the counterman darted out through the rear door to keep him in custody.

Then a howl of sorrow and rage went up from a man in the canoe. "God . . . help . . . my son. . . ."

Lindy whirled back toward the canal and saw the body of a small boy hanging limply over the side of the canoe, his hands dragging in the water. The young man steering the canoe had also taken a bullet, though his wound was less serious; he was clutching one shoulder and calling helplessly to the docks. "What's happening? What's going on?"

Heedless of the lethal exposure, Konecki charged into the open, heading for the entrance to the Safari ride, a gate leading to the canalside. "What's the matter with all of you?" he screamed at the other marshals. "Stop this guy. Now! Do you hear me?"

Hypnotized by Konecki's daring, the others came up quickly behind him.

Crouching at the edge of the canal, Konecki called to the

petrified canoe passengers. "Get down flat in the boat. You, too, kid," he instructed the young man still trying to steer. "Let it drift."

Heads went down out of sight. The limp body of the boy draped over the gunwale was dragged onboard.

Two empty dugout canoes were tied to the landing dock. While one man armed with an automatic carbine covered them, Konecki loaded his team of marshals into the boats. Then he untied them, giving each boat a hard push so it would glide across the canal to the far side, the shore of the island.

During all this activity, no firing came from the hidden gunman.

Konecki ran back to Lindell and they watched together as the marshals fanned out and disappeared into the jungle.

"Bastard's gone, I'll bet," Konecki muttered. "He's had five minutes head start to get out of his blind and disappear."

"Your men may have a rough time anyway," Lindell observed. "There are still the animals: a couple of lions, tigers—"

"They're either asleep or dead," Konecki said confidently. "The hit man must've done something to keep them out of his own way, used knockout darts or poisoned food."

They remained still for another minute, listening. There were no shots.

"Gone," Konecki whispered, shaking his head.

Someone had called local police to the scene. Within minutes heavily armed squads were swarming through the area. Most of them joined in the search with Konecki's team; a few were detailed to shepherd the badly shaken customers to makeshift recovery stations, where they could sit and have coffee until statements could be taken.

Konecki led Lindell through the bustle to the juice stand where Vereste was waiting in the custody of two marshals. On the way they were accosted by a state police captain. He was pale and thin, and his uniform hung loosely on his spare frame as though he had only recently returned to duty after an illness.

"Which of you is Konecki?" he said sharply as he came up to them.

"Me."

"I've been told that you're the man in charge."

"That's correct."

The policeman introduced himself as Captain Albert Waitely, New Jersey State Police. Then his tone hardened. "Now, Konecki, suppose you tell me exactly what it is you're in charge of. What the hell's been going on here?"

Konecki explained his special role in the federal anticrime scheme. "We came to pick up that man," he said then, and pointed to Vereste, who was standing ten yards away.

The captain stared at him.

"Know who that is?" Konecki asked.

"Yeah," Waitely said quietly. "He lives a few miles from here in Silver Hills; that's in my district. If he's doing a squeal, it's no surprise they went crazy trying to knock him out." He glanced away from Vereste to check the activity on the midway. A police ambulance was nuding its way through the crowd, the siren emitting an unearthly yawping as if the machine were desperately gulping for breath. Waitely's gaze settled again on Konecki. "Christ, marshal, if you sat and thought about it for a month, you couldn't have picked yourself a worse place in the whole goddamn state to do the touch."

"Vereste called it, not us. Obviously he wanted the crowds for extra cover."

Not far away, the ambulance came to a stop beside the body of one of the dead marshals. On the canal dock a trio of policemen were transferring the body of the little boy from the canoe onto a stretcher.

"Sure got his extra cover, didn't he?" Waitely said tightly.

"How's the boy?" Lindy asked.

"Who are you?" Waitely snapped, ignoring the question.

"My name's Lou Lindell."

"You look familiar." Waitely paused, trying to place the face.

"I was—"

Konecki cut in. "He's part of our team, captain. Now what about his question: how's the boy?"

"Killed instantly," Waitely said flatly, diverted from Lindell. Then his anger boiled up. "We should've been called in on this, Konecki. If we'd been here helping with security this might not have happened. I'm telling you, heads are going to roll because you didn't take the proper precautions; and if anybody asks me about it, I'll gladly tell 'em where to swing the axe."

Konecki nodded, almost sympathetically. "I'd do the same in your shoes, Captain. But this is standard procedure for us. We couldn't have let you in on the pickup, and you ought to be able to guess the reasons."

"Leaks, huh," snarled Waitely. "Well, cutting yourself out of our help doesn't seem to have plugged any holes. You'd be smart to tell us your next move."

"We're taking Vereste out of here. The cars are standing by."

"I'll arrange an escort," Waitely offered. "I can give you a couple of squad cars and a few bikes."

"Thanks," Konecki said, "but I'll pass. Best to keep the party private."

Waitely's glare became icier. "I have clean men for you. But, okay, be a smart-ass. It's your funeral." He started away and saw the bodies being loaded into the ambulance. "Yours and a few other people's," he added, before moving on to confer with a subordinate.

The policeman's words stung Lindell. He thought back to last night, the call. If only he hadn't been so damn eager to get Vereste in, he would have bargained over the meeting place, cared about the peripheral dangers before it was too late.

"C'mon," Konecki said, with a tug on Lindy's arm. "We've got to get Vereste on the road."

"You take him from here, Gabe. I'm sick of it."

"I thought you were going to take the whole trip. I've gotten special clearance from the AG to attach you to the program."

Lindy shook his head.

"It could make a difference if you drop out," Konecki argued. "Vereste has some kind of fix on you. He might sing better if you're his baby-sitter."

"I'm sorry."

Konecki hesitated. Then he walked away to huddle with

94

the marshals who were guarding Vereste. One of them spoke quickly into a two-way radio and half a minute later a cortege of three unmarked beige cars came down the midway, which was now cleared of people and cordoned off. The front and rear cars were already occupied, four men in each. The middle car contained only a driver. Konecki climbed into the front seat on the passenger side, while Vereste and his two escorts got into the back.

Lindy watched the cars move off. Then he went to the edge of the cluster of people standing around the ambulance, police, doctors, and a man in slacks and a sport jacket. A stretcher was just being slid into the rear of the ambulance. On it was a long black plastic bag. The man in the sport jacket, tears running down his cheeks, caressed the bag as it went past him, and sobbed the same vague question, over and over:

"What kind of people? . . . What kind of people?"

SEVEN

In the brochure put out by the real estate company which had developed Silver Hills, the colony of expensive homes was described as "a new concept in living, combining the carefree joyful feeling of open country with the reassuring security of twenty-four hour protection." In specific terms, this meant that each of the modern homes built to owner's specifications at costs ranging between two and four hundred thousand dollars stood in three acres of grounds divided into oak woods, velvety lawns, tennis courts, and glittering free-form swimming pools; and, moreover, that the entire community of eighty houses was enclosed by a fourteen-foot-high electrified chain mesh fence, with the entrance through a gatehouse constantly manned by two armed guards and linked by direct intercom to each residence. If the fence was cut through at any point, breaking the electric circuit, an alarm would be triggered in the gatehouse; there was also a panel of TV monitors watched over by the guards, receiving pictures from the forty television cameras which scanned the colony from high in the oak trees.

Bart Vereste's particular needs in a home were met perfectly by Silver Hills, an unremarkable coincidence considering that the profitable real estate development was a legitimate offshoot of other Francini interests. That the Verestes were, in effect, the landlords of Silver Hills played no part in their acceptance by the other residents, because the Vereste's financial involvement in the project was a secret. On the other hand, the community knew from the televised hearings of the Ryle Committee that Bart Vereste was more than a successful corporation lawyer; but still this knowledge of his affiliations had done nothing to harm the Verestes' standing

96

in the community. Those who knew about Bart only from their newspapers or from watching him on television might think of him as an odious figure. But the secure, well-off families who saw firsthand the way Bart and Ginnie lived—as peacefully and respectably as themselves—were more amused than horrified by the committee revelations. The women of Silver Hills knew Ginnie as a willing participant in their fund-raising coffee klatches; the men knew Bart as an easygoing scratch golfer, generous with valuable stock market tips. They saw no reason to sever relations, nor—most of them—to prevent their children from attending the swimming and tennis parties given occasionally by the Verestes' son and daughter. Only those who did not have the privilege of knowing the Verestes, of seeing how well they fitted into the community, would have been inclined to shun them.

On the afternoon when Bart Vereste was surrendering himself as a government witness, Silver Hills presented its customary quiet appearance. Men were at their offices, women were shopping or at the beauty parlor, children were at play in the large gardens behind high fences. Only domestic employees remained in the houses, occupied with cleaning or cooking. If it had not been a Thursday, there would have been no witnesses at all to the activity around the Vereste house on Sterling Drive. On this day, however, Pete Breibart was putting in his one afternoon a week as a gardener at the Dorisson's, burning the waste and tending the lawns and hedges. The Dorisson house was situated diagonally across Sterling Drive from the Verestes'. Accordingly, as Pete was clipping the front hedge, he saw the moving van turn into the Verestes' driveway. Thereafter, he glanced frequently across the street, keeping close track of the comings and goings of the four men who had arrived with the truck. Like others who lived or worked in Silver Hills, Pete knew about Bart Vereste and did not condemn him. Why should he? What if Vereste ran the numbers or had some connection with the people who did? Was anything wrong with that? Pete himself put a quarter down every morning at the newsstand where he bought his newspaper. Two years ago he had hit the six-hundred-to-one full payoff, and collecting that hundred and fifty bills was the most exciting moment of his

97

life. Pete couldn't think badly of a man who had something to do with the numbers, but he couldn't help being curious about him. So he watched as the moving men carried three long coffinlike crates into the house, and watched as they made a further three trips from the truck to the house with three large black trunks. Then, after the men had been in the house for ten or fifteen minutes, Pete saw them emerge carrying three more black trunks back out to the van; he could not imagine that they would be the same trunks that had just been carried inside.

But that seemed to complete the job. The truck drove off and the street was quiet again. Pete's full concentration reverted to clipping the hedge. He did not look up from the task until a whiff of acrid smoke came to his nostrils. Not ordinary smoke. The fumes penetrated right to the back of his throat, made it feel raw and dry. Pete had smelled something like it whenever he accidentally threw anything plastic into the Dorisson's incinerator along with the leaves and paper. The incinerator was going now; maybe he'd done it again, thrown in an empty fertilizer bag. Pete started around the the back of the house. But as he walked, he caught sight of a line of smoke seeping from under the closed door of the Verestes' garage.

He ran straight over and put his hand to the metal door to open it. As soon as his palm closed around the handle, Pete yelped with pain. The handle, the whole damn door, was hot as a frying pan! Pete whipped out the pair of work gloves jammed into his back pocket, wrapped them around the handle, and tried to lift the door. It was locked.

Blowing on his blistering palm, Pete ran to the front door of the house and pushed the button to ring the bell. There was no answer. He kept leaning on the bell. Someone had to be home. Someone had let the moving men in, had taken the call from the gatehouse and cleared the truck to proceed through to the house.

Still, no one came to answer the door.

Pete ran around to the back of the house, tried the rear door with the same negative result. Spotting a leaf rake propped against the back wall of the garage, Pete grabbed it up and was about to swing it through the kitchen window when he stopped himself. This was Silver Hills. He didn't dare break in. If he was seen, his actions misunderstood, he could be blamed for the fire. Pete dropped the rake and ran around to the front of the house again and then up Sterling Drive toward the gatehouse.

At the same moment a black limousine with U.S. Government registration plates was turning into the entrance to Silver Hills. One of the security guards leaned out of the gatehouse toward the driver's window. A wallet was flashed open, exhibiting a golden badge.

"U.S. marshals," said the driver. "Mrs. Vereste is expecting us."

"Don't mind if I check, d'ya? Don't like to have our people bothered without their permission."

The marshal nodded to the security guard, and shrugged to the other man in the front seat of the limousine.

The guard went to his phone and pushed the intercom button tagged with the Vereste name.

"You say she's expecting you?" the guard asked, when he received no reply on the intercom after two minutes.

"Keep trying," the marshal said. "She's there."

"Yeah, I suppose she's busy. There was a moving van went in and out a while ago." The guard left his finger on the intercom button. He removed it only when the second guard distracted him.

"Hey, Stan, what's this?" The second guard pointed out the gatehouse window at the figure running in their direction, screaming frantically.

"What's he saying, Dave?" asked the first guard.

"Fire! There's a fire." The second guard pushed a fire alarm button connected to the nearest firehouse.

The two marshals in the limousine exchanged a quick glance.

"Get in with us!" the driver shouted at the two guards.

The security men piled into the back seat of the limousine before it shot through the gate. The car screeched to a halt to take aboard Pete Breibart, then roared on through the privileged serenity of Silver Hills.

EIGHT

Dom Francini was spending the afternoon at Belmont Park. By the end of the seventh race his losses amounted to eighteen thousand dollars. And at that he had to admit he'd been lucky. Steve Drapetto had called this morning to tell him about a horse that would be juiced in the fourth; somebody's third cousin was on the split box to switch the urine sample after the race. It was a sure thing. If Dom had not bet that one, he would have been down another twelve k. Good old Steve, count on a one-armed man to know the five-legged horses. Unfortunately, it wasn't enough of a break to keep Dom from plunging into one of his blackest moods. He didn't mind losing the money; there would always be more of that. What gave Dom heartburn was the sheer insult of being proved wrong, time after time, by dumb animals. This was the repugnant paradox that kept him and so many others in the brotherhood always coming back for more: They could outsmart people anytime, yet these damn animals could fool them.

What added to Dom's annoyance today was that Sal Raguza, the soldier he had brought along to the track, was on a winning streak. Sally Rags made a fair chunk now and then running gambling junkets to the Caribbean, but he normally couldn't afford to bet in the same league as Dom. Yet he was already up eleven big ones for the day. Dom's only consolation was to make winning a very unpleasant experience for Sal.

"Why didn't you tell me the fix was in on that one, Sally?" Dom would ask menacingly each time the soldier picked a winner.

"Jesus, Dom, that wasn't no junk race. I guessed right, that's all. You coulda bet with me, I didn't stop you."

100

To ease the tension, Sal had tried to press a thousand of his winnings on Dom—"for the ride to the track"—but Dom had refused it. He got more pleasure out of keeping Sally Rags on the hook.

As Dom and Sal sat in the clubhouse looking over the card for the eighth race, Steve Drapetto appeared beside their table.

"Hey!" Dom boomed brightly. "Just the man I need. I didn't know you were coming out today."

"I wasn't going to," Drapetto said grimly. "I only arrived a minute ago. I rode out with Don Valerio."

Dom tensed. Ligazza had often expressed his disapproval of the races, especially for those who bet excessively. Public display of large amounts of cash invited trouble, either in the form of investigation by the Revenue men who circulated around the tracks, or as the source of resentments within the brotherhood, divisive jealousies between those who had the luck and those who didn't. Gambling was a fine way for the Organization to make money, Ligazza proclaimed, but only the biggest fools would make suckers out of themselves. He had frequently chided Dom about his betting habits at gatherings of the Commission. The most nettlesome feature of these castigations was the way in which Don Valerio inevitably held up Joe Francini as an example to be emulated. Joe had been a *gentiluomo;* if only there were still more around like Joe. Dom often felt that Ligazza regretted the leverage he had exerted with the *Commissione* for Dom to be picked as Joe's successor instead of Bart. But then Ligazza had done it only out of respect for Joe's own wishes.

"What's Don Vee doing out here?" Dom asked guardedly. "He always shits on the track."

"We came for you," Drapetto said flatly. "Give Sally your car keys. You'll ride back with us."

Dom hesitated.

"Now," Drapetto said forcefully.

Ligazza's Rolls-Royce was waiting in the special enclave reserved for officials of the track. No mistaking the number plate, VL-1. A fine one he was to talk about ostentatious public display, Dom thought as he approached the shining wine-colored car. Ligazza had the balls to ride around as if he were the goddamn governor.

But Dom gave Ligazza a polite, deferential greeting as he stepped into the Rolls and settled beside the old man on the rear seat.

Ligazza acknowledged Dom with an imperious nod and said nothing.

Drapetto placed himself sideways on one of the pull-up seats, partly facing around to Dom. Then the car got under way.

Dom perceived that Ligazza was in a white-hot fury. He waited, expecting the conversation to open with another reprimand for his gambling excesses.

"What have you told him?" Ligazza said finally, speaking to Drapetto.

"*Niente.*"

"About what?" Dom asked anxiously. Suddenly he felt an atmosphere of doom in the car like the mood in a hospital ward of incurables.

Ligazza regarded Dom coldly. "Not quite two hours ago, your *consigliere* surrendered himself to federal marshals."

The implications were immediately apparent to Dom. His heart skipped a beat, the outer extremities of his immense body felt numb. "Shit," he muttered, "I guess we might as well all leave the country."

"Let me not hear that kind of talk!" Ligazza said sharply. "Run like rabbits? We'll stand our ground and beat this challenge as we have any other. The law grinds slowly, Don Domenico; it is at the mercy of those who move swiftly, with bold strokes. So we will stay and fight, all of us. We will find Bart Vereste and destroy him. If any of us are arrested, we will make the bail and continue the hunt."

"We should have hit him before," Dom growled wrathfully, one of his hands slamming down on his broad thigh. "But you wouldn't go for it, neither of you. Thought we couldn't do without his brains, all his fancy schemes for—"

"Yes, you called it," Ligazza cut him off quietly. "We wondered, in fact, if you had gone beyond that—had put out a contract?"

"I couldn't," Dom grumbled. "You know that. He was guaranteed by you."

"It's nice to hear you respect the rules. But the fact re-

102

mains a contract was out." The old man's brilliant gaze bore down hard on Dom Francini. "Somebody evidently knew Vereste's intentions and tried to cut him down first."

"Not me," Dom replied, puzzled by Ligazza's aggressive tack. "But wouldn't it be smart if I had?"

Ligazza glanced to Drapetto. They were judging him, Dom knew.

"We'd be better off, wouldn't we?" he insisted, a tremble creeping in.

"If it hadn't been botched," Drapetto replied. "Bart's meet was set for a place called Wonderworld—a big new fun park not far from his house. There was a mechanic on hand and he went for the hit right there. The trouble is he missed, badly. He took out two fed marshals and a seven-year-old kid, but Vereste didn't lose a drop of blood."

"You understand, Fisherman?" Ligazza chimed in. "Bad enough our man goes over—probably the most valuable man we've ever lost—it also happens in such a way that the public appetite for his information will be magnified a hundred times over. No one cares if we use our guns to kill each other. But wait and see what happens when the death of one innocent child must be avenged. Read the editorials in the newspapers being rushed onto the streets at this moment. We've given the crusaders a martyr, a rallying point. Whatever Vereste can tell them will be that much more hungrily gobbled up, indictments more quickly sought, judges that much harder to reach—"

"Well, it wasn't my play!" Dom shouted.

"And the fire?" Ligazza pressed on.

"What fire?"

"The failures of the one who struck at Bart may have damaged us," Ligazza railed, "but perhaps his success was even worse!"

"Success? What—"

Drapetto cut in. "About the same time Vereste surrendered, a fire broke out in his home. A real pro burn job, we gather from the news. They found three bodies in the ashes; just enough of them was left to tell there were two females and a male."

Dom swallowed hard, sending a ripple across his accordion

chin. The only person he'd ever felt any family attachment to was Ginnie. Knowing she was unhappy in her marriage had contributed to his dislike of Bart.

"I'd never have done that," Dom murmured.

"Of course not," Ligazza said dryly, unpersuaded that any act of violence was beyond Dom Francini. "The point is that it severely damages our counterattack. If his dependents had lived, they would also have been harbored by the government. Instead of having one trail to follow, we would have had four. The wife, the son, the daughter—each had worlds of their own from which they would have to separate, each might have left distinct clues to where they were headed, the identities they would assume. These extra benefits have been lost to us."

"Maybe that was the idea," Drapetto said. "Bart had them burned."

Ligazza gloomily eyed the traffic which had congealed around the Rolls as it drove nearer the city. "I don't think he was capable of such an atrocity. It smacks more of the vendetta."

There was a silence. Dom understood now what was agitating Ligazza. The prime suspect for the hit on Bart and his family had to be Rocco Gesolo. Ligazza could not acknowledge that, however, without being faced with the dilemma of whether to discipline Rocco.

"This shooting may have screwed us up," Dom said at last. "But at least it busted things open. Without that, it might've been weeks before we realized Bart was a fink. You know how Uncle Sugar works these days. They sneak a guy away to a tree-house somewhere, keep him talking night and day. You never know there's a squeal on until the swoop comes. But we know from the start. We've got a chance to choke it off before Bart spills too much."

"Presuming we find him," said Ligazza as he turned from the window to Dom. "Hard times require harsh methods, Don Domenico, and there are none harsher than yours. The Commission charges you personally with the responsibility for hunting down the offender."

"Me?" Dom protested. "But this is too big, Don Vee. It should be handled right from the top, by you."

"He was your man," Drapetto said. "Therefore, the responsibility for his actions must be yours. Of course, you won't be on your own, Dom. None of us have any higher priority than finding Bart and whacking him out. You can call on the help of any man in the Organization from anywhere in the country."

"But I don't know where to start, who to—"

"Emergency is the mother of invention," Ligazza paraphrased. "You'll bring to the task a determination out of which I'm sure we can expect positive results. You must, Don Domenico, there's no other way. Naturally, I'll be available for consultation; in fact, I shall insist on daily progress reports. So don't worry, *mi amico,* you aren't alone."

But he was, Dom understood; he had never been so alone. They were all shaken to the roots by Vereste's run, even the mightiest, even Ligazza. They needed the sacrificial goat and he was it. As long as the plague lasted, as long as they couldn't strike directly at Bart, his own life was mortgaged. If he didn't bring Bart to justice, he would take the hit himself.

But there was no refusing a charge from the Commission. There were only two choices: find Vereste, or die for failing.

Shakily, Dom voiced the respectful compliance demanded by custom. "I will do whatever the Commission asks of me. Vereste will be found and punished."

"*Bene,* Domenico," Ligazza said. "I knew we could count on you."

The Rolls had halted in a solid jam of cars. Ligazza looked out the window again. "*Dio,* look at this traffic," he declared irascibly. "Why doesn't somebody do something about that?"

NINE

Lindy had been keeping half an ounce of grass in his apartment, the remains of a Christmas present given to him by the actress. Previously it had been reserved for an accompaniment to their sexual explorations; since breaking off with the girl, Lindy hadn't touched it.

Tonight he was using it to anesthetize himself. Unable to satiate a masochistic hunger for the radio and television news about the Vereste surrender, he sought something to make it more tolerable. He had started with a couple of shots of Scotch, but the liquor had brought him farther down, intensified the morbidity. The grass worked better. It dulled his feeling of personal responsibility.

Earlier, listening to the first news reports, he had blamed himself for the whole inventory of death—not only the three Wonderworld killings, but the annihilation of Vereste's close family. His cooperation in the scheme had brought it on, his eager willingness to parley with the informer. Only now did Lindy realize the tumbling cataracts of blood that could flow through the dam broken with Vereste's defection. Even the gardener who had discovered the fire at Vereste's home was said to be under federal protection, a marked man in case he had witnessed anything which would help to identify the murdering arsonists. But what good was federal protection? The Vereste family were supposed to have had it.

As the evening wore on and Lindy subjected himself to hearing the gory facts repeated, watched the films brought in by television news teams—dried blood on the midway, police scouring a fake jungle for spent cartridges—the marijuana soothed him, dulled the ache of guilt. The gentle hallucinogenic effect fuzzed the line between fantasy and reality, be-

106

tween the *Movie of the Week* and the eleven o'clock news. It was just another Mafia melodrama. He had been part of it for a time, but he could close the book.

The door buzzer called Lindy out of his drifting thoughts.

Ciel Jemasse was standing outside. He had mediated for her in obtaining a lease on the penthouse. There had been no static yet from other tenants, but Ciel had scarcely moved in; the lease had come through only three days ago. A lifetime ago, Lindy thought, as he looked at her now.

She was wearing faded jeans and a man's frayed button-down shirt, hugely oversized, obviously a hand-me-down from her ex-husband.

"Is it too late for a neighborly visit?" she asked. "I tried calling, but your phone's been busy all night."

"I left it off the hook," Lindy explained.

"Oh." She took a closer look at him. "You all right, man?"

"Sure. Come in." He stood back from the door.

She hesitated. "Nothing important, you know. I was just unpacking my crates, hanging pictures; and it was so nice, Lindy, I wanted to tell you—to thank you." She stepped back. "But I can see it's a bad moment—"

"Don't go. It's a bad moment, all right, but the company would make it better."

She came inside and he closed the door. The dialogue of the late-night movie, a gangster film, was reverberating loudly through the apartment. Lindy went into the living room and Ciel followed, hovering uncertainly in the passage from the small entrance hall.

"Drink?" Lindy asked as he switched off the television.

Ciel came farther into the room. "If you're having one."

"I'm not." He picked up the joint smoldering on a plate beside a half-eaten sandwich and held it out to Ciel. "You go for this stuff?"

She stared at it a moment, then shook her head. "Not often. It always reminds me of the shit my sister's gone through for a few kicks. I know it's not the same, not in theory. But that does kinda make it harder to enjoy."

Lindy nodded and stubbed out the cigarette.

"Hey, baby," Ciel said quickly, "I'm not preaching."

"I know." Lindy smiled. "How is your sister, anyway?"

107

Ciel waggled two crossed fingers. "So far, so good. She came downtown today and I took her out to lunch. She looks real fine, putting on some weight. I think I did the right thing, moving out." She sat on the sofa, and watched Lindy until he had seated himself across from her. "Now, why don't you tell me what's bugging you?"

He sighed. "Heard about those shootings today?"

"I saw a headline on a paper when I was riding home on the bus. Big Mafia character went to turn himself in and all hell broke loose. What's that to do with you?"

"I was there," Lindy said. "I was the middleman."

She gazed at him, sympathetic but not completely comprehending.

He sketched in the story of his involvement, from the first phone call to the last bullet.

When he was finished, Ciel crooned softly, "Wow, baby. You've had a day, all right. But if your Mister What's-His-Name, this informer, if he can really come up with the goods, you've got nothing to feel bad about. They ought to give you a medal."

"That was the way I had it figured," Lindy said ruefully, "until today. This was practically a dream come true. Two years I'd worked for the government of my country, trying to lift up the rocks a little, scrape out the bugs crawling around underneath. It didn't amount to a thing. But Vereste was going to change all that, was going to make it seem worthwhile. Maybe that sounds crazy, because this time I didn't do anything except take a couple of messages. But you see, he wouldn't have picked me if I hadn't been on the committee, so the time I put in meant something, after all. Finally, it gave me this chance to help."

"And you did, baby, you helped plenty."

"I don't know. Is it worth fighting these guys if ordinary people get caught in the cross fire? We'll see. The government has had informers before, and they haven't made a real dent. This one's supposed to be different, the new model, bigger and better. But is he really? Maybe that's just some hype I fell for, and sold myself on while I was selling everybody else. In the meantime, while I wait to see what Vereste is worth, I've got to live with what I saw today; a little boy reduced to a lump of meat in a body bag. It's pretty hard to believe Vereste was worth that."

"And that's why you're tearing yourself up!" Ciel said with a harsh, accusative edge. "Man, you come uptown with me. No meat there, but plenty of bones. Skeletons! Nine, ten years old, some even younger; skinny, wasted kids standing around the streets and trying to figure out where to grab a little green. Not a dime for a candy bar, baby, but four or five dollars for a jolt. And where do you think it comes from? Sure, we've got nice black boys and Spanish gauchos dealing off the decks. But who's the Man who really puts it on the street, lays out the millions to keep it all comin'? And who's got the law in their fist, who's been paying for years to pull the teeth on any legislation that would make a difference?"

"Look, you don't have to tell me." Lindy moved out of his chair, escaping from her assault.

"No. I bet you've seen all the statistics," she went on, unrelenting. "You could probably tell me how many of those skeletons become corpses. But that doesn't move you. One little white boy catches his on a day out with daddy, you get haunted. There's nothing so touching about the little nigger bastards who OD every day in tenement halls."

Lindy was at the window. He stared down at the city streets, slick with a spring rain.

His silence screamed at her. She rose and went to him. From behind, she reached out to touch him, and then drew back. "Lindy, I—I've got this stuff eating at me, you know, because of Avril, because I'm running out myself, and I don't see what else there is to do. But it's crazy getting it off on you. You're the last guy who deserves it. Forgive me."

He nodded without looking at her.

She was turning to leave when he spun and caught her arm.

"Stay."

His hand slid down to hers. She held on a long time, her fingers playing delicately with his. Lindy pulled her closer.

"No," she said, gently resisting. "I'd like it. I've had it on my mind. But not tonight. Not only because it's extra hard to be alone or because we have to prove the differences make no difference."

109

"It isn't that."

"Are you sure?"

He smiled and shook his head.

"Neither am I," she said. "Let's wait for a time when we are."

They released each other.

"Guess I'll get back to my decorating," Ciel said. "Nothing like putting pictures on the wall for working off hang-ups."

He walked her to the door.

"I may be out of town for a while," Lindy said as she went out. "I'll call you as soon as I get back."

They watched each other until the elevator came.

After he closed the door, Lindy went straight to the phone.

"U.S. Marshal Service," the voice answered his call. "Night duty."

"Can you tell me how to reach Gabe Konecki?" Lindy asked. Immediately there was a sharp click on the line; Lindy thought he had been disconnected. Then the night duty officer came on again:

"Who is this?"

"Lou Lindell."

"I can get a message to Marshal Konecki. He'll have to call you back."

Lindy understood. Gabe was at the safe house. They had to be suspicious of anyone trying to wangle phone numbers or locations. The click he'd heard was probably some kind of automatic trace being switched on.

"Tell him I've changed my mind," Lindy dictated his message. "Tell him I want in."

Konecki called back twenty minutes later. His voice came through with an echoing, metallic quality, and there was a high-pitched background whistle; not an ordinary phone line, Lindy thought: electronic, probably, and scrambled.

"I'm real glad about this, Lindy," Konecki said. "Vereste was pretty unhappy to hear you weren't going to be around. You're his handpicked contact, after all. He still wants to do his talking through you. Hasn't given us much since we tucked him in."

"It is rushing things a bit," Lindy remarked tartly, "if you expect him to talk right after his wife and kids have been wiped out."

Konecki paused, as if repressing a defense. "He's not suffering, believe me. He'll open up anyway, sooner or later; he's got no choice. But if you're around, someone he trusts, it'll be sooner. And we need quick results, Lindy, need them bad. The way things blew up this afternoon we're under tremendous pressure to justify taking Vereste. And that's without anyone being wise yet to the deal we gave him. Before that gets out, we've got to have a few bosses under arrest, something to balance the books."

"How do I find you? I'll leave in the morning."

"Can't do it like that. Security. I'll have to arrange transport. I'll give you an early call tomorrow and tell you where to meet our ferry service." Konecki added quickly, "Lindy, do you own a gun?"

"Hell, no. What do I need a gun for?"

"Look, I was on the point of calling you when your message came through. Something's been nagging at me, and you've got to know about it."

"Give."

"Well, it's obvious there was a leak before today's meet. Not long before, I'd guess, because the way the hit was staged it must've been a last-minute desperation move: the publicity didn't do us any good, but considering Vereste came through, it probably hurt the Mob even more. So where do they go next? It might well depend on what else they can learn through the leak."

"You mean, they might know the location of the safe house?"

"No," Konecki said definitely, "I'd swear that's still secure. We've been extra tight with that information—sealed orders, the works—and every man here is a charter member of the program. It would be fairly easy, though, for the wrong people to get your name. You've been hopping around Washington for more than a month, talking up this golden opportunity. Anyone looking for Vereste might come after you for a key to his hiding place."

111

"But I couldn't tell them."

"They don't know that. All they know is you're heavily tied in."

"Christ," Lindy said, "can you tell me where to find an all-night gun store?"

Konecki gave a short laugh. "No cause for panic. You're in the best place for now—off the street. And from tomorrow you're under our protection."

"That still leaves tonight."

"I'll see if I can connect with a couple of our men down there, put them on picket duty. It's late and I may not round them up, but I'd rather not bring in police or FBI. There are too many cops on the take, and once the Bureau has you under its wing they won't let you go anywhere without tagging along. You know how Vereste feels about them."

"Okay," Lindy said. "I can make it through one night."

"You've got a night doorman in your building, haven't you?"

"Yes."

"Tell him to give you advance warning if he sees any unlikely visitors lurking around," Konecki suggested. "Now go to bed and don't worry. I'll give you your wake-up call bright and early."

"Thanks. But I'll be sleeping with my eyes open."

They said goodnights and hung up.

Lindy checked the locks on the front entrance and a service door behind the kitchen. Then he called the night doorman and relayed Konecki's instruction.

He struggled uncharacteristically over the chore of packing some clothes for his trip. How long would he be at the safe house? Where was it, in what kind of climate? Finally he sorted out a minimal all-purpose wardrobe, crammed it into a valise, and went to bed. Lying in the dark, he wished Ciel were there beside him. Her rages had reminded him of the reasons for taking Vereste; her sorrows had given him perspective on the sacrifices—among which, Lindy was coming to realize, might be the loss of his own life.

TEN

The phone rang at a few minutes past seven.

Dom Francini was deeply asleep, having been up until after three, trying to plot strategy for the search with a few of his chief lieutenants and enforcers. Dino Forte had been at the house and Ottavio Stirelli and Tommy Aleppo. Dink, Stirrups and the Leper, as they were known more familiarly. (The giving of nicknames was no longer a mere affectation of Mob life; in the years since the FBI had started wholesale bugging of homes and offices, code references to people and places had proven a valuable means of circumventing the use of names that would be evidential.) Sally Rags had stayed in, too, after delivering Dom's car from the track. And Carlo "Dagwood" D'Agobbrochi had arrived late, after flying straight home from a Miami holiday upon hearing the news.

Among them, however, they had produced no hopeful plan for quickly locating Vereste. It would be a long and arduous task. They would have to grill anyone who had talked to him lately, look through his papers—if they could find any of value that had not been destroyed—and track down minute clues. As Stirrups had succinctly stated it: "We're gonna have to work like a squad of fucking detectives."

In the manner of infantrymen on the night before a big battle, they had passed the hours until three finding ways to keep their minds off the problem rather than working to solve it. Drinking, griping, playing occasional rounds of poker, cursing Vereste, avoiding the sorry admission that their mission was futile. Since the government had started making special efforts to protect its witnesses, not one of them had been picked off.

When the jangle of the telephone cracked into Dom Fran-

113

cini's consciousness this morning, it frightened him. This must be Ligazza calling, already demanding a progress report. Who else would dare to disturb him at this hour on his private line? Dom remained on his back, his thick eyelids glued shut by sleep. But the phone rang insistently. At last he flopped over and grabbed the receiver.

"Yeah?"

"Don Domenico, this is Jack Trandi."

Dom knew Trandi. He owned a bar out on Route 57 which had been used now and then as a meeting place. "Trandi! You wanta lose your head? What the hell kind of hour—"

Trandi interrupted the tirade. "I apologize for waking you, Don Domenico. But I have information that may help you to find Bart Vereste."

Dom pressed his ear harder to the receiver. "Spill it."

"A state police captain who was at the scene of the walk-in has provided the names of two men who worked the contact. One is the fed marshal who took Vereste into custody. The other was Louis Lindell."

"Lindell?" Dom rummaged in his fogged memory. "You mean the same guy who sat with the Ryle circus?"

"The same. The way I hear it, Vereste was pulled out by a crowd of marshals. They drove him to an airport, and he was flown off to an unknown destination. But Lindell didn't go along for the ride. He was seen leaving Wonderworld on his own."

The value of the tip was obvious. Lindell must know something, but unlike others involved in the operation, he might still be in circulation, accessible.

Dom hurriedly thanked Trandi and hung up. There were other calls to be made.

Lindy was dressed, ready to go. He had received his early wake-up call, but not from Gabe Konecki. The voice on the line at seven-thirty belonged to Dick Jenner, Tom Ryle's general factotum. An informal press conference was to be held this morning in Ryle's senate office, Jenner had said, eleven o'clock sharp; the senator would like Lindell to be on hand. Could he catch an early plane to Washington?

Despite urgings from Jenner that began to take on a

114

threatening undertone, Lindy had been noncommittal on the phone. He had his own idea of where the priorities lay, but he needed to check them first with Gabe. By half past eight, however, Konecki still hadn't called. Lindy knew he couldn't linger another minute. If possible he had to get to Ryle before the press conference, make a last-minute pitch for cooperation. It was crying against the wind, perhaps, but if there was the least chance that Tom could be dissuaded from publicly blasting the Vereste deal, it had to be tried.

Lindy took his suitcase with him. He could contact Konecki's office when he got to Washington and make new arrangements for a ferry to the safe house.

Passing through the lobby of the apartment building, Lindy noted that the doorman was not around to whistle up a taxi. It was the hour, he surmised, when the shifts were changing. He went out to the sidewalk and turned toward the nearest corner. The building was on a westbound street intersecting Second Avenue. At this hour of the morning a heavy stream of taxis flowed downtown along the avenue. Most would be occupied, taking early-bird executives to work, but it was not yet the peak period. Lindy was sure he'd quickly find a ride to the airport.

As he walked toward the intersection, the door of a green Buick parked at the curb abruptly swung open in his path.

"Lindell?" a voice paged him.

He glanced toward the car as a man stepped out. Neatly dressed, and with a recently acquired tan, the man did not seem especially menacing. Lindy assumed he was part of the team Konecki had said he might put on picket duty. But then he canvassed the rest of the scene, saw the doorman sitting in the back of the car with a nervous, prayerful expression on his face. The doorman, Lindy realized, had fingered him.

He took a quick step toward the man beside the car, enough to put him within reach. Then, pivoting his body to put his full weight behind the move, Lindy swung the valise in his right hand. The man threw up his hands to take the blow, but the impact of the suitcase knocked him off balance. He staggered backward and plopped onto the sidewalk in a sitting position. Before he could rise, Lindy threw the loaded baggage at him and ran.

Reaching the corner, Lindy turned right, heading uptown along Second Avenue. Since the traffic ran one way, downtown, the car would not be able to follow.

After running a block, Lindy looked back. He had not dared to pause to hail a taxi.

The man with the tan was sprinting in pursuit, a gun in his hand. But Lindy supposed the gun would not be used except to put muscle into the demands that would be made if he were caught. If they needed him for information, they wouldn't fire wildly and risk killing him. He stepped up his pace, put enough distance between himself and his pursuer to try for a moment to flag down a taxi. The cabs passed by him, one after another, all occupied.

He ran on before the distance shrank critically between himself and the gunman.

But the next time he glanced back, Lindy saw that the green Buick had not been deterred by flow of traffic. It had made the wrong-way turn into the avenue and was racing uptown, playing a persistent game of "chicken" against the downtown stream of cars and cabs and trucks. And winning all the way, with each oncoming vehicle swerving out of its path to avoid collision.

Then, miracle of miracles, Lindy spotted a free cab. He ran into the street waving his arms and the yellow Ford pulled over. Lindy jumped in.

The driver leaned back, putting his ear to the plastic antirobbery shield. "Where to, bud?"

"Airport," Lindy panted. "LaGuardia. Move!" Through the windshield he could see the Buick coming on, a block away, the man running on foot even nearer.

But the taxi hadn't moved yet, the driver hadn't thrown the clock. "Sorry, mister," he said, shaking his head. "I don't go to the airports. Especially LaGuardia. No percentage. Not enough flights. You drive all the way out, then sit around waiting for the next—"

Lindy had gathered enough breath to shout, "Twenty dollars. Just get moving, please!"

"Hey relax, bud, you'll live longer. You got me wrong if you think I'm trying to jack up the price. I got principles. I just don't go to the airport."

116

The hood with the gun had run between two parked cars into the street on the driver's side. Another ten seconds and the Buick would be blocking off the other door. No more time to waste discussing ethics with the hackie. Lindy barged out into the traffic. He ran across the avenue, dodging and spinning to escape being bounced off passing cars, a matador in an arena of a hundred metal bulls.

The gunman tried to follow. But he was not so lucky, not so nimble. A car fender grazed him, hurling him to the asphalt. Other cars swung wide to avoid crushing the human obstacle in their rush-hour race.

Lindy reached the opposite curb and doubled over, his lungs burning. How the hell could you run in this goddamn city? There was no oxygen left, for Christ's sake. Gulping and gasping, he looked around for a place to hide, something to carry him away from danger. The Buick had proceeded up the avenue to the point where the gunman had fallen. The car's driver, a runty specimen with a stained fedora, was out helping the dazed gunman to his feet. Their prisoner, the doorman from the apartment building, took advantage of the moment to leap out of the car and run away.

A half-block farther uptown Lindy saw a bus arrive at its regular stop and begin taking on riders. He hauled in another lungful of air and scrambled to the stop. Glancing back as he tacked himself onto the line of boarding passengers, he saw that he was not being chased. The gunman and his runty companion were standing in the street beside their car, watching him.

But as soon as the bus moved on, the two hoods got back into the Buick, which began executing a U-turn to follow the bus along the avenue.

Incredible! Lindy thought desperately as he caught sight of the maneuver through the bus window. They had visibly displayed a gun, driven against the traffic, yet no one interfered. Wasn't there a single cop around to step in?

What could he do next to evade his would-be kidnappers?

The bus approached its next stop, two blocks down the avenue. Lindy hadn't recouped enough wind to get back on the street and run. Through the rear windows, he could see that the Buick was just completing its turn and zooming downtown to catch up. It jumped a red light, narrowing the gap.

Lindy had remained by the fare box, near the driver. Now he leaned over to the uniformed man at the wheel and asked politely:

"Would you mind skipping this stop, driving past it?"

The driver shot a quizzical glance at Lindy, but said nothing as he applied his foot firmly to the brake and brought the bus to a smooth stop in front of a pair of morning riders. They came aboard, the doors closed, and the bus moved ahead. Meanwhile, the Buick had pulled abreast. It coasted along at the same speed as the bus, the gunman looking up from the passenger seat. From the taller vehicle, Lindy stared down into his smiling, confident face.

"Don't stop again," Lindy said roughly to the bus driver. He paused, searching for a way to explain the urgency of his command.

"What do you think this is, Mac? A private express for you? We stop every two blocks."

"Listen, damn it, I'm ordering you to cooperate. I'm—I'm a deputy U.S. marshal and I've got to get away from those men." Lindy pointed down at the Buick under the driver's window.

The driver looked over at the car. "Oh, sure. I recognize them, marshal. Aren't those the James boys, Frank and Jesse?" He turned, smirking, back to Lindell. "And I'm Evel Knievel and this is my jet-bus. But we still stop every two blocks. Now move to the rear, Jack, I'm getting tired of you."

The next stop was coming up. The driver's foot moved to the brake.

How did you crack through? There were so many nut cases in the city these days. What made the truth stand out from the ramblings of crazy men?

As the bus slowed enough so that the driver would not quickly lose control, Lindy leaned over the guardrail separating the driver's seat from the passenger aisle. Slamming his hand against the man's neck, he vised his fingers into the throat and gripped hard. "Keep going," Lindy said. "You've got to keep going."

118

The driver obeyed.

Passengers waiting to disembark at the rear door shouted as the bus passed its stop, then angrily rang the bell signal again and again. A couple of older women who had seen Lindy's attack retreated from the front of the bus and whispered warnings to the people around them.

"Okay, Mac," the driver croaked through his constricted windpipe. "I'm going wherever you want. But let me breathe."

Lindy pulled his hand away.

The Buick was still alongside, keeping pace without difficulty. Lindy looked ahead on the avenue. There was still room to maneuver through the traffic.

"Faster," Lindy urged. "Get away from that car."

"It's only a bus we've got, pal. We can't beat a car, no way."

"Try! Floor it!"

If he had to get stuck in a bus, Lindy discovered, he had picked the right one. Given the limitations of the cumbersome vehicle, the driver was an excellent jockey. With the first burst of speed, he squeezed through a gap between two trucks, leaving the Buick jammed up several car lengths behind.

For the next ten blocks, the bus kept up a good bouncing pace. Then the two hoods were alongside again in their car. They matched their speed to the bus until, farther downtown, the traffic halted at a red light.

When the light changed and the traffic in front of the bus moved on, the Buick roared ahead and turned broadside across its path, blocking it.

"What now?" the driver asked shakily.

The tanned gunman bolted out of the car and prowled along the side of the bus where the doors were. Any second, Lindy guessed, the hood would shove the nose of his revolver through the rubber seam in the front door and order the driver to open up.

"Keep going," Lindy said.

"Mister, there's nowhere to go! This thing don't turn wide enough to get around that car."

"Ram it, then. Push it out of the way."

The driver stared at Lindy for a moment. Then he pulled

119

up a handle beside his seat and ducked under the guardrail into the aisle. "If that's what you want, you do it." He pointed to the handle. "That's the hand brake. Just let it off and give her gas, it's automatic."

Lindy took the driver's seat without protest. As he had anticipated, the gunman stopped outside the front door.

"Lindell," shouted the tanned thug, "we want you! Open this door or I'll start putting bullets in there!"

Passengers who overheard the threat started to scream and cower.

Lindy eased down the handle for the emergency brake.

The gunman fired a shot upward through a side window. It went on through the roof without hitting anyone.

At the shot, Lindy's foot hit the accelerator pedal. The bus charged ahead into the side of the Buick. Lindy saw the runt at the steering wheel take the impact. The little bastard had been sitting there so damn sure that no one could match their brutality. The bus smashed through the body of the car, twisting the wheel around so that it pinned the driver against the seat.

"Dagwood!" Lindy heard the runt screaming. "Dag, help me!"

But he kept his foot down hard on the gas pedal. The bus continued pushing into the car, collapsing it, crushing the driver. Finally the ramming forward motion flipped the wreck aside.

The bus surged on down the avenue.

There had been a few wild shots, but no one had been hit. The attack on the car had caught the gunman off guard. He hadn't taken aim, had stopped thinking of capturing Lindell in favor of helping his comrade, his "family."

The shaken passengers rode in dumb silence as Lindy drove on another ten blocks.

Then, picking a corner at random, Lindy braked to a stop.

"How do I open the doors?" he demanded of the driver.

The driver pointed to a lever under the window. "Push it forward."

The doors hissed open. Lindy stood and turned to the cringing passengers, wanting to explain. But confronted with the horror on their faces, he knew there was nothing to

120

say. In their minds he was the killer, the fugitive. Who could tell the difference? Off-duty cops, out of uniform, were always shooting each other down in the streets.

He fled to the sidewalk and, reading the street sign, found he was at Forty-sixth. Slipping away through the heavy crowd of people heading to work in the thousands of offices in the area, he picked up a cab a block farther downtown, and told the driver to take him to the airport. This time there was no objection.

Emerging from the elevator, Lindy saw instantly that he was too late. The press conference had begun, to an overflow audience. Newsmen unable to pack themselves into Ryle's office suite were spilling into the corridor of the Senate Office Building. There was an auditorium on the ground floor which could easily have accommodated the crowd, Lindy knew; but Ryle, the showman, preferred the electric atmosphere of an SRO cracker-barrel session in a smoke-filled room.

Recognized immediately by several reporters in the corridor, Lindy had to bargain his way into the suite by promising statements after the conference. Eventually he had pushed forward through the antechamber to the doorway of the inner office.

Although it was nearly eleven-thirty, the conference had apparently started late. Ryle was at his desk, spectacles on, still reading from the prepared statement that would precede a question period.

". . . which for so long," the senator was declaiming in his Sunday-best oratorical style, "have been a significant force behind a decline in our social standards, the root cause of a vast catalogue of social evils among which is the perversion of government itself at every level—municipal, state and federal. It is within our power to stop this erosive process; it has always been within our power. And now, it is my view, we have come to the time when that power must be exercised unequivocally." Ryle took off his reading glasses and looked up at his audience. "Gentlemen, your questions."

From the fragment he had heard, Lindy believed that the process Ryle had condemned in his statement was the same

121

that he had decried over their lunch: the erosion of the law by grants of immunity, pardons, treating amicably with the enemies of society. It was not an unreasonable position. But it was hard to stomach after what he himself had been through less than three hours ago. The frantic chase by two hoodlums determined to learn Vereste's whereabouts had reconfirmed Lindy's original feeling that the deal would prove worthwhile. Indeed, he had committed himself irreversibly to that position, had conceivably sacrificed his career to it. He had seriously injured—very possibly had killed—a man in support of his belief. In legal terms he had committed murder this morning.

And here he was seeing his plan demolished. Without Ryle's support Vereste's terms could not be met, the Mafioso would remain silent. Yet Vereste would live out his days safely in government custody for if one informer were to be thrown back to the wolves, the government would never get another. Pondering the wreckage of his career and Konecki's and the waste of innocent life he had seen yesterday, Lindy became vaguely aware of the babble of newsmen around him.

It was only when Mack Sunderland's dominating figure rose, and an assault was launched on Ryle, that Lindy woke up to what had been happening. Sunderland was enough of a heavyweight to couch his question in an editorial statement of his own without being called out of order:

"Senator, there's no doubt that the country would be a healthier place without organized crime. I think most of us here have applauded your past positions. But from what you've said this morning, it seems you're taking a radical new direction. We had a situation yesterday where ordinary citizens were literally caught in the crossfire of the war on crime. It's not the first time, of course, but what happened in this case could have been avoided if enforcement agencies hadn't rushed ahead with this public-be-damned attitude. And yet, earlier you called for"—Sunderland referred to a note pad in his palm—"'. . . facing the cost of an all-out battle, whether calculated in toil or tears, in money or men.'" Sunderland lowered the pad. "Senator, I don't think I've ever heard that kind of saber rattling used in relation to a domestic problem. Do you really justify what happened yesterday in those terms? Does the taking of one Mafioso mean so much? And if

122

so, what kind of ultimate costs are we talking about in this 'all-out battle'?"

Sunderland had evidently voiced the questions of all present. The other reporters stopped straining to be recognized and sat back, pencils poised.

To Lindy's amazement, Ryle began his response with a number of points lifted from the pages Lindy had submitted with the cassette, and went on to adapt other things that had been said over lunch. The purpose of the press conference, Lindy realized now, was to quell the criticism, not raise it to a new pitch. Ryle was *defending* the Vereste deal! Doing it even though the Wonderworld shootings had made such support even more politically questionable than Ryle had thought it would be when he had earlier refused his cooperation.

"So," Ryle concluded after spouting some statistics, "if you're asking me whether I justify stopping that kind of drain on our national resources, I say an emphatic *yes.*"

Sunderland started to interrupt. "But you've glossed over—"

Ryle cut him dead. "With specific regard to yesterday's tragic events, I cannot condemn the procedure that was used to bring in Mr. Vereste. How should the authorities have acted differently? They went to meet a man who offered to give himself up. What happened then was not their fault. Bear in mind, gentlemen, that the trigger of the gun that killed so heartlessly was being pulled by the very Organization which I have said we are long overdue in finally and totally eliminating. And why did they make this desperate attempt to liquidate our witness? Sources of mine who were instrumental in arranging the surrender have told me that the information we gain will furnish the means to destroy the effectiveness of the Mafia—the so-called Cosa Nostra, the Mob, the Organization, the Syndicate, call it what you will. If there is such an unprecedented inroad to their secrets, then I don't think there's any doubt that taking this one man is the most important coup in the history of law enforcement in this country."

"And what about the cost?" Sunderland's voice boomed over the sudden explosion of a hundred other questions. "What are we giving Vereste in return? You mentioned having a line to someone who arranged the surrender. What were the conditions?"

Ryle hesitated. "I wasn't told that."

Sunderland held the floor. "But he did have a price?"

"I assume so," Ryle said. "Every informer has. But giving some consideration to witnesses does not represent a departure from the government's established policy. In fact, Mr. Sunderland, contrary to your judgment on my position, I don't see that there's anything new about my or the government's making the strongest possible effort to solve one of the country's most serious problems."

"I'll tell you what's new!" Sunderland shouted. A wave of other voices drowned him out, but he called louder, demanding to be heard. "I'll tell you, Senator, if you really want to know—I'll tell you what's new!"

The other reporters yielded. Sunderland was acknowledged to be the best-informed journalist in town. He was plugged in all over to secretaries and special assistants and filing clerks who used him as a conduit, a means of exerting influence above their station; then of course he also had his friends among the cabinet members, who leaked information as it suited them to gain acceptance for their policies or to put pressure on their enemies. Now perhaps, in his anger, Sunderland might blow one of his own scoops. The room became very still. Sunderland stood glaring at Ryle, taking a moment to batten down the hatch on his temper.

Ryle preempted the pause and tried to make Sunderland's outburst appear rude and foolish. "I'm sorry, Mr. Sunderland. I didn't mean to ignore you. But I had the crazy idea that some of your colleagues in this room might also have a question or two."

"I hope to God they have plenty," Sunderland rallied. "And that they get some decent answers. Because there are things I've been hearing about this situation that bother the hell out of me. Some are unsubstantiated so I'll leave those aside. But one fact I have checked out is that the middleman in the dealings with Vereste—I expect he's the source you've already mentioned—was the former counsel for your investigating committee."

Though Sunderland had not mentioned his name, Lindy became the focus of many eyes in the room.

"Now maybe the rest of you would like to give a round of

applause," Sunderland went on, "but I'm not so sure it's a great stride forward when the legislative branch starts playing gangbusters, trying to enforce the law as well as make it. Is that putting it too strongly? Then what's Tom Ryle doing here, putting his prestige on the line to endorse the Vereste deal? And why is he the mouthpiece for conducting a total blitz against organized crime?"

The other newsmen began to look mystified by the virulence of Sunderland's attack. Whatever the possible flaws or dangers in an all-out effort against organized crime, they could not see that it would be anything but basically positive. But then, Lindy guessed, the others might not know all that Sunderland did—the unsubstantiated inside dope that might even include the amount of the payoff.

In touch with the sympathies of the majority, however, Ryle dared to goad Sunderland. "I can't see why you're getting so hot under the collar, Mr. Sunderland. Unless you have some reason for wanting American people to go on living with a major crime problem."

Sunderland's powerful temper was coupled to the rigid control that very big men were forced to develop. He ignored the innuendo and kept to the issue.

"I'm one of the American people, and I'd rather go on living with a crime problem than without the Constitution. We've seen the vigilante mentality infecting our enforcement procedures more and more. Cast aside certain principles of conduct and the strain on the system may reach a breaking point. When you talk about wiping out the Mafia in an all-out battle, Senator, what comes to my mind is that the last time they were dealt with in that consummate manner was by Mussolini, in a fascist Italy."

It was far worse than any attack Ryle had anticipated, Lindy thought, but no more than a preview of the points Sunderland would probably keep hitting in his widely syndicated column as he chewed down to the bones of the Vereste deal.

Ryle's sleek, silvery facade had lost its sheen. He looked ashen, weary, and there was no snap to his retort.

"Was there a question in there somewhere, Mack? Or were *you* giving a press conference?"

125

"Yes, Tom," Sunderland said, acknowledging Ryle's amiable tone, a reminder that away from this arena they had enjoyed an acquaintance based on mutual respect. "Here's my question: what the hell are you doing mixed up in this?"

Ryle tried to speak. His voice cracked. He cleared his throat and the answer came in a quaver. "My duty, son. I'm trying to do my duty."

In the tortured delivery and the accusing glance fleetingly shot toward the corner where he stood, Lindy detected that Ryle was somehow an unwilling hostage to his role. He had played the part Lindy had asked of him, yet he was hating himself for it.

Sunderland ceded the floor and bulldozed his way out of the office. As though a bad-mannered boy had finally left a birthday party, the conference continued with a deliberate effort to pretend he had never been there. No attention was given to the negative points he had raised. The implicit consensus was that Sunderland had gone wildly overboard. Could a major offensive against vice and drugs and other forms of corruption be bad? Even if Sunderland didn't like Tom Ryle's new fire-and-brimstone gangbusting style, others did—it made for good headlines—and they used their questions to elicit more of it.

But Ryle's responses had become listless, desultory. And when Dick Jenner took his cue and announced that the conference was over, the room was cleared without much objection. Those men who understood from Sunderland's reference that Lindy had been the middleman immediately turned their attention to him. But before he had time to answer any questions Jenner plucked him out of the tide of reporters ebbing toward the corridor.

"Could you stay, Lindell? The Senator wants to see you."

Jenner led Lindy back to the inner office and closed the door behind him.

He was alone with Ryle, who stood in a corner pouring himself a drink from a small bar. At the sound of the door closing, without looking up, Ryle said:

"Get what you wanted, boy?"

Lindy felt a hostile bite in his old mentor's question. "Look, Tom, I'm sorry about the way things blew up with Sunder-

126

land. But what did you expect? I never asked for this kind of grandstanding, a press conference, battle cries. Sure, I wanted you to speak up for the deal, if and when it came under fire. But you went way beyond that. To be honest, I think you went much too far, begged for trouble. This stuff about an 'all-out battle'—Christ, that *is* vigilante talk. If that kind of noise comes out of Washington, it can have a dangerous effect all over the country. It's damn lucky no one beside Sunderland picked up on that."

Ryle turned from the bar and came across the room carrying a tumbler almost filled with neat whiskey. His hands were shaking so that the amber liquid sloshed out of the glass. Lindy realized this was the outward sign of a consuming rage only a second before the whiskey splattered in his face. He shut his eyes to clear the stinging drops and heard Ryle spouting a stream of abuse.

"You goddamn glory-grubbing backstabbing sneaking son of a bitch Judas. You've got the nerve to give me your sanctimonious bullshit about going too far!"

Stupefied, Lindy groped for a reply. By the time his vision returned, Ryle had made a trip to a table in the corner and was coming at him again, waving a folder. "You tell me what choice I had with this being shoved at me!" Ryle swung the folder, slapping Lindy hard across the face with it. The contents scattered onto the floor. Dropping the empty cardboard file, Ryle slouched away.

"Tom," Lindy appealed quietly, "I don't know what this is about, I swear. What are you hanging on me?"

Ryle said nothing.

Then Lindy saw the hunched, defeated shoulders jiggling, heard the choked, rhythmic lowing of Ryle's suppressed sobs. He knelt to scoop up a handful of the scattered papers.

There were some photostats of records from the Melville County Savings and Loan Association, some endorsed with the signature of Thomas Ryle; these bank sheets were dated 1945 and 1946. Underneath Lindy found a photostat of a tiny news clipping, cut from a small local paper, by the look of it. The report read: "On Wednesday last Miss Laura Lee Priddie was found drowned in Kowatchee Creek. The creek was swollen due to the recent heavy rains." A handwritten note on the photostat margin gave the source as "Zaneville News, June 9, 1946." Lindy shuffled through other photostats, and more bank sheets and personal checks of Ryle's dated from the late forties through the early fifties, without increasing his comprehension.

Lindy went to Ryle. "Tom, what is all this? I've never seen any of it."

Ryle collected himself, squared his shoulders. "You didn't have to see it to use it, you lowdown—"

"For God's sake, if you're going to keep cussing me out, at least read me the charges! What are these papers, how were they used?"

Ryle inspected Lindy. The crinkles around his narrowed suspicious eyes slowly smoothed out. "Maybe you didn't know," he muttered at last. "But you started the process, son. You went against me after I warned you. So that meant I had to be kept in line. They had to go out on a limb to do it, but the temptation was too great. All those triumphant headlines, arrest after arrest, a new age of glory for the Bureau. They were too hungry for that to quibble over—"

"The Bureau?" Lindy said. "You mean this material came from them?"

"Well, shit, you know about their files. Who doesn't know? Every bit of dirt they can suck out of the air."

"But that was Hoover's garbage. Those files have been destroyed."

Ryle shuffled to his desk and slumped into his chair. He laughed, a dry mournful sound with no mirth in it. "Destroyed," he echoed. "And whose word did we have for that?"

"What's in the file, Tom?"

"Hell, what isn't. If I ever spit in a public place, it's probably on the record. Most of it wouldn't mean shit to the primmest Kentucky widow. The one that carries the punch, though, that there is a honey. Something that happened with a girl I knew."

"Laura Lee Priddie?" Lindy prompted.

Ryle nodded slowly. "Laura Lee," he said, chanting it almost, as if to summon her spirit at a seance. "Laura Lee. My

God, so long, long ago. . . ." He trailed off, but Lindy could see he was remembering the girl, the story. When it was all there, living inside him again, Ryle went on. "I was working in the hometown bank—same one I bought later, after I'd worked my way up. In those days, though, I was just a clerk; the first job I got after I came home from the war. One afternoon, end of summer, I was sent out to the Priddie place to discuss a loan. A hundred dollars to get them through a drought we'd been having. When I arrived, the girl was there alone. She wasn't anything special, just a cotton-grower's daughter, dirt-poor and dumber than a mule. But I was still making up for all the years I'd spent on a minesweeper. Laura Lee was supposed to be a kind of collateral for the loan, I figured, and I accepted it. Oldest story in the book. Ten weeks later, her old man he came into the bank and told me Laura Lee was in foal. He knew I couldn't marry her, that I was already engaged elsewhere. All he wanted was a thousand dollars to square things, a one-time payment either to pay for Laura Lee getting fixed up right, or else cover the extra expense of feeding the child if she wanted to keep it. No question of blackmail. Priddie was being decent with me—we're all decent folks where I come from. I didn't have the thousand, of course, but I knew where to borrow it. Though not exactly in the official way. An unborn bastard isn't the best collateral for a bank loan. I suppose, technically, you'd call my method of borrowing embezzlement. Except that I paid it all back over the next twenty-two months, every damn penny, including the standard rate of interest. Priddie was as good as his word, too. I never heard from him again, except when he came into the bank to repay the hundred dollars after he'd sold his crop. We only talked bank business, nothing else. By then Laura Lee had drowned herself. It—it was a little after when the baby would've come. . . ." He paused and glanced with moist eyes at the papers on the floor. "Never found out if she had it or not. I looked all through that file for that one piece of information. The one goddamn thing I'd like to have known—and it isn't in there."

Lindy moved up closer to the desk. "Tom, I swear, if you were pushed into that press conference in return for hushing up old country tales, I had nothing to do with it. I couldn't have thought of it. I'd never expect you to knuckle under to this kind of crap."

"If I hadn't, they would have leaked the story, one way or another. A man from the Bureau made that very plain. He dropped in on me late yesterday morning. It was before the Vereste surrender, but he knew it was coming. I gather he was the Bureau's liaison on the deal; he had been to a briefing before coming around to visit me. He was crystal clear about the kind of cooperation they were expecting at my end."

"But for *this!*" Lindy said with disdain, tossing his handful of paper down on the desk. "You could have stared him down, Tom. It's ancient history. The money was paid back; there's no proof of paternity. You're too big to be hurt by unsubstantiated gossip."

This time when Ryle laughed the trace of a lilt reappeared. "You may be the top of your class, Lindy. But Lord, when it comes to politics what you've got in your head wouldn't fill a flea's twat. Right now there's a demon craving for truth in this land. Folks don't seem to care how they get it or where it comes from or the damage it does. They don't even care what they do with it after it's out. They just want to know everything, to know the truth is still there to be had, like kids on Christmas checking their new presents under the tree. Maybe it'll be a good thing in the end. What it means for the moment is that any man with a secret can be brought down with the first whisper."

Listening, Lindy realized he was also a prisoner of the process he had begun. He could hate the methods Konecki had used to guarantee the deal, but if he backed out of cooperating, he would feel worse than if he went ahead.

"Tom, I wish I could make it up to you."

"You can't, son. But you might as well see if you can make it count for something. The only men who haven't been suffering lately are the honest crooks, the ones who haven't kept their crimes a secret. I guess it is about time we lowered the boom on them, too. Now get out of here," he added brokenly, "and don't come back."

Lindy went slowly to the door. He looked around before

going out. Ryle was coming around his desk, but not to call him back. Eyes fixed on the contents of the file littering the floor, the senator was oblivious to Lindy. He walked into the midst of the scrap, sank down, and started to sift through it.

Lindy left with that image branded on his mind: his old friend on his knees, not so much examining the evidence of the man he had been, Lindy thought, as searching for proof of the man he had hoped to become.

ELEVEN

The Lear jet rolled to a stop in front of the low shed that served the small airport as a terminal building. Through the plane's windshield Lindy read the sign identifying the airport's locality. It was the first indicator he'd seen of the area to which he had been flown.

There had been little delay in arranging transport after he checked in at the Washington headquarters of the Marshal Service. A helicopter had lifted him direct from the parking lot to Dulles airport. Then the jet had whisked him here: Plattsburg, New York, Municipal Airport. Another helicopter was waiting on the runway, rotors turning—apparently the last link in the ferry. Lindy saw Gabe Konecki standing near the helicopter.

It was a mild, sunny spring day. Dressed in denims, Konecki for the first time resembled an approximation of his peacekeeping predecessors, men who had worn the badges a century ago. As Lindy left the jet, Konecki came forward to meet him. At his approach, Lindy's hands clenched into fists. He wanted to lay into Konecki, punish him for Ryle's humiliation. But there wasn't enough spare adrenalin to fuel the impulse for more than a few seconds. It had all been used up this morning. On the flight, a low-grade shock reaction had set in. Lindy felt weak, devoid of any will of his own.

He had killed a man, he knew now. At the Washington HQ he had given the Marshal Service a full report on the hoods who had tried to kidnap him and the means by which he had escaped. The Service had checked details with the New York police and had learned that Lindy's victim was Salvatore Raguza, an odd-jobs man from the same crime family as Bart

132

Vereste. They had also been able to tell Lindell that Raguza had died in a hospital of his injuries.

"I gave you a call at home," Konecki said first, "but you'd already left for Ryle's press party. I heard you had a rough trip."

"You might say. It's not quite every day that I'm forced to kill a man."

"It was him or you, Lindy. What do you think would've happened if they'd taken you off that bus? When they were through trying to pound an answer out of you, they'd have given you a lead headache and dumped you in a building foundation—just one more jerk with a Park Avenue office building for his tombstone."

Lindy shrugged. "Somehow that doesn't make me feel less like a murderer. But I guess Vereste might as well have one of those on his new team; he's already got an embezzler and a blackmailer." He started past Konecki toward the helicopter.

Konecki grabbed him back. "So Ryle filled you in. Well, I warned you, didn't I? If we want to get our money's worth out of Vereste, we pull no punches."

"Even the low blows."

"You wanted to take Vereste; you were pushing for it. When I said I'd deliver Ryle you were satisfied. You didn't seem too concerned about how I made good, as long as I did."

"Yes," Lindy said, "I should have worried. I just keep forgetting there's no conscience anymore."

Ten minutes after the helicopter left the ground it was traveling over a region of richly-forested mountains cradling numerous ponds and sparkling streams, the nearest thing to a virgin wilderness Lindy had ever seen.

"Where are we?" he asked.

He was sitting in the seat next to the pilot, Konecki behind him. They had not spoken since the takeoff.

"The mountains below us are the Adirondacks," Konecki replied. "In the whole group there are forty-six peaks of more than four thousand feet, including Mount Marcy, highest in New York State. We've taken over a ranger station in the middle of the region for our base. There are no roads

133

going in. It's accessible only to climbers and hikers. Unless, that is, you can drive a chopper." Konecki tapped the pilot, a gangly young man with a crew cut and a large nose illuminated by a sunburn. "Take us down closer, Snoot. Give Mr. Lindell a chance to appreciate Mother Nature."

The pilot dropped his craft to skim the treetops and the surfaces of the lovely small lakes, fluttering over the contours of the landscape like a dragonfly. Konecki grinned when he saw Lindy braced in his seat for a crash.

"Relax, Lindy. Snoot was six years in Vietnam. He could take this eggbeater sideways between raindrops without getting wet."

"Have we got the army in on this, too?"

"We're getting some cooperation. Snoot and his machine have been detached for as long as we need him."

"And who else would be 'detached' if we needed?" Lindy's tone was critical. He was remembering the way Mack Sunderland had denounced the prospect of all-out war on the Mafia.

"Why should we need anyone else?" Konecki said blithely. "The odds are heavily against anyone coming after Vereste on this turf. To start with, they've got the problem of learning where he is. I don't think they can crack that within a few weeks, and by then we expect to be moving in court. Of course, that's where we can expect trouble, but nothing we can't handle with existing procedure."

"But surely they'll try to cut him down before he ever gets to a courtroom. They'll stop at nothing to pinpoint where he is now; I've already seen the proof of that. And if they do, they'll come on foot, by chopper, whatever it takes to make sure they silence him. They've got as much money to fund an expeditionary force as any small nation."

Konecki smiled. "Can you see gutter rats fighting on this terrain? If they're dumb enough to try, let them come. It'll be a massacre. Ever hear of Igloo White?"

"Sounds like a popsicle."

Konecki laughed and turned to the pilot. "Want to tell him, Snoot, or should I?"

Snoot shrugged laconically, content to remain one of his machine's moving parts.

134

"It's a network of tiny electronic sensors," Konecki explained. "You can plant them in trees, bushes, underground, anywhere. The Pentagon developed the system to track guerrilla movements in the Asian wars. The sensors are seeded around a perimeter—in our case, two miles on every side of our base. If anything warmer or colder than its surroundings moves in that sector, we can spot it, analyze it by computer, and find it in the dark."

"It rings a bell now," Lindy said. "Isn't this the billion-dollar gadget they dubbed the electronic battlefield?"

"That's Igloo White," Konecki affirmed. "At least we got something out of that war."

"With all respect to Snoot," Lindy argued, "I'm not sure we did. That electronic jazz didn't work very well when it was used in Nam. In fact, I seem to remember reading that once the Cong learned to recognize the equipment, they could always fool it by planting buckets of warm human urine in the vicinity. That would send the B-5s flying off to bomb a valley full of nothing but pisspots."

Snoot laughed in a way that seemed to verify the item.

Konecki dismissed it crossly. "I don't ever see a pack of mobboes being quite so clever at guerrilla tactics. And so far the system has worked perfectly. We've been able to track the movements of every hiker that enters the safe area."

"Why not close it all off to the public? Why all this fancy dancing to keep it open for the nature lovers?"

"It's too large an area to shut down effectively, except by methods that would attract too much attention. We're satisfied with our security arrangements as they are. In addition to the electronics, there's a compound fenced off around the ranger station with two dozen men to patrol it."

The helicopter rose steeply to clear a high peak capped by a smooth rocky summit. As it floated down the far side, Konecki pointed forward.

"There's our home, sweet home—code name Sweetheart." He chuckled. The name had obviously been chosen as a nose-thumbing gesture to any critics of the Vereste deal.

Ahead, Lindy saw a clearing at one end of a lake which looked from above like a gigantic blue-steel monkey wrench. At the center of the clearing stood a cluster of square buildings, constructed of dark timber in a pseudo-log-cabin style. As the nerve center for a modern, electronically-monitored security operation, Lindy thought, it was good camouflage. If the placid rustic setting was not enough, a carefree holiday atmosphere was added by a couple of tennis courts and a boathouse on the lake. Three canoes and a sailing dinghy were pulled up on the shore. Lindy could also discern two figures darting around one of the tennis courts, engaged in a match.

"Wow," he remarked, "if you want any more pigeons, all you'd have to do is send out brochures."

"We try to make the confinement as pleasant as possible," Konecki said mildly.

When the helicopter settled on the ground, a different aspect of the mountain retreat came into view. Posted on porches, invisible from the air under the cabins' projecting eaves, were men with carbines slung over their shoulders. Other guards were posted in log lean-tos that nestled in the trees at the edge of the clearing. Also set back in the forest were some prefabricated Quonset huts, and a hangar for the helicopter. From one of the huts came a humming sound which Lindy guessed belonged to a portable generator.

"Want the tour now?" Konecki asked as they left the chopper.

"Up to you. I thought you'd shove me right in with Vereste."

"He'll keep awhile." Konecki started toward one of the smaller outbuildings. "He really does act as if he's on a vacation. I've never seen a mug this cool. Even yesterday, after he almost had his head shot off, he wasn't rattled. Know what he did as soon as we got here? Presented us with a list of books he wants. Said he's been looking forward all year to this chance to catch up on his reading. And you should see the titles—history, economics, political theory, everything from Keynes to Kissinger. I never saw a Mob guy before who read anything but *The Godfather* and the racing form."

They mounted the wooden steps to the wide porch of the first cabin. The interior of the cabin consisted of only one room, knotty pine peeking out on all sides from between the steel and glass panels of sophisticated electronics equipment.

136

Computers, radar, and communications systems were lined along the two side walls and on either side of the entrance. At the center of the room was a control console for these units monitored by a bland professorial type in black horn-rimmed spectacles whom Konecki introduced as Jerry Harpe.

The rear wall had been given over to a separate system, the Igloo White. Linked to its own bank of computers was a large glass screen with illuminated grid markings and a thousand twinkling green pinpoints forming a rough circle around a glowing blue nucleus. The system was controlled from a console which was presently under the watchful eye of a stubby, cheerful man named Willy Dyskowicz.

"How's it working, Dice?" Konecki asked after the introductions. "Mr. Lindell is a little worried that some hiker's going to throw the system out by relieving himself in the vicinity."

"You know," Dyskowicz said brightly, "they did have that problem in Vietnam."

"I know, I know," Konecki said sourly. "Forget I mentioned it. What have you seen today?"

"Usual traffic. One party of three just set down a camp inside our northern line. Up there." Dyskowicz pressed a button and a red pinpoint of light toward the top of the grid flashed on and off. "I sent Burville out for an eye check. He should be calling in any second."

The computer tapes clicked over quietly. Dyskowicz volunteered some instruction to Lindell. "Those are readings coming in from the sensors. The input tells us if the source is living, moving. By calculating exact amounts of heat, vibration, and noise levels, we get a readout on the size of anything live that activates the system, enough to tell if it's bird, animal, or human."

A beeper tone sounded from the console.

"Here's Burville," Dyskowicz said, flipping a toggle switch.

The field transmission came through a speaker. "Ranger-four to Sweetheart. Do you read?"

"Read you, Burv."

"Party of three on coordinates GL seventeen, N five checks out as man, woman, child on camping expedition. They've

137

pitched a tent and intend one-night stay. Any more activity or should I come in?"

"Activity nil, head for home." Dyskowicz switched off the receiver.

"Doesn't that give you away?" Lindy asked Konecki. "Checking credentials on everyone who gets near you?"

"It wouldn't bother any real campers," Konecki replied. "We've dressed up our field patrols as forest rangers. It would be perfectly normal for a ranger to happen across a campsite. They're always roaming the territory, looking for fire hazards or hunting violations." He clapped Dyskowicz on the back. "Thanks for the show, Dice."

Guiding Lindy back into the sunshine, the marshal went on with his spiel. "The rest of the small cabins are bunkhouses for our men, or storage for food and ammo. And that's the lodge." Konecki steered toward the largest building in the compound, at the crest of a gentle slope. "Our best guest accommodations. Vereste and his family are quartered there, along with you, me, and a few staff."

One phrase had hit Lindy with jarring effect.

"Family," he said. "Did you say Vereste and his family?"

"Wife and children."

Lindy stopped in his tracks, speechless.

Unaware that he had said anything remarkable, Konecki continued ahead. Then, noticing he was walking alone, he turned back.

"Oh, I forgot," he said calmly after a quick reading of Lindy's expression. "You weren't in on that. A little magic trick we performed." He motioned Lindy over to a point from which they could see the tennis court behind the lodge. The two figures Lindy had seen from the air were now recognizable as two women. "The wife and daughter," Konecki went on. "They play a lot. The son, on the other hand, he's not much of an outdoor type. The thing that interests him most is our electronics setup. He's spent hours talking with Dice. Knows something about it, apparently, worked with computers in college."

Finally Lindy summoned his comment. "I don't get it. Pretending to kill them off. For what? What difference will it make?"

138

"All the difference, we hope. At this point the Mob would do anything for revenge against Vereste. There will be open-ended contracts out on him and anyone he might care about. But there's no need to write tickets on people they already assume to be dead. That makes it much easier to provide three innocent parties with new identities and put them safely back in circulation. If they exercise some caution, they might even pick up the pieces of their old lives, see people they knew before. They couldn't do it otherwise. Their old friends would be staked out by the Mob, watching and waiting for the Verestes to show up."

"So who got burned instead? There were three bodies found in the ashes."

"Two women and a young man who'd died in federal prison hospitals within the past three days. There were no relatives to claim them."

Lindy ambled on again. "My God. I never imagined you'd go to such lengths."

"We've always got to go a little bit farther than the other side," Konecki said, unapologetic.

"Didn't the family have any objection to being 'killed off?'"

"They weren't given a chance to think about it. Now that they're dead, they realize the advantages. Only the daughter's a little piqued—Bits, they call her. She's left a guy behind that she wants to marry. But she's accepted now that this way he's safer while she's out of circulation. And when she does get back to him, they'll be able to live a normal life."

"Unless," Lindy put in, "the guy gets tired of mourning before that happy day arrives."

"She says he can be trusted with the truth. In a couple of weeks we'll run a check on him, and cue him if we're satisfied. Shouldn't be a problem; he's just a college kid."

They mounted the steps to the lodge porch, Lindy still shaking his head.

Inside the lodge, few alterations had been made from the appearance it must have presented in its time as a ranger station. The large front room used for lounging and dining was decorated with comfortable, unelaborate furniture. Imitation Indian rugs were scattered over the varnished pine floor, and survey maps of the Adirondack region were tacked to the walls. The main source of charm and warmth was an enormous fieldstone fireplace. This was flanked by two doors, one leading to the kitchen, the other to an L-shaped corridor running down one side of the lodge and around to the rear. The bedrooms were all along this hallway. Also, Konecki said, there was a room equipped with the best army field hospital equipment, and two trained nurses—the only female staff at the compound—were in attendance.

"In case of battle casualties?" Lindy asked.

Konecki reminded him then that Vereste had requested plastic surgery for himself and possibly the others.

The bedroom to which Lindy was conducted was decorated with spartan austerity: an iron-framed camp bed and a wobbly chest of drawers.

"Well, this is the way it ought to look," he observed. "Like a prison."

"The next room along is Vereste's. I thought it would be nice if you were close, in case he feels like talking in the wee small hours."

"Very considerate."

"After you get changed into your country clothes," Konecki said, going to the door, "I'll chaperon your reunion with the great man."

Lindy remembered suddenly that he had no clothes but the rumpled suit on his back. He told Konecki what had happened to his baggage.

"In that case," Konecki responded, "you might as well go right in. Have a nice long chat. That'll give me time to round up some spare threads from the troops. There ought to be someone who wears your size." He went back into the corridor with Lindy and gestured to Vereste's door like a headwaiter showing his best table. "Go to it, Deputy."

Lindy glared at Konecki. "Don't call me that. I'll get what I can from the man, but I don't want to be one of you, Konecki. Understand?" He turned away and moved to Vereste's door. He waited there until Konecki had walked away. Then he knocked.

"Who is it?" Vereste called from inside.

"Lindell."

The door swung open quickly. Vereste wore a broad, welcoming smile.

"Glad you could make it," he said. "I've missed you."

At twilight Dom Francini's Cadillac turned off Route 57 into the parking lot of Trandi's Glass Bar. As if in welcome, the neon sign went on as the car pulled up by the door.

Ottavio Stirelli got out from behind the wheel and went to open the passenger door for his don. Tommy Aleppo let himself out of a rear door.

Usually, Dom liked to drive himself. But this evening he had been too nervous. Several times during the day his heart had been struck by bursts of palpitation, and each time he was sure it was the coronary that the doctors had warned would inevitably kill him. Again he swore to himself that he would lose the ninety pounds they advised as a necessary minimum. If he lived to lose it. The more fateful condition at the moment was not his obesity, but the difficulty of finding Bart Vereste, and the day's events had made that problem more critical. After pulverizing Sally Rags, Lindell—their only lead—had skipped clean away; now, no doubt, he would remain permanently out of reach. In addition, Don Valerio had called to inform Dom that a gathering of *capi* from every part of the country was beginning to take shape, could be expected on short notice within the next two or three weeks. Most of the men, Ligazza had said, would be vulnerable to prosecution if Vereste told everything he knew. They were ready to meet any demand on their men or money if it would silence the informer. But first they had to know where he was. Dom was expected to tell them when they convened.

Even with the added pressure, however, Dom had seen the first glimmer of light behind the black wall of pessimism. Last night his mind had been too frozen by fear, too clogged with desperate stratagems for self-preservation, to plot useful methods for saving the whole Organization. When Dagwood had said that finding Vereste was going to take skilled detective work, Dom had felt hopeless. Soldiers of the brotherhood could be counted upon for strong-arm duty, but not for shrewd, patient tracking. Given a year, perhaps, or a list

141

of the right heads to break, they could find any man. But Vereste had to be found now, yesterday, and whose head did you break to get the answers?

But then this afternoon, Dom had been struck by the elementary insight in Dagwood's remark. If finding Vereste was going to take police work, then the police could do it. Wasn't it a cop who had given the tip on Lindell?

"Is he here?" Dom rumbled at Jack Trandi as he entered the bar with his two bodyguards.

Trandi, a small man with hair dyed black, was sitting at the counter made of glass bricks which gave his establishment its name. He pointed to the rear of the long gloomy space, lit only by dim blue bulbs behind the glass bricks and an assortment of promotional signs for different brands of beer.

Dom strained to make out the shadowy figure in the farthest booth. "Christ, why don't you put some lights in here, Trandi? It's worse than a foggy night on the Sound. What's his name?"

"Waitely. Al Waitely."

Dom Francini gestured his bodyguards to take seats at the bar and started toward the back.

"Don Domenico"—Trandi stopped him—"I would like to offer a suggestion for dealing with this man. The way to get results is not to push too hard. He's got mixed feelings about being on the pad."

"Oh, yeah?" Dom snarled. "He didn't take mixed money. It was all green."

"He's got a sick wife," Trandi offered. "He does it to pay for her treatment. He couldn't afford it otherwise."

"Well, that's good to know. Let's all hope she doesn't die so we can keep him working." Dom proceeded to the rear. The space in the booth was too narrow to accommodate his girth. He shouted to Trandi to bring him a chair.

Waitely didn't look up as Dom stood over the table. Even when Francini had been accommodated with a seat, the policeman continued to stare into his beer.

"I hear," Dom began, "you got troubles with a sick old lady."

At last Waitely turned to Dom Francini. "Let's keep her out of this."

142

"Why?" Dom said implacably. "She's the reason you're here, ain't she? What's her problem, Al?"

Waitely hesitated. Trandi had warned him about Dom Francini before the meeting, the man's legendary cruelty. He answered the question: "Bad kidneys. She goes to the hospital twice a week to have her blood washed by a machine."

"And I'll bet it costs a fucking fortune," Dom said sympathetically. "Fucking doctors got the biggest protection racket going, don't they? Pay—or die. And you know what the bastards do with the money? They gamble it away with us. The biggest losers on all our junkets, Al, they're all doctors. Remember that. You sweat to come up with the fee, and those pricks piss it away with us. They wind up borrowing to meet their nut, and next thing you know the only way they can meet the vig is to suck more out of their patients. So don't feel too bad about taking our money, Al. It's just your own coming back."

Waitely glanced up bleakly, said nothing, and then finished off his drink.

"Trandi!" Dom roared. "Bring this man another of the same."

When the beer was in Waitely's glass, Dom went on. "Here's my offer, copper. Give me what I want and I'll lay down enough cash for you to get the Mrs. an operation, buy your own machine to wash her out, whatever you need to put her straight."

"Look," Waitely said after a moment, "I gave you Lindell's name. That's all I know."

"That was your good deed for yesterday," Dom said harshly. "I appreciate it, but it took us nowhere. You've got to come up with something else."

"How can I? Why pick on me?"

"Your jurisdiction also covers the area where the Verestes lived, doesn't it?"

Waitely nodded warily.

"I want you to conduct an investigation," Dom continued. "Squeeze anyone who had contact with the Verestes—including the wife, son and daughter—anytime in the last few weeks. There's a chance they knew in advance where they'd be hiding out and they were loose with the secret, accidental-

143

ly dropped a hint. So you cover all their neighbors, lovers, girl friends, and see if you can come up with something."

"I can't do it," Waitely protested. "If I scramble around looking for leads to Vereste, how long would it be before somebody ties me to you?"

"And how long will it be if you sit back and let Vereste talk? He knows who's on our pad; turning over the list must be part of his package." Dom reverted to a gentler cajoling tone. "Listen, Al, if you handle it right you'll be in the clear. You'll advertise this as a homicide investigation. Nobody'll be surprised if you try to get a make on who did the torch job. As a matter of fact," Dom added, "while you're at it I wouldn't mind knowing who lit the fire. That guy who turned in the alarm, a gardener or something—he must have picked up a clue if the feds have put him under their wing. But you could get to him easy enough in the line of duty."

Waitely took a sip of beer, then sat with his head hung over the glass, silent.

"Now get this," Dom erupted. "I'm not asking, I'm telling. But what the hell is it I want? If your barracks commander gave the same order, you'd be creaming to carry it out. Well, okay, so it comes from me. That still ain't no reason to do any big conscience number."

"No," Waitely mumbled, "no reason."

Dom leaned on the table and pushed himself up from his chair. "Then get on it fast. Find me some footsteps and I'll see your wife gets fixed up perfect." Dom emphasized the promise by joggling Waitely amiably by the shoulder.

The policeman ignored him again. In other times, Dom would've ordered a man taken to pieces for such a snub. Today he allowed it. Waitely would play, that was the main thing.

"I'll drive," Dom told Stirrups as they left the bar. He felt much better now. On the real ocean he might be a lousy fisherman, but when he threw his lines out into the filthy sea of humanity, Dom Francini had a powerful intuitive ability to sense when he was about to get a strike.

144

TWELVE

The illusion of vacationing at the sort of rugged summer retreat where city dwellers pay extravagantly for the privilege of roughing it extended to the way that meals were served at the lodge. A single long table in the big front room was reserved for dining. There, half a dozen of the guard contingent sat down to eat side-by-side with their charges. Separate provision would have been made for the Verestes if they preferred, but they seemed to welcome the company and the atmosphere of a party. Though a rota system had been arranged among the marshals to share cooking and washing, both Ginnie and Bits Vereste had offered to pitch in. They were in the kitchen tonight along with the staff nurses, preparing supper as some of the men assembled on the porch.

Bart Vereste was not outside, Lindy saw when he joined the waiting group. But Snoot, Dyskowicz, and Konecki were all present; and a dark intense young man of about twenty, whom Lindy took to be Mark Vereste. They sat apart in weather-beaten cane rockers or on the porch steps, talking little, watching a candy-striped sunset die in the west. The night was turning cold.

Konecki came over to Lindy and nudged him toward the end of the porch.

"Thanks for the clothes," Lindy said. They had been in his room when he finished talking to Vereste, but he had not seen Konecki until now. Lindy felt a grudging reluctance to release his information—which Konecki was so eager to have that he was ready to knock down any obstacle that stood in his way.

"Don't thank me," Konecki demurred. "The pants are

145

Harpe's; the shirt comes from a guy named Finch. We'll do better for you tomorrow. The chopper goes out daily for mail, papers, provisions. Give me a shopping list."

"It'll be a short list if I get the right drift from Vereste."

"Oh?" Konecki looked worried. "Don't tell me he knows so little he can spill it overnight."

"No, he'll live up to your expectations. He says, on a rough estimate, he's got enough to break fifteen or twenty top men and two or three times as many in the second rank. He gave me a few sample names, without telling me what he's got on them. Almost every one came up in front of the committee, but we couldn't find a thing to nail them with."

"If the lode's that rich," Konecki said, "you ought to buy skis; we could be here taking dictation till there's snow on those mountains."

Lindy shook his head. "You could be in court in weeks. It depends on how fast you pay, not how fast he talks."

"What do you mean?"

"Vereste has so many facts and figures to turn over that he couldn't keep them all in his head. He's been collecting the stuff for months, putting it down someplace where it can be instantly retrieved—but only by the right people."

"What's the gimmick?"

"Computer," Lindy answered tersely, with a meaningful glance over Konecki's shoulder.

Looking around, Konecki saw that Lindy had indicated Mark Vereste. "You mean sonny boy did some extracurricular work in his college computer courses?"

Lindy nodded. "Daddy planned such a big score he couldn't memorize what he wanted to sell, and collecting that amount of paper would be too dangerous. But he was always hearing valuable tidbits, or having important paper go through his hands. All he had to do was pass everything on to junior, keeping a few facts in his head, or else scribbling them down. Once the data was punched into a memory bank at the boy's college, Vereste could forget it, destroy notes, return files, whatever would keep him in the clear. Mark Vereste has been into computers for a year or two, I gather; maybe that helped nudge his father into the idea."

"So it's all programmed," Konecki murmured hungrily. "We don't even have to interrogate the son of a bitch. He tells us which buttons to push and the info can be read off a screen."

"A dream squeal," Lindy confirmed. "Bank account numbers, books on corporations the Mob has taken over and sucked dry, serial numbers on black money and hot negotiables, numbers of checks that played a part in laundry transfers. Vereste claims if you break down some of his stuff you could trace a thousand-dollar bill dropped on a crap table in Vegas all the way to the pocket of a Turkish poppy pasha."

"The first time in history a machine turned fink," Konecki chuckled, giddy at the thought. "All of them—we're going to put all of these bastards in the slam."

"Slow down," Lindy cautioned. "Let me finish telling you about this computer. It's a particularly advanced model—the college had some government grants to pay for it, incidentally—and the memory core has the capacity, theoretically, to store a few billion facts. In other words, you don't just stick in your thumb and pull out a plum. To get the data you want, you have to punch in a very complicated, specific code relating to a particular program."

"I'm with you," Konecki said placidly. "It's actually the codes we have contracted to buy from the firm of Vereste and Son."

"But there's a new clause in the contract. Vereste wants his money up front. No pay, no play."

"Wait a second!" Konecki hissed, fighting to repress his explosion so he would not be heard by others on the porch. "That wasn't the—"

"The deal?" Lindy interrupted. "No. At least, not the way he led us into it. But you can see this makes better sense from his point of view than waiting around while you take an accounting of what his information yields to Revenue. If he opens secret accounts for you, steers you to records, there may be enough evidential material to stand up in court without his testimony. Once he plays his trump, he knows he'll be at your mercy. And he's afraid the government wouldn't keep its part of the bargain. There's no written agreement, after all."

"Tough." Konecki said. "He'll have to go with us now. He's got no choice."

"And you do? Come off it, Gabe. What if he refused to

147

talk? You were the one who educated me about the possible effects of a dud pigeon. How do you justify what's been done so far? How do you explain the next fifteen years of grocery bills for Bart Vereste? Or this?" Lindy waved vaguely at the compound. "What's this Shangri-la costing the taxpayer? Twenty, thirty thousand a week? Do you close it down and let Vereste get blasted? You told me, too, that once you lose an informer, it'll be a long time before you attract the next one. The program would probably lose its appropriation long before then. You're getting a lot of flak as it is. Everyone's calling for results. When Ryle talked yesterday about all-out war on the Mafia there was only one man in a roomful of pretty smart people who raised an argument against it. So tell me, how do you make Vereste back down?"

"Christ," Konecki admitted, "it's a nightmare." He turned then to study Mark Vereste, who was now in conversation with Dyskowicz.

"I can't say yes or no," Konecki went on at last. "It has to go to the AG, and frankly I can't see him initialing this. It was different when we thought Vereste would get his taste *out of* what we pulled in." He paused. "Of course, if Vereste would give us a sample of what's to come, a free appetizer to prove it isn't a con . . ."

"I have a feeling he will," Lindy said. "He's thought this through so well, I'll bet he's even got it ready."

"Put it to him in the morning."

Someone near the lodge entrance shouted that dinner was on the table, and the men at the other end of the porch went inside.

But Konecki didn't move. He was suddenly appraising Lindell critically, as he had on the first day they had met.

"Tell me, friend," he asked Lindy, "what gives you such loving insight into Vereste's intentions? For that matter, why did he pick you to broker the deal? We never did clear that up. If it was only for the Washington connection, he could've done better. Yours turned out to be pretty cold."

"I asked him about it myself," Lindy said pleasantly, overlooking Konecki's implications. "He said he's had a special feeling about me ever since his appearance before the committee. 'A sense of identification' was the way he described it."

"Identification? Where the hell would he get that from?"

"Because, according to him, I was doing the kind of work he thinks he might've done if he hadn't gone crooked."

Konecki stared in amazement at Lindy, then broke into a laugh as he moved toward the door. "'Life dealt me a bad hand, Father,'" he declaimed, cornily dramatic. "Jesus, I thought that pitch went out with Pat O'Brien movies."

At the dinner table no concession was made to the circumstances which had brought the company together. It was a friendly, lively gathering, almost surrealistically normal, Lindy thought. True, it was the second night most of the same people had been together, and the stiffness would have broken down to some degree. But at this table no barriers appeared to exist at all between the warders and the internees. "One big happy family" was the phrase that came to mind.

A marshal named Perry, who seemed to be the youngest— and for that reason had been assigned more as a companion to the Verestes than as a guard—bantered with Bits about her play that afternoon in the tennis match he had chaperoned. At another end of the table Mark Vereste was in a serious discussion with Willy Dyskowicz about future applications of computer technology. Snoot and the two nurses were exchanging information about the history and geography of the Adirondacks, and planning a possible mountain-climbing lark if they could arrange a day off together.

Strangest of all was the conversation between Konecki and Bart and Ginnie Vereste. The Verestes were asking, like any two concerned householders, about the extent of damage to their property from the fire that had been deliberately set. Ginnie Vereste was particularly concerned to know the fate of a collection of needlepoint she had made over the years and kept in an upstairs closet. Bart was informing Konecki that he did not expect to forfeit his ample fire insurance because of the government's extreme ideas on how to protect witnesses.

After dinner, people helped themselves to coffee from a table in front of the big fieldstone fireplace, ablaze with a crackling log fire. Some of the other guards who had been on duty, or who had eaten separately in dining facilities attached to the bunkhouses, joined the company; chess and

149

card games were begun. A number of the men gravitated to the porch where a folding Ping-Pong table had been set up. When Lindy went out, he found that Vereste had taken command of the table by virtue of a superior forehand smash; all comers were being roundly trounced.

As Lindy watched, Konecki came up beside him. "You look like something you ate disagreed with you."

"Not something I ate. But the rest of it is kind of hard to swallow: La Cosa Nostra Summer Camp for Boys and Girls. Everybody's having such a goddamn good time."

"How would you treat 'em? Ball and chain in a damp dungeon?"

Vereste polished off another challenger and a cheer went up from a couple of the spectators. Lindy saw some money change hands.

"Anyone else?" Vereste crowed.

"Somebody's got to beat this mother," Konecki muttered and went to pick up the free paddle.

Lindy turned away from the game. At the opposite end of the porch, he saw Ginnie Vereste sitting under a gas camping lantern, occupied with another piece of needlepoint. She was an attractive woman, he thought, with lovely soft features. The unique pressures of her former existence had told on her, though, made her look older than the thirty-nine years that was her recorded age. There were deep worry lines across her forehead and her jet-black hair was streaked with gray. Elementary plastic surgery, a change in hair color, some lessons in makeup, would improve her appearance considerably. The process would be an agreeable way to begin her new life.

Lindy went along the porch and stood at an empty rocking chair next to hers.

"May I?"

"Of course." She gave him a warm, genuine smile, and looked back at her needlepoint, a floral design.

Lindy sat down. A roar went up from the Ping-Pong spectators as a point was scored by whoever had the most money riding on him.

"You don't seem to mind being here at all," Lindy said.

"Why should I? It's the first peace I've known, the first time I've felt safe in—in my whole life." Her hands stopped

150

working. She paused as if to repeat the statement silently, a revelation even to her. Then she resumed her stitching. "I only wish I'd broken away sooner. I guess Julie got all the brains between us."

"Julie?"

Ginnie Vereste glanced up. A bit startled, Lindy thought, as though lulled by the unaccustomed security, distracted by her pastime, she had let some forbidden word unconsciously escape her lips.

"My twin sister," she answered slowly, "Giulietta. She ran away more than twenty years ago, right after I was married. She must have done what I'm going to do now, changed her name, started another life. They never found her." Again she picked up her stitching. "How long will we have to stay here? It's nice, but I don't want to live too long in a cage."

"You're not a prisoner. This is only for your protection. If you want, once you've been covered with an identity, I guess you could be resettled anytime, you and your children."

"Soon," she said. "I hope it can be soon. You know, I have another sister."

"Rina," Lindy supplied. Giulietta Francini was listed in the file as missing and untraceable, but the second sister was still a cause for concern. She was in an institution for the mentally retarded near St. Louis, an exclusive establishment which also provided care for defective offspring of American families far more distinguished than the Francinis. Quite probably, Rina was not the only Mafia child to have the benefit of this kind of skilled and expensive attention. The habit of inbreeding among crime families, especially in the last two generations, when secrecy had been more rigorously preserved, had led to a high incidence of retardation and other genetic flaws.

"Yes, Rina," Ginnie said sadly. "I go to see her eight or nine times a year. She looks forward to those visits so much. I don't want her to suffer too long, to think that I'm never coming. . . ."

She trailed off and Lindy let the silence last, watching the slow spread of color in her pastel design. It was astounding, he thought, how ordinary she was—they all were—when you looked closely.

151

Finally, he broached the subject which had impelled him to speak to her.

"Why," he asked, "do you think your husband decided to become a witness?"

She looked at him in surprise. "He's the one to ask about that."

"I did."

"Well?"

"He said it was for the money."

"You find that hard to believe, for what you're paying him?"

"Crime paid him well, too. Not *as* well, perhaps, but more than he could spend. There had to be something more to push him into turning his life upside down. When I asked him, I had the feeling he was holding back."

"Why do you have to know?" Ginnie Vereste said, turning away. "Isn't it enough to have his information?"

"It would be, if he was giving it away. But the way he's holding us up, there's some worry about whether it's simply a racket. In fact, the whole deal could break down because his motives are suspect."

"In what way?"

"One theory is that he's been sent by the Mob to do a very special hatchet job. We'll pay, come up empty-handed, the story will be made public—and that'll be the end of government funding to pay and protect Mafia informers."

"My God," Ginnie Vereste scoffed, "if that were true, would they have tried to kill Bart?"

"They missed," Lindy said simply.

Ginnie glared at him.

"Look, I'm sorry," Lindy continued, "but nobody can take it for granted when a man like Bart Vereste suddenly changes sides. That's why I'm talking to you. I don't want to see what he's got go to waste. I don't know why he should hold back anything that would clinch this deal. But if there is something, I ought to know it. The more I understand his reasons, the more I can pass along, the quicker this could go through."

Ginnie laid aside her canvas and wool. "I've been sitting too long," she said. "How about taking a walk?" Without

152

waiting for his answer, she stood and went down the steps at the end of the porch. Lindy followed quickly and they walked toward the lake. Around them, in the darkened guard shelters at the rim of the compound, the tips of lighted cigarettes glowed, a comforting reminder of protective presences. The boisterous cheers and hoots of the Ping-Pong competition receded in the background.

As they neared the edge of the lake, a bright beam was suddenly flashed across their faces.

"Oh, sorry, folks," said a voice behind the light. "Have to check, you know."

They continued on to the boathouse dock. The lake was dark except for a single tiny flicker on the far shore, the cooking fire of some campers, perhaps. The stillness was broken only by the occasional soft splash of a leaping fish. A half-moon frosted the rising mist with enough reflected glow so that Lindy and Ginnie Vereste could dimly see each other.

"You know Bart wouldn't want me to do any talking on my own," Ginnie began. "But I'm grateful for the way we're being treated, the chance to start over. Where I can, I want to cooperate. But you mustn't ask me anything about the business side."

"His reasons," Lindy said. "That's all."

"All right. I can't see why he even held out on explaining them. Male vanity, I guess. Or maybe because of some polite notion that personal matters should be left out of it." She shrugged. Then, staring out across the lake, she told the story:

"Last Easter, Bart and I went to Florida with the children. At the hotel where we stayed, there was a girl, the daughter of a man named Rocco Gesolo. She was there for the holiday with her parents, and we all spent a lot of time together. You see, Rocco's also—"

"I know who Gesolo is," Lindy said.

"Then you can imagine the dangers in what happened between Bart and the girl, Marianna Gesolo. She was only seventeen, a few years younger than his own daughter. I'm sure Bart would have preferred to avoid the affair. But well, the girl is . . . I know it's unfashionable to talk about sex objects these days, but I can't think of a better way to describe her:

153

she's one of those magnificent animals who are created to be loved. In every way but one she was shallow and undeveloped as a woman. But in that one way—physically—she had come fully to flower, gave off the irresistible perfume of perfect ripeness just at this moment when Bart was exposed to her at the hotel. And he had reached an age when the interest of such a girl—whether it was love, infatuation, or the need she had to be released—was overwhelmingly flattering."

From the detachment with which she outlined the causes of the affair, Lindy perceived that Ginnie Vereste had surrendered her husband without protest. Yet the apology she made on his behalf also bespoke a remnant of love.

"Of course," she went on, "their lives, certainly his, depended on keeping their mutual attraction a secret. But I knew. When you live with a man long enough, you can tell if he's around someone who excites him. I could smell it on his skin. And the girl, perhaps I could sense what she was feeling because I'd been where she was, in love with Bart, at almost the identical point in my life. As soon as I realized what was happening, I tried to warn Bart. Oh, I didn't mind if there was someone else. We'd reached a stage long ago where that wasn't an issue. But *this*? It was insane. If I had figured it out from being around them, sooner or later Marianna's father would figure it out too. When he did, he might kill Bart straight off, and that could set the stage for more killings, a war between families. The only thing that prevented it in the beginning was Rocco's blind spot. Fathers often fail to realize how deeply their children feel. I know something about that from experience, too."

"But Bart ignored your warning," Lindy said, calling her out of the old memories.

"I can't be positive. We never spoke again about Marianna Gesolo. But many weeks ago, when he told me he intended to become a government witness, I assumed it was because of her. Bart knew this was the only way to break free and eventually marry Marianna."

"But if that's what he wanted, he should have brought her into custody with him."

"I think he planned to, originally."

154

"What changed his mind?"

"Nothing. It simply became impossible. Bart never told me, but I know that Rocco Gesolo finally discovered the affair. A few weeks ago I heard from some well-meaning friends that Bart was in trouble because of it. Marianna had been removed from her school and was being kept a virtual prisoner by her father, tutored at home, allowed out only in the company of bodyguards. Bart, meanwhile, had been given *un biglietto,* a ticket; that's what they say when a man is notified to appear for judgment by a group of bosses. Rocco had submitted the case to the Commission. If they found Bart guilty then Rocco would be permitted to punish him without having it spark off a full-scale vendetta between families."

"If this was several weeks ago," Lindy observed, "then Rocco's permission must have been denied."

Ginnie nodded. "I think Bart always knew it would be. He was never very worried about the ticket as far as I could see. Either he was sure that Rocco couldn't prove his suspicions, or he realized he was considered too valuable to kill."

Lindy pondered. "Then Bart could have continued working with them as before, without worrying."

"Perhaps he could have," Ginnie conceded. "But by then he'd gotten the idea of informing. He'd seen the possibilities of enriching himself, and with Marco he'd worked out the machinery for collecting a tremendous amount of information to sell. He didn't want to throw all his plans away. Besides which, he'd been given a new incentive to destroy our little world of strict, old-fashioned traditions. It had denied him a right he would have had in ordinary society: to love and marry for a second time, take the girl he wanted." She paused. "And I suppose he was thinking of me, too, and the children. This way we can all have second chances."

Lindy thanked Ginnie Vereste for her cooperation and they walked off the dock together. As they came to the sloping grass that led up to the lodge, however, she excused herself, explaining that it would be wiser if she walked back alone. Lindy understood that she didn't want to risk being seen by her husband returning from an intimate stroll in the dark. Ginnie Vereste was not free yet.

155

Lindy lingered at the bottom of the hill. Distantly, on the lighted porch, he could see the throng around the Ping-Pong table. The tenor of raucous cheers from opposing rooting sections indicated that a close exciting match was in progress. Lindy turned away and gazed across the peaceful lake. He didn't particularly give a damn who won.

In the morning, Lindy approached Bart Vereste and relayed the condition Gabe Konecki had imposed: the quality of the information must be proven beyond doubt before there could be any further consideration given to payment. Vereste agreed instantly; the condition, he boasted, had already been foreseen and provided for. He suggested then that both his son and Konecki be invited to participate in a meeting where details of these arrangements could be fully discussed.

The meeting began as a lecture on elementary computer technology given by Mark Vereste. One of the neatest aspects of the scheme he had devised with his father, explained the young man proudly, was that the information the government wanted could be safely retrieved from its place of storage without going anywhere near it. Modern large computer systems were routinely provided with facilities for making data links, a technique which utilized telephone lines so that a console located thousands of miles away from a memory bank could be used for data retrieval. The fortuitous presence of computer equipment as part of the security arrangements—a convenience the Verestes had not anticipated, though they had naturally counted on government access to data systems—meant that Konecki's condition could be satisfied on the spot, once a network of data links was set up.

As he went on, the interest that Mark Vereste had taken in Dyskowicz and the equipment in the electronics cabin of the compound was seen to have been a purposeful intelligence-gathering exercise. He had ascertained that there was an existing data link between one of the consoles at the safe house and the memory bank at FBI headquarters in Washington. A similar link, said young Vereste, existed between the central computer at his college and several government agencies in

Washington which wished to draw directly on research data. One such agency, Vereste knew, was the National Institutes of Health, but there were others, affiliates of the Pentagon and the Central Intelligence Agency (or so rumor had it among the students). In any case, if the existing links with terminals in Washington could be hooked up to each other, a chain would be completed allowing a console at the safe house to make a retrieval demand directly on the college memory bank which held Bart Vereste's secrets.

Willy Dyskowicz was brought into the meeting and verified what Mark Vereste had said. With quick cooperation between those who controlled various links in the chain, by this afternoon, or tomorrow at the latest, Mark Vereste could sit down in the electronics cabin and punch in his codes, and the information would light up the screen within seconds.

"Just a taste to start with," Bart Vereste reminded them now. "As the Moustache Petes used to say, enough to wet the beak."

Then he outlined the procedure to be followed afterward. There were seven full parcels of information—programs that would transmit data for up to half an hour at a time. For each of these parcels, a prepayment would have to be deposited in a bank in Switzerland. Each payment would be calculated as an agreed percentage of the amount the government would gain, either in cash or in back taxes, by using the parcel of information. If the government became dissatisfied at any point, it had the option of suspending its purchases. But there could be no possibility of the government's making fraudulent payments for what it decided to buy. Vereste had prearranged a contact in the Swiss bank of deposit. Until Vereste received telephone confirmation of each deposit from his contact man there, who would identify himself with a different code word for each of the seven separate deposits, the computer would keep its secrets.

The meeting broke up then. Dyskowicz had volunteered to handle technical arrangements for the data link network, and Konecki stayed behind for a moment to consult with him on these. The Verestes went out together. Lindy followed alone.

When Konecki emerged from the cabin, he found Lindell

157

standing outside, watching a canoe that was gliding away over the calm lake, paddled by father and son.

"They move well together, don't they?" Konecki said tartly.

"Perfect coordination." Lindy agreed.

They continued watching, in silence, the swift knifing glide of the Indian boat, the sparkle of wet paddles in the sun.

An outboard motor suddenly buzzed to life along an outlying shore. A rubber boat emerged from the shadow of an overhanging tree and scooted rapidly toward the center of the lake on a path that would intercept the canoe. Lindy took a reflex step forward and glanced anxiously at Konecki.

"Ours," the marshal said imperturbably. "The whole lake's inside our perimeter. There's an armed launch in the boathouse, too. And, just on the off-chance the Mob sends in a submarine, we've got a couple of guys who are ex-frogmen."

Lindy laughed. "You've thought of everything, haven't you?"

Konecki continued gazing across the lake, an unhappy, suspicious expression on his face. "Wouldn't it be nice if I had," he said.

"If you're still worried about whether or not Vereste is working for himself," Lindy said, "I think I can tell you something to settle your ulcer." He went on to report what he had learned about the Gesolo affair from Ginnie Vereste. Then he drew some conclusions. "That clears up what the motive is, aside from money. I think it also covers why the shoot on Vereste came how and when it did. Rocco Gesolo never accepted the verdict the bosses handed down in Vereste's favor. He must have started tracking Vereste, his lust for revenge eating at him. But he knew if he killed it would probably mean a war—and certainly his own death, as punishment for defying the will of the bosses. All he could do was keep a watch on Bart and hope that he might someday get an opening that would leave him in the clear."

"And he got it," Konecki amended excitedly, "because he was watching Vereste at the same time our boy was watching you, making the first contacts. Geloso got onto that, figured out that Bart was planning to fink—"

"And by catching him in the act, he'd have his revenge, and be a hero in the Organization."

158

There was a silence. Konecki's excitement fizzled. "Why didn't he just tell the Organization? Let them handle the contract?"

"They'd let him down when he'd gone through channels about his daughter. He wanted the satisfaction of doing the job himself, his way."

"And what about catching Vereste in the act? Exactly how did he manage that? He was set up at the rendezvous before Bart got there."

"If he knew Vereste had made a touch with me, he might've bugged my phone."

"Maybe," Konecki said. "We'll check it out. It would ease my mind on a few points if it adds up. Though, I don't know. . . ." He glanced toward the canoe again.

"For Christ's sake," Lindy cried, exasperated. "He's agreed to prove the information is genuine. You know what his reasons were for turning around. What else is bothering you?"

Konecki turned to Lindy. "That game," he said slowly.

"What game?"

"The Ping-Pong game I won last night. I could've sworn he gave it away, just to make me feel good."

THIRTEEN

Why couldn't the whole city be air-conditioned? Dom Francini thought as he stepped out of his car in front of the apartment building on Fifth Avenue. Not just the cars and houses, but the streets, the whole goddamn world? For a man of Dom's bulk even a few moments in the gritty swelter was a form of torture. It was only mid-May, but today was freakishly hot. Those bombs, Dom cursed silently, that's where the trouble started. Snow in April, heat waves in May. The guys who thought of those fucking bombs should be hit.

He was dripping wet by the time he had crossed the sidewalk. In the lobby of the building, Dom paused to wipe his face with a handkerchief. But he was still perspiring heavily as he rode up in the elevator to the penthouse. Perhaps he should have waited in the lobby until he cooled off. It was unwise to be seen sweating; it might be interpreted as a signal of fear, of defeat. Dom was already late, however, and Don Valerio hated to be kept waiting.

The elevator stopped at the penthouse, and the door opened directly into the grandiose foyer of the triplex apartment.

Waiting to receive Dom was Ligazza's principal bodyguard, Jerry Logibbio, a lumbering pyramid of a man popularly known as Giblets. He ushered Dom across the foyer to the living room and pointed at a door leading out to the terrace.

"He's working the farm," Giblets said in a commiserating tone.

The sprawling rooftop which wrapped around Ligazza's apartment had been totally covered with a deep layer of soil, tons of it. In addition to the decorative plants and shrubs

160

which were the conventional landscaping for the luxury penthouses of Park and Fifth, Ligazza had cultivated an orchard of dwarf fruit trees and a large vegetable patch. He favored growing those varieties which would flourish in his native Sicily. In fact, the earth in which they were rooted had reputedly been imported from that distant island at great expense. In one corner of the vast terrace Ligazza had also constructed a small stone hut and a number of wooden pens modeled on those that could be found on the farm of an ordinary Sicilian peasant. Here he kept chickens, rabbits, and goats.

This grand folly had been assailed frequently by other occupants of the apartment building on the grounds that a multitude of health and building codes were being violated. And on another front, one or two of the old Don's associates had occasionally dared a mild joke about his curious hobby. But Ligazza had taken both the serious complaints and the ridicule in his stride. The health and building inspectors who came to the penthouse had never verified a single violation of their respective ordinances; and the friendly detractors were generally silenced by a taste of the delicious cheese which the old man produced from the milk of his goats. To those who expressed a genuine admiration for Ligazza's achievement, he would modestly reply that it was quite unremarkable. Rooftop agriculture was being practiced by many in the city these days—not usually on the same scale, of course, though an heir to a General Motors fortune was said to have a penthouse farm similar to his.

Before abandoning the air-conditioned living room, Dom paused to remove his jacket and undo another button on his sport shirt. He could see Ligazza's lean figure in a far corner of the terrace, stooped over a patch of green. The old man was wearing a tattered white shirt and a pair of dark suit pants and the same kind of white straw hat worn by the old *paisani*. Crazy old creep, Dom thought. Why the fuck didn't he go back there if he missed it so much? Or was he so close to being a god that he really believed he could bring the place to him, lift the island out of the sea and raise it up into this polluted sky? Was that why he wasn't scared when everyone else was?

161

Dom moaned as he opened the door to the terrace and a solid wall of heat slammed into him, tumbled around him, began squeezing the water out of his body. He thought of retreating, sending Giblets to ask Don Valerio if they could talk inside. But he knew that would be a tactical error. Ligazza was at his most relaxed and approachable when playing with his incredible toy.

Dom went toward Ligazza, passing slowly through the areas of shade under a line of plum trees.

Ligazza raised his head as Dom's shadow fell over the vegetable patch. "Ah, Don Domenico. Stay there. I don't want my finocchio murdered under your feet." He continued pulling weeds, working his way along a row in Dom's direction.

Dom felt the rivulets of sweat pouring down his body, tickling the creases in his rolled flesh. Yet on Ligazza there was not a single bead of perspiration to be seen.

"Well, don't keep me waiting," Ligazza coaxed buoyantly. "What is this exciting development you've come to report?"

"Don Vee, I've had a cop running an investigation for me. The results are in."

Dom explained then how he had put the police machinery to work for him twelve days ago, and followed with some of the less spectacular findings made since by Captain Albert Waitely.

The policeman had located the daughter of a family in Silver Hills who was friendly with Bits Vereste and knew that she was involved in a serious romance with a student named Danny Behrens, a senior at a New England men's college. Other gossipy neighbors had provided Waitely with the names of two men who had probably had affairs with Ginnie Vereste. The latter had both convincingly denied having seen or talked with Ginnie on an intimate basis at any time in the past few months. On the other hand, Waitely had established that it was probably the Behrens boy who had been with Bits on her last night before the fire. The guard on night duty at the Silver Hills entrance gate had checked Bits through at some time after two A.M., and remembered her being with a young man who was driving a car with a Massachusetts license plate.

162

"So you think it is possible"—Ligazza interrupted himself to tug at a truculent weed—"that the girl would have given her *amante* a forewarning of her need to disappear with her father, even to the extent of telling him where she would be?"

"And that's not all," Dom declared. "I think she could've told him she was going to play dead."

Ligazza threw aside a handful of weeds and straightened up. "Play dead?" he echoed.

"Don Vee, this cop Waitely, who's doing the legwork, he has the idea that all the Verestes may still be alive. From what he.tells me, I go along."

Ligazza came along the row to where Dom stood. "You look hot, Don Domenico. Perhaps we should sit in the shade until you tell me more about this." He conducted Dom to a bench under a grape arbor.

There, Dom Francini filled in the details.

Waitely's suspicions had been aroused when he went to interrogate the gardener named Breibart who had turned in the fire alarm. Breibart had been under federal protection since then at a Holiday Inn. The marshals who kept the gardener constant company had balked at Waitely's request to take a statement from the witness. But Waitely had broken down their resistance: if the witness was under protection from possible reprisal by the murderers, why wouldn't his protectors readily cooperate to see that the threat was eliminated, the murderers apprehended? At last, after consultation with their head office, the marshals had yielded and allowed Waitely to question Breibart in their presence. In that session, Breibart had described the events leading up to his discovery of the fire. A curious fact struck Waitely: where Breibart spoke about the comings and goings of the men from the moving van, he mentioned having seen three large crates carried in, and three similar containers carried out not long after. Although moving and storage companies did supply containers for packing, they could not have been filled with personal belongings in the span of ten or fifteen minutes that Breibart recalled was the period during which the van remained at the house. The anomaly was sufficient to

163

send Waitely to the county morgue to attempt a positive confirmation of the identities of the three charred bodies removed from the fire. Forensic experts had advised him that this would be possible only with the assistance of dental records, to be compared with fragments of jawbone that had survived incineration. Waitely had secured dental charts and X rays from the files of two dentists in the community who had attended the Verestes, but there had been no chance to make the comparison. Before he had appeared at the morgue with the records, the bodies had been impounded by federal authorities and removed to a place unknown. Waitely had been unable to take his hunch any farther.

"In short," Ligazza observed, "there is not a shred of evidence to support his notion that the bodies may have been substituted."

"Which," Dom replied, "is the best proof, if you ask me. Why would the feds tie a cop's hands? It must be because they didn't like what he was about to grab onto. Don Vee, you said it yourself, that fire aced us out of some of our best shots at tracing Bart. It would've been a smart move to con us into believing that his family was dead."

Ligazza thought a moment. "So there may have been two separate actions against Bart and his family. The man who tried to shoot him had nothing to do with the fire."

The new theory, Dom realized, lifted a burden from Ligazza. He had been forced to suspect Rocco as the source for an independent contract against Bart, but found it abhorrent to believe that his *consigliere* had callously eliminated the whole family as part of his revenge.

"Very well," Ligazza went on, "say all the Verestes are alive. What then?"

"The way I see it, Don Valerio, it's past the point where I can handle this alone. Four days ago a Revenue team showed up at one of our banks in Mexico City; with a little paper work they got cooperation from the Mexies to grab two accounts on a John Doe action. You know what it means. The stoolie has started to unload. Gardia called me in a panic to say that Bart had originally opened the accounts for him; they were handling in and out action on his Latino coke

164

trade. As of yesterday the balance added up to one-point-two million. Gardia thinks he's personally in the clear, but he's not sure. How much more can Bart give them? How long can we hold out if he strips all our cash? We've got to move like lightning, Don Vee, and that means I need your push."

"You'll have plenty of help, Don Domenico. Plans for the full convention are almost finalized. Mike Sardi has given his hotel for the purpose."

Every day for two weeks Ligazza had been saying the convention of bosses was imminent. Was it only to pressure him? Dom wondered. It was true that such a gathering would have to be carefully arranged, couldn't be rushed. The specter of the Apalachin fiasco still hung over every convention that was held.

"It sounds great," Dom said automatically. "But meanwhile we've got to use every day."

"What do you recommend?" Ligazza asked agreeably.

"We've got the name of this Behrens kid. We know he goes to school in New England and he drives a car with a Massachusetts plate. With the right connections at the license and registration bureaus that's enough dope to find him in a day."

"I see. That's Sciavone's territory, so you want him to handle it."

Dom nodded. "I figure if Bits cared for the guy she didn't leave him in mourning. When his tongue is pulled he might tell us if she's alive, and where to find her."

"I'll arrange it," Ligazza said quickly. "What else?"

"You know my brother's youngest kid, Rina. She was born stupid and nobody could keep her since Joe died. She's been living in a special home out in St. Louis. She means a lot to Ginnie though. Ginnie's always going out there to visit."

"I can't imagine Ginetta would be fool enough to trust Rina with a secret on which so much depends."

"I'm sure she didn't. But that wasn't my idea. St. Lou is Charlie Toccato's, right?"

Ligazza murmured confirmation.

"If Charlie could fix a snatch on Rina," Dom continued, "take her out of the bughouse, it would put the pressure on

Bart to clam up. I mean, assuming Ginnie's alive, she'd have to square it with Bart; she'd know his silence was the price for getting Rina back alive."

The old man's thin dry lips arched down with distaste. "I doubt if that would work," he said.

"Maybe not. But even if it's a hundred to one against, we can't afford not to try it."

"And you would use someone of your own blood in this way, in such a *gioco d'azzardo,* an almost hopeless gamble?"

Dom faltered under the intense, demanding gaze of Ligazza's bright blue eyes. He groped for his already sopping handkerchief and wiped it over his face and neck. The old bastard, he thought, always making such a holy fuss about blood, family, respect. Even now! Christ, what had started the trouble in the first place?

"I don't like to suggest it," Dom answered. "But there's so few angles to play. I've got one more, but I don't think it's worth much."

"What?"

"You know about this character Lindell, who was in on the Vereste deal. He's wise we're gunning for him now, so he's also disappeared. There's a good chance he went down the same hole. We'll try and find anyone who was tight with him, see if they know where he is."

"Yes," Ligazza said, "do that." Then he left the bench and walked back into his vegetable patch.

Dom stood, too, but clung to the shade of the arbor. "And about Rina," he called, "what is your decision, Don Valerio?"

Ligazza walked between the rows of green and bent down. He worked without speaking for several minutes. Then Dom Francini went to the edge of the patch. "Don Valerio, time is short. You must—"

"I must pull the weeds," Ligazza cut in harshly, without looking up from the task. "I'll let you know what I have decided."

The program was running, the first sizable compilation of data for which Bart Vereste had been paid. Twenty minutes earlier, Mark Vereste had come into the electronics cabin and punched in a retrieval code on the computer console. It

166

was that simple. The boy had walked out then, leaving the data system to function on its own. Since then the neat rows of names and dates and numbers had been lighting up the screen, in front of which sat Konecki, Lindell, Dyskowicz, and a couple of other marshals assigned to monitor the various electronic functions. Simultaneously, the facts were being seen and conveniently recorded on the FBI computer which was part of the data-link network.

The program had started with a list of some companies in which Mafia bosses owned silent controlling interests, followed by a breakdown of which men were involved with which company and the exact means and methods which had been used to acquire ownership. Then there had been details from company accounts showing how they had been used as conduits for illegal earnings. By falsification of records on money-losing operations, transferring funds to cover subsidiary losses, huge sums had been swallowed up in seemingly allowable tax write-offs. Although the system was complicated and required deft hands on the books, it involved less risk than the more elementary methods of simpler times, when couriers had been sent out of the country with bundles of cash. The amounts had grown too large to be shifted so crudely; in any case, too many of the men who could have been used as couriers were under observation by federal authorities. The answer had been to adapt the "creative accounting" used by all corporations to minimize taxes, conceal losses, plump up earnings—whatever would impress the stock market and conserve profits.

The payment to Bart Vereste for this first parcel of information had been one and a half million dollars. The appropriation had been quickly approved by the Justice Department after Bart's "free sample" of data had opened up the Mexico City accounts, especially since the amount of cash thus recovered had contributed all but three hundred thousand of the price. The rest of the money to pay Vereste had been diverted (with little compunction) from funds originally earmarked by the government for other uses. It was anticipated that the first program would pay for itself many times over. Vereste was making good on his promise: the bosses who had concealed illegitimate earnings would be lia-

167

ble for long terms of imprisonment on multiple charges of tax fraud. The names of two big men in the East, Ricavole and Gardia, had already come up, along with others operating in the Midwest and New England. More than a dozen men who stood lower in the hierarchy had also been listed as involved in the fraud, stock manipulation, and extortion through which business holdings had been acquired.

The flow of information had finally banished Konecki's skepticism. The quantity was too great, the quality too fine, for Vereste to have hoped to peddle anything phony; it could all be easily checked. Nevertheless, to be on the safe side, Konecki intended to continue buying the parcels one at a time, using the proceeds from one, hopefully, to cover payment for the next. Vereste would, in effect, always be paid with Mafia money.

Though the dealings had become mechanical, Bart Vereste had insisted on doing his talking through Lindell. Lindy had agreed to stay on through the processing, though he regarded his involvement now as more of a punishment than an honor. Perhaps, he speculated, Vereste's quirky "sense of identification" had to include not only negotiating with someone he thought was like himself but corrupting him as well. Certainly Lindell's participation had knocked the pedestal of idealism from under his feet. He knew now there was no way to accomplish anything without violating some principle. And as he watched the letters and numerals appearing before him, he had an odd sense of losing a cause rather than winning. There were the names of men he had once questioned fruitlessly for hours on end, now at last rendered liable to punishment. Yet he could feel no thrill at having broken them this way. They had not cracked under interrogation or the power of legislation, they had never surrendered to the police. What had defeated them was simply putting their trust in one disloyal man.

Lindy was about to leave the electronics shed when an electronic teleprinter started to chatter. Willy Dyskowicz got up from his chair and went to check the incoming message.

"Hey," Dyskowicz said gravely, "have a look at this. From the Bureau." He tore off the printout and brought it over to Konecki.

"Shit," Konecki whispered hotly as he read.

168

Lindy turned from the door.

"Danny Behrens was found cold by a roadside two hours ago," Konecki said, addressing himself to Lindy. "Somebody must've gotten the idea he could give them a lead on this place. When he had no answer they threw him away like a piece of used chewing gum. He'd been broken to pieces and there were four slugs in his skull."

Lindy grabbed the printout and read it for himself.

"You were supposed to stay ahead in this game," he sneered, pushing the paper back at Konecki. "Couldn't you have figured that one, for God's sake?"

"There's a limit to how far we can spread our net," Konecki snapped. Then he added with restraint, "We were sending a man there, you know that. Just a few more days. I talked to the girl about it. She asked us not to bother Behrens until we were ready to tell him everything, not to hang around him otherwise. As it was, his parents didn't approve of their match, wanted to bust it up. Bits figured that putting him under protection could've been the last straw."

"The last," Lindy muttered. "She'll have some new ideas on that, I guess." He glanced at the computer screen where the precious data was still rolling. "Jesus, they'll do any rotten thing to turn that off." Suddenly he whirled back to Konecki. "Gabe, if the Mob wanted to break open Danny Behrens, then they must know—"

"Know what?"

"That Bits is alive—all of them."

"No. That's one lucky thing. We hadn't told him yet."

"But suppose they knew, anyway. They could've expected Behrens to have some communication from Bits while she was here, as he would have in a few days. They were squeezing him to find out where she was."

"How could they know she was alive?" Konecki said doubtfully.

Lindy advanced on him angrily. "I don't know. But the boy's dead, damn it. Somebody made connections somewhere. You'd better think hard and plug any other goddamn holes, because there's one hell of a lot of murdering bastards looking for a way in here."

Konecki sat mute and scowling for several seconds. Then he marched to a filing cabinet in a corner of the cabin, yanked it open and pulled out a file. He scanned it briefly, shoved it back in place and slammed the drawer shut. Turning to Dyskowicz, he barked, "Send an all-red to HQ. I want a couple of men sent pronto to that place where Mrs. Vereste's sister is parked. She'll be listed as Rina Francini; the address is Winterman Institute, St. Louis. If we have no one on the spot, tell them to liaise with the Bureau and use people from their St. Louis office." Konecki rubbed his fingers together, conjuring any other precautionary thoughts. Dyskowicz was already seated at the teleprinter, tapping out the instructions to the operator in Washington. "Better have Washington phone ahead to the Institute right now," Konecki added. "Instruct them that Rina Francini is not to be allowed off the premises until our men get there."

Dyskowicz finished typing and an acknowledgment rattled back immediately.

Konecki turned palms up to Lindell. "That's the only one I can think of."

For a minute they gazed gloomily at the computer program, the cause of it all.

Then Lindy asked, "Did the son have a girl friend?"

"No one as far as we know."

"You ought to ask him again about his friends, ask all of them. They may come up with a few names once they hear what happened to Behrens."

"Look, Lindy. I don't think there's any sense in—"

Konecki was interrupted by a buzzing signal on a radio-telephone linked to the Washington headquarters. He snatched up the receiver.

"Yeah, speaking," he said, and then listened for what seemed a long time. "No, never mind," he said finally. "The Bureau can take it over." As he lowered the phone, he murmured, "The bastards."

"The Bureau giving us trouble again?" asked the taciturn Harpe.

"I didn't mean them. It's the C.N. They've got Rina Francini."

They had done it without force or violence. At eleven o'clock that morning a man identifying himself as a cousin of Rina's, Victor Francini, had arrived at the Institute and

170

asked to withdraw the girl from resident care. In a meeting with the administrative director, he had explained that the family wanted Rina with them during a period of "personal difficulties." Familiar with Rina's background, the director was prepared to accept the euphemistic excuse. He knew that Ginetta Vereste was listed as the party responsible in all decisions about Rina's care and treatment; he also knew—though Rina had not yet been told—what had happened to Mrs. Vereste and why. Bart Vereste's surrender as a government witness was still a topic in the national news. The director followed Mack Sunderland's column, which had sparked off a heated controversy by reporting that, according to reliable sources, Vereste was being paid millions of dollars for his information. If he was that valuable a witness, the director realized, reprisals for Vereste's defection might even include the retarded sister of his wife. Thus the director could understand Rina's family wanting to place her under their personal protection. Relieved to eliminate any risk that the Institute's name would be dragged into the unsavory affair, the director had authorized Rina Francini's immediate release in the custody of her cousin.

Descriptions of "Victor Francini" concurred in reporting that his behavior with the girl had been very loving and patient. He had carefully packed everything in the room she occupied, every article of clothing, every scrap of paper. And, according to a woman therapist on the Institute staff who had helped prepare Rina for her departure, she had been repeatedly assured by her cousin that she was not going away forever: she would be back soon, and while she was gone she would be staying with family. Rina Francini had been very happy to go then. She had carried some of her own baggage to the waiting limousine.

The details dribbled in on the teleprinter. After an account of the way in which Rina Francini had been peacefully kidnapped, the machine started spewing out a long and discouraging list of specific efforts to trace the victim. Checks on rail and air terminals, hotels and motels, rousts of known Mafiosi for interrogation, all with negative results.

Lindy stopped reading the printout. "They'll never get her back that way," he said drearily to Konecki.

171

"There is no other way," Konecki replied. "You think we're going to erase the stuff we've already put to the computer?"

"Use it and they'll kill the girl."

"Then we'll sit on it until she's found."

"And if you don't find her—can you sit on your golden egg forever?"

There was a silence. They turned to look at the console which had been screening the Vereste program. The program had ended without anyone noticing.

Lindy walked out of the cabin. As he went down the porch steps, he saw Ginnie Vereste stretched out in a beach chair on the boat dock, convalescing. Ten days ago a U.S. Navy anaplastic surgeon had been brought into the safe house to do a job on her face; nothing radical, but it had produced startling results, taken ten years off her appearance. Bart Vereste had undergone more extensive surgery and had since kept to himself in his room.

Seeing Ginnie serenely reclining, Lindy realized that no one had thought to tell her of Rina's kidnapping. Was it Konecki's intention to impose a blackout, not to let anything rock the boat? Ginnie's influence on her husband might still be sufficient to make him withhold the information he had not yet sold.

But why wait to see what Konecki would do? She had a right to know. Lindy went down to the lake.

She heard his footsteps on the dock and turned toward him. There were still some slight discolorations from the surgery that had smoothed out her skin, but they were fading into a tan. She would have no trouble finding a man, Lindy thought, if she wanted one. Ginnie Vereste might have a very good life ahead of her.

"Hello." Her smile came quickly, then faded as she sensed his tension.

"We've just been notified . . ." Lindy paused, drew a breath. "Rina's been kidnapped."

Ginnie Vereste choked down a cry and bolted upright in her chair. Then slowly she rose and went to the tip of the dock. Facing out toward the lake, she said: "Tell me everything."

172

He told her not only about the kidnap, but also about Danny Behrens' murder.

The relative calm with which she took the news was a revelation to Lindy. Ginnie Vereste had lived for so long with the possibility of violence shattering the lives of those she loved that her nerves were calloused, as much as if she had been fighting a war, seeing cruelty and death every day. There had been a brother slain years ago in an outbreak of hostility between families, Lindy recalled; maybe all her tears had been used up then.

When Lindy had finished his report, Ginnie asked:

"How much has Bart told you so far?"

"Quite a lot," Lindy admitted. "But only a fraction of what he's offering."

"Then it's too late to pay their ransom, isn't it? They want total silence, nothing less. You'd have to give them Bart in exchange for Rina, grant immunities to everyone he's already implicated. Of course, it's impossible, I know that. There's only one thing to do. Take what Bart can tell you, and use it, all of it. The sooner the better."

"But you know what will happen to your sister."

"She'll be all right. If holding her hostage fails to stop Bart, they'll let her go."

"You can't believe that."

"I *have* to." Her voice broke, a hint of the emotion concealed by a massive exercise of will. "I don't suppose you can understand. I'm here, helping you, but I'm still one of these people you want to destroy. I've grown up with them, loved them. . . . Oh, yes, one part of me hates them, too, longs to be free. But if there was only that, it wouldn't have taken me twenty years to find my way to a place like this. There's still that part of me that simply refuses to believe they are monsters. It doesn't matter how much evidence you put in front of me. It didn't matter when I was told my father had ordered men killed; he was never a killer to me. Even when he tried to keep me from marrying a man I loved, I couldn't hate him—or if I did, I forgot it as soon as I understood that he had some good reasons." She ran clawed fingers through her hair, as if to reach down inside her head and untangle her thoughts. "It's crazy, perhaps. But I can't help seeing

173

their side—that everything they do is according to rules, reasons. Oh, yes, against the laws of the land, but not ungoverned by any code. They have their law. Whoever violates it will be found and punished; there are no grants of immunity. In that system, it is we who are the criminals—Bart, myself, my children—as surely as any Mafioso is to you. And our crimes are no less monstrous. We aren't merely threatening to put men in jail, destroy their rackets, take their money or possessions. We're bringing down a way of life—everything they understand—smashing traditions, destroying a world." She paused and Lindy could see the two selves that fought within her changing places. "I don't sympathize with them. But I know they are men, human, not without feeling. They will stop at nothing to defend themselves; but if they see it was senseless to take Rina, they will return her, unharmed."

"What does sense have to do with it? Did it make sense to kill Danny Behrens?"

"In their terms, yes. He would have been a witness against whoever assaulted him. Rina's handicaps would rule her out as a reliable witness."

"I wonder if your daughter will understand so well," Lindy said acidly. He didn't want to hurt Ginnie, but she seemed to be goading him with her reasoning, seeking some response from him that would validate her feelings.

"Of course she won't," Ginnie said. "But I'll talk to her. I don't want anyone else breaking the news."

Lindy felt she wanted to be alone now and started to go.

"You will keep talking to Bart?" she said urgently.

"I don't know."

"You must! And use what you get; don't wait."

Lindy hesitated. "You know, if you hadn't given your people credit for knowing where to draw the line, you might have warned us to protect your sister before this happened."

"Perhaps. But why didn't someone else think of it, anyway?"

There was no blame in the way she said it.

Lindy had no answer. But walking away from the lake, he realized she had not needed one. She had only meant to remind him that expecting boundaries of decency to be observed was a universal error, a common mistake of the species.

174

FOURTEEN

Charlie Toccato was one of the first people interrogated in connection with the kidnapping of Rina Francini. On the afternoon of the day she had been taken from the Winterman Institute, two FBI agents had called on the dapper Mafia chief at the sixty-two-lane bowling alley in East St. Louis from which he governed an empire with interests in meat packing, grain storage and detergent manufacture, as well as the more usual business of the underworld. The FBI had been hounding Toccato for years, fruitlessly trying to establish his responsibility for any number of criminal activities. The Bureau had no doubt that if the eastern Commission had ordered Rina Francini's disappearance as a lever against Bart Vereste, then Toccato had handled the job. But they were also aware that there would never be a scrap of evidence to that effect. If any strong-arm tactics were used to coerce confession, they could be equally certain that a team of the smartest lawyers in the Midwest would work up a crushing case against the government. The best they could do was harass him.

Toccato received the agents cordially. He had been interviewed so often in the past by the same two men that they were all on a first-name basis. Toccato supplied the obligatory denials, parried cynical comments with the repeated plea that bad things really *could* happen in this part of the country without his knowing about them, and in twenty-seven minutes the interview was over.

The two agents returned daily.

On the fourth day, Toccato was not at all surprised that the interview covered exactly the same ground as the day before. These were familiar harassment techniques, a joke to be borne with good humor. Charlie Toccato's glossy façade was still intact as the FBI agents prepared to leave his office.

Then, at the door, one agent said: "Oh, Charlie, have you heard about Phil Ricavole?"

Toccato said he hadn't.

"Picked him up in New York a couple of hours ago. Had all we needed to book on a new tax rap—a lot stronger than the old one."

"Poor Phil," Toccato said lightly. But he knew it was a heavy turn. He knew where the new rap had sprung from: Vereste's information must be coming through.

"We lost him, though," the second agent said.

Toccato brightened. "Yeah? Too bad."

"Only in a manner of speaking, actually. His bail was set at two hundred big ones, but Phil managed to get a lawyer there with the cash forty minutes after he was booked."

Toccato laughed. "That's Phil. He doesn't waste time."

"No, he doesn't. He knew he was boxed and he didn't want to spend a day in jail, now or later. As soon as he got home, he put a shotgun in his mouth and sprung himself, permanently."

Toccato paled. He didn't doubt the report. Most men would have stood up, but Phil was supposed to be dying anyway.

"Gardia, too," said the first agent. "We got him today. He's still alive, though."

"For the moment," supplied the second member of this Mutt and Jeff routine.

The agents went out.

Toccato stayed in his office until evening. Then he went down the back stairs to the basement of the bowling alley, where the controls for the automatic pinsetters were located. The teenager who supervised the controls, the son of one of Toccato's soldiers, was honored to be asked for a favor by the *capo*. The boy left immediately through the main door of the Bowlaway Lanes and drove his Dodge Charger from the parking lot to the restaurant six blocks away where Toccato had told him to wait.

Leaving by the service door normally reserved for taking bar deliveries during the day, Toccato walked the six blocks through back streets and took over the car, sending the boy back to his job with a new hundred-dollar bill in his pocket.

176

For twenty minutes, Charlie circled through the darkened commercial section, satisfying himself that there was no second car on his tail. Then he headed out of East St. Louis, crossing the bridge from the Illinois side of the Mississippi River into Missouri. In St. Louis, he stopped at a "company" garage to make some phone calls before continuing his seventy-mile journey.

"What's the word?" asked Melo Predante, a short balding man with a lumpy pneumatic torso of the kind which is formed by solid muscle layered over with fat.

The man whom Predante was addressing, Paul Nicastro, had just hung up the telephone after talking with his don and Melo's, Charlie Toccato. Nicastro was the sincere, soft-spoken gentleman who had masqueraded as Rina Francini's cousin to secure her release from the Winterman Institute. The small house in which she had since been imprisoned was attached to the rural tree nursery owned by Predante, who had also acted as chauffeur on the snatch.

"Bad," Nicastro answered his companion. "Vereste has started to spill. Uncle Sugar grabbed two *capi* today. One of them took it so hard he went home and whacked himself out. Everyone's shook. There's a big meet shaping up back East and Charlie's going."

They were standing in the shabby kitchen of the house, lit by a badly flickering fluorescent tube.

"What happens to the girl?" Predante said, as he went to the refrigerator and took out a can of beer.

Nicastro shrugged.

"Want one?" Predante pointed to a second can while the refrigerator was open.

Nicastro shook his head and Predante closed the refrigerator.

"I guess we dump her cold," Nicastro said. "But I don't know. It's touchy because she's blood. Charlie'll be here in an hour, he'll tell us how to handle it. Meantime he wants us to go through all that stuff of hers again, make sure there's nothing that ties to her sister."

"Christ, isn't once enough?" Predante moaned. "Does he really think they'd blow Vereste's hole that easy?"

"They're shook, Mellie, I told you. Charlie was told to dig

177

again, and he's telling us. And this time he says go through everything, not just the letters and gifts, but all her clothes, everything."

They went to the upstairs room where Rina was kept and listened for a moment outside the door. They could hear her humming softly, and then quick scratching noises on the linoleum floor. On the first day the girl had been uncontrollable, like an infant having a tantrum. But she had been instantly pacified when Predante had thought of putting a kitten in the room with her, one of a recent litter from a cat that roamed the nursery. Since then Rina had been utterly docile, moonily playing with her pet all day long.

Predante unlocked the door and the two men entered uneasily. They had spoken a lot to each other about the girl, admitted being spooked by her. That firm, appealing woman's body; and the face of a madonna, disguising the mind of a child. Both had been tempted to use her perversely and both had resisted, though Nicastro had come extremely close to succumbing. The girl had neglected to call out once when she needed the toilet and had wet herself. Nicastro had run a bath, had led her to it with the idea of leaving her to wash herself. But she had insisted on being helped, undressed, scrubbed. He had obliged. A fantastic piece of ass, he had thought. If only you never heard her talk. He had fought down the impulse, though. She was blood, and under Charlie's protection.

When her jailers entered, Rina was lying on the floor of the room, the kitten frisking around and over her. She had been left to dress herself, and her clothes were, as usual, carelessly worn. Tucked halfway into a red skirt was a plain brown blouse with only one button done, and she had on no shoes or stockings. The men tried to ignore her as they went to sift through the luggage piled in a corner. Rina paid no attention to them. She understood now that the early promises of "Gin-gin" coming to meet her had been lies. But she had stopped caring. The men had given her a nice playmate, and had taken good care of her.

As before, the search turned up nothing that would help trace Ginnie Vereste. But this time, afraid that Charlie would be angry if they left him empty-handed, Predante and Nicas-

178

tro set aside a few things anyway. A collection of post cards, a souvenir ashtray from Atlantic City, a diary filled with Rina's childish scrawl, some old snapshots. Useless miscellany, they knew, but their *capo* might want to bring it east as proof that he had carried out his orders.

Then, as Predante was rummaging through the clothes, he noticed one item that struck him as genuinely significant. It was a vest made of sleek horsehide with a distinctive black and white pattern, lined with a creamy-textured leather. Most interesting was the label sewn in at the nape: "Dallen's, Oklahoma City."

"Hey, look at this," Predante displayed the vest to his partner.

Nicastro went and took the item, stroked it appreciatively. "Pinto pony," he said, "like those western guys wear in the rodeos. Looks new."

"Compared with the rest of her stuff, this thing sticks out a mile," Predante observed. "What do you think she's doing with it.

Rina had sat up, was watching the two men hawkishly.

"I don't know," Nicastro said. "Maybe it's a present she got a hundred years ago and she just never wore it. She wouldn't get much chance. Not too many rodeos in that bughouse."

Predante giggled.

"Mine," Rina whined suddenly.

The men ignored her.

"And what about that label," Predante remarked. "Oklahoma. Who the hell would she know down there?"

Rina leaped to her feet and rushed at them, reaching for the vest.

Predante blocked her way. "We must be on to something, Paulie."

"Where did you get it, sweetheart?" asked Nicastro, dangling the coveted vest beyond the girl's reach.

She flailed her hands wildly and Predante caught her wrists.

"Mine," she bawled. "Give, give—"

"Hey, hey, girlie," Predante crooned, "be nice. All we're asking is one little thing: tell us who gave that to you."

The girl stopped wrestling against Predante and he re-

179

leased her. But she pouted silently, refusing to speak. The kitten came and rubbed against her ankle and she kicked at it, so that it scampered away under the bed.

"This is very important to us," Nicastro said gently, patient. "You must tell us. Understand?"

"It's mine," she mumbled.

"We know that. But who gave it to you? Who do you know in Oklahoma?"

"Nobody. Don't know Okoma."

Under ordinary circumstances, the men would have departed now from calm persuasion. It was pointless to beg and cajole when pain could produce instant results. But the girl was a special case. Fighting against their practical instincts, they tried again to reason.

"You didn't buy that for yourself, did you?" said Nicastro.

"No. Came in a box. Present."

"Nice. When did the box come?"

"Don't remember."

Predante grabbed her chin firmly, forcing her to look at him. "Sure you remember. Tell—"

"No!" Rina screamed, and slashed her fingernails down one side of his face. As Predante rubbed at his cheek, then inspected the blood in his palm, the girl ran to the door and pulled feverishly at the knob. Predante recaptured her, however, before she got the door open. Holding her in a bear hug, he swung her around so she was facing Nicastro.

"I'll ask once more," Nicastro said once more, stepping up in front of the girl, shoving the vest up to her eyes. "Who gave it to you?"

"I can't, I can't," Rina shrieked. "Can't tell anything."

Nicastro slapped the girl across the face with his empty hand. For a moment she was stung to silence, then she began to whimper, her head hanging down. Nicastro asked the question again. When the girl continued to sob, he pulled her head up by the hair. This time Rina retaliated, bringing a knee up sharply in Nicastro's groin. He lurched back, massaging himself.

"Little bitch," he hissed.

The girl struggled furiously, making odd barking noises with her exertions. Predante had to squeeze tightly to keep

180

hcr from wriggling out of his bear hug. The pressure and the movement of her body on his began to excite him. And then, in a mirror on a dresser across the room, he caught sight of himself and his prisoner. Her twisting and jerking had caused the fabric of her skirt to work up over her thighs. The simpleminded girl had not bothered to dress herself with underwear. Predante's organ hardened, strained in his pants. He pumped his hips unthinkingly, jolting the girl forward. Facing her, Nicastro also responded to the sight of her nakedness. The two men exchanged a glance, daring each other to begin.

"Charlie's going to want her dumped, anyway," Predante said. "And I'll bet she's still got her cherry. Seems awful she should die without ever having it. . . ."

Rina went on writhing, barking.

"We'd better find out about that horsehide first," Nicastro argued. "I've got a feeling it really means something."

"We'll find out," Predante said, still grinding into the girl's buttocks. "Girlie's gonna be so grateful, she'll tell us everything." Keeping one arm braced across her chest, he slid the other down under the skirt.

The girl went abruptly silent, rigid, her legs stiff yet not closing against the hand caressing her vagina.

"That's it, doll," Predante soothed.

Nicastro moved around her at the front, opened the blouse and fondled her breasts. The men continued using the girl together. She yielded to each demand they made on her body until they had satisfied themselves.

At last, she dragged herself nude into a corner and sat on her haunches, hugging herself, rocking back and forth on her heels and lowing softly. Predante and Nicastro stood up from the floor and put on their pants. Then Nicastro walked across to where the black and white horsehide vest had fallen. As he picked it up, Predante said:

"Screw that, Paulie. It's probably nothin' anyway. We better forget it now, leave her alone."

"No. It means something. Charlie'll want to know."

The girl looked up when Nicastro was standing over her. She stopped rocking and stared with wide unblinking monkey-eyes. Nicastro started to crouch toward her. Then the

181

girl screamed, a horrible raucous scream like none the men had ever heard before. It ripped out of her with such force, it seemed her throat must hemorrhage and a fountain of blood would spew forth with the sound.

"For chrissake, Paulie, stop her!" shouted Predante.

Nicastro had reared back, speechless. Now he stooped and slapped the girl. She toppled off her haunches, thrashed on the floor, and continued to scream. Nicastro turned to Predante and called through the unearthly noise.

"It's some kind of fit."

"Com' una strega," Predante responded. "She's puttin' a curse on us." He ran to put a hand on her throat, stifle her wind. "Finished girlie. No more. *Basta!"*

He was not prepared for the strength in the arms which reached around behind his head and forced it down, down into her open mouth, which then pressed hard over the small bit of fleshy cheek and corner of Predante's lower lip that had descended into it. Then, with all the fearsome inhuman strength of the hysteric, she clamped her teeth tightly shut, biting deep into the tissue caught between them. The burst of pain immobilized Predante, made him release his hold on her throat. His next impulse to howl in agony was contained only because his mouth was partially pinned shut, and his straining attempt to open it made her teeth tear deeper into his lip. He tried to pull away, to push her off, but the girl clung on, teeth clenched, gnashing, tearing. Predante lost all awareness of what his hands were doing. They groped wildly at the face sealed against his. He drove a fist into her throat, punched everywhere, but her jaws remained locked.

And then finally he was free. The grip against which he had strained all the muscles of his bull neck and hefty shoulders held him no more. Falling back, Predante put his fingers automatically to the wounded lip. It felt numb, wet, jagged. His eyes focused again on the girl's face.

Now, for the only time in his life, Melo Predante experienced the outer limits of numbing terror. For clamped in Rina Francini's mouth, he saw a flapping sliver of pink like a tiny fish, and he knew it was a piece of himself.

"Cannibal!" he roared. "Fuckin' *cannibal!"*

He chanted the same words over and over as he began to kick and stomp the girl's body.

Nicastro moved to stop the attack. "Melo! No!" He tried unsuccessfully to pull Predante away. "Enough, Melo!"

"No, Paulie, no. Not for what this fuckin' cannibal did." In answering his companion, Predante became aware of the terrible garbled pronunciation caused by the disfigurement of his lip. His frenzy was recharged as he went on savaging the inert body at his feet. Realizing that Predante might turn on him if he tried to interfere further, Nicastro backed off to a window and looked out into the darkness. After some minutes, Predante's barely intelligible cries became more muffled, faded to silence. The attack was over.

Nicastro turned. He had seen a lot of people pounded, but never anyone so brutally as Rina Francini had been. Nicastro felt sick.

Predante was at the dresser mirror, staring at himself. "Look at me, Paulie. I'm a freak . . . a freak. . . ." He started to sob. "Chris', I even talk like a freak."

When Charlie Toccato arrived he was met at the door by Paul Nicastro and told what had happened. Predante was still in the bathroom where he had locked himself after the murder. He could be heard from within now and then, wracked by bursts of self-pitying sobs.

Though Toccato glared with evident fury as his underling began his narrative, by the time Nicastro had finished the dapper don appeared resigned. In fact, he was not. He had come tonight to question Rina Francini for himself, after which he would have ordered her dropped, unharmed, at some place where she would soon be found. The kidnap having failed to buy silence from Vereste, the crime was not to be compounded with murder. In accepting his assignment from Ligazza, Toccato had given his word that Rina Francini would not be hurt.

It was pointless, however, for the don to remind his men of this now. He merely assured Nicastro that there was no harm done and ordered him to dispose of the body carefully with Predante's help. Then, taking the package of oddments which Nicastro had prepared, including the horsehide vest, Toccato left and drove back to St. Louis.

Two days later, before journeying east, he issued the contract. Special instructions were given so that the emasculated bodies of Predante and Nicastro would serve as warning to any who were tempted in the future to violate so terribly any woman of the blood.

Yet, ironically, the object which had led to the trouble proved to be the key in tracing the whereabouts of Bart Vereste.

FIFTEEN

In the quietest hour of a moonless night, Bits let herself out of the lodge through the window of her ground-level room. Skirting the compound, ducking low each time she came near a guard shelter along the fence, she managed to reach the lake without raising an alarm. She waded slowly into the icy water until she felt it soaking into the hem of her short nightdress; then she began to swim. She paddled slowly out toward the middle of the lake, the wet material clinging to her body, restricting her movements, tiring her quickly.

Except for the advanced technology at the safe house, she would have succeeded in drowning herself. But the lake area was covered by an infrared scanning device, to guard against any night penetration of the compound from the water. The night duty man in the electronics cabin had seen the gray figure moving across the black screen. He picked up a walk-ie-talkie and alerted one of the pickets, who was parked at an outward point along the lake shore in a motorized rubber boat.

The commotion woke Lindy. He switched on the lamp beside his bed and looked at the clock. Four-eleven A.M. He got out of bed and, peering into the corridor, saw Konecki in his bathrobe conferring with one of the two staff nurses. When their conversation broke up, Lindy asked Konecki what had happened.

"The Vereste girl was just fished out of the lake," Konecki replied. "Says she had an irresistible urge to take a solitary swim, a girlish caper with no sinister intentions."

"Not impossible. Sleepless night, the call of the wild."

"Bullshit," Konecki proclaimed. "You've seen her. She's

been like a zombie since she heard about the boyfriend's murder. Blames herself. The usual psychological whiplash."

"How is she now?" Lindy asked.

"Okay. *Too* okay, for that matter. Everything under control, not the least bit insulted because we sedated her and put a nurse in the room to watch her. Yup, she's all quiet and wrapped up—like a time bomb." Konecki paused. "Feel like a drink?"

There was more to the offer, Lindy suspected, than camaraderie in the wee hours. "Sure, why not? It won't be easy to get back to sleep."

There was an abundance of liquor on a sideboard in the main room. They each poured themselves a different brand of whiskey and sat down on opposite sides of the fireplace. A fire of fresh logs was blazing, evidently left over from the first efforts to warm Bits Vereste after she had been brought in from the lake.

"Of course," Konecki said, after a sip of his drink, "if we take our eyes off her for a second, she'll try again. The idea's still there; you can see it in her eyes."

"And if she succeeded," Lindy commented, "you know it would take a little more of the shine off your badge."

Konecki eyed Lindy tolerantly. "I'm not worried about her succeeding, pal. We can keep her alive if we have to, watch her around the clock, put her in a straitjacket if it comes to that. And it might. The nurses' opinion is that Bits Vereste is on the brink of a total breakdown. We'll get a doctor in here tomorrow for a more expert reading, but I don't have any trouble accepting the diagnosis right now. Obviously, it isn't entirely the fault of the Behrens killing. That just lit the fuse on a lifetime of accumulating internal conflict." Konecki tossed down a swallow of whiskey, more than it was possible to enjoy. "It's amazing she's held together this long, I'd say; a goddamn miracle that any halfway decent kid who grows up in a Mafia family doesn't become a raving schizo. Christ, how *do* they square it with themselves?"

"How do any of us," Lindy said, "living in this world?"

Konecki shrugged. "Anyway," he sighed, "this kid's about to go under unless we get her out of here, away from the pressure, back to real life. Her mother knows it, too. She was onto me about it tonight, five minutes after they brought Bits

186

in here. She's ready to take their papers and get out, she and the girl."

Lindy perceived now that Konecki was ready to let them go. What still eluded him was why the marshal needed to ask his blessing. "Real life," he said, "could be a tougher place for the Verestes to survive than in here."

"With legitimate documents in new names," Konecki rebutted confidently, "it's a one-in-a-million shot they'd ever get stung, providing that they're careful where they settle, and stay away from the big cities where the hives are. We have the proof, Lindy. We've resettled a few people now and not one has been found." He hesitated. "The one precaution we've always taken is to give escort, someone who helps the pigeons find a safe nest, and gives us a full report so we can always keep surveillance, at our discretion."

So that was it. "And this time," Lindy said, "you want me to perform that service."

"No, I don't *want* you. I'd much rather it was one of my regular men. But Mrs. Vereste has turned down the escort. She'd prefer, whatever the risks, to manage her own disappearing act so we'll never know her final destination."

"She must be afraid of leaks from our side. Did you tell her about the bug?"

Lindy's earlier conjecture to account for the Wonderworld shooting had proven correct. An inspection of the phones in his apartment had uncovered an electronic bugging device—planted, it was assumed, by someone in the pay of Rocco Gesolo.

"Naturally, I told her," Konecki replied, "but it didn't help. She's adamant about doing this her own way. But I think she'd reconsider if you offered to be the shepherd. You've established good rapport; she trusts you. I think she's influenced, too, by the faith her gentle spouse has in you."

Lindy dawdled thoughtfully with his drink. "Maybe she should have the right to get lost on her own, especially if the odds are as much in her favor as you think. With her address sitting in your files, she'd never feel free. She's been watched by one kind of vulture all her life. What'd the difference be if she put herself under another set of eyes? She'd rather go it alone than know she hasn't gone anywhere."

"I understand," Konecki said, "and I sympathize. But,

well . . . listen, Lindy, you've been down enough on this operation lately so that I thought it was better to hold out on a couple of recent developments. But you'd better know now." Konecki fortified himself with another swig from his drink. "Yesterday two St. Louis hoods were found dead outside of St. Louis. They'd been tortured before they died—castration was one of the particulars—and a rumor was around, rather carefully spread in certain hangouts, that it was punishment for killing Rina Francini. That much of Mrs. Vereste's guess was correct, it seems; someone high up had put a bond on the girl and made good on it. But when it came to the crunch, that didn't keep Rina Francini alive. Chalk up another black mark on our record; put it next to my name if you want. But the point is it's tough out there. Whatever my carefully worked out equations are, I can't send the Vereste women away without taking some precautions." He spread his hands, at a loss. "I wouldn't send them out at all, except it's tough in here, too."

Konecki drained his glass and went to pour himself a refill.

He was genuinely anguished by the choices, Lindy thought.

"You think she'll be safe traveling with me?" Lindy asked. "My face isn't exactly unfamiliar to her enemies, and I'm not in the mood to have it renovated."

"I don't imagine you'd object to our makeup experts providing some temporary disguise: eyeglasses, gray in the hair, that sort of thing."

"Is that enough?"

"To cover the loose ends, it is," Konecki replied. "You only have to be on public view for a day or two. What's more important than disguises, in any case, is making a sensible travel plan. The Mob may have a lot of eyes, Lindy, but not nearly enough to watch every crossroads. You can travel safely incognito as long as you stay away from big cities, route yourself through secondary airports. We will, of course, happily provide our own transport to the farthest point that Mrs. V allows."

"All right," Lindy agreed at last. "I'll talk to her."

Konecki hoisted his glass, as if in a toast. "Thanks."

There was nothing left then, none of the banter that had

come easily at the beginning of their association. Lindy left Konecki drinking alone, staring at the area maps on the wall.

Pausing outside Ginnie Vereste's bedroom, he heard muffled conversation from within, her voice and a man's. Mr. and Mrs. Vereste were talking like any concerned parents about how to deal with the problems of their daughter. Lindy returned to his own room. He got into bed and turned out the light. But sleep would not come. It crossed his mind after a while to take a swim, but he knew it was out of the question. It couldn't be done without setting off some goddamn alarm.

The incongruous holiday atmosphere of the safe house had finally been dispelled. Breakfast was a grim interlude, not the chatty gathering of staff it had been on previous mornings. Men straggled in, gulped their coffee, and went to their posts. Guarding the Vereste family had become the stern, joyless business Lindy had imagined it would be from the start.

Ginnie Vereste came to the table while Lindy was drinking his coffee and took a seat beside him. The two marshals who were also at the table inquired solicitously about Bits, and Ginnie told them she was still asleep. After a minute's awkward silence, the marshals excused themselves.

Alone together Ginnie gave Lindy a tense, vulnerable smile.

"Konecki told me you want to leave," he said.

"Yes. Very much."

"He can't let you go on your terms, though."

Ginnie said nothing. She stared into her own cup.

"I can understand the need you feel to get out," Lindy went on, "but you have to make concessions."

She glanced up. "Last night," she said, "after . . . after what happened, Bart came to my room. We talked about it. And then . . . then we made love. He wanted me and I gave in."

Lindy could say nothing. He didn't understand why she had wanted to tell him.

"I don't know what brought it on," she continued, averting her eyes. "Shared sorrows. One more for old time's sake.

189

Animal need after being in this cage. Or perhaps I was a stand-in—because the body he really wants is denied to him now." She was plainly thinking of Marianna Gesolo. "Or maybe he told me the real reason. He said the change"—absently she ran her fingers down the side of her face—"had attracted him to me again. He said that when this was over, he . . ." She swallowed the rest, not wanting to hear the promise emerge senseless and unbelievable in the light of day. "I still love him, you see. Whatever he's done, I could never turn against him, because I'm responsible. What we once felt for each other is responsible for making him what he's become. But I don't want to go back. Not to him, not to the life we had. I want something better."

Lindy received the message now. Leaving wouldn't be only for her daughter's sake, Ginnie was saying; she had defined a new future for herself, had found the will to pursue it, but the seeds of hope could still be blown away by a breath of passion.

Ginnie glanced over her shoulder, making certain they were still alone. Then she continued:

"We have a place to go—to come to rest, to heal. A home, waiting for us, like a promised land. Except it's forbidden to me if my going would threaten the people who already live there."

"You make it sound as if there's a spell on it or something."

"In a way, there is." Ginnie's face darkened. She put down her cup and clenched her hands together, knotting and twisting the fingers so that she winced with the self-inflicted pain. "I've never told this to anyone," she went on at last, "not even Bart. Four years ago, during those few days when he was in Washington to testify, I received a telephone call at home. It was from my sister, my twin sister, Julie. She'd been watching the hearings on television. Seeing Bart had triggered it. If nothing else, knowing he wasn't at home made her less afraid to call. The phone number was unlisted, and she'd pulled some strings to get it. The man she's been married to for twelve years apparently has a fair amount of money and influence. That was one of the things she told me about when we talked. Also that she's got two kids, lives in a beautiful house, and that she wished we could see each other again. She said she had a pretty good idea of the kind of hell

190

I was living in, and was willing to try and share her happiness with me, if ever there was a way." Ginnie shrugged, not because she was resigned now, but had been then: a twitch of memory. "In that one conversation, we worked out our plan for keeping in touch without anyone knowing, which we've done ever since. When I was faced with the chance to make a break, of course I told her about it. The things she had to say in return made it a lot easier. More than advice. She offered to help me set up again—to provide not only friendship, but a place to live, even the money to get into some kind of business of my own." Ginnie grasped Lindy's hand. "You see what a rare chance it is. To be able to go to someone who's already lived through the break, could guide us through it. It goes without saying, though, that I couldn't take it if it meant exposing Julie, telling anyone where she is or who she is now. She's never even told her husband the whole truth."

Lindy nodded slowly. "You've got damn good reasons for traveling solo," he admitted, "but they wouldn't cut any ice with Konecki."

"I know that. I wouldn't tell him this even if I thought it *would* make a difference. But he'll let us leave here with you."

"You'd trust me with Julie's secret?"

"No," Ginnie said quietly. "As soon as you had us on neutral territory I'd want you to cut us loose."

Lindy couldn't think with her begging eyes on him. He left the table and went to a window. Outside the sun was shining, sparkling on the lake. A paradise of blue sky and green mountains. But today it looked shoddy and uninviting, like a poster that had hung too long on the wall of a two-bit travel agency. It was a prison for Ginnie Vereste; the whole world would be a prison unless he gave her the chance. Didn't he owe it to her?

And what did he owe himself? Suppose he collaborated with her, and then she was found by her husband's enemies, used and killed as others had been. He was already on trial for too many murders in his own mind: for the victims of a hit man who had wanted Bart Vereste, for Danny Behrens and Rina Francini. Not only Ginnie and Bits but Julie Whoever-She-Had-Become and her husband and two children might be added to the list.

Lindy turned back to Ginnie Vereste. "I'll do it on one

191

condition. You trust me down the line. I'll have to take you to the last stop. If I'm satisfied you'll be safe there, I'll leave and never say where I was."

"I can't agree to that," Ginnie said unhappily. "It means exposing Julie."

"She wants you to have this chance," Lindy coaxed.

Ginnie shook her head.

"Call and ask her," Lindy urged.

"From here? They'd have to know where I was calling."

They were rapid footsteps on the varnished pine floor. They turned to see the nurse who had been attending Bits.

"Mrs. Vereste," the nurse said, "your daughter's awake. It would be a good idea if you talked to her. Especially about last night. She needs to let that out."

"I'll be there in a minute," Ginnie said.

The nurse left the room.

Ginnie took several very deep breaths, as though preparing for a long swim underwater. Then she stood and nervously smoothed down her dress.

"It will help Bits to know that we're leaving," she said to Lindy before walking out.

On his second day after arriving in New York, Charlie Toccato was invited to be a guest aboard Dom Francini's boat. He brought with him his bodyguard, Ignazio "Snowman" Gambereste. The fishing party was further complemented with three of Dom's men, Stirelli, Leporello, and Giorgo Teddina, who would handle the helm.

With the boat heading out to sea and their respective bodyguards amusing themselves fishing from the stern, Dom and Charlie settled themselves in the salon. Dom opened the package that Charlie had brought with him and spread the contents on a table.

"What a fuckin' load of junk," Dom pronounced the collection. "You got some nerve bringing this, Charlie."

"I didn't pick it out, I told you."

"Postcards! Look at 'em. The earliest one was canceled two months ago."

"You wanted to see her mail. That's all there was."

"And this ashtray. Shit. 'Atlantic City.' You really think the feds put a *casa privata* under the boardwalk?"

"That's all there was," Toccato repeated angrily.

"If the girl had to be iced at least you could've made it count for something."

Charlie screwed his dark eyes to Dom's puffy face. "Is that why you're breaking my balls, Dom? You know that wasn't my fault. I did what I could to square it."

Dom ignored Charlie and held up another article from the package of Rina's effects, the pony-hide vest. "And this? What's this doing in here?"

"Look at the label."

"Oklahoma City," Dom read aloud. "So?"

"You never know. Check the store, go through sales records, see who comes up as the buyer. It looks new enough."

Dom brooded. He knew what he had hoped to find when he asked to have Rina's belongings sifted, but he hardly dared to believe this was it. "Checking those records is a pig of a job," Dom grumbled. "Do you jerk the police in Okay City?"

Toccato shook his head. "Oklahoma goes through the Hot Springs office."

The investigation gimmick would shave days off a records check. Sales slips wouldn't have to be stolen from the store, or gone through during closing hours by a couple of men sent inside. They could simply be impounded by the police on some pretext. But Dom was leery of using the police a second time. The Waitely investigation had almost backfired disastrously. The cop had delivered the goods, all right. But he had been stricken with guilt afterward. The day he had heard about Danny Behrens' murder, Waitely had taken his police revolver and killed his wife in her bed, then turned the gun on himself. His suicide note had confessed to Mafia association, and specifically named Dom, Jack Trandi, Vereste, and six other men on the state police force whom Waitely had known to be on the pad. Fortunately, however, his fevered final thoughts had blocked from his mind the elementary fact that police were apt to be first on the scene of a combined homicide and suicide. The letter Waitely had left propped up prominently on a bedside table had conveniently disappeared.

Dom put the vest aside. "I'll follow up on this one, Charlie. Let's hope it turns into something."

"Let's hope," Charlie seconded. "For all of us."

Dom chortled, curiously provoked by the remark. "Yeah, all of us, Charlie."

"What's so funny?"

"Nothin', private joke." Dom raised himself out of his chair. "How about a little sport?"

Toccato demurred with a tug on the lapel of his gray silk suit. "I expected this to be strictly business, Dom. Didn't dress for fishing."

"Didn't stop Snowman," Dom laid a heavy hand on Toccato's shoulder. "Come on."

"I'll watch," Charlie compromised.

On the stern, Leporello and Stirelli were seated beside each other in the two fighting chairs, each steadying a rod in the holster, long black diagonals of high-test line trailing far out behind the boat.

"Where's Snowman?" Charlie said.

Leporello glanced around and shrugged.

"He went in for a drink," Stirelli said.

"One of you guys give Charlie a chair," Dom commanded.

"No, Dom, I told you—"

"You've gotta try, Charlie. I have a feeling you're gonna be lucky."

Stirelli was already out of his chair, standing beside it like a barber waiting for his customer. Dom prodded Charlie Toccato by the elbow.

"Please, Don Carlo. It's a superstitious thing with me. My guests must fish with me."

Leporello gave his chair to Dom as Charlie reluctantly took the place vacated by Stirelli.

"First thing," Dom instructed, "you've got to make sure your line is still baited." He started to reel in, watching Charlie until he imitated the action.

"Christ, this is a hard pull," Charlie said.

"There's a lot of drag from the water," Dom explained.

They wound in for a moment without speaking.

Then Dom said, as if it were small talk, "You should've heard Ligazza when he got the news on Rina. I've never known the old man to go so *pazzo.*"

"You told him how it happened, didn't you?" asked Char-

194

lie, his words broken by shortness of breath as he struggled to turn the reel handle.

"Sure, sure. And I told him you squared it. But he went on raving. He's flipped over this whole honor bit, Charlie. Well, he always was, but it's ten times worse since Vereste started blowing the whistle. It's been no picnic for me, I can tell you. I owe for it, he was my man. I'm on a short string with Ligazza, Charlie. And he's always going into this number about Bart, about how there's no respect anymore for the word, the blood, each other. If we still had it, he says, we could even survive this big squeal. Thirty, forty years ago there were informers, too, he remembers. But they never scratched us. Now Bart goes in, and everything starts to fall apart. You know we got word that Gardia's trying to make an immunity deal? When he saw what the Feebies had on him, he cracked. Now he's threatening to spill on a dozen other guys—not the *capi,* there's something sacred, at least—but he may talk enough to get a few years shaved. That couldn't have happened twenty years ago. Not even five."

"Okay," Charlie said, "so Frankie's a fink, too. Don Vee ought to save his screaming for that. What's this big beef about Rina?"

"I don't quite get it myself," Dom confessed. "Sure, she was my own blood. But she was only a dummy, let's face it. Ligazza doesn't see it that way, though. He says it's all connected, one kind of disrespect leads to another, we'll come through only if we enforce the Word to the letter. That's why he says you're not through making good, Charlie, because you didn't keep your guarantee on Rina."

"It sounds to me like the old man's getting soft upstairs," Charlie said, bewildered. "But all right, if I owe him I'll square. What does he want now?"

"Hey, Charlie," the Leper interrupted, pointing off the stern. "Looks like there's something on your line."

Toccato had not been paying attention. When he turned, he saw a dark shape near the surface, white water breaking around it like rapids over a stone.

"Help him, Lep," Dom said.

"No, I got it," Charlie said, straining. "It's no fish, though Looks like seaweed or something." He reeled in another six turns on the handle before the thing was close enough to identify. The rushing water alternately tossed the head up and submerged it, but Charlie had been able to glimpse the ganged hooks, one barbed tip coming through Snowman's throat, the other through the shoulder. Charlie's hands froze on the rod. He fought to repress a stammer as he warned Dom:

"You don't dare. Touch me and you'd get yours tomorrow. All of you." His voice grew shriller, he felt his limbs tingling with the electricity of terror. "I got two hundred guys behind me, they'll come after—"

"It's squared, Charlie, from the top." Dom motioned languidly to Leporello who grabbed Toccato from behind.

"Jesus, Dom," Charlie started to whimper. "Don't. Name anything. I've got a couple of million. Anything."

Stirelli brought the hooks and handed them to Dom.

"Please," Toccato sniveled, "for God's sake. The gun, Dom. If you have to, then . . . " He gagged on his own fear. "Only please . . . Oh, God. . . ."

Neither Toccato's pitiful begging nor his last earsplitting shrieks deterred his executioners from carrying out the sentence. This was their justice. An absolute, never needlessly delayed or diluted with mercy.

That night Dom reported to Valerio Ligazza, who in turn consulted the Hot Springs office. The next morning Hot Springs called Dom directly with their directions on how to proceed. Within hours a member of Dom's family was on a plane for Oklahoma City. On arriving, he contacted a sergeant of detectives named Gallinson and, in a later meeting with him, turned over the vest which had belonged to Rina Francini.

By representing the article as a clue in a murder case, Detective Sergeant Gallinson gained the immediate cooperation of the management of Dallen's department store. A buyer in sportswear was particularly helpful in narrowing the probable date of purchase for the pinto vest. She pointed out that since the article was made of real pony fur, it could not have been sold within the last two years. Since that time, conservation lobbies had hardened consumer resistance to genuine hides, and the store had handled only synthetic pony. Judg-

196

ing by the condition of the vest, the buyer guessed that it had been among the last of its kind to be sold in the store.

Records for the sportswear department covering the period between two and four years in the past were stored at Dallen's warehouse. This was opened to the police and permission given for a thorough search of files. By concealing the true purpose of their assignment, the detective sergeant was able to divert twelve regulars from the police force to assist in sifting the sales slips. In a single afternoon, they unearthed forty-two copies of receipts pertaining to sales of genuine pony-hide vests. Forty-one out of the forty-two sales had either been charged, or paid by check or credit card. Only one customer had used cash and had refused to give a name. Seven of the purchasers had arranged prepaid mailing of their purchases to addresses outside Oklahoma, and the addresses were recorded in a space specially provided for this purpose on the receipt. In one case, the mailing address given was: R. Francini, Winterman Institute, 18–24 Coombes Way, St. Louis, Missouri. The purchaser was an account holder, Mrs. Byron Pleyer of Niles, Oklahoma. She had evidently sent the package as an anonymous gift, a note on the receipt specified "no card."

The Pleyer name struck a vaguely familiar chord with Detective Gallinson, so he had the morgues of the daily papers culled for references. The combined yield of marriage and birth announcements, articles on land-zoning fights, reports on the efforts of ranching lobbies to improve federal subsidies, and of various chamber of commerce and political dinners, produced a picture of Byron Pleyer and his family. He owned twenty-four hundred acres of land around Niles, half inherited and half acquired in the past twenty years. Operating under the title of Sundown Ranch, Incorporated, Pleyer conducted a notably successful agricultural and cattle-breeding enterprise. He was a substantial contributor to political, conservation, and cultural causes, but preferred to keep a low profile. He had been married for sixteen years and had two children. On the occasion of the Ranchers' Association dinner given two years ago to honor Pleyer, a picture of him had been taken along with his wife and children. Gallinson had the picture photocopied.

Additional research at the marriage and motor vehicle

registries revealed that Mrs. Pleyer's first name was Jill, that she was thirty-nine years old, and that the couple had been married by a county judge, with Pleyer's older brother and the judge's wife as the only witnesses; also that Mrs. Pleyer had claimed on her marriage certificate to be an orphan, raised by an aunt in South Dakota who was deceased at the time of the marriage.

On the evening after receiving the vest, Detective Sergeant Gallinson drove across the Oklahoma state line into Arkansas and met with his Hot Springs contact. After turning over the dossier he had compiled on Jill Pleyer, Gallinson was handed a gratuity of two thousand dollars.

On the same evening, to oblige Don Valerio Ligazza, who had transmitted Don Francini's request, three veteran enforcers were sent out of Hot Springs to take up surveillance of the Sundown Ranch in Niles, Oklahoma.

SIXTEEN

The Breezy Isle Hotel occupied its own island in Chesapeake Bay a short distance off the Maryland shore. The island was linked to the mainland by a causeway which had been built at state expense well before hotel construction had even started and had opened with ribbon-cutting ceremonies presided over by a governor who had gone on to become a vice-president. A subsequent ruling in a zoning dispute had designated the causeway to be part of the hotel property. Thus, on this weekend, it was possible to insure the absolute privacy of the hotel's guests by having uniformed armed guards at the causeway gates checking off each new arrival against a master list, even though unwanted transients were not likely to show up. Officially the hotel was still under construction, not scheduled to open until next spring. By spring, it had been hoped, state laws would have been conveniently altered to permit casino gambling on the premises. But because of Bart Vereste, the change of the law and the opening of the hotel were two of the lesser uncertainties among those that confronted the men whose names were on the master guest list—a total of one hundred and six top Mafiosi, bosses from around the nation and their seconds.

It was the largest congregation of crime princes that had ever been held. Bigger than Apalachin, bigger than Tahoe, bigger than Grand Bahama. As before, there were acknowledged dangers in concentrating so much of the Organization in one place at one time, and so the meeting had been repeatedly postponed. But finally the risks of delaying the convention outweighed any other consideration. The mass of men empowered to formulate an immediate policy for dealing with the crisis came together. Of course, the precautionary

199

measures taken by those traveling to the convention also exceeded any that had been taken before. It had never been forgotten that Apalachin had been needlessly blown when one New York State cop had his suspicions aroused by an overabundance of limousines with out-of-state registrations suddenly showing up one day on the road of a remote rural area. Since that fiasco, transport to the conventions was carefully disguised. On this occasion, the Maryland overlord, Mike Saldi, had instructed scores of his soldiers to drive inconspicuous cars to a number of different rendezvous points around the state, or just over the boundary in Delaware and Virginia. There they had picked up the men arriving by car, train, plane, bus, and boat, and driven them back to Breezy Isle. Because the hotel had not yet opened, it had not attracted federal surveillance and was thought to be the safest place in the country for the men to convene.

Their mood as they gathered was in sharp contrast to the buoyant optimism that had prevailed during past meetings. Then the discussion had been about expansion, diversification of interests, and the means by which a president could be reached and manipulated. Even the arbitration of bloody jurisdictional disputes, for all their negative aspects, had not clouded a basically rosy atmosphere, since the disputes by their very existence evidenced the lush pickings to be had for those who would seize them. This time, however, a deep pessimism colored the words and thoughts of the underworld figures who clustered in the bars, or met for informal caucuses in their suites. In the minds of many was the idea of retiring permanently from Mob life. The bravest and most positive thinkers favored at least a tactical retreat, a total suspension of illegal activity until the government had finished its prosecution of all cases arising from the Vereste squeal. Later the damage could be inventoried in a calmer atmosphere. Then, with a reasoned appraisal of surviving assets and manpower, the Organization could be reconstructed on a new power base. Several bosses had already begun acting unilaterally on this premise. Millions of dollars in sharking funds had been taken off the street, drug connections had been choked off and shipments ended, illegal gambling operations had been restricted or closed down. And a harsh policy of assassination had been instituted to eliminate any men who were known to be vulnerable to prosecution and were likely to volunteer information once in custody.

These practices not only had failed to alleviate the crisis, but had also contributed to the momentum of deterioration. Defections increased as the rank and file fled to hiding from the real or imagined vengeance of their *capi*. Those who nervously stood their ground were striking precipitately against their brothers. Chains of command were breaking down; families were killing each other off from within. Meanwhile, in areas where the Mob had loosened its hold over vice and drugs, their rivals had quickly taken up the slack. With the authorities concentrating their attack on the Mafia, the blacks and Latins had expanded overnight without meeting any resistance.

Daily the destructive cycle accelerated, became more vicious and irreversible. If the government drive did not succeed in destroying the Organization, its own presently ill-conceived defensive strategies might do the job.

A pitifully short roster of bleak possibilities confronted the Breezy Isle convention. Either there must be a resolution to retrench peacefully in order to conserve resources and contacts for a future resurgence, or something must be done to find Bart Vereste, and very soon. Even if it was too late to cancel the prosecutions the government had begun to schedule, convictions might be less likely if the principal witness had been silenced. Finding Vereste, furthermore, would restore morale, revive the vital confidence that the Honored Society could ultimately defeat any challenge and remain above the law.

Minutes after Dom Francini arrived, while he was still exchanging sober greetings in the lobby, he was sought out by Rocco Gesolo.

"The old man's waiting," Gesolo said.

Francini didn't have to be told the crux of the impatient demands that would be made by Valerio Ligazza. Five and six times each day since the watch had been placed on the Sundown Ranch, Ligazza had called asking for reports. Ligazza could have called Hot Springs direct—for it was from the Office there that Dom got his information—but he preferred to remain aloof from the secretarial work. He only wanted to hear positive results, predigested, easy to swallow. He also wanted Dom to remember that finding Vereste was his responsibility.

Ligazza was occupying the grandest suite at the hotel. As the crisis deepened, his aura had shone even brighter. He was the Great Survivor, not only the symbol of past prosperity but the essence of hope; if the old man was willing to fight on, at an age when the spirit could so easily fail, then survival could not be far out of reach. In the corridor outside Ligazza's rooms, other bosses, ruthless wielders of vast power in their own right, waited quietly, almost meekly, for an audience with Don Valerio. They nodded to Dom as he was escorted inside by Gesolo.

"Well?" Ligazza accosted Dom as soon as the big man set foot over the threshold. "Anything?"

Ligazza was seated in a high-backed chair before the expanse of glass that overlooked Chesapeake Bay.

"I've told you every time," Dom replied, exercising control. "I will let you know the moment—"

"You saw them out there," Ligazza cut in icily, nodding toward the door. "You know why they wait. Not for advice. Not to hear plans for the future. They've given up any cure for the plague but a miracle. They wait like peasants outside the church for someone to say 'Your prayers have been answered, return to your homes and all will be as it was.'" Ligazza paused to fiddle in his lap and Dom noticed that there was a blanket spread over his legs. Dom felt oddly embarrassed, for as long as Ligazza had been known to his worshipful confreres as "the Old Man," he had never actually worn the trappings of infirmity.

"But there is no miracle," Ligazza went on gravely. "The weight of their hope crushes me, Don Domenico. I have nothing to tell them. Nothing! Except that in the middle of nowhere, three men are sitting in turns by a dusty roadside."

"That's all there is," Dom said. "They might as well know it."

"And on that they should rest their hopes!" Ligazza said scornfully. "Rocco, share with Don Domenico some news of the day."

202

Gesolo moved to stand by his *capo*. "Nineteen of the men invited here will not be attending, including three from the Commission. Januzzi flew to Costa Rica two days ago, Di-Gangia disappeared to an unknown destination, and Serrembe was hit. Splits and hits account for all of them, except Bustoratto; he had a coronary, keeled over and died in his sauna."

"And even that, perhaps, was a form of suicide," Ligazza commented. "In recent weeks, Busto had developed the habit of sitting in his sauna for hours on end, subjecting himself to the intense heat for as much as half a day."

"Asshole," Dom smirked. "As if he didn't have enough heat on him already."

"Yes," Ligazza said coldly, "you're quite right, Francini. His behavior was most illogical. But so are we all who sit and wait for your miracle, *matti*, madmen."

"Listen, I'll get us to Vereste," Dom said hotly. "I haven't been following a wrong hunch. You've seen the picture; that dame living on the ranch is my niece Julie. I had a buzz she couldn't cut herself off completely, and I was right."

"Too bad it's Bart Vereste we must find, not your long-lost relatives."

"One will lead to the other. Work it out: Rina went into the institution fifteen years after Julie skipped. So how did Julie know where Rina was to send her presents? She must have made a touch sometime in the past five years with Ginnie. And that means when Ginnie moves out of her hole, sooner or later she and Julie will touch again. My money's on Ginnie turning up at that ranch. Julie stayed lost for twenty years; where she buried herself is going to look like the safest place in the world for Ginnie to settle."

"When the feds turn her loose," Rocco put in sharply. "That could be months from now, a year—after the trials are over."

"Not if I know Ginnie. But, of course, if you wanted faster action we don't have to wait 'til she's untied. We can take Julie today, her whole goddamn family, hold 'em hostage and force the feds to trade Bart and drop charges in return."

"No!" Ligazza said vociferously, eyes blazing. "The kidnapping and murders have accomplished nothing for us except to make the public more unforgiving. They've tolerated

203

us in the past, even at times showed a certain sympathy, as long as our battles remained private. Now, because we have begun acting like terrorist hooligans, they are flooding their representatives with telegrams, expressing their support for the hard line of Senator Thomas Ryle. And that makes our friends in Washington afraid to put their heads up. If we move at all now, it must be with extreme care, within prescribed limits."

Dom paced the room. "Christ almighty, what do you want? You ask for results, but you won't go after them. All this bullshit about limits, staying within the code."

"Without it we die—are already dying."

"And with it?" Dom whooped derisively. "You're getting senile, old man."

"Careful, Dom," Rocco said protectively.

"What do you call it, then?" Dom demanded. "He's living in the past, isn't he? Traditions, rules, laws—maybe they worked once. But see all the good they do us now. Tell him, Roc. You see it. The rules don't exist anymore, not for anyone. If the cops had ever paid for information before the way they're paying now, how long could we have kept our secrets? But they wouldn't do it. They couldn't weaken us until their own limits broke down. And Christ, see how well they do without them. And still"—Dom glared at Ligazza—"you jabber on about keeping ours!"

The old man was very still, his lips compressed with fury. Then as if to deny his age, emerge reborn from a shriveled cocoon, he pushed the blanket off his lap and stood erect. Moving to the window, he watched the gulls wheeling past outside.

"There's no point in argument," he said at last. "It cannot change the facts. We have lost."

Dom turned to Rocco, comparing their reactions to see if he had heard correctly. Gesolo stood expressionless.

"Lost?" Dom murmured.

"We've taken a sounding," Gesolo said. "The majority feeling favors closing down operations completely until we've got a positive fix on Vereste, or until the storm blows over."

"You can't do that," Dom entreated Ligazza. He was arguing for his own life as much as for the survival of the Organization.

The old man reared back slightly, affronted; he could do whatever had to be done.

"Roc, you understand," Dom said, his hands reaching out. "Let things get rusty and we'll have no way to fight back even when we do find Bart. Look at the walls they've built around finks before; and he's worth fifty times any of the others. So it's going to take a lot of men and money to knock him out. We'll have to fight like an army, equip ourselves with the kind of stuff those Arabs use. We can't do that unless we keep the men tight, keep the money coming in for a war chest. Treasury's been grabbing cash right and left. We'll be broke pretty soon without tomorrow's profits."

"Good points, Dom," Rocco conceded. "You can make them again when the full convention assembles tonight. But we've already covered the same arguments in our meetings with the men. They can't keep taking knocks because you've got a hunch to play; you never did well enough at the track. It's time to write off Bart Vereste as a bad debt, cut and run and try to come back later when it's all quiet. Don Valerio will endorse that policy tonight at the assembly."

For a moment Dom could not breathe. He had heard his death sentence. If Ligazza called for retreat they would all follow. And Dom would be the scapegoat. He had been given a chance to make good on the betrayal of his lieutenant, but he had failed. He would be the final sacrifice offered by the brotherhood to purge their demons.

It was for this, Dom realized finally, that Bart had spared him, had continued withholding from his squeal the information that would have locked Dom away in the comfortable care of a prison.

"So, it's finally happened," he seethed, finding his wind again. "They've dried up and dropped off. The old man who told me he would never run has become an old woman, without balls, without heart! He could fight, but he prefers to say it is finished."

Dom moved toward Ligazza, who remained at the window, calmly looking out at the gulls.

Gesolo stepped into his path. "You're not helping yourself, Dom."

"We'll see. I'm not so ready to lie down anymore, not because this old woman says I should." Dom backed toward the

205

door. "And I'll find others. Not everyone could have turned soft and gutless. You'll see tonight. I'm walking in with an army behind me."

Dom flung open the door. The ten or twelve men who had been outside waiting to see Ligazza were still there. They stared at Dom, unmoving. They had overheard the challenge he had issued, but none stepped forward in support.

As he turned into the corridor, Dom heard Ligazza's taunting farewell: "*Buon' fortuna,* Don Domenico. See if you can raise an army without pointing it at an enemy."

Dom took the elevator to the lobby. As it started the descent he was still churning with furious resolve. But within seconds, he had accepted the futility of defying Ligazza. The old man was right. There was no realistic alternative he could offer, merely the slim hope of a miracle. As he stepped out into the lobby, the first thought in Dom Francini's mind was to keep walking, get out, disappear. Now or never. Give Don Vee or Rocco a chance to think and they would close off his escape routes.

Dom crossed the lobby to the exit which led to the garage. He had almost reached it when a voice close behind boomed his name and a strong hand slipped under his arm.

"Francini! Been looking for you."

Was it possible? Would they make an example of him right here, with a dozen of the brotherhood looking on?

Dom turned slowly.

Mike Saldi was behind him. Saldi had boxed heavyweight in his youth and had the marks to prove it, a scarred and misshapen face made that way by his earliest opponents, honest boxers who had refused to take fixes—"dead honest," as Saldi described them when he told anecdotes from his sporting days. He had a winning smile, though, and now it adorned his face like a rose on a garbage heap.

"Hey, hey. What're you giving me such a mean look for, Dom? I'm bringing you good news. At least, that's what the guy on the phone said."

"What guy?"

"Didn't give a name. Says he's been dealing only with you and that's how it stays." Saldi pointed to a rank of paneled phone booths near the reception desk. "Take it through there. He's still on the line—long-dee from Hot Springs."

Heading for the phones, Dom started to laugh quietly. Don Valerio would not have his way tonight, after all. Let him come to the assembly and dig his own grave, moan like a widow and tell them all to save their pennies. Dom would have his army. He felt a miracle coming on.

Marty Grecco had driven back to the motel to phone in to the Office. Their instructions had been to sit tight. For half an hour Marty played cards with the two other men who had shared watch. Then the phone rang and he answered. Although he was the youngest and slightest of the three, he held seniority by virtue of his greater reputation as an enforcer, more kills to his credit.

"The Office told me the news," said the voice on the phone. "This is Dom Francini."

Marty knew the eastern don by reputation. He replied obediently to the big man's demand for a detailed summary of what he had seen an hour ago.

"We're perched on a hill just off the main road, right across from the entrance drive to the ranch. That still puts us a fair distance off from the house, though, because the driveway's a long mother—the whole ranch takes up half the fuckin' country—but my orders were not to get in so close, it might tip we're around. With a good scope, though, and being up on this hill, we've got a pretty nice look-in. A few minutes after one o'clock I see this car drive up to the house and two broads and a guy get out. I couldn't swear it at the distance, but I'd lay an easy ten-to-one the broads were the same ones as in the pictures the Office gave me."

"I don't want to hear odds," Francini said quickly. "This has got to be a dead cert."

"I'm telling you good as I can. I think the broads are Vereste's old lady and the mouse. But there's no way to clinch it, not unless we go inside. They're kinda disguised, you know. Like their hair is different; big mama's gone light brown and the kid is a blonde."

"Listen to me, gunboat. If you go in and you're wrong, you've given away our last chance for nothing."

"You're the man," Marty replied. "Tell me to hang back and that's what I do."

There was a silence.

"I need it now," Dom grumbled, more to himself. "What about the guy? You sure there was only one? That's not much of an arm."

"*Uno solo*, no mistake. But you know. . . ." Marty added tentatively.

"What?"

"I'd swear I'd seen him somewhere before. Like maybe on television."

"Everybody's on television, gunny. Think! Where'd you see this one?"

Marty rummaged through a mind bricked up with square images; when he wasn't working he spent all his time watching the tube. "Got it," he said, surprising himself. "It's the smart-ass who was asking the questions in Washington, back when they—"

"Beautiful," Dom broke in. "I'll buy. You got enough push to go into the house right now?"

"I don't know. There's a lot of muscle around the place during the day, y'know, ranch hands for the animals. We'd be better off calling in a couple more guys."

"How long would it take to get 'em there?"

"Depends on who's around. I'd have to check with the office. Maybe by tonight, tomorrow the latest."

"You'll have to go in without 'em, then."

"Okay," Marty said thoughtfully, "I guess we'll be cool with three. The cowboys don't hang around too near the house."

"You know what we want," Dom said. But even with Marty's affirmation, Dom took no chances. He rattled off his instructions once more.

"And no mistakes, gunny," he said before hanging up. "This is the last chance. The very last."

Ginnie's fears had proved groundless.

She had traveled with Lindy as far as Oklahoma City without sharing the secret of their ultimate destination. Then, at the airport, she had called ahead to her sister, letting Julie know that she and Bits were on the way, and that they had been forced to accept an escort. Terrified as she was that Julie would retract the offer of a home, a haven, Ginnie had not been able to deny her the opportunity.

208

But Julie—known now as Jill Pleyer—had accepted Ginnie's explanation of the necessity to bring Lindy; after twenty years of living undisturbed outside the sinister circle of her heritage, she could allow herself the luxury of feeling secure. The only assurance she needed was that Ginnie would refrain from the smallest hint of their true relationship to each other and the life they had once shared. Her husband and children must never know anything of her background. The possibility of upsetting them was Jill Pleyer's only worry. She knew from experience that it was possible to take up a new, safe identity—and she had not even been blessed, as Ginnie had, with government-certified documents. Hearing that Ginnie and Bits were both equipped with valid passports and birth certificates, Jill readily assumed the reponsibility of receiving them into her home.

As they drove to the ranch in a rented car, Ginnie told Lindy about the foundation the sisters had laid in anticipation of an eventual reunion. During the past couple of years Jill had occasionally reminisced to her husband about the cousin with whom she had been raised in South Dakota, the daughter of the aunt who had taken her in after her parents had both been killed in an automobile accident. Jill had also told her husband how much like a sister she felt toward the cousin, though they had not kept in close touch. And more recently there had been talk of reestablishing contact, of the cousin's unhappy marriage, and the possibility that someday she might need a place to stay, to start over.

When the car drove up to the large main house of the Sundown Ranch, Byron Pleyer came out, arm around his wife, to greet the new arrivals. A freckle-faced fifty-year-old with red hair showing the first tinges of gray, Pleyer was a modest, friendly man prepared to take everyone at face value. Even if he had not been primed to extend his largesse, Lindy guessed, Pleyer would have acted no differently. There was not a trace of charity or patronage in the unreserved welcome he gave "Janine Cabel" and her daughter. The surname was presumably a married name which Ginnie would keep even after her divorce came through. For her own rechristening, Bits had adopted the first name "Diane." Lindy was also introduced under the alias of "Larry Dillon," a friend of Janine's who had been coincidentally traveling west on business and had wanted to help her get properly settled.

As he observed the reunion of the sisters, their tearful, joyful embraces, Lindy was glad he had made his bargain with Ginnie Vereste. It would have been a crime if she had been forced to begin again anywhere but here, where so much love had been waiting. Bits, too, had recovered an animation she had not evinced since hearing of Danny Behrens' murder. She was going to be all right.

Ginnie's airport call had given enough advance notice for a festive lunch to be prepared. With the tears spent, and only the smiles remaining, the Pleyers, Janine and Diane Cabel, and their friend Larry Dillon sat down around a table on the poolside veranda. The Pleyer children would not be home until evening, Jill said; they were spending the day at the country club.

There were one or two rough patches during the meal. Several times Byron Pleyer looked across the table, comparing his wife and her cousin, and remarked, "I can't get over how much you two look alike." But he said it more with amusement than amazement, and Jill Pleyer consistently defused the observation by responding with calm repartee instead of panicky evasion.

"Darling," she scolded her husband at last, "you're going to insult Jan if you keep that up. You can see she's much younger than I am."

The plastic surgery had indeed made Ginnie appear to be several years younger than her twin, barely old enough to have a grown daughter. Lindy would have thought it impossible for the women to sustain their lie, if he had not reminded himself that, in several senses, their lives depended on it. He had to admire Jill Pleyer for joining the masquerade, shouldering the strain of it, when it would have been so much easier simply to shut her sister out. Her sacrifice gave Lindy his first direct experience of the undying familial devotion that created the Mafia originally and kept it invincible for so long.

Jill Pleyer had just poured the coffee when the mood of happy reunion was forever shattered.

The three men who appeared on the veranda each came from a different direction. The slick young one who had stepped through a door from the house had his gun pressed into the ribs of the servant who had admitted him. The other two, who had circled around to the rear of the house through the grounds, pointed revolvers at those around the table.

An angry reflex jolted Byron Pleyer up from his chair. "What in goddamn hell! You—"

Lindy caught Pleyer's arm, pulled him down. "Don't."

"Good advice, daddy-o," said Marty Grecco, as he pushed the petrified maid into an empty garden chair. "Stay on your ass, all of you, or you're dead."

Ginnie looked to her sister in abject desolation. "Forgive me," she whispered, barely able to form the words through trembling lips.

Julie Francini could not speak. The gun pointing at her was a wand which had transformed her happy reality to a nightmare with a single wave.

"Murderers," Bits mumbled. Then the accusation burst from her in a scream and she leaped at one of the bigger men, clawing at him. "*Murderer!*"

The gunman defended himself, swiping the gun into the side of the girl's head. She crumpled to the flagstone paving, not quite unconscious but severely stunned. Ginnie stifled a cry.

"Just tell me, for God's sake," Pleyer said. "What do you want? Tell me and you'll have it."

"You can't give it to us, daddy-o," Marty Grecco said, and turned to Ginnie. "Ain't that right, Mrs. Vereste."

Julie dissolved into quiet sobs, as Byron Pleyer looked from Ginnie to his wife in consummate bewilderment.

Ginnie passed a burning glance over the three gunmen, each representing a mere fraction of the evil she could destroy if she remained silent. Then her eyes lowered, she went slowly around the table, taking stock of what she could save if she talked.

Bits pulled herself up, caught a pleading eye-signal from Ginnie to stay quiet, and huddled in defeat.

"Let's not drag it out," Marty Grecco snapped at Ginnie.

"Talk fast and it won't be painful. We've got orders from the Fisherman not to hurt you, if you cooperate."

Ginnie trusted the code, Lindy remembered. She had believed that Rina would not be hurt, but she had not yet been told the suspected outcome of the kidnapping. Should he tell her now?

Ginnie had already made her choice. "I'll tell you anything you want to know."

The interrogation proceeded. Grecco asked Ginnie to reveal not only the location of the safe house, but, to the best of her knowledge, the number of men detailed to guard it, their shift arrangements, the type of weapons she had seen them carrying, the extent of ammunition stores, and the access routes.

From the thorough nature of his questioning, Lindy understood that the assault being contemplated to reach Bart Vereste might be a large-scale mobilization of Mafia manpower along military lines. He noted with relief that, either deliberately or inadvertently, Ginnie had neglected to mention the electronic warning system which defended the safe house. Whatever hostile forces might be arrayed against Konecki and his men, they would at least have advance warning of the danger.

When Marty Grecco had finished questioning Ginnie, he asked where to find the nearest telephone. Pleyer pointed to a weatherproof box at the far end of the veranda. Grecco used the phone for several minutes, speaking in muted tones, his back to the table while his two silent companions kept their guns on the company. Though only an occasional word was audible, Lindy realized that Marty Grecco was relaying Ginnie Vereste's information.

"That's all there is to it, folks," Grecco said jauntily when he returned to the table. "We got what we came for." His eyes swept slowly around. "Now at this point, frankly, I'd like to kill every one of you."

Jill Pleyer gasped. Her husband put his hands firmly on the edge of the table, a subtle preparation for some kind of last stand, making ready to push the table over.

But Grecco understood perfectly. He glanced at Pleyer and smirked. "No, not yet, daddy-o. You're not going to die

212

today, because it's not up to me. My orders are to leave you untouched. The question is whether you die tomorrow." He turned to Ginnie. "Your uncle wants you to have a chance, since you've cooperated. But you understand: you've got to keep on cooperating. The phone lines are cut, and the cars will all need some attention from a good grease monkey before they run again. But those are only minor inconveniences, to make sure we get a smooth ride out of here. The major inconveniences will come if you say a word to anyone about what's happened here. If you did. . . ." Grecco shrugged.

"If we did?" Pleyer demanded sharply.

"They'd come back," Jill cried desperately. "They would, or someone else. And they'd do it then: kill us all."

"That's right, Mrs. You and daddy-o and your two children and"—he nodded to Ginnie and Bits—"you two ladies."

There was a silence. One person present had been conspicuously omitted from the roll call of death. But, as Grecco moved around the table toward Lindy, it became clear that the omission meant no reprieve.

"You, TV star—I hear you're the one that started all the trouble. My man says we owe you for that."

The lithe, angular gunman prodded Lindy in the back of the neck with the muzzle of his revolver. "On your feet; you're traveling with us." He chuckled. "Part of the way."

Lindy stood.

Ginnie whispered hopelessly. "No. . . ."

"Isn't that sweet?" Grecco cooed. "You've got a friend." He prodded Lindy hard in the ribs with the gun.

Lindy moved. If he were to attempt escape it could not be here. The idiosyncrasies of Mafia custom had allowed a protective bond for the women. But the fate of Rina Francini gave evidence that it was a frail provision. If he tried to save himself, it would probably cost the lives of all the others.

Pleyer, coiled in his seat, muttered under his breath. "Rotten scum. You won't get away with this."

Marty Grecco paused. Still keeping his attention partly on Lindy, he flicked a sidelong glance at the rancher. "You don't believe me, do you? Well, tell the man, Mrs. Vereste! Tell him!" Suddenly Grecco was shouting, a hoarse, rabid sound.

213

"Would we think twice about coming back to finish all of you if he doesn't play ball?"

"He means it," Ginnie murmured. "Someone will come."

Grecco nodded and wiped some drops of spittle from his lips with the edge of his sleeve. Then he gestured his two silent partners to join him in retreat and they faded around a corner, pushing Lindy ahead of them.

For a minute no one left on the veranda could speak. A squeal of tires sounded faintly from the drive in front of the house.

Pleyer broke the silence. "They're going to kill Dillon, aren't they—Dillon, or whatever his name is?"

Julie was staring at the table in front of her, unable to move, buried alive under the collapsed structure of past and future.

Ginnie nodded.

Pleyer got to his feet. "I don't know if I'll ever understand why this happened. But I know for sure you don't just look on while—"

"No!" Julie cried suddenly. "We've got to leave it. Please. They'll do exactly what they said if we interfere. Think of the children."

"God, woman," Pleyer thundered savagely. "Don't make it worse! As it is, you've got a mountain of lies to account to me for. We'll cross over that, maybe. But not if you add this to it—telling me to shut my eyes to murder. You ought to know me better than that." Quietly, he added, "Even if I didn't know you."

He walked into the house.

The complexities of running the vast ranch had been simplified several years ago by the installation of a two-way radio system. From a transmitter in his office, Byron Pleyer could be in immediate contact with the men who patrolled his herds in pickup trucks. Marty Grecco had not known about this system, so it had escaped destruction. And now Pleyer went to the transmitter and put out a general emergency call, asking for acknowledgment from all of the four mobile units. When they responded, he told them quickly what had happened, asked one truck to pick him up at the house, and gave the others directions to block off the gunmen's escape route.

Although Pleyer could not describe the vehicle in which they were traveling, the gunmen were not so long gone that they could have reached a road which did not skirt his ranchlands. He knew just how they could be stopped.

After instructing his men, Pleyer went to his gun cabinet and selected a high-velocity clip-loaded rifle. Then he went out to wait for the pickup.

Lindy was in the back seat of the Plymouth sedan, pinned between the shaky young man who had been the spokesman and one of the stocky older men.

"Which way you want me to go, Marty?" said the third man, at the wheel.

"Just keep driving. We'll look for a river, or a canyon."

"We shoulda done it back there," said the heavy man on Lindy's left.

"Witnesses," Marty explained.

"Shoulda iced them all."

Marty shrugged. "The big don said nix. Only this one."

It was a peculiar sensation for Lindy, hearing his murder discussed with such cool, practical detachment. Seated between the two thugs, each with a gun pressed into his side, he knew that no escape was possible. When they found the convenient moment to do their work, they would finish him. He felt almost as though he was already dead, a ghost listening in on the conversations of the living. How many men had felt like this before him, had taken a last ride between Mafia gunmen? Five hundred, a thousand? No, in all their eighty or ninety years of existence it must be more. Two thousand, perhaps five thousand. At this moment, his realization that there had been a sort of ongoing war for almost a century was strangely crystallized. When he had sat in Washington, interviewing the bosses with their fine clothes and perfect manicures, he had not really understood the magnitude of their evil, never quite connected the corpses with the corporate image the murderers cultivated. That was something you couldn't understand until you were about to become one of their victims.

Resigned as he was to take their bullets, Lindy was nevertheless not prepared to be an easy target, a lamb led to

215

slaughter. If he grabbed one of the guns, there was a chance of wounding one of the men before the second man fired into him. Or was it better to dive forward, he wondered, grab the wheel and spin it, try to flip over the speeding car? He was considering the options when the driver moaned in annoyance:

"Oh, shit. Look at this, will ya?"

A couple of hundred yards ahead, the road was blocked by a herd of cattle being driven from one side to the other.

"Christ, Marty," said the man on Lindy's left, "whatta we do?"

"Relax," Grecco said. "Just stop the car and wait, Zig. The road'll be clear in a minute."

"They're blockin' us, Marty. That red-headed prick must've told them—"

"He wouldn't be that crazy. He knows we'd come back and wipe them out; somebody would, anyway."

They sat for half a minute while the steers, piling up in the road, began funneling toward them.

Had Pleyer arranged it? Lindy wondered. There was little enough reason to hope so. The best bet was always on apathy, the will for self-survival. The Mafia generally counted on public fear and indifference to carry out their hits without being identified by ordinary citizens. Had any warrants been sworn out against the men who had chased him through New York City in the morning rush hour, had any descriptions been issued?

A pickup truck, hidden until now in the cloud of dust raised by the shuffling herd, came rocketing into view and drove along the side of the road, heading toward the Plymouth. There was no longer any doubt that this was a blocking maneuver. The man at the wheel of the car zoomed into a U-turn to escape the truck.

Lindy heard a shot fired. The truck was almost abreast and he could see that the man in the passenger seat had a rifle pointing at the sky; he had fired a warning shot.

The return fire was not so kind. The man at Lindy's left took careful aim through his window and squeezed off two shots that turned the face of the rifleman in the truck to a red mask. The rifleman slumped down out of sight.

216

With the car under siege, Lindy realized he was excess baggage, liable to be killed and tossed out at any moment. But at this instant, the man on his left was facing through the open window, his gun over the sill. On his right, the young reptilian type still had his gun placed firmly against Lindy's side, but he was also diverted, looking out the other window in search of any threats coming from other directions.

The chance might not come again.

Whipping his left hand across his stomach, Lindy grabbed the barrel of the revolver in his ribs, and jerked at it so the aim was shifted forward. The young gunman immediately squeezed the trigger. The bullet nicked the fleshy heel of Lindy's hand which was clenched tightly around the muzzle, overlapping it. But the pain of the flesh wound was not enough to make him release his hold. He clung on, strengthening his grip with the other hand, pushing the gun away. At the same time, by throwing his body hard to his left, Lindy hampered the other man in his attempt to turn from the window.

But he could feel that the gamble was lost. The heavier man was twisting around. As Lindy grappled for the gun, he yanked at it blindly, forcing another shot to be triggered off.

Suddenly the car was skidding wildly, out of control, throwing all the men in a tangle. The driver had steered off the road, wasn't steering at all. In the spinning, rocking capsule of massed bodies, Lindy had a flashing glimpse of a small black hole in the back of the driver's seat. The second shot must have gone through into his body.

The car rolled over, the press and pull of gravity crunching its occupants together. It somersaulted twice and came to rest on its left side. Lindy heard the whirr of a wheel spinning free, slower, slower. He felt twitching movements on top of him; beneath, a wet stillness. Then more noises. Motors, doors slamming, a babble of voices, pounding on the metal overhead.

And someone saying, "You snake-eyed son of a bitch. I ought to kill you."

Above, through an open door, Lindy saw a dark shadow holding a rifle, the muzzle pressed to the ear of the young gunman. The shadow became recognizable as Byron Pleyer.

Other shadows appeared, reached down and roughly seized Marty Grecco, dragging him out of the car. Lindy climbed out, assisted by Pleyer. Looking back, he saw the third man in the back seat had been thrown partially out of the side window and been mangled under the car.

"You all right?" Pleyer asked.

"Think so."

Lindy stood, supported by the rancher, and watched as Marty Grecco was bound with rope by a couple of ranch hands, then loaded into one of the three pickup trucks pulled up around the wreck.

A ranch worker came over to Pleyer and handed him a bottle of whiskey. Pleyer passed the bottle over to Lindy. "Have a little first aid, Mr. Dillon. And you better have something for that hand, too." He gave Lindy a clean handkerchief from his pocket.

Lindy bound his bleeding hand, and drank from the bottle. He felt the jumbled pieces of himself begin to merge again.

Handing the whiskey back to Pleyer, he said. "My name's not Dillon, by the way."

"I kinda figured it wasn't," Pleyer said. "Maybe while we head back to the house, you could tell me what this was all about."

A ranch hand had been able to splice together the severed telephone line so that Lindy could call Washington and report that the safe house had been blown. He left the phone number at the ranch and minutes later Konecki called back.

"For Christ's sake, Lindy," Konecki demanded angrily at the start. "What the hell are you doing in Oklahoma, and how did the wise guys get on your tail?"

Lindy patiently explained who the Pleyers were and why Ginnie Vereste had wanted to be with them. "There wasn't anybody on our tail," he concluded. "They'd traced the missing Francini daughter and were here waiting for us to show up."

"Oh," Konecki said simply, his sheepish tone passing for an apology.

"Listen, Gabe," Lindy went on quickly. "They asked Ginnie a lot of questions, and she had no choice but to answer them all—not just your address, but how many men are guarding Vereste, what kind of firepower. Understand? They know enough now not to send in merely a couple of goons with handguns. They might even contemplate a kind of guerrilla-type action to reach Vereste, a lot of men, well-organized. If I were you I'd pull up stakes."

"Why should we?" Konecki said calmly. "We know they're coming now, we can be ready. They sure did us a big favor leaving you alive, giving us a chance to set our traps."

"That wasn't the original idea. I just got back from an old-fashioned ride."

"And what about the family," Konecki asked, concerned. "Any casualties?"

"Not really. No physical damage, anyway. The reasoning was that they'd keep their mouths shut. And they would have—with one exception."

"Mrs. V?"

"No. She made her choice when she answered the questions. It was her brother-in-law who blew the whistle. He didn't know enough to be scared. At least, not then." Lindy added with a glance at the closed door of Pleyer's office. Elsewhere in the house the rancher and his wife were having a heart-to-heart, trying to patch together a new reality.

"We'd better put them under a blanket," Konecki said.

"There's some cops here now."

"I wouldn't leave them to cops. I'll call the Oklahoma Bureau office. You said one mobbo survived. We'd better make him our responsibility, too, clamp down on any news that we've got him."

"Why?" Lindy asked.

"We don't want the Indians to get the idea that we might be expecting them do we?"

"But if they know you're prepared, they might call off the attack."

"Exactly what we don't want. We can handle anything they send against us. This could be a golden opportunity to pick off a good share of their enforcement arm."

"You talk as if you wanted this to happen," Lindy said accusingly.

219

"Wanted it? No. But since it has, we'll make the most of it. Don't trouble your conscience about it, pal. You're out of it now."

Out of it? No, Lindy thought. He had been in at the beginning, he was in all the way. Almost like a premonition, it struck him that he could never understand the law of the land, what it had—or would—become, without returning to the safe house.

SEVENTEEN

At the Breezy Isle convention, Valerio Ligazza had been shamed, if not utterly disgraced.

Dom Francini had kept to himself the information received in Marty Grecco's telephone call from the ranch, had allowed the old man to go through the day espousing the cause of retreat to the men who paid him court. In the evening, the bosses had gathered in the hotel ballroom. Seated at round tables, with the members of the Commission at a dais across the front of the room, the Mafiosi arrayed themselves as if for a fund-raising dinner on behalf of some benign charity. Then, after Ligazza had risen on the dais and begun to address the somber audience, Dom had crassly shouted him down, announced that he had learned where Bart Vereste was being held. Without Francini having to say it, a suspicion was instantly conveyed to the audience that Ligazza had known this and suppressed it; that secret agreements had been made among the Commission members, under Ligazza's command, to let the Vereste squeal run its course. Pandemonium had erupted in the ballroom. Without fuss, Ligazza had left the dais, implicitly abdicating his place at the head of the Honored Society. Motioning Rocco aside, the old man had also surrendered the reins of power over his own family. His exit from the ballroom tacitly acknowledged that in the battle to come he would play no part, just as he would no longer share in the fruits of any victory.

And in the sudden reversal of mood, the Fisherman was elevated to the role of messiah. If hope was on the street again, then Dom must be the dealer.

When order had been restored, the revitalized convention turned to planning revenge on Bart Vereste. No one disagreed with the speech made by Dom Francini in which he assessed the strategic requirements. The problems of reaching this informer were unprecedented. Vereste was being held in a veritable fortress, inaccessible overland except on foot, guarded by twenty-four men, with a helicopter constantly standing by to bring in reinforcements if needed. Accordingly, the invasion force had to be large and well-equipped. Not merely twenty men, but fifty; perhaps a hundred, if the men could be found. Even a favorable troop ratio of five-to-one could be canceled if the authorities picked up a whisper of the invasion plan and shuttled extra men into the safe house. Fortunately, when pledges were taken from the assembled *capi*, an aggregate total of well over fifty enforcers was seen to be a realistic possibility.

Money for the war chest was pledged without reservation. Though cash on hand had been slashed by recent Treasury raids on the bank accounts, over three million dollars were volunteered when Dom Francini made a plea for funds. The men who parted with their spare cash knew they would be reimbursed many, many times over if the crisis could be properly met and overcome. And at least three million dollars might be needed to acquire the kind of firepower that Dom Francini was advocating.

In fact, as the offensive was discussed more and more in military terms, the contribution of ideas devolved increasingly upon those men present who were veterans of American wars in Europe and Asia. At last it was recognized that a special command group should be named, distinct from the Commission, although the Commission would continue to be responsible for funding and other "political" aspects of the operation. As the senior war hero of top rank, Steve Drapetto was chosen to be field commander. He selected his officers from among others who had experienced actual combat. Rocco Gesolo was one of these; and, in consideration of Rocco's as yet unsatisfied hunger for retribution against Vereste, he was designated second-in-command.

Toward midnight, with toasts of wine gravely sipped, the full assembly adjourned, leaving the detailed planning in the hands of the *giunta di guerra*.

Drapetto, Gesolo, and their officer corps spent the rest of the night discussing their strategy. The answers they sought

222

were not immediately evident. The Organization had never, in the past few years, succeeded in reaching a prime government witness; and now they could not afford to fail. By dawn they had formulated a plan and scheduled the attack for five days hence. This was the earliest possible time, allowing for proper reconnaissance and arming to be carried out in advance, and time to notify and muster the soldiers coming from all over the country.

Starting at five-thirty in the morning, a series of men were called from their rooms to appear in Drapetto's suite. In the revived spirit of optimistic camaraderie, this was already being called "the War Room."

The first to be summoned was Jerry Valvitani, *capo* in the upstate New York confederation. Cadaverously thin as a result of a thyroid condition, the fifty-year-old Valvitani was further debilitated by a horrendous stutter. The impediment accounted for his nickname, "Chatter"—usually shortened to "Chat"—which carried appropriate echoes of the fact that two out of the three men Valvitani had ordered killed for untimely remarks about his handicap had been machine-gunned.

He arrived at the War Room dressed in bathrobe and pajamas and saluted sleepily as he entered, half-joking.

"*C-c-commendat-dat-dattori!*"

"Sorry to get you up so early, Chat," Drapetto said seriously.

"*N-n-niente.*"

"Please. . . ." Drapetto motioned Valvitani to a vacant chair beside him in the uneven semicircle formed by the other seated officers.

Drapetto went straight to the point, sparing the upstate New York boss the ordeal of any small talk. "I don't know if you're personally familiar with the Adirondack region, Chat, but it falls within your jurisdiction—Albany and points north." Drapetto unfolded a New York State road map someone had hastily scrounged for the planning session. "You can see it here," he said, sweeping a finger over a section marked Adirondack Park.

Chat Valvitani took the map and held it. "Yah," he said, "that piece is m-m-m-m-m-m-mine."

"On a map of this scale," Drapetto went on, "we can't see

223

exactly where Vereste is holed. But it's good enough to narrow the location down and give you an idea of our problems. Vereste's wife said the house was originally a ranger station, that it was on a lake, and that she'd heard someone say it was at the foot of a range of mountains called the MacIntyres. This map doesn't indicate ranger stations, but the mountains are marked here." Drapetto pointed. "As you can see, there are six or seven lakes in the vicinity. We know that there are no roads going into the lake we want, so that limits the choice to these three, accessible only by trail: Lake Colden, Henderson Lake, or Preston Pond. The first thing we've got to do is send a few men up there—get them going this morning, if possible—to eliminate any doubts about the spot we're aiming for and to study the terrain. A couple of men can pose as campers, one or two others might charter light planes from local airports, make a couple of overflights to get the layout—doing it, of course, in a way that doesn't arouse any suspicion. We want you to supply the reconnaissance, Chat. There's a lot of walking to do so they should be young, lower-echelon guys. On the off-chance they'd be picked up, they should also be absolutely lily-white, no records; if anyone checks them out, they've got to pass for complete outsiders." Drapetto took the map and folded it. "That's the order, Chat. Can do?"

Valvitani nodded. "No p-p-p-p-p-p—"

"Problem," one of the officers boldly assisted.

Valvitani ignored the interjection and continued. "If you w-want the youngest and c-c-c-cleanest, how about I get k-k-k-kids. I mean, m-my *sotto* he's got t-t-two boys, sevent-t-teen and n-n-n-nineteen." He went on to mention a few other sons of his family members who were already serving apprenticeships and would willingly take the reconnaisance hike.

"That's a good angle," Rocco said. "But it might piss off some of their mamas."

"Your m-m-mamma didn't stop you from j-joining, eh?" Valvitani rejoined.

The men laughed and Valvitani's suggestion was ratified. He left to phone the orders immediately.

The next four bosses brought to the War Room were from

224

states scattered around the country. The common denominator in this group was that each controlled a territory where there were large government military installations or ordnance depots.

As gambling and prostitution have always been more important than chapel or USO shows for relieving the tedium of military duty, the Mafia has long-standing connections with the armed services. Lately, with the interest a few greedy officers had taken in drug-dealing among enlistees, the Mob's leverage had grown.

Now Drapetto proposed this leverage be used to the full. By threatening some guilty officers with exposure, canceling the gambling debts of others, and adding lucrative payoffs for those who would cooperate, he had no doubt that government stores could be opened to provide the attack force with sophisticated weaponry. Even with substantial payoffs, this method promised to be faster and more economical than purchasing arms through established wholesalers; it had the added advantage of threatening the government with an ugly scandal if the source of the weapons should ever be successfully traced.

The four *capi* charged with acquiring armaments were also told to sift their families for young veterans with experience in handling the newer weapons; the attack could not be postponed long enough to allow for training.

Though one *capo* in the supply group was dubious about his ability to meet the order in the limited period remaining before the assault, the other three were confident. One spoke of a supply sergeant who had been his connection for drug sales on a large base in his territory; another held a forty-seven-thousand-dollar marker from a brigadier general.

"Of course, there's a limit to what I can get," joked one of the bosses. "Don't expect any ballistic missiles."

The others laughed. The man who spoke controlled a southwest territory where there were several known missile sites.

"We don't need any tanks, either," Drapetto retorted. "The basic requirement is for lightweight automatic weapons with plenty of ammunition. If you can unlock the right doors, we could also use some of the special gadgets with a bigger punch. Things like heat-seeking rocket launchers. We'd give a big chunk of the budget for three or four of those; they'd improve our ability to blast the place at night."

"Wait a second, Steve," Gesolo said. "I didn't know we were thinking in those terms. We want to get in there and kill Bart. But if we blast the place too hard, we'll have to stand for another twenty murder raps."

"What else can we do, Roc? We can't make a selective hit. We don't have the time or talent to infiltrate a bunch of clever commandos who'll whack Bart and vanish into the night. He's obviously too well defended. We've got to hit the place hard, level it, and not worry about who gets hurt."

"But twenty raps are harder to beat than one," Rocco said.

"Are they? The principle's the same every time: innocent until proven guilty. And the way we're laying this out, either they won't be able to prove it—or they won't want to."

"I'm with ya," said the southwestern *capo*. "It's no different from any other contract. It may have our trademark on it, but that doesn't mean we can be nailed."

Drapetto looked slowly around the semicircle; the other men murmured accord.

The four bosses of the supply division were dismissed to initiate their quest for equipment.

Just before he went out, the one who had been least cooperative paused.

"Steve, there's a hot wire I've got with a captain who holds the keys on an army warehouse. He's helped me lift a shitload of stuff, but I didn't think until a second ago there's anything we could use. He's only in the Quartermaster Corps; what he looks after is mostly furniture, stationery, now and then some booze. But I just got a flash: part of the warehouse is used to store uniforms."

"Uniforms?" Drappeto responded. "Hey, don't get too carried away with the military gig."

"I wasn't thinking of it for a kick," the *capo* said earnestly. "We're gonna be moving a lot of guys into a fairly small area, and we want to move them with their pieces. This may be a hit-and-run, but if our guys are expected to go a few miles on foot, it's gonna leave them exposed for a few hours at least. And if they're in civvies, toting all that metal, the game is up.

They can't say they're out hunting deer with that rocket shit you were talking about. But if they're in uniform it's a whole other thing. This mountain area we're aiming at sounds like the kind of place the army might use for training maneuvers. Say we put our guys in regular GI gear; then we get a few trucks, give 'em the right kind of paint job. We could move the men together, right out in the open, without getting the local cops worked up. Simplifies transport and rendezvous, and once they're in the woods they've also got a cover story to tell."

Drapetto pondered.

"I don't think the army uses state parks for maneuvers," Rocco said.

"The army does any fuckin' thing it wants," said one of the staff, speaking with the authority of a veteran. "By the time any cop would think of checkin' road movements with the fuckin' Pentagon, we'd be gone."

"It clicks with me," said another man.

Drapetto mediated. "It might be an angle. But we'll reserve decision. In any case, let's get the uniforms."

"How many, Steve?" asked the *capo* who would supply them.

"Make it a hundred, to be on the safe side."

The last man to be summoned to the War Room was Don Carmen Pontone. It was only a few minutes past seven o'clock when Drapetto called Pontone's suite, but the Florida boss was already wide-awake. A short, vibrant man of fifty-nine, he was noted for his long working days, sleeping no more than four or five hours each night. But this was not the biggest reason that he occupied a very special niche in the brotherhood's hall of fame.

Along with Charly Lucky and others who had helped to prepare the 1944 invasion of Sicily, Pontone was one of the few Mafiosi who had actually been sought as an ally by the United States government. The genesis of this curious alliance lay in the warm relationships Pontone had established with many of the émigrés from Castro's Cuba who had found asylum in Florida. The passionate dedication of these men to overthrow the Communist leader and his regime gave them a community of interest with all the racketeers who longed to see the wide-open Havana of pre-Castro days restored. There was, in fact, a triangle of factions seeking to overthrow Castro, the third side being the Central Intelligence Agency. Its operatives had been sent to contract with the boss of the Florida Mafia when the agency wanted a hit man—either one of the boss's own men or a Cuban he would select and train—to assassinate the Cuban head of state. (When a leak about the scheme made a splash in the press, it was said that the agency's representatives had been acting outside their authority; but Pontone could have told a different story—he had spoken twice on the phone to a deputy director at Washington headquarters.) Though the half-million-dollar contract had been canceled without explanation only days before it was to be carried out, Pontone had been consoled by his share of the quarter-million-dollars paid in advance.

Today, Pontone was sought as the most likely source for a couple of helicopters and pilots. Prior to the Bay of Pigs, several groups of Cubans had been equipped with helicopters by the CIA and trained as pilots. While the ensuing fiasco had ruled out another invasion, the helicopter units had been maintained under the guise of air-taxi services; they were still on call for such tasks as air-sea rescue of Cubans who tried to escape from their island to Florida in small, sometimes unnavigable boats. At other times, the helicopter units were free to accept whatever charter work they could find. Pontone had frequently availed himself of their services to have cash and drugs moved around the Caribbean. Police authorities throughout the area were conveniently reluctant to interfere with these taxi services because of their Agency connection.

But when Drapetto explained his current plans for the helicopters, Pontone did not respond with immediate enthusiasm.

"This thing sounds like it's getting over-organized," he said grumpily. "You've got maybe a hundred guys going in on foot. Now you want wind-machines so you can fly over on a bomb run? If y'ask me it's—whataya call it—overkill. Send the machines or send the men. Why both?"

"A tried and true military principle, Don Carmen," Drapetto answered. "Ground troops need air cover; air attack should be supplemented with ground support. If we could get big enough choppers to fly all the men in, we could toss that rule aside. But what's available is small stuff, only big enough to carry four or five men and the pilot. The best way to use them seems to be to load some rockets in, to blast the safe house from above. After that happens, anyone left alive in the house is going to scatter, fan out; and one of those people might be Vereste. That's where the foot soldiers come in. They'll be positioned in a ring around the target area. Anyone who tries to escape will get picked off."

Pontone scratched his chin. "Sounds like maybe you know what you're doing," he relented. "But that don't mean I can help. My spics have the last word, and they'll probably want to stay clear. It's one thing to do a quick hop with five or ten keys of smack. It's another kind of tamale to go dropping bombs on the feds. Don't forget who bought the Cubies their toys, for Chrissake."

"Not for a minute," Drapetto said. "That's exactly why we want them."

Pontone mumbled something inaudible, evidently an uncomplimentary remark on Drapetto's mental condition.

"Hear me out, Don Carmen. There's a good chance that one of these machines will get shot down. Then it becomes evidence: trace the charter back to us and we get slammed with a mass murder charge. But if we use CIA hardware, the feds will have to sit on the truth. You think they want to prove that one government agency paid for the means to bomb another? Or that the spooks have a connection with us? They're in so much trouble now they can't stand any more knocks. They'd sooner hush up the whole attack, even if it means letting us off."

After a moment, Pontone grinned. "Well, well, I guess you boys didn't stay up all night for nothing after all. But I've still got the problems of convincing the spics. I can't use your reasoning to romance them. They've got some loyalty to the spooks, y'know. On top of which we don't want to make them think in terms of getting shot down."

"We don't have to give any explanations to them," Drapetto asserted. "What's the usual bite on a smack run?"

"Depending how much they carry and how far, I pay anywhere from twenty up to fifty k."

"All right, let's pay enough so the pilots can do one more

229

job and never have to work again. Make it two hundred fifty big ones for each man and machine. You think they'd give us an argument?"

"They always argue," Pontone replied lightly, "it's in their nature. But for a quarter mil apiece," he added, "it ought to be a very short argument."

By midmorning the word had been passed throughout the hotel: the convention was to disband. Drapetto's military command would remain in close contact, coordinating the operation. All others were to return to their individual headquarters and be prepared to supply men and money at a moment's notice.

Starting at ten o'clock and continuing until noon, the guests were chauffered away to diverse points, retracing the discreet itineraries which had brought them to Breezy Isle.

Among the first to leave was Valerio Ligazza. Passing through the lobby, he paused briefly to clasp the hands of the bosses who were mingling there, exchanging final notes before departure. The intensity of Ligazza's farewell, the misty cast in his eyes, was not lost on those who saw him walk away, still proud and erect. He would not be seen in their circle again; an epoch had ended. The old man would no doubt return home at last. After commanding an empire, having some of the leaders of the most powerful nation in the world in his thrall, he would end his days sitting at a table in the café of a small village on a poor, dusty island. And strangest of all, they knew he would be happy there.

The surveillance of the ranch by federal authorities had begun, shared equally between the United States Marshal Service and the FBI. Henceforth at least one man from each agency would be in the house at all times; others would accompany any of the principals whenever they left the ranch, including the Pleyer children. These procedures would be maintained indefinitely, certainly until the Mafia trials were over.

Lindy had stayed on at the ranch overnight and through this morning, hoping to provide some friendly counsel that might ease the torment of the Pleyers and the Vereste women. The dream of peaceful reunion, of building secure new lives, was in ruins. Yet there were valuable tokens to be found in the wreckage. Byron Pleyer had not rejected Julie because of her massive lie. In view of the background Lindy had given him—and with the events of yesterday as proof of the Mafia's ability to find any of its lost sheep, and subject them to the perennial threat of death if not the actuality—Pleyer had been sympathetic to his wife's desperate fiction. And the rancher was not inclined to cower because his refusal to remain silent had marked him as a target for future gangster retaliation. When Lindy suggested it might be advisable to relocate, Pleyer bridled:

"Leave my home? Why the hell should I? Hell, there never would've been a Sundown Ranch if my daddy and his before didn't have the guts to stick right here. You think this country's ever been any different? There's always been some greedy lowdown bastards tryin' to scare us off. Squatters, railroads, oil companies. Shit, no matter what kinda sons of bitches are out there now, they can't be worse than what we've seen before."

That fighting spirit had been a balm for Ginnie and Bits Vereste. Instead of running away for another try at anonymity, they had decided to stay at the ranch. Julie, even more than her husband, had begged Ginnie not to go. Assured by Lindy that there was very little likelihood that he had been followed when he brought the Verestes to Oklahoma from the safe house, Julie was willing to admit that some past carelessness of her own might be at fault.

Late in the afternoon, Lindy flew out of Oklahoma City. His plan for traveling back to the safe house called for connecting in New York with a flight upstate to the Adirondack fringe. Before departing, he was to phone the arrival time and place to Washington for relay to Konecki so the helicopter ferry could be waiting.

At Kennedy, Lindy booked a seat on the nine-fifteen to Glens Falls, and then went to a phone booth. When he was inside the booth, however, his first impulse was not to call Washington.

In the past couple of weeks she had hardly crossed his

231

mind. He knew it was not a whim that had made him want her, but lately there had been no room in his thoughts for any life outside the cloistered world of endangered witnesses. Tonight, when he allowed himself to think of Ciel, he wondered if what existed between them could be strong enough to supersede all the arguments against taking it further. Was love enough to simplify anything?

Perhaps the sound of her voice—whatever words she used—would tell him.

He dropped the coin into the slot, and then remembered he didn't know the telephone number at her new apartment. He dialled the "information" operator and asked for it under recent listings.

"I'm sorry," the operator told him, "the number for C. Jemasse has been delisted."

"You mean, it's unlisted?"

"I mean what I said," the operator replied, narrowly within the company's limit of permissible insolence. "The subscriber has paid for a standard listing, but our permission to give out this number has been withdrawn until further notice."

"For what reason?"

"It is not my business to know, sir." The operator disconnected.

Lindy replaced the receiver. Ciel's decision to cut herself off from unwanted callers disturbed him. He could guess the probable cause. There had been some unpleasantness in the building as news of the black girl in the penthouse spread among the other tenants.

Lindy looked at his watch. There was less than an hour before his flight, no hope of getting into town and back to the airport in time.

He would catch a later flight, Lindy decided. He had to see Ciel, to know she was all right.

He was delayed at the building entrance by a doorman, a new employee who conscientiously forced Lindy to state the cause of his visit before proceeding to the elevators. When Lindy introduced himself as a tenant and supplied his name and apartment number, this produced a flutter from the doorman.

"Oh, Mr. Lindell. You've been away, haven't you?"

232

"Yes."

"You know, they've been looking for you."

"Who?"

"The police."

Lindy could think of a few possible reasons, most of them very bad. "What did they want?"

"About that burglary in your apartment."

That hadn't been one of his guesses. "Burglary? When?"

"Ah, that's right, you were away. A couple of apartments in the building were broken into. Yours was one—"

"And the other?" He asked, his voice rising with anxiety.

"Penthouse E."

As he had feared, Ciel's. Lindy ran for the elevator.

Riding up, he castigated himself. Idiot! The people close to Bits and Ginnie Vereste had been tracked down and slain in the Mafia drive to find Bart, yet he had never imagined there was any danger to Ciel. He should have warned her! Obviously not a single stone had been left unturned. His own apartment had been ransacked for clues to his whereabouts. Then Ciel's, because somehow they had learned of his help to her. Through a doorman, perhaps, the same one who had fingered him on that morning a few weeks ago. Christ, where didn't they have contacts, strings to pull, lives to squeeze? Or maybe they had simply broken into his office, found the copies of the lease which he had co-signed—

The elevator opened to the top floor. Lindy pounced on the button for the doorbell of Penthouse E and gave a long, long ring. But no one came.

His spirit sank. Konecki's words on Danny Behrens echoed through his mind: "Thrown away like a piece of used chewing gum." Was she any more likely to be left alive? No life was sacred; no one was spared who blocked the crime princes from their ambitions.

He leaned on the button again, refusing to believe she was gone, afraid to go back to the doorman and ask.

Then he heard a movement on the other side of the door. A click as the metal latch of the spy hole was slid open so that the visitor could be inspected.

Even before the door was thrown open he heard her cry: "Lindy!"

Then her arms were locked around his neck, her cheek

233

warm against his. As they kissed, he felt her begin to tremble, slightly at first, escalating in seconds to a violent uncontrollable quaking. Their lips separated. She loosened her hold and moved her head down against his chest.

"I must be improving," he said. "I never had a kiss do that to anyone before."

She had started to sob, but now she laughed with it, faintly. The quaking subsided. He held her until she moved back, pulling him inside the apartment.

He noticed the plaster cast on her left hand when she used it to push the door shut. A murderous rage crackled through him.

"Cool it, baby," she said, catching his blazing glare at her injured hand. "It'll be all right. Come in and—" Abruptly, she stopped leading him into the living room. "Oh, God, it was all to find you, don't you know that? You shouldn't be here. If you've been—"

"The pressure's off," he said calming her. "They know where Vereste is."

She made him take a drink before she would tell him what had happened. Lindy glanced around the living room as Ciel poured two Scotches and some of the story told itself. There was a color television console with a shattered tube, and several ruinous slashes in the new velvet sofa and suede chairs she had bought. The square chrome-framed coffee table in front of the sofa had no glass in it.

Ciel handed him his drink and they sat down together on the sofa.

"Damn it," Lindy said guiltily, "This is my fault. It just never crossed my mind that you'd get dragged in."

"How could it, man? It was sort of a case of mistaken identity, you know. They got the idea I was your mistress because you'd helped get me the apartment."

"But how did they know?"

"Oh, Lord, what don't they know! Where don't they have someone who can be used!" She waved her plastered hand at her ruined belongings. "You think this is all there was to it? Honey, it didn't start or end there. First they tried diplomacy, a little peaceful coexistence, shall we say." She took a quick gulp of her drink and continued. "A couple of days after the last time I saw you, I got a call from my ex. Buckie

234

said he wanted to drop over and see my place, have an informal housewarming for old time's sake. We're not too close these days, but tight enough so it seemed natural, so I gave him the green light." She smiled ruefully. "Some housewarming. He was running errands, that's all. He was sent to find out what he could about you, where you'd gone."

"Buck Gracey? What's he got to do with the Mob?"

Ciel cast her eyes down, as if the shame was her own. "He's been working to rig the point spread in some of the big games—you know, passing wide at the crucial moments, and like that. I never knew. All that time we were married I thought Buck was a real straight cat. But it goes way back to before then." She looked directly at Lindy. "It's the one good thing about all this, learning that Buckie was never his own man. Makes me feel better about a lot of stuff I used to hang on myself. They always had him under the gun, simple as that. This time they figured he could be useful to open me up. If he hadn't come to hassle me, they were going to leak the truth about some of those games to a couple of big sports columnists or the football association."

"And when you couldn't tell him anything?"

"Buckie knows when I'm leveling. We talked, and he believed me. He took the story back to his man and he was let off; he'd done what was asked—and he's much too valuable to throw away while he's still a star quarterback. But with me it was another story. Round two was Avril."

"Oh, Jesus," Lindy sighed.

"A man stopped her on the street one day outside Mama's house. Up to then she'd been good as gold, stayed off the shit. But then this cat offered her a free deck, and a lot more where that came from if. . . ." She broke off.

"You don't have to finish this," Lindy said.

"But I do." Ciel struggled to continue. "You've got to hear it all. I remember how torn up you were about bringing in this cat Vereste because of side effects. And I want you to get it clear, baby: you've got nothing to regret. If you help to crush these motherfuckers be glad. Because there's nothing they won't do, nowhere they won't put their foot in, if we don't stop them."

"It's funny you have to remind me," Lindy mused. "I started out with the same feeling. But I didn't know the things we'd have to do to stay out front. We turn ourselves into gangsters in some ways. And for what? Wipe out one rat's nest, there's always another. You might as well keep the status quo. I only wish I'd realized it sooner. How do you think I feel bringing this down on you, and your sister?"

"You haven't heard me complain, have you? As for Avril, honey, they've owned her forever since the first jolt. You think there was a chance she wouldn't have crumbled sooner or later? All it took was some dude waving a taste at her. Poor kid. I hardly know whether to feel glad or sorry she couldn't collect on her big free bonus. Oh Lindy, if you'd seen her—it ripped my heart out. She was down on her knees to me, pawing the floor like a dog. But I had nothing to tell her." Ciel took a reinforcing sip of her Scotch, then leaned forward to set her drink down on the coffee table. She caught herself as her hand went through the empty chrome frame. With a small, bitter laugh, she said:

"There we are, round three. By then, I suppose they were starting to believe me. But they had to be sure. A week ago when I got home from work there were two of them, sitting and waiting, drinking my booze calm as you please. A doorman had given them the passkey. He told the police later these crumbs had a connection to his union; he didn't dare refuse them. When I came home the show started. Every time I gave them an answer they didn't like, they'd bust up a little more furniture. Finally, as the saying goes, last but not least—" She raised the hand encased in plaster. "They held it against a door frame, said if I didn't tell them where you'd gone they'd smash my. . . ." She faltered.

Lindy reached for her hand. "Okay, never mind," he said softly.

She pulled away, shouted savagely, "No, goddamn it! If you care anything about me, listen. Get down off that clean white pedestal and learn to hate these bastards!"

Lindy sat back, turned away.

"They asked me once more, the same question. I had only one answer, as you know, the one they didn't like. So they made good on the threat. One guy held me, and the other one closed the door—hard as, . . . I fainted from the pain, and when I opened my eyes they were gone."

236

Lindy got up from the sofa, paced the room aimlessly. "We'll get them," he said. "If you can pick them out of a line-up, find a picture in the mug files."

"*If* the police show me the right pictures, *if* they pull the right men into a lineup. Let me tell you the last round. Next day, when I felt well enough to call the cops, they sent around a detective lieutenant to take a statement. Lovely guy. But he wasn't nearly so interested in getting down a description of my attackers as asking me things like whether I'd been in touch with you to tell you my troubles; and if not, why not? Wasn't it true I was your mistress? You dig, baby?"

Lindy felt sick. The whole society was rotten, from top to bottom. And yet he wondered if the cure wasn't worse than the disease. "At least you won't be bothered anymore," he said quietly. "They found out what they wanted to know by another route. Any day now they'll send the guns to try and kill Vereste." He stopped pacing, looked down at Ciel. "But you want to hear the good news? They're being set up for a fall. We know they're coming, and everything's going to be thrown against them. I have a feeling that the ones who come will be massacred to terrorize the ones who don't. How about that for a plan: no trial by jury, no due process, no prisoners taken—just a body count."

He waited, expecting he had touched some sense of justice, an awareness of the dangers of going too far.

But all she said was, "Amen."

She would not talk anymore about the attitudes that divided them. They went on trying to reach each other, but in a silence of soft touches, soothing away the anger and doubt.

At last they made love, in the bedroom with all the lights on. They had to be able to see each other, Ciel said; their differences should not be forgotten simply because they became invisible in the dark.

He woke first the next morning, and watched her as she slept. Then he rose, showered and dressed. She was still sleeping when he was ready to go.

He would have liked to confess the love, but not the hate she demanded with it. So he left without waking her.

237

EIGHTEEN

As the helicopter landed in the compound, Lindy saw Konecki emerge from the electronics cabin and stride forward with a welcoming smile. The aspect of villainy which he took on now and then for Lindy had vanished again, a chimera.

"It's been lonely around here without our conscience," the big marshal jibed as Lindy jumped to the ground.

"From what Snoot tells me I haven't missed much. Not a sign of activity from the other side."

"The temperature just started to rise," Konecki said, steering back toward the electronics cabin. "A small plane flew over about twenty minutes ago. We got the markings and checked registry at Civil Aeronautics. It belongs to a flying club in Tupper Lake, a town about twenty miles from here."

"What does that prove?" Lindy asked. "There must be plenty of private flying enthusiasts who'd detour over these mountains for the scenic view."

"Right," acknowledged Konecki, "and there are quite a number of small airfields in the park with planes for hire. But this was the second overflight in two days, and it seemed to come in a trifle on the low side. So I followed it through the glasses and, far around the other side of the lake, I saw it bank sharply as if to double back without making a second pass directly overhead. It looked to me like we were the farthest point on the flight plan, but we weren't supposed to know."

"You think they might be looking for an opening to make a landing, try and steal Vereste alive? It would help them a lot if they could find out exactly how much he's unloaded."

"Sure it would. They'd love to go over him. But taking him alive is beyond their capability. Their main priority now must

238

be to make absolutely certain Vereste gets killed very dead. Those were reconnaisance flights, Lindy. Somebody up there is mapping our layout for the attack."

"If they're that careful, they must have put in ground surveillance, too, for a close look at perimeter defenses."

Konecki shrugged. "Haven't seen a sign of it on the Igloo. I'd guess they started some kind of steady watch as soon as they had a fix on the place, but for now it must be limited to a couple of guys on a mountain using a scope. That's enough to tell them how strong we are."

Lindy swept a glance over the compound. "They ought to be delighted then. Theoretically, they could send an army in here ten or twenty times as strong as your defense force. How many soldiers can the Mob call on? Four, five thousand?"

Konecki laughed. "That total includes every fat old slob who ever took the oath. The only ones we have to worry about are the enforcers, the hard core. Nationwide, they don't add up to more than a couple of hundred. And the Mob would be lucky to get fifty of those on this job. They're not the sort of boys who'd volunteer for hazardous duty. They'll want to be paid, the way they would for any hit; and the price could be extra high to compensate for the extra risk. To get fifty men for this one night's work the bill might come to over a million."

"The moneys' there," Lindy said. "You'd better get some reinforcements."

"We don't have room to put a hundred new lodgers," Konecki argued. "With surveillance and those recky flights the other side would spot any buildup right off. Once they saw men swarming the compound we'd have lost our main advantage—the best advantage in any fight—the element of surprise. Right now, they don't know we're expecting them and we don't want them to know. That's also why I've kept Vereste here; if they spotted him being moved out, they'd call off the invasion."

"You're not worried about the element of surprise swinging their way, if they can pounce before you have a chance to prepare?"

"Can't happen," Konecki said smugly. "The Igloo will tell

239

us when they're moving in. As soon as we have them at the point of no return, we call in reinforcements—drop some in here by chopper, move in others at the enemy's rear. The old pincers play."

They had reached the electronics cabin. Konecki led the way in and stopped before the huge screen of the Igloo White system. Dyskowicz was in his accustomed place at the console.

"Any change, Dice?"

"See for yourself." Dyskowicz tuned a couple of dials, heightening the intensity of the illuminated lights on the grid. Amid the myriad green pinpoints showing sensor locations, three red spots stood out on or near the perimeter.

"Only three," Konecki mused. He turned to Lindy. "We had four last night. Finch did the ranger bit, looked them over. All innocent camping parties—three happy families and one group of teenage boys on a hike. The kids must have pushed off and the families haven't broken camp yet."

Lindy switched his attention to the data-link console. It was inoperative at the moment, abandoned by its operator, Harpe.

"Have you got all the programs down?" Lindy asked.

Konecki shook his head slowly. "Only four. I gather you haven't seen Mack Sunderland's column in the past few days."

"No. Why?"

"He's been blasting the Vereste deal. God knows where he gets his information, but the sources are Grade A. Seems to know exactly how much we're paying Vereste and where the money is coming from."

"Where is it coming from?" Lindy said. "You never did ask for a special appropriation, come to think of it. And if you've got four programs, the total must be—"

"We've paid out five million eight hundred thousand, to be exact."

Lindy whistled. "How? Whose money is it?"

"More than half comes from Mafia accounts opened by the squeal. Unfortunately, since the value Vereste places on his information includes a percentage on tax claims—money we haven't seen yet, and may never see—the accounts can never cover the whole nut. The balance has been siphoned off from regular departmental budgets—FBI, Treasury's Narc division, Customs, Border Patrol—there's enough fat to cover us. But somehow Sunderland has traced every transfer. He's demanding a congressional investigation, says that sucking these budgets has weakened all our enforcement agencies."

"So," Lindy sighed, "you may not be able to finish buying Vereste's package. Almost half his information could stay locked in the computer."

"It could happen," Konecki said flatly. "Though it's still a toss-up. We're not without allies on the Hill. There are the guys who never believe anything Sunderland says; and there are the guys who hate him either way; and the ones from sunny green states where crime isn't an issue, so they won't want to get into a fight about it. And then there are the men who'll follow Tom Ryle's lead—who'll say that we've pumped billions into countries we haven't saved, so why not a few million more to save our own? Altogether they might add up to a fair scrimmage against the old-fashioned tight-ass crowd who'd oppose paying Vereste on principle, no matter what was at stake." Konecki paused. "But I guess, in the end, we'd lose. And while the handwriting is on the wall, no one's signing any more checks for Bart Vereste." He gave Lindy an earnest glance. "Maybe you understand now why we're making the most of our chance to cut down the Organization's strength on the battlefield."

Did he understand? Lindy wondered. Could he really look on unaffected while Konecki converted the defensive mission of protecting a witness into a cold-blooded strategy of liquidating the opposition. Did the practical gain compensate for any adulteration of the law?

"Gabe," Lindy appealed suddenly, "if I could persuade Vereste to turn over the rest of the package, no strings attached, then would you take him out of here—and do it with a lot of noise?"

"You mean, so there'd be no confrontation?"

Lindy nodded.

Konecki hesitated. "I guess I could settle, if Vereste would. But you're dreaming, Lindy. It's never been anything but a racket with him. A way to settle some grudges and get rich

241

into the bargain. He won't do any favors to save the lives of a few gunnies."

"I'm not sure he's so heartless," Lindy said. "Remember what triggered this whole deal? A love affair. He lost his cool over a schoolgirl. And his sentimental streak doesn't end there. My guess is that he chose this way to settle his grudges not only for the money, but because it gave his wife and daughter a chance to start over."

"You might be right," Konecki admitted. "The only time I've ever seen him upset was when I told him the news from Oklahoma. He almost cried. First I thought he was rocked because the Mob had found him. But he didn't mind at all for himself, as it turned out. It was the women he worried about. Cussed me every which way for not protecting them well enough."

"Where is he now?"

"At the lodge. Reading in his room, probably." Konecki laughed to himself. "He's into biographies of the Caesars all of a sudden. Talks about them every night at supper."

Lindy went up to the lodge and changed out of his suit. Then he knocked on Vereste's door.

Vereste appeared wearing a crisp white tennis outfit. "Well, well," he clucked, smiling crookedly. He managed somehow to convey with this greeting that he was aware of Lindy's travails during his absence from the safe house and that he was no more than mildly amused at the ordeal of being taken for a ride.

Lindy stared at Vereste, startled by the change. The face was almost completely healed from the plastic surgery. The reshaping of nose and eyes made the Mafioso unrecognizable from his former self. Yet more than these externals had altered. There had been a greater change within, a transmutation of spirit reflected ineffably in some difference of bearing. Before Vereste had seemed merely ice-cold; now he had become diamond-hard.

"Can we talk?" Lindy said.

"I was about to meet my son on the court," Vereste replied briskly. "We're getting too damn soft lying around this resort. If you want to talk, walk over with me."

They went through the main room of the lodge, where Vereste grabbed up one of the tennis racquets provided for general use.

"All right. Talk," he snapped as they emerged into the bright sunshine.

"You know," Lindy began, "there's been some trouble finding the money to buy the rest of your information."

"Trouble?" Vereste said flippantly. "In a rich country like ours."

Lindy passed over the sarcasm. "It'll stay in the computer, doing nobody any good, unless you give us the rest of the codes."

"*Give* you?"

"That's right. Gratis."

They walked in silence for a moment. Ahead, on the tennis court, Mark Vereste was warming up against a practice wall. The sound of the ball rebounding ticked off the seconds.

Slowly, Vereste said, "What makes you think I'd do that?"

"Why shouldn't you? You don't need money anymore. You've already wrung enough out of the government to live like a king for the rest of your life."

"There are kings and kings, Lindell. And then, there are emperors. I've just been reading about a few, and I wouldn't mind being one myself. I haven't earned my way into that league yet."

Lindy studied Vereste. Was this the source of his changed aspect? His ego was soaring to rarefied altitude because he had negotiated with the government at a top level and had gotten everything his own way.

"The Caesars had their legions," Lindy said. "No matter how rich you get, you're always going to be one man—alone. Your treasure could be very hard to enjoy if you've left too many enemies in circulation, and you've got no protection."

Vereste chuckled dryly. "Oh, shit, Lindell, you're not pulling the old protection racket on *me*?"

"Sorry, did that sound like a threat? It's merely a report on the way things are. There's been a lot of backlash to our deal with you. A wave of sentiment is building against any further cooperation. Keep holding the government to ransom and the backlash can only get stronger. The end result is likely to be that the protection program is canceled and you're left out in the cold."

"You wouldn't dare," Vereste flashed. "That's violating a treaty."

Another trumpet blast from the ego. Was he imagining it, Lindy wondered; or did Vereste, in classifying himself as party to a treaty, mean to elevate himself to something greater than a mere individual, an entity that could deal with a government on equal terms, a power unto himself?

"There's nothing sacred about the deal with you, Vereste," Lindy said harshly. "If you can't be used one way, then you'll be used another—and tossed on the garbage heap if your uses are exhausted. Can't you see it happening already? The money's drying up and you won't talk, so you're being used as a decoy. Your old buddies know where you are, and they're coming in to try for the kill. But they're being set up. There's been a top-level decision to throw everything against them, blow them all away. The only way a massacre can be stopped is by moving you out. But it won't be done unless you finish talking."

Vereste stopped walking and stared at Lindy. "That's your real reason, isn't it? Your conscience is bothering you. Suddenly you can see what any man on the inside sees from his cradle: that the good guys commit their own kind of crimes. And you want to stop them. Well, you're crazy if you think I give a damn. Let every two-bit mechanic who comes gunning for me be pounded down to a damp red piece of earth. I'm happy to be the decoy. If I had the Mob's welfare at heart I wouldn't be here, would I?"

Vereste started to walk on, but Lindy caught him roughly by the arm and spun him around. "And why am *I* here?" he raged. "You wanted me because—how did you put it?—you 'identified,' had some blurred memory of what it felt like to be a decent human being. So can't you identify at all with a desire to spare the bloodshed, find a better way? I know you've got some scores to settle. But I thought you chose this way partly because it was better than murder."

"I did," Vereste said quietly. "But this time I don't have to do the killing."

Vereste continued on, and Lindy followed to the edge of

the tennis court. On the far side, Mark Vereste had interrupted his practice and stood watching them.

"You ought to think it over," Lindy said. "Or you may defeat your own ends."

"That would depend," Vereste retorted coldly, "on what my ends are."

Lindy watched them for a few minutes, playing tennis like any father and son on a Sunday at the country club. Walking away, he thought again of Vereste's final retort. Was Vereste claiming to harbor some unsuspected ambition beyond all imaginings? Or was this more wild boasting, germinated in the same distorted notion of self that could confess to aspiring to a station above kings? Lindy began to suspect the exact nature of that curious revolution of spirit he had detected in Vereste. In his isolation, cast adrift from any standard of morality, with no beacon of law or loyalty or love to steer for on either side, the man was probably going mad.

The center of Mafia activity in the days leading up to the target date for the assault on the safe house—a date which Drapetto had dubbed V-Day—was now in the rear office of the Floor Magic carpet store, one unit of a suburban shopping complex owned by Valerio Ligazza. Years ago the old man had given a lease on the store to Rocco Gesolo, in the event it might be useful as a betting shop or numbers bank. Gesolo had chosen to maintain the store as a strictly legitimate enterprise against the time that he might urgently need an absolutely clean front. Now the time had come, and Rocco had volunteered the store for the command post. To the office behind a showroom lined with rolls of broadloom and linoleum came the telephone calls, progress reports from the bosses who had been given strategic assignments.

First to meet his responsibility was Carmen Pontone. On the day after the Breezy Isle convention had disbanded, the Florida boss called to say that two Cuban helicopter pilots had signed on. After some discussion between Gesolo and Steve Drapetto, a return call went out to Pontone with instructions to be relayed to the pilots. They were to begin moving north in time to be standing by on Thursday evening at a small airfield outside the town of Gloversville, New York, fifty minutes flying time from the target. The attack would be made on Friday night.

On Tuesday and Wednesday more of the equipment requisitions were filled. In return for covering the sudden disappearance of one hundred M-16 automatic carbines from the stores in his charge, a supply captain at an army training base in Ohio had accepted cancellation of a nine-thousand-dollar marker, plus an additional cash payment of seven thousand dollars. At this price, the weapons were being purchased for less than cost.

A much smaller payoff to a different source had procured the uniforms which had been suggested as a possible cover, though it was still not certain that they would be used.

The biggest score had been chalked up on Wednesday morning at two-thirty. It was then that a trailer truck belonging to the Excelsior Waste Removal Company had presented an official entry pass, endorsed by the acting base commander, at the main gate of the U.S. Army Ordnance Depot near Greenley, Virginia. Once on the grounds of the sprawling installation, the vehicle proceeded to move unchallenged in and out of the loading bays of those warehouses which had been specially marked on a hand-drawn map in the possession of the truck driver. At each warehouse the sentry on duty was shown the necessary authorizations. There was one zealous private who insisted on verifying permission for the truck to take its load with the night duty officer. He was satisfied by a telephone call: the Excelsior Waste Removal Company was a known independent contractor with the base, and the presence of its vehicle and employees were fully in order. Even when the sentry reported that it was not waste being put aboard the truck, but twenty cannisters of napalm, he was reassured by his superior that there was no irregularity. And there the matter was left. At this hour of the morning the private was not going to get his ass chewed for waking up the Pentagon to report that napalm was being driven out of Greenley by an independent contractor. Strange it might be, but the event was obviously endorsed by the brass. No doubt it was tied up with a covert operation, perhaps in concert with the intelligence divisions, DIA or CIA. Waste removal, the private mused, could easily be a euphemism for their kind of business.

After nine minutes after four, the truck stopped on the way out of the main gate to have its passes stamped in accordance with regulations. The gate sentries took their duplicates and waved the driver through without inspecting the cargo. The latter, in addition to the napalm, consisted of sixty-two thousand rounds of M-16 ammunition, several cases of anti-personnel multi-fragmenting phosphorous grenades, two 50mm machine guns, a variety of communications equipment, and four heat-seeking rocket launchers with ammunition for a total of twenty-six firings. The total cost in payment to those who had authorized the theft beforehand and would later alter or misplace warehousing records and lading bills in order to conceal the loss of this comparatively minor amount of materiel had been two hundred and ninety-five thousand dollars. Another bargain.

On Wednesday afternoon, Rocco Gesolo informed Bobby Lamartine, manager of the Floor Magic store, to post signs in the window advertising a special sale this evening.

"Make them real big signs," Rocco ordered, "and make sure it causes a stir. Call it something like . . . like a 'Midnight Madness Sale.' Sixty percent reductions on all business between seven P.M. and midnight closing time."

"Sixty percent, Roc? You're gonna lose a fucking bomb!"

"We'll make it up later. Just do it, Bobby!"

While many businesses in the shopping center stayed open late, the volume of costumers was often small, especially after nine o'clock. Rocco had wanted to be sure of having a crowd, and his Midnight Madness Sale did the trick. From six o'clock on the store was crammed with bargain hunters, and the parking area in front of the store was constantly full. Accordingly, no special notice was taken of the seventeen men who drove up between seven-thirty and eight o'clock, parked their expensive cars in the nearest available spaces, and made their way through the crowded store to the office at the rear.

At eight o'clock sharp the meeting was called to order by Steve Drapetto. He looked around at the assembled faces when the room was quiet.

"We're missing a couple," Drapetto observed, turning to Rocco. "Didn't you tell them no later than eight? We've got a lot to do."

247

Before Rocco could reply one of the other men spoke up. "Tedesco and Sanguinetti won't be coming. The Feebies picked them up this afternoon."

Drapetto nodded grimly. "Well, let's do our work well tonight, so we can stop this shit once and for all."

First on the agenda was Rocco's report on the equipment situation, concluding with an inventory of the goods collected at the Greenley Ordnance Depot which were now on their way to the Gloversville staging area. The applause and enthusiastic whoops of approval which greeted the news went unheard outside the office in the melee of yapping customers.

Then, to report on troop commitments, Drapetto called on those staff officers who had been acting as liaison to various families around the country, handling details of recruitment. No soldier was being asked to donate his services. The job was to be done, like any hit, on contract for a payment of twenty thousand dollars up front. Normally, each man would also have received guarantees of legal fees and family support in the event he suffered prosecution, injury or death as a result of his assignment. But in these hard times, if the mission to kill Vereste failed, such guarantees would be meaningless. Thus, to the degree that those who joined the task force were willing to accept less than the best terms—even the cash payment was not up to the standard of the best hit men, who might be paid up to forty thousand dollars for a night's work—they did evince a certain amount of esprit de corps. And when the recruitment reports were completed and the troop commitments tallied, it was an agreeable surprise to find that a total of eighty-nine men had enlisted in the attack.

"That's fine," Drapetto declared. "We'll manage easily with that number. Especially on the firepower we've got now."

To maximize the firepower, Drapetto had always intended to apply standard tactical procedure and divide the full force into smaller units which would converge on the target from different directions. Forming these separate squads, however, had to be done without the benefit of being able to rate individual aptitudes under simulated field conditions. This left only two rather imperfect criteria for choosing specialists and arranging the soldiers into distinct, balanced units. One was the gossip about the abilities of various individuals that could be contributed by the men present at this final strategy meeting—a reasonable body of knowledge, since the Organization's best gunmen floated around the country, doing jobs for many families other than their own. Secondly, Drapetto had asked his recruiting officers to take careful notes detailing the age, physical condition, special skills, and recent military service (if any) of each enlistee.

As these résumés were read aloud they revealed that a high percentage of the men were veterans of Vietnam. Few peacetime careers could satisfy the taste for violence which this war had cultivated in its participants, and thus many of those young veterans who had family affiliations with the Mafia had drifted easily into becoming its contract killers. They were a different breed from the older men who did the same job—more trigger-happy, more bloodthirsty, harder to control, some of them even on drugs. In fact, there had been a growing debate about the danger they posed to the brotherhood, which had strived too long for respectability to be pushed backward into primitive struggles by members who relished killing for its own sake. The trend had so alarmed some older bosses that they had recently begun importing obedient young Sicilians to hold the Americans in check, sometimes elevating these immigrants quickly to superior positions in the hierarchy. Until Vereste's defection had provided a focus against which these antagonistic factions could unite, the increasing friction between them had threatened to explode and possibly tear the Organization apart from the inside on a scale not seen since the thirties. The danger was now postponed, but it was clearly reflected in the troop résumés read out at the planning session. Among the eighty-nine soldiers, only eleven were of the older generation. The balance was divided between the immigrants, eager for the opportunity to distinguish themselves and earn rapid advancement, and the Viet vets, hungry for the action.

Weighing the need to eliminate any internal squabbling on the mission and yet to place authority in the hands of those with military training and recent experience in handling sophisticated weaponry, Drapetto, Gesolo, and their staff were a long time at the task of designating the separate squads. When the lists were finally set, two officers from the planning committee were assigned to each of the four squads; they would be responsible for contacting their men later tonight, instructing them on the rendezvous to be made on Friday evening.

Finally, Drapetto briefed the staff on the map work and timing governing the mission. Unfolding two large maps, he taped them to a wall; one showed the larger geographical features around the target area—now established as Lake Colden—and the other was a detailed ground plan of the compound. Both maps were marked according to the information which had been gathered by the reconnaissance over-flights and by the four boys who had hiked extensively around the perimeter of the compound.

Before the meeting broke up, telephone calls were received from the drivers of the equipment trucks reporting that they had reached their standby points, at motels near Gloversville. There was also a call from Silvio Urbani of Massachusetts, to say that he had filled Drapetto's request for fifteen surplus army trucks; these would be given fresh coats of khaki paint and driven through Thursday night to arrive at the staging area by mid-Friday. Gloversville had been selected for this purpose not only because it lay on a good secondary road that headed directly north into the heart of the Adirondacks but because there was an army installation near the town. Drapetto had decided, after all, that the Mafia task force would travel disguised as a military unit on maneuvers.

When the men emerged from the office into the Floor Magic showroom, the sale had just ended. The showroom was cleared of customers, sales staff, and stock. Bobby Lamartine caught Rocco by the arm. The pudgy store manager knew exactly what had been taking place in the rear office, but after spending six hours in the thick of crazed rug buyers, he was too dazed to think of anything but the sale. "Don't ever do that again," he said to Rocco, gesturing at the shambles around them. "We've never had anything like it in here. It was murder."

"You ain't the only one, Bobby," replied one of the planning committee as he left. "Our business was murder, too."

Lindy had been keeping to himself. He read in his room, walked alone within the perimeters of the compound, bolted

250

his meals with a minimum of conversation, and went to bed early. Once he had taken a sailing dinghy on the lake, but he rebelled at any pastime which perpetuated the absurd pretense that the place could be a pleasant resort. Others on the staff had begun to feel the same way; one man's solitary moodiness went unnoticed in the prevailing tension as they watched and waited for the expected assault. The only person who showed no symptom of nervousness was Bart Vereste, though his son came a close second.

For Lindy, the compound seemed now like an island bewitched, under a black spell that gave its inhabitants bizarre and ugly perspectives on morality, impossible to see from any other vantage point. Still, he could not bring himself to leave before the climax of the Mafia drive to find and punish Vereste. At moments, Lindy recognized within himself a perverse, vicious desire to see the effort succeed—for Vereste to be killed, his asylum destroyed. Amid all the damage to life and law, why should Vereste go unscathed? Why indeed should he profit, be pampered, entertained, enriched? Perhaps the irony would be tolerable, if Vereste had not reveled in it so blatantly. The bastard hadn't a trace of humility. He had played the drum to which they all marched, and now had begun to believe that he was above all men, almost superhuman. When he finally put down his drum, he would then be conveniently reincarnated, given a new identity, so that in effect he would become his own heir, benefiting from his own rich legacy. Vereste's new self, unlike his wife's, would probably endure. She had been undone by sentiment, a longing to reestablish old sources of love, but he could probably live without such sustenance.

On Thursday afternoon Lindy, dozing on the dock in the sun after a long exhausting swim in the icy lake, was startled by quick, heavy footsteps. Raising his head, he saw Gabe Konecki coming toward him. They had barely spoken since Lindy had admitted failure in gaining any concessions from Vereste.

"Tomorrow," Konecki said when he was standing over Lindy."We're being hit tomorrow. I thought you'd like to know."

It took a moment for the significance of Konecki's prediction to sink in. Then Lindy asked, "And how the hell do you know—in advance?"

Konecki smiled, satisfied by having drawn Lindy back into the game. He reached into the breast pocket of his denim shirt, brought out a folded slip of yellow paper and handed it down. Taking it, Lindy saw that it was the carbon tear sheet from a teleprinter.

Konecki sat down as Lindy read the message:

28/5 1:32 PM BU D.C. HQ SPECIAL TO SWEETHEART—URGENT

N.Y. OFFC REPORTS ANONYMOUS PHN CONTACT CLAIMING C.N. AFFILIATION. N.B. SOURCE INSIDE—WARNS AGGRESSIVE ACTION COUNTER SWEETHEART COMMENCING FRIDAY NIGHT—N.B. FRIDAY 29/5—OPPOSITION STRENGTH REPORTED EIGHT-NINE MEN, HEAVILY ARMED, PLUS AIR SALIENT.

REPEAT SOURCE ANONYMOUS. REQUEST FOR ID REFUSED AT CONTACT. NO GUARANTEE A.D. GOLDEN BUT ADVISE FULL ALERT.—PHONE INIT. 2:30 PM BUREAU DIRECTOR FOR FURTHER DETAILS. PLEASE ACKNOWLEDGE AND STAND BY------------ OPR J.D.B.

Lindy looked up in mute astonishment.

"That was only the beginning," Konecki resumed. "When the tip came in everyone in Washington was out to lunch. The operator sent this message on his own initiative. Since then the brass has been rounded up and I've been on the phone getting details. Quite a few little zingers. Describing these boys as heavily armed is the understatement of the year. Among other things they've got their hands on there's some napalm and a few Bird Dogs to send against us."

"Bird Dogs?"

"Heat-seeking rockets, the latest model. They're fired from a hand-held launcher about as easy to use as a water pistol, and they're equally effective air-to-ground or overland."

"Holy shit! Where do they get stuff like that?"

"Buy it, steal it. Who the hell knows? How does any terror-

252

ist fill his stocking? If Al Fatah can do it and then get received at the UN, I guess the Mob sees no reason not to update their arsenal. Let's just be damn glad we know what we're up against."

"Christ, yes," Lindy seconded. "It's a godsend. But why? Assuming it's a genuine tip, what's the motive?"

"We figure the source is pretty well placed—from the sound of it, he might even be in on the planning phase of the operation—and he's afraid of coming up soon on Vereste's list. By helping us, he can ask for better terms if he's ever pulled in."

"But he didn't give you his name."

"He doesn't have to," Konecki remarked. "He's the only one who'll know we had this tip. If it ever comes to the crunch, then the fink will take credit. Nobody else would."

Lindy thought. "Couldn't it be a fake? You know, phony intelligence to give their surveillance a chance to check your responses? They cry wolf, then let you sit until your guard is down, and hit you later."

Konecki shook his head. "I don't think they'd be so cute. This is the Mob, Lindy, not the Allied Forces landing at Omaha Beach."

Lindy continued to puzzle over the development. "I can't read it the way you do, Gabe. Maybe it is a real tip, but there's still something weird about it. You say the source must've been motivated by fear, that he was looking to put some favors in the bank. But without this advance information, could you have prepared for an attack on this caliber? You stood to be on the losing end; Vereste would've been buried. And a man who helped plan the operation would have realized that sooner than anyone. So why should he be afraid?"

Konecki shrugged tentatively. "He couldn't count on a sure thing, he was hedging his bets."

"He's doing more than that," Lindy insisted, "much more. He's helping set up his own side for an ambush—helping you keep Vereste alive. Isn't he? And asking nothing in exchange. That just doesn't make sense."

Konecki stood up. "Whether we can read the motive or not, pal, the rule of thumb is never look a gift hood in the mouth. The Bureau judges the tip to be the real thing, and they actually spoke to the man. So we'll act on the basis of what he's told us."

"Well, thank God for that," Lindy sighed. "Where will you move him?"

Konecki blinked, uncomprehending. "Move who?"

Lindy stood slowly and examined Konecki, saw that the big marshal was practically vibrating with excited anticipation. "You still intend to keep him here—to deliberately invite this kind of blitz? My God, where do you draw the line?"

"At the point where we can't handle it," Konecki replied. "But we're on top of this. When Snoot goes out on today's mail run, he's really sneaking over to the nearest Air Force base; there's one right outside Plattsburg. We're getting some anti-aircraft missiles of our own along with a few experts to work them. We'll also have 'black boxes'—electronic jazz that can screw up incoming shots. For ground defense, we'll have National Guard."

"And that's all you think I'm worried about," Lindy said tightly, "holding them off?"

"It's all you should be worried about!" Konecki shouted. Then he went on, quietly, restraining himself. "Listen, Lindy, if we run away, put Vereste in another hole, do you think they'll stop tracking him? Sooner or later, one way or another, they'll make a battleground. It's better to finish it here, now. We don't want rockets falling on the steps of a federal courthouse."

"Bullshit," Lindy proclaimed hotly, "that's your excuse. You can't care what happens outside the courthouse without caring about what goes on inside. And you don't. You're more interested in trial by the gun, the big showdown. That's why you're making the stand here, isn't it, marshal? This is your chance to relive the good old days; it's the O.K. Corral all over again. The only difference is you don't play anymore with six-shooters. Now it's napalm and Bird Dogs and black boxes."

"We are back on the frontier," Konecki answered steadily. "Face it, Lindy. The bad men have taken over the town and this is the only way to clean them out. When they're gone, then we can pass through this territory and head back to what some people call civilization."

254

They were distracted suddenly by the drilling scream of the helicopter starting up, the rotor revving faster. The machine rose into the air and its shadow passed over the dock as it wheeled around above the lake and vanished behind a mountain.

"Off to civilization," Lindy muttered, watching it go. He lowered his eyes then and realized he was talking to himself. Konecki was walking up the hill toward the lodge, on his way, no doubt, to tell Vereste the good news.

NINETEEN

Shortly after sunrise on Friday morning the early phase of Plan Valentine, the coordinated defense of target Sweetheart, went into effect. Units of the National Guard from four localities at different compass points around the Adirondack region, a total of seven hundred and forty men, were dispatched by truck convoy toward the target area. As it was not known from which direction the attack would come, all sides were being separately covered by forces outnumbering the forecast total of Mafia invaders. By ten o'clock in the morning all Guard units were in place, within a half hour's drive of the junction between highways and trails leading into the target. For the rest of the day, they were to bivouac in the concealment of thick forest awaiting further orders. Their company commanders remained in constant radio contact with Sweetheart.

At the safe house, the Igloo White system was monitored with special vigilance. While it was anticipated that the Mafia would not move into the area until after dark, there were other reasons for concern about movements within the defense perimeter. Innocent campers had to be cleared out before any hostile action erupted; if any such people were unwittingly enmeshed in the fighting and suffered injury or death, this would compromise the government's intention to keep the operation a secret after it had been carried out. During the day the electronic screen registered the passage of several hikers and the arrival of two parties who planned to establish overnight camps. The latter were approached by a "ranger" before they could hammer in their first tent peg and advised to seek another, safer campsite. A family of bears was roaming this area, they were warned; only last night they had entered a campsite and savaged a woman and child to death. The story invariably sent the campers hurrying off to pitch their tents many miles away.

When darkness came down, the battleground was empty, ready, and waiting.

Rocco Gesolo and Steve Drapetto traveled upstate together, riding comfortably in the backseat of a limousine while Rocco's bodyguard Johnny Baldone, handled the wheel. Their destination was the Sunnyview Motel outside Gloversville, which Chat Valvitani had booked for the night to serve as the forward command post. Other motels and cabin colonies in the vicinity had been taken over for the use of the enforcers who would be arriving throughout the day.

The drive from New York City took almost six hours, but Gesolo and Drapetto passed the time easily, making last-minute battle plans and then gossiping about the changes in the Organization brought about by Bart Vereste. Passing through Saratoga, where they had enjoyed many lively excursions in the past, the two men turned to nostalgic reminiscence of the fifties and sixties, when they were young and had begun their climb through the ranks of the Honored Society. A golden time, when they had lived in a separate world sufficient to itself, going its way without any interference from the outside. The early seventies had been good, too, they recalled; the country had been so steeped in corruption that the dons were able to rub elbows with political leaders and heads of government agencies, all members of the same club, each one taking his own piece of the pie. Could the future be as lush as the past? Even when Vereste was dead, there would be many problems to solve. Warring factions would have to be brought under control and culled out; the old men who had clung to power too long would have to be retired. Looking forward to the task of rebuilding and reorganizing, the two dons could admit that even before Vereste challenged the survival of their order, it had needed to be realigned with modern realities. The defector had been a symptom as much as a cause.

At a few minutes before seven P.M. the limousine arrived at the Sunnyview Motel. The car drove past the reception office

257

without stopping and without the manager's coming out to inquire about its new guests. In arranging the accommodations, Valvitani's lieutenants had prospected the rural community to find the seedier places off the main roads, owned or managed by people who would happily accept a thousand dollars in return for being uninquisitive.

When Gesolo and Drapetto entered cabin five of the motel, the air was already thick with cigarette smoke. Prior arrivals included the officers who would be commanding the attack squads, a fat sweaty man named "Boney" Grandevita, who was an expert at setting up betting wires and had been brought in tonight to oversee communications, and Ottavio Stirelli, representing Dom Francini, who had remained comfortably at home. Absent though he was, Francini was still the man ultimately responsible for the operation. He had traced Vereste; and when the rat was dead, he would get the lion's share of the credit.

The mirrored dressing table of the cabin's bedroom was serving as the communications center; on its walnut-grain formica top sat a compact transceiver designed to be used in tandem with the pocket field radios which had been part of the Greenley haul. At the controls of the instrument was a longhaired youth with a Zapata moustache, dressed in chino pants and a tee shirt with a faded pop design. Presently he was engaged in testing the equipment, tuning into messages of no consequence which were being transmitted from other motel "barracks," or sending out requests for these test transmissions.

Eyeing the radio operator, Drapetto pulled Boney Grandevita into a corner. "Where'd you get him?"

Grandevita knew what was bothering Drapetto. Longhaired kids weren't favorite choices for anything but trigger jobs.

"Don't worry, Steve. You know Maury Aiello, the guy who does all the bug work. This is his son. Learned his stuff in Vietnam."

"He's not a hophead, is he? We can't have a hophead in here. There's too much riding—"

"The kid's cool, Steve. But even if he wasn't, we'd be lucky to have him. That radio is fancy gear, something new; Billy's the only guy I could come up with who could sit right down and make it hum."

Drapetto went over to Billy Aiello and introduced himself. Then, taking the measure of his experience, Drapetto asked:

"Aren't you running an unnecessary risk, doing so much testing? The cops might pick up our traffic."

"No chance, man," Aiello replied. "This is fantastic stuff you've got. It broadcasts way over the top of any regular police frequency, right at the ultrasonic border. Even if the cops did tune up that high, without a converter all they'd catch when we talk is a high-pitched whistle."

Gesolo moved over from a conversation with Stirelli. "Hey, what was that about the cops?"

Drapetto repeated what he had just been told about the radio. Rocco's concern outwardly disappeared and he returned to his other conversation.

The room continued to bustle with radio tests, comings and goings of visitors from other barracks, and dozens of telephone calls. Grandevita knew how to tap directly into the telephone company's overhead lines to provide supplementary service on any number of extra phones. Of course, if operated over the long term, the dodge would eventually be traced. But it was safe for periods up to several weeks. Tonight, as many times before, the Organization was able to operate its additional wires on equipment acquired through contacts at phone manufacturing plants; twenty-eight extra lines were working out of the command center, free of charge. There were calls to and from Dom Francini, to satisfy his appetite for up-to-the-minute reports; to and from bosses in distant cities, desperate for assurances that the operation was proceeding smoothly; and from late-arriving enforcers as they checked into their motels. The two Cuban helicopter pilots also checked in regularly from a phone in the hangar of the small airfield nearby where their machines were parked. And calls went out to the drivers of the truck transports, who were standing by in the garage of a large supermarket which belonged to an upstate chain controlled by the Valvitani family.

By eight o'clock, the boisterous jangle began to subside. Only one hour remained before the wheels began to roll. In cabin five of the Sunnyview Motel, the phones were turned off while Drapetto talked over the timetable once more with his field officers.

At nine o'clock the troops were given their first general order: to proceed by car in groups of five and six to the supermarket garage. There, they changed into uniforms and were issued weapons and ammunition. Other field aids—compasses, radios, night-vision scopes—were parceled out among those who had experience in using them.

At ten o'clock the truck convoy left the supermarket garage for the drive north. At the same time, two rocket crews went by car to rendezvous with the helicopters.

Within the first half hour of its journey, the convoy was spotted by a pair of state policemen cruising on night patrol. Ordinarily the police would have drawn their own conclusions about the military traffic: there were several bases in the northern section of the state and troops were frequently shuttled around on light training maneuvers. But tonight the patrolmen did not have to guess about the convoy. Earlier in the day all state and municipal police functioning within the Adirondack region had been notified of special maneuvers the governor had authorized for the National Guard. Hours ago, the patrolmen knew, four units of the Guard had been on the roads; the line of trucks they saw now was obviously a late supplement to the same exercise.

At eleven-thirty the trucks came to a junction, where they divided into four separate groups. Each group would follow a different route, transporting one squad of men to one of four trailheads. The attack force would thus converge on the house from all directions, one of the four squads being emplaced on the far shore of the lake, so that all escape would be blocked even if there were an attempt to move Vereste by boat.

At one forty-two a transmission was received at the command center from the last squad to reach its assigned trailhead. Billy Aiello called Steve Drapetto to the radio.

The Squad's leader, Joe "Santa" Santucci, a *sottocapo* from Los Angeles, sounded irritable as he spoke to Drapetto.

"It's goddamn dark out here, Steve, and all the men are frozen stiff. How long have we got to make this walk?"

Drapetto was not surprised that some of the earlier high spirits of the men had evaporated. At last they were coming to grips with the reality of their task. For three and a half hours they had been riding on hard seats while the cold night air whipped through the canvas-covered trucks. Real army conditions. Many of the men had faced them before, but they had never been asked to do nearly so much on a Mob contract.

"You've got four hours to make it to the target," Drapetto replied sharply. "You could walk on your hands and there'd still be time to spare. You've only got six miles to cover, and some of the other guys have ten."

"Six miles," Santa moaned. "I don't think I've ever been on a hit before where I walked more than twenty paces."

"Stop bitching and start walking," Drapetto ordered. "I want you all in position to blast by five-thirty. We're timing the choppers to fly over then, so don't be late."

"Okay, okay. We're on the way."

"Better check with the other three squads," Drapetto said to Billy Aiello after the contact with Santa. "Let's be sure they're making progress. The way these guys are complaining you'd think we asked them to cross the desert without water."

The checks established that all groups were moving up, though the advance was slow. Even with infrared scopes the darkness was causing problems. One soldier had tripped over a stone and twisted his ankle; unable to continue, he had been left to crawl back to the trucks by himself. The muddy mountain trails were chilling the feet of even the best marchers, since few of the men had thought to wear boots and had come in their everyday street shoes.

"We've got some guys muttering about turning back," one squad leader told Drapetto. "Maybe I should let them go. We don't want to start shooting at each other before we get to the target."

"Listen," Drapetto warned harshly, "you tell those cream puffs anyone who turns back now gets taken out. One between the eyes, personal from me!"

Just like the real goddamn army, Drapetto reflected afterward, the same fucking discipline problems.

Glancing around the room as he moved away from the radio, Drapetto saw that only Grandevita, Stirelli, and the two bodyguards who had arrived with himself and Gesolo were present.

"Where'd Rocco go?" he asked.

Stirelli answered. "Went out to see if he could find a road house still open, to buy himself a drink. Said he was gettin' closet-phobia or something, from being cooped up."

Drapetto looked questioningly at Johnny Baldone, Rocco's bodyguard. It was uncommon for a don to travel in strange territory at night without a man to back him up.

"He's calling home," Baldone explained. "You know how he worries about his old lady and the girl. Especially the girl. Always checks in, wherever he is."

"Whatsa matter," Grandevita cracked, waving at the phones sitting atop every surface in the room, "he had some trouble finding a place in here to make his call?"

"He never likes anyone around when he talks to them," Baldone said. "I guess he's embarrassed, being so hung up on them." There was a silence, then Baldone voiced the thought running through all their minds. "Well, shit, if he hadn't been, we wouldn't be here tonight, right? All he had to do was let his precious goddamn daughter fuck Vereste, and the son of a bitch would never have sold us out."

A semi-blackout was in force at the compound, giving the appearance that all but a skeleton force of regular sentries had retired for the night. But not a single person slept. Even Vereste and his son were staying up, though there was no sign of a crack in their bravado. In the company of two marshals, they were playing chess beside a warming fire in the lodge.

In every other quarter of the safe house, behind windows blanketed to darken them to the outside world, the separate components of the defense network were being keenly monitored. The two army technicians who had been shuttled in with the ECM black boxes—electronic counter-measures— were isolated in the boathouse, where their sensitive equipment would not interfere with other electronic systems. The speedboat with a front-mounted machine gun, which until now had been kept inside the boathouse, was moored at the center of the lake, ready to roar quickly to any point along the shore. Aboard, boosting its already considerable firepower, was one of the Bird Dog crews that had flown in with Snoot. Two other rocket launchers were positioned within the compound.

Lindy was keeping the vigil in the electronics shed, along with Konecki, Dyskowicz, Harpe, and two army men—a radio officer named Sutter and a leathery-faced specialist in antiguerrilla tactics, Brigadier General Oscar Hagen—who were assisting in liaison with the National Guard. Only occasional snatches of conversation broke the long silences while the men stared at the Igloo White screen, mesmerized by the thousands of green lights, heat sensors that, as yet, registered no enemy presence inside the three-mile radius.

At seven minutes past two A.M., they were jarred out of their trancelike concentration by the ringing of a red telephone, the direct line to Bureau headquarters in Washington. Konecki answered in hushed tones, as though the vigil was a ritual he was loathe to disturb:

"Yeah, speaking . . . No, nothing yet." Then suddenly he cried out excitedly. "No shit! When?" Ear to the receiver, he relayed the cause of his outburst to the other men in a muttered aside: "The Bureau just had another tip. From the same guy. . . ."

Konecki went on nodding and muttering as new details were fed to him. "Yeah . . . yeah . . . got it . . . check. Anything else?" He was about to hang up when he snapped out another question. "Hey, did your source ask for credit yet?"

As he cradled the receiver, Konecki looked across at Lindy, who had been following the conversation intently, and gave him a puzzled shrug. Then he spun toward the army radio man.

"Sutter, get all Guard commanders on the horn. Pronto."

"Anything I can help with?" Hagen put in pointedly, piqued at having his authority bypassed.

"Thanks, but I'll handle it," Konecki replied flatly.

In seconds Sutter had the Guard officers standing by. Konecki grabbed up the microphone:

"Listen carefully, please. This concerns every one of you. The opposition are now known to be heading into the area from four directions, though they have not yet penetrated near our perimeter. Note the following trail sources and proceed immediately to the one in your sector. We will use all four units to pursue." Consulting a map, Konecki then read off coordinates and road directions which would take the Guard units to the necessary trailheads. He continued, "There is one more piece of information which must be communicated without fail to every man in your command. Our informer tells us that the enemy are wearing regulation army battle dress and could easily be mistaken for friendlies. You must take measures to eliminate this confusion. Please acknowledge message received and understood."

A babble of consternation came through the radio as soon as Sutter switched to listening mode. At last one voice took precedence.

"Marshal Konecki, this is Captain Boseen, thirty-first NG, Utica. Let's be sure we've got this straight. You say the enemy is dressed so we can't tell their men apart from ours?"

"That's the situation, captain."

"Then we can assume they know there's real army on the scene; they're disguised for infiltration."

"I don't think so, captain. It's more of a coincidence. Our information is that they posed as army so the police wouldn't question their road movements. The important thing now is that something is done to make the distinction."

"Well, what the hell you suggest, marshal? Go home and get into our tuxedos, or just strip down to our birthday suits?"

"Improvise, captain," Konecki said impatiently. "Put a handkerchief around your arm, pull your pecker out and tie a yellow ribbon on it. I don't give a shit what you do, but fix it so you don't shoot each other up while the gorillas get in here and kill the rest of us."

"Aye, aye, sir," said the captain.

"Marshal," another voice came on, "this is Colonel Perkins, Schenectedy Guard. What are your orders for pursuit? You want us to overtake and shoot on sight? Or should we track at arm's length until further orders."

"Stalk them at a distance, colonel. We've also been told that two choppers will be coming over. But they won't take off until the ground troops are closer in; their attack is supposed to coincide. If we give ourselves away too soon, the helicopters might turn back, or even stay on the ground; and we'd never find them. Let's try and bag everyone at once."

"Roger," said the colonel. "We'll track on tiptoe until you give us the word."

The other commanders signed off after confirming their understanding of the procedure.

"You're goddamn lucky to have that informer, marshal," General Hagen observed as Konecki returned to his chair before the sensor screen. "Without him you might have been in big trouble. And you say he's anonymous?"

"That's right, general. We don't know who he is; we don't know what he wants."

Hagen shook his head. "Sounds too good to be true." Hagen opened his mouth as if to add something, but then he shrugged and leaned back in his chair. No one was asking for his opinion; these smart-ass civilians could paint themselves right into a corner if that was what they wanted.

Silence descended over the shed again.

The question plagued Lindy: why had there been a convenient tip-off of such vital assistance to the authorities right before the attack? Could it be to settle some internal vendetta? What grievance could there be against all those whose one common goal, at the moment, was to save the Organization, in which, seemingly, the informer held some power?

Or was it more elementary: someone wanted to insure the survival of Bart Vereste. One top Mafioso was rooting for the Organization's most treacherous defector, wanted him to succeed. Perhaps they were partners. Vereste had insured himself against the Mob's tracking him down, had teamed up with someone who would stay inside, play guardian angel if the need ever arose.

But Vereste had been found on a fluke, a thousand-to-one shot. Would he have shared the rich proceeds of his squeal simply to guard against the remote outside chance of being traced?

Why else would he need a partner?

A cry from Dyskowicz brought Lindy out of his introspection:

"There it is! Three miles out on the eastern flank."

At the right of the screen an indicator light had turned red. Every man sat forward on the edge of his chair.

It was 4:06 A.M.

Now a series of indicator lights changed from green to red, tracing the progress of a column of intruders toward the blue light at the center of the screen representing the safe house. As the march moved on past the sensors, the indicator lights on the board would change back to green.

Dyskowicz pushed a button and instantly several lines of data were flashed onto a small cathode screen set into his console. He read out the figures. "If they keep up their present pace, the East Side Boys should be at our gates by five-eleven. The column is estimated to consist of between twenty-seven and twenty-nine men. The sensor also picked up a high-frequency signal of some kind."

"Must be a radio," Sutter contributed.

"Twiddle the dials again, Sutter," Konecki directed. "See if we can catch their transmission." They had tried several times already without success.

Sutter tuned through the full range of frequencies again, then shook his head. "Sorry, sir. Not a thing. Unless they're sending on a cuss-box."

"What's that?" Lindy asked.

Hagen answered sharply. "CUSS is short for converted ultrasonic system. If the Mafia was able to get its hands on that, gentlemen, I can tell you there will be serious repercussions within the army. The equipment is still classified and in very limited supply."

"For a radio," Lindy muttered disgustedly, "there'll be repercussions. Doesn't it worry you that the Mob also armed itself with heat-seeking rockets?"

"Those," Hagen said, absolutely deadpan, "they could've got from the Russians."

The discussion had momentarily distracted the men from the sensor screen. When they looked up again, two more columns were showing in the western and southern quadrants.

266

"Looks like they're putting in some guns on the far side of the lake," Konecki commented. He picked up a walkie-talkie and alerted the crew in the speedboat.

Ten minutes later, along the same path of lights that had shown the enemy's eastern salient, the sensors registered a second sequence of identical changes showing the movement of the tracking National Guard unit. Soon the same thing happened behind the second and third enemy columns.

It was four forty-two when the first red lights appeared in the northern quadrant. As the fourth enemy column advanced toward the safe house it was computed to consist of only fourteen men and, perhaps as a result of its size, to be moving faster. By five thirty-eight all attack forces were expected to be at the edge of the compound.

At five-sixteen a telephone rang—not the Bureau line this time, but a green phone which had been reserved for contact with an Air Force radar tracking station.

Konecki answered.

"Christ, it's about time," he said after listening a moment. The other men understood that there had been a radar sighting of the air approach to the target. But they were shaken out of any sanguine assumption that the situation was under control by a sudden burst of furious shouts from Konecki:

"He said *what?* . . . Then, by God, do it! . . . I don't care how high you have to go; you get that authorization. . . . Maybe not, but if you don't we will; that mother has got to be shot down if he gets anywhere near us."

Konecki banged down the phone and gazed with evident stupefaction at the other men as he related the news. "They've spotted two craft heading this way. First thing they did was send out a radio request for ID. Made it through Civil Aeronautics, so the pilots would take it for a standard check: air control routinely ask for ID on aircraft that haven't filed a flight plan. On the first try they got no reply. So the request went out again. The second time they raised an answer from both pilots. Some answer! The creeps read out their registration numbers, and then they said their flight was connected with secret government business. Can you imagine that? Secret government—"

"But who's gonna believe that bullshit?" Dyskowicz said.

"Wait till you hear the rest," Konecki went on. "Air Force did a quick check on the registrations through central records. The numbers belong to an air-taxi firm based in Florida, and they have special coded prefixes giving them clearance to travel without filing flight plans. Our friends at the local AF base say they've seen similar qualifications before, on Agency covers."

"Agency?" said General Hagen, an awed murmur. "You mean *the* Agency?"

Konecki nodded. "How's that for a can of worms? The air base has sent up two jets for an eye-check. Originally they were supposed to handle the choppers for us, force them down, shoot them down if necessary. But if they authenticate those numbers by sight, we won't get that help. The military know the shit's going to fly over this thing, one way or another, and they don't want any sticking to them."

"But the Agency couldn't have authorized the use of those choppers," Lindy argued. "They must be stolen, like the rest of the stuff. Or the pilots are moonlighting."

"Probably," Konecki agreed. "But these days no one would bet on it. Which leaves us with those two machines coming in to bomb us in twenty minutes—not enough time to get official permission to shoot. Even if the right people could be found in their own beds at this time of night, there wouldn't be any snap decisions. Another Agency abuse to account for. They'll all be going crazy." Konecki pondered a moment. "Well, if it's got to be hushed up, I guess there is no better way than to bring them down right here, try and sink them in the lake."

Grabbing up the walkie-talkie, Konecki warned the rocket crews and the black-box specialists that they were definitely going to deal with an attack from the air. Then he barked at Sutter:

"Contact all NG units."

While Sutter called them, Konecki glanced over the sensor screen. The first of the enemy columns was just moving into position at the edge of the compound. The others were only minutes behind. When the choppers came over all hell would break loose.

Sutter held up the microphone. "Waiting for you, sir."

Konecki snatched the mike. "Boseen, Perkins, all of you, close the gap on the double. Get right on the enemy's tail, but don't let them know you're there. The second you get the order to fire, you've got to be in position to stop them from lobbing anything in here."

The instructions were acknowledged. One Guard commander added a question:

"Boseen, marshal. The way I reckon our present position relative to the enemy, they're already sitting right on your fences. Seems to me you're cutting it a bit too fine if you leave it any longer before we take preventives."

"Not much longer, captain. But we want everything and everyone in our sights before we open up. Now close in tight and stand by." Konecki crossed back to the green phone, barking into the walkie-talkie as he moved. "Finch, you read me?"

"Ho, Gabe," came the reply. Finch was one of the two marshals in the lodge guarding Vereste.

"How's everything up there?"

"The subject is in trouble. His son's about to checkmate him for the seventh time tonight."

"We're all in danger of being outplayed, I'm afraid. Move the Verestes down to the boathouse. The ECM gear is in there, so that's the last place that ought to be bombed. Whatever happens we want to keep our witness healthy."

"Roger."

Konecki was dialing the radar tracking station even before Finch signed off. "AF, this is Sweetheart. How far off is trouble? . . . And they're authenticated? . . . Sure, we understand. We'll handle it. But let's keep this line open. We want constant readings on their position." Konecki turned to Hagen. "General, what's the range on those rockets?"

"Dead on at anything up to a thousand yards."

"And how safe are we with the black boxes?"

"They'll cause considerable deflection, move the incomings off target. But of course they can't make a rocket do a U-turn."

"Then we're not under an umbrella? The enemy could miss what they're aiming for and still hit something else in the compound?"

Hagen nodded.

Konecki handed him the phone. "This is open to radar. They'll give you the chopper positions. Two minutes before they're in range, you start calling out a countdown."

Hagen took the phone.

"We're three for four now," Dyskowicz announced.

Konecki swiveled around to face the Igloo White screen. Three of the four Mafia columns were on the line marking the inside perimeter. The gap between them and the second sequence of lights showing the Guard positions was visibly narrowing.

The marshal drew a deep breath and sat down. There was nothing to do now but wait.

In the tense silence, the riddle rose again into Lindy's thoughts. What common interest did Vereste share with someone still inside the Mafia? Didn't Vereste want to destroy them, all of them?

All of them?

Suddenly the vague suspicion began to take on sharper outlines. A theory formed, a notion that conveniently explained everything that had happened, and was happening. Was it a delusion? Concentrating on a simple idea, like looking into a bright light, could be blinding rather than illuminating, inspiring imaginery patterns to float across the mind's eye.

"The fourth enemy column is on the fence," Dyskowicz announced. "We're boxed in."

There was hardly a pause before Hagen added, "We have a two-minute countdown to range." Holding the phone with one hand, he unclipped a walkie-talkie from his belt with the other. "Hagen to ECM, we have aircraft at range plus ninety seconds . . . approaching from southwest sixty-nine degrees. Begin scan sixty-five to seventy-five."

Lindy pulled himself to his feet and started toward the door.

"Where are you going?" Konecki snapped. "All hell's about to break loose out there!"

Lindy ignored the warning and stepped out of the shed. He didn't want to hear the execution order given; it felt too much like being a willing accomplice to murder. He heard Konecki call after him. Then Hagen saying:

"One minute to range."

Across the compound, Lindy could dimly make out the boathouse. He could imagine Vereste now, laughing to himself. A Caesar on the brink of empire. Lindy took a step forward. Would there be a better moment to confront Vereste, question his motives? If the battle got hot enough, he might get rattled, admit the secret he had kept to himself on quieter days.

"Thirty seconds," came Hagen's voice from inside the shed. And he went on ticking off the remaining seconds, one by one.

Lindy turned to scan the sky in the southwest. The helicopters were going to come in over the lake, and try to put their rockets right through the front door. He saw nothing there but a few clouds, faint elephantine shapes silhouetted by a quarter-moon.

But he could hear them.

And then they appeared, banking around the side of a mountain on the far side of the lake.

Hagen was screaming. "Range . . . range. . . ."

Lindy saw a trail of fire in the sky like a tiny meteor. Then a second. They bore in toward the compound, one aiming for the lodge, the other at the staff sleeping annex. But their swift, straight trajectory was suddenly afflicted with a kink, and the rockets went corkscrewing off to one side, both plowing into open ground. They detonated in whooshes of yellow flame that rolled upward and disappeared into the air like a magician's billowing handkerchiefs.

The incoming salvo was answered immediately from the ground. From two separate points in the compound the comet trails rose; another went up from the center of the lake. Two seconds later, they hit their targets in the sky over the water. The helicopters burst into oval suns, throwing out burning fuel and exploding ammunition like solar flares. Then they feathered down into the lake. Bubbling, sizzling noises came from the hot scraps of metal as they met the water and sank.

On all sides now there was shooting, filling the forest like the sound of thousands of branches splintering off the trees. From across the lake came the rumble of the speedboat motor and the chatter of machine-gun fire.

It went on and on.

271

To save Vereste.

At last it was over. An ominous, leaden silence came down, the silence of death.

Then voices began to call faintly somewhere deep in the surrounding woods. Across the compound, lights went on in the lodge. The blackout was over.

Konecki would say they had won, Lindy thought, and there was nothing to prove otherwise.

TWENTY

Lindy woke and peered at the travel clock beside his bed. It was just after noon. When the shooting was over he had retreated into sleep. He had not wanted to watch the cleanup operation that he knew must follow the uncompromising annihilation that had taken place.

But it haunted him anyway. Throughout the hours after dawn the sounds of constant activity in the compound penetrated to his room, intermittently dragging him into a half-conscious awareness where fact and nightmare merged. He heard helicopters flying in, taking off, removing the dead—and the living prisoners, if there were any. Before the sun rose too high, the battleground was to be cleared, the appearance of verdant wilderness restored for the nature lovers who would trek through.

As Lindy lay awake, the theory he had begun to develop last night—that Vereste was cooperating with someone inside the Mafia, working in tandem for something more than money, more than revenge—came back to him. Delusion or deduction? In the absence of any proof, he had not confronted Vereste with it, after all. Mere accusations would be meaningless. Lindy had only to remember his experiences with Vereste before the Ryle committee to know that this cool, unflappable adversary could not be rattled by interrogation. Under the pressure before last night's attack, there had been a chance he would crack. But that chance was gone. How then could his true ambitions be unveiled? Could there ever be any proof? Especially when Lindy's notion was founded not so much in fact as in the intuition that he understood Vereste as no one else did. Perhaps his bitterness over his own failed ideals gave him a greater insight into Vereste's charac-

273

ter, the direction Vereste had taken, and the man he might have become if fate had not begun twisting his soul twenty years ago.

But intuition alone would mean nothing to Konecki, who had to be told precisely how he had been used.

Then Lindy thought of Vereste's accomplices. One was anonymous and out of reach. A second was Vereste's son, who—probably unaware of the full extent of his father's design—had dutifully supplied his expertise without demanding explanations, because like his sister he wanted out.

But there was a third accomplice, easily accessible and in possession of all the answers. And, Lindy thought, if he could only frame the right questions, the answers could not be withheld.

He dressed hurriedly and left the lodge. The compound looked deserted under the bright midday glare. Most of the men, Lindy realized, must be catching up on their sleep. He hoped someone would be in the electronics cabin.

Fortunately, Harpe was on duty. He sat at the console of the data-link to the central FBI computer, staring at its small screen. Then he became aware of Lindy's footsteps on the cabin's wooden floor and glanced up.

"Morning," said the lean, bookish computer operator.

"It's afternoon." Lindy saw now that Harpe, bleary-eyed and unshaven, had evidently not been relieved since last night. "I'd like to ask that computer a few questions," Lindy said. "Could you work the punch keys for me?"

"Have you cleared it with Gabe?"

"No. I didn't want to bother him on this, not yet. It's just a hunch I'd like to follow through."

"What's it about?"

"Vereste's information. I want to analyze it a little, break it down."

"How do you mean?" Harpe said. "You know these machines are temperamental. You can't just say sing me a song, you have to say what kind of music you want to hear. They don't perform if you've only got a general idea. To do an analysis, you've got to know what you're trying to learn from it, formulate an approach."

Lindy hesitated. He knew what he wanted to dig out. But to impart the full substance of his suspicion, he felt, would be a mistake. At best, it would be rejected as nonsensical, a waste of time. At worst, it would be resented.

"Suppose we start from this angle," Lindy suggested, "run a list of all the men Vereste has tagged for us, see if there's a common denominator."

Harpe laughed. "Well, sure there is. They're all in the Mafia."

Lindy kept it serious. "Something more than that. I assume the Bureau has an in-depth profile of every active top Mafioso in its data bank. Couldn't we compare them?"

Harpe pondered, then translated into the machine's terms. "You want something like a computer profile of Vereste's average victim—if there is such a thing."

"And of the survivors. Cross off the ones Vereste has given us from the total list, and we can also get a picture of how much of the Organization is left."

"I'm still not quite sure what you're aiming for," Harpe said, "but I'll see if I can help. You'll have to wait, though, till I finish running these programs."

Lindy had noticed the lines of names and figures rolling across the screen. He had surmised they were checks on the men who had been involved in the Mafia's attack last night, who had now been identified. But Harpe said he was running programs. That classification had been mentioned in only one context at the safe house.

"What are they?" Lindy asked quickly.

"The last four."

"You mean Vereste's—"

"Yup. He sort of cracked up when the fireworks were over. I guess he never imagined the Mob would be able to mount that kind of offensive. It must've scared him, and he didn't want to leave himself open to it happening again. Begged Gabe to fly him out of here today, find him a new nest. And he gave us the rest of the codes to milk the computer, no money down. This is the seventh and last program going through now. Ought to be finished any minute."

The bastard. He had believed that there would be no more money coming through, had been ready to give up the information. But not to save any lives. He had waited until the men who came gunning for him were destroyed.

It tied right in.

And Vereste would be flown out to another safe asylum. Today! Lindy recalled the appearance of the compound, how deserted it seemed this morning, and remembered the roar of helicopters rupturing his sleep.

"Are they still here?" he asked quickly. "Vereste, Konecki—"

"Should be, but not for long. Gabe was planning to lift him out around one o'clock."

Lindy sat impatiently as the program ran to the end.

Then Harpe turned to him. "Okay, I'm yours."

No, Lindy thought, you're his. Damned if we're not *all* his.

"Let's start with a profile on the men he's fingered," Lindy directed.

The computer operator raised his hands over the keyboard, kept them hovering in the air for a moment like a pianist about to strike the opening notes of a virtuoso piece. Then he started to tap out the request.

Leaving the electronics cabin, Lindy saw that the helicopter had been moved into position for a takeoff from the grass in front of the lodge. Lindy ran ahead up the slope.

He burst into Konecki's room without knocking. The marshal was packing his suitcase.

"I looked for you," Konecki said. "Got some good news."

"I know your news."

"Well, smile. It means you're sprung. There's nothing more you can do for us. You'll be taken out of here later today, along with young Vereste."

"Why isn't he going with you?"

"His father wants him to join his mother now, go back to school."

At last Vereste was going his way alone. That tied in, too.

Lindy took a sheaf of papers from his pocket and thrust them at Konecki. "I made these notes at the computer. Before you fly away with your precious witness, you ought to know what's in them."

Konecki reached out slowly. A quizzical expression remained on his face as he riffled through the notes.

"They don't speak to me."

"Then let me give you the bottom line," Lindy said grimly.

"You've been on a contract for Mr. Vereste. We all have. He's turned Uncle Sam into his hit man."

"What the hell are you talking about?"

Lindy snatched the notes back. "It's all here. He's been clobbering certain elements of the Mob, and favoring others; centralizing power by redesigning the geographical jurisdictions; wiping out cash resources of some families, while leaving others untouched; and, of course, amassing a fair amount of venture capital for himself. To sum it up, he's given the Organization the first really complete realignment and renovation its had since the Castellammarese Wars of the thirties—remolded it to be run more efficiently, along modern lines, by younger men."

"And I suppose," Konecki offered dryly, "since he's the mastermind, he expects to get the cream. Next time the Commission meets, he'll walk in, apologize, explain he really did it for their own good, everybody'll kiss and make up, and he'll be made the boss of bosses."

Lindy, ignoring Konecki's belittling tone, answered straight. "No, he'll stay the way he is—out of sight, anonymous, protected. And he'll still get the cream. He's going to run things by proxy, through a front man. Long ago he lined up someone who's in a position to ascend the throne, but who's willing to let Vereste be the power behind it."

Konecki smiled. "The latter being the same guy who tipped us on the battle plan."

"He'd be the odds-on favorite."

Konecki's smile faded. He studied Lindell carefully. "Jesus, you're dead serious, aren't you?"

"So's the computer."

"The answers you get out of a computer are colored by the way you ask the questions. If you had this cockeyed notion going in, Lindy, then the computer could easily rubber stamp it for you. But it isn't telepathic. It can't read Vereste's mind."

"You're wrong, Gabe. There's no better way to analyze his motives. Because he used it to kill off the competition. He put everything into it, made this an electronic vendetta, the Computer Vespers." Lindy glanced at his notes. "Let me give you a quick profile that fits all the men Vereste has named, with the exception of Frank Gardia—and let's say he was the pro-verbial rule-prover, deliberately thrown in to fudge the pat-tern. Every other man is over sixty-five years old, either born abroad or raised in the old-style Italian ghettoes of our cities, uneducated beyond a rudimentary level; and in the last year or two, all of them have been beefing up their families with young talent imported from the old country, boosting them over the homegrown product, creating potential heirs in their own image. Get it, Gabe? They're the old guard, the last conservatives. Vereste is cleaning them out, along with their loyal lieutenants."

Konecki laughed lightly. "And you needed a data bank to give you that? Shit, they've got to be the old guard. Vereste gave us what we wanted most, the top echelon. Naturally it took time for them to reach the top. And time, I'm reliably informed, makes people old."

"Yeah, I've even heard it makes people die," Lindy re-joined shortly, his anger growing at Konecki's refusal to lis-ten with an open mind. "For that matter, a lot of the old men have died off; the next generation has started to take over. There are quite a number of new bosses in their forties and early fifties, men raised in this country with some of the ad-vantages, not so hooked on the secret society mumbo jumbo. But the process is incomplete; the guard hasn't changed over all the way. That's resulted in a lot of internal dissension. For the past couple of years there's been constant static between the old men and the young; only small rumbles so far, but al-ways on the verge of exploding into something bigger, all-enveloping. What Vereste did was to push the transition through faster, to the end, but without tearing the Mob apart from the inside. Compared to past reorganizations, this one has been as neat and tidy as a corporate reshuffle at General Motors. Because he gave them an outside enemy to focus on. Us. We made most of the hits."

Konecki was shaking his head, incredulous.

Lindy searched through his notes. "Look, I did a geo-graphical breakdown. The way the territories were carved up is going to be entirely changed. Instead of three New England families, there'll be one. There were four in the Midwest, but when all the new information goes through,

278

they'll be down to two. No change in the Far West, but that's never been choked with competition. Now consider this state, New York: seven families down to four. In New York City alone there have been five families since God created Luciano. Suddenly two have lost all their officers, but three haven't been touched."

"Right," Konecki pounced. "And the three that have ridden it out are the Drapetto, Ligazza, and Francini families. I'd sure like to hear how that fits in with your hot idea, Lindy. Drapetto may be one of the young turks, but don't tell me Ligazza isn't old guard."

"The oldest," Lindy agreed. "He's seventy-nine or eighty, far enough gone to be left to die on his own—or maybe happy to retire, if he's given a nudge and looks around and sees that none of his cronies are left. For all we know, he may have stepped down already."

"And Francini," Konecki persisted, "I suppose you've pegged him as the front man for his *consigliere*. You really think he could hope to get away with that?"

"No. He's not the front man. My guess is Vereste is leaving him to Mob justice. As Vereste's *capo*, he's responsible for the defection in his ranks. If Dom Francini can't make good on finding his lost sheep, he'll go down himself. Any day now."

"You're doing well," Konecki acknowledged. "An answer for everything. Now maybe you can tell me how our duel at dawn suited the master plan. Don't tell me we did Vereste a favor by blowing away a major portion of the Mafia's enforcement arm."

"I wouldn't go so far as to say Vereste figured that into his operation," Lindy replied evenly. "But I'm sure it smoothed the way to a takeover."

"How?"

"You said yourself, Gabe, that the men who came in here amounted to only a portion of the Mob's armed strength. What do you think determined which enforcers joined the march, and which ones stayed home. Wouldn't the majority of those who volunteered to snuff Vereste be from the families who'd already suffered most, were hungriest for revenge? And they're the very ones Vereste wanted to stamp out. By losing their enforcers, they're weakened all the more."

279

There was a pause.

Then Konecki said, "God, Lindy, you must be good in a courtroom. You can argue anything, can go from pleading one side of the case to the other and hardly miss a beat. At the start of this deal you were all for it, the big booster, talked yourself and everyone else into believing it was the dawn of a new day. Oh, I understand the impulse: this was the chance to make up for all your wasted years in Washington. But now, because the victory doesn't look so sweet—because it never does in the end—you're making us the villains, the murderers, the dupes."

"Yes," Lindy declared, "we are. We set ourselves up for it by throwing away too much of the book. *We.* I admit it, I got suckered in, too. But at least I can see it now. Why can't you? Look at what we're giving Vereste. A bankroll, immunity from prosecution, a new face and identity that nobody in the street knows. And we're prepared to safeguard that identity—have to, in fact, for fear of sacrificing credibility to protect any future informers. The witness will be allowed to testify in camera, under his old name. The day the trials are over he'll walk away to start a new life. Or maybe just a new version of the old one."

"How could he, Lindy? We'll be watching him."

"Sure, up to a point. Watching, listening, taking his pulse. Exactly the way you've done for years, to all the big names in the Organization. You've stood outside their houses rain or shine, bugged their phones night and day, rousted their friends, squeezed their families. And hardly ever laid a finger on any of them—until the informers started coming. Now we've got the daddy of them all. But tell me, Gabe, when he's through testifying, if what I say is true, who'll inform on him? Only one man on the inside will know who he is, where he is, what he's become."

"The hypothetical collaborator," Konecki scoffed. "That's where it finally falls apart. If Vereste did dream up something like this, who could he get to agree to it? The man had to be established at a high level, someone in whom Vereste had ultimate trust—a close friend. And they must have spent time together, a good deal of time, cooking it up. Would the Mob have any trouble finding the man who fits that description? Any good friend of Vereste's is already being watched like a hawk by his brothers; he's on probation. If they ever make contact again, they're both dead."

"Unless," Lindy said, "it's a friend who became an enemy—his worst enemy. The one man nobody would ever suspect, because he'd already tried to kill the squealer once."

Konecki paused, turning the idea over. He moved slowly to an open dresser drawer, stood by it a moment, then lifted out a stack of shirts. Then he went back to the valise which lay open on the bed and continued packing.

Lindy waited for some response. When it didn't come, he walked to the bed and slammed the lid down on the valise.

Dropping the clothes, Konecki's arms went out from his sides, rigid, hands flexing. "I don't buy it," he said quietly, "that's all."

"No, you can't. But not because it won't hold together. You can't, because it scares the shit out of you, because you can't see what to do about it, because you'd have to admit that you're—"

"Because I can't see the point in worrying about what happens tomorrow!" Konecki shouted.

They faced each other tensely.

A knock on the door broke the silence. Konecki stomped over and opened it.

Harpe was outside, the tear sheet from a teleprinter in one hand. He read the anger in Konecki's face, then looked past him and got the same message from Lindy.

"Oh," he murmured, "sorry to interrupt. But I thought you'd want this, Gabe, hot off the wire."

"What?" Konecki snapped.

"State Police were called to a motel in a place named Gloversville, not too far from here. The proprietor was found dead this morning, shot. When the cops checked through the place, they found one room full of telephones, and a stolen army radio. Looks like it must've been the command post for the Mafia action. Whoever was there obviously heard their boys getting creamed over the radio, so they scattered. The proprietor was promptly iced so he couldn't ID any of his guests for the night."

Konecki shook his head. "Beautiful people," he whispered.

"And that's not all," Harpe went on. "There was a big hit only half an hour ago, out on Long Island. Dom Francini. They got him at home, blew up the whole house, probably with a couple of leftover rockets."

Konecki took the tear sheet and scanned it. "Thanks, Harpo," he said then. "Get some rest now. Wake Dice and tell him to take over."

Harpe nodded and left. Konecki closed the door, walked back to the dresser and began transferring more clothes to his suitcase.

Lindy waited another moment, hoping something might have changed. He had called it perfectly with Dom Francini. Why not the rest of it?

But Konecki said nothing.

Lindy went to the door. As he opened it, Konecki said:

"Even if you were right, Lindy, what could we do about it now? Kill him?"

Lindy slammed the door without looking back. In the corridor he turned unthinkingly toward Vereste's room. The question echoed in his brain, tingled on his nerves. What could you do?

Vereste's room was empty. The drawers turned out, the bed stripped.

Lindy went outside. From the porch, he saw Vereste, standing at the end of the dock with his son. Evidently they had strolled down there to say their good-byes. Lindy walked toward the lake, but stopped halfway, putting himself on the path Vereste would have to take to board the helicopter.

Vereste spotted him then. Interrupting the conversation with his son, who sat down in a deck chair, Vereste walked off the dock alone and climbed the hill.

"I guess you've heard I'm leaving," he said as Lindy approached. "I couldn't go without thanking you for all your help."

"I set it up perfectly, didn't I?" Lindy said ironically. "But don't thank me yet. I'm not going to let you take the big prize."

Vereste hung back, kept a distance between them as if sensing an aura of danger around Lindy.

"What prize?" he asked, expressionless.

282

"An empire. Isn't that what you want now?" Lindy stepped closer to Vereste, closing the gap. "I know your history, what happened when you married, how it made you over. You never came to terms with it, did you? Somewhere inside you remember what it was to feel clean, but you know you can never have it again. So this is the only way to go: if you have to be one of them, put them all under your heel; make them all sorry, one way or another, that they didn't leave you out of it long ago. And while you're at it, use the rest of us, shit on the system, prove that no one is clean. Maybe then you can live with yourself—when you can believe there never was any virtue to lose in the first place."

"You're imagining things, Lindell."

"Oh? Did I imagine that someone on the inside helped to save your skin?"

"He must've had his own reasons."

"Like the guy at Wonderworld had his own—for missing you. Was that really just bad aim? From a gunman who could pick off the two men walking on either side of you, one shot for each, and then a kid to chalk up that extra quota of headlines that made us so hungry for your talk? He could do all that so efficiently and yet never get his sights on you?"

Vereste opened his mouth to speak, but then snapped it determinedly shut.

"What were you going to say?" Lindy goaded. "That you're sorry about the kid, you didn't know who'd get it in the crowd, left all those details to your partner?" He moved up on Vereste. "It's Gesolo, isn't it? He didn't really mind about his daughter. You invented a feud, so no one would suspect he's working with you."

Vereste smiled thinly, lips compressed.

"Not a word," Lindy demanded, "not even going to take the Fifth?"

Vereste looked off to one side, then the other.

When Vereste began to speak, Lindy realized that he'd been checking to make sure they were out of earshot, removed from anyone who could bear witness to his confession. "I don't mind telling you now, Lindell. You've almost got it right. All except the part about Gesolo. Oh, yes, Rocco minded plenty about his *cara figlia*. He found us in bed

283

together, you see, the first time it happened for us, in Florida. Almost killed me right there. Would have, if Marianna hadn't told him about all the others. College boys, beach boys, waiters, gas station attendants, a procession of them, going way back, starting when she was thirteen. Always carefully selected, of course, from outside the Honored Society. She's some little number, all right. I wasn't the seducer, she was. And all the time Rocco'd been planning a white wedding with some royalty from the *amici*, figuring that would help him take over as the number one when Ligazza died. When she told him the truth—in language that left no doubt about what she was—Rocco was so wild at her, he let me off. He was even grateful when I said I loved her, wanted to marry her. It was that, of course, which led us into some mutual bitching about the bullshit traditions that tied everyone in knots. Rocco was especially worked up about it because he had Ligazza over him, and the old man looked like he'd live forever. So then we started getting ideas together." He shrugged amiably. "And you started getting phone calls."

He had told it coolly, arrogantly. Not a confession, after all, but a boast. He had been unable to resist taking the credit because there was still nothing to stop him.

Lindy's simmering frustration boiled over. He swung, connected, his fist pounding into the leering, gloating face. He felt something snap under his knuckles, and then remembered the surgery, the realignments of bone and skin barely healed.

Vereste went down immediately, put his hands over his face, cowering.

But Lindy would not let him surrender. He reached down, grabbed Vereste by the shirt, dragged him up, and then clubbed him down again. And fell over him, hands going to the throat.

Then Lindy was pulled away roughly. Around him he saw Konecki, Snoot, Finch. They all had a hold on him and were breathing hard, having sprinted from somewhere unseen during a span of time that had not existed in Lindy's universe.

How long had it been?

His eyes focused on Vereste, sprawled on the ground, his son kneeling over him.

He was taking in air in quick, desperate gasps. Not dead.

"My God, Lindell," said Finch, who was tightly gripping Lindy's arm. "What the hell got into you? A government witness! And you'd have killed him if we hadn't pried you loose."

Killed. Murdered. Not simply his foot on a gas pedal this time, thought Lindy, not even in self-defense. But with his bare hands. Savagely, primitively, for revenge.

And that, too, would have been a kind of victory for Vereste.

"What do we do, Gabe?" said Finch, clearly referring to the treatment of Lindell.

Konecki glanced down at Vereste. "You all right?"

Vereste lifted his eyes to stare at Lindy. "Never felt better."

"Put him on the chopper," Konecki told Finch.

Vereste stood, with his son's help. Mark Vereste looked fiercely at Lindy until his father pulled him away. Accompanied by Finch and Snoot, they walked toward the helicopter.

Konecki and Lindy were alone. "You really would have finished him."

Lindy nodded.

"Anyone who saw it would know," Konecki continued, "and would swear to it. That's a serious charge, attempted murder. Especially when the victim's under government protection. At the least, you'd be disbarred; on the heavy end, you could draw time in the slam."

"He admitted it, Gabe," Lindy said. "I told him I knew what he was angling for, and he admitted it. He and Gesolo cooked it up together."

Konecki nodded placidly. "Good, Lindy, I'm glad you had the satisfaction of knowing you're right. But it doesn't change anything. We still need him. We'll use him as long as we can, and then . . . we'll see. It's too soon to worry about his angle. For now, we just play ours."

"But you don't have one. That's an illusion. In the end, you'll be right back where you started." Lindy paused. "No, not even that. You'll be way behind. The law will be a joke.

The Mob won't need to own the judges anymore, not while the men on top know they can always turn the law around to work for themselves."

"I don't see it that way," Konecki said. "But if that's what you believe, then do something about it. Change the law, make it work better. Don't expect guys like me to do it. We're only the enforcers."

"Funny," Lindy said, "I thought that was a Mob word."

There was a silence.

Konecki turned and waved a signal to Snoot, who was sitting in his pilot's seat, looking out the front window of the chopper. Framed in one of the windows behind him was Vereste, still smiling.

The helicopter motor coughed, whined; the rotor turned, spun faster. The artificial wind whipped across the field.

"See you in Washington," Konecki said, and started away.

"You bet your ass you will," Lindy shouted after him. "And Vereste will, too. Tell him!"

Konecki climbed aboard the helicopter, the door closed. Finch and Mark Vereste backed out from under the turning rotor, the marshal standing as a buffer between Lindy and the son of the man he had almost killed.

The helicopter rose straight up a long way before it began to glide forward. Lindy watched the ascent and swore inwardly:

You won't get away.

He mustn't get away. Let one man be immune, above the law, able to twist it to his own ends without punishment, and the whole system was poisoned.

But the way to stop Vereste was not by gun, by primitive force. Sure, you could kill him, but someone else would step right into his shoes. He wasn't really one of a kind. There was only one way to stop Vereste, what he represented.

The law must be made to work. Not with tricks, not with prizes. By and for itself.

Maybe Ryle's way. In Washington. A haunted city, perhaps, but not a ghost town yet. Tomorrow he'd get to Tom, tell him the end of the story. He might be given another chance—if he begged for it. And if the chance wasn't there, if Ryle couldn't forgive, there were other ways to go. To Mack

286

Sunderland, others, anybody who would listen. It would add up.

Lindy started toward the lodge; he had his own packing to do. Behind him, the noise of the helicopter motor reverberated out of the mountain valleys. From the porch, he looked back once more, searched the horizon. But the machine was gone, the sky was empty. Only the drumming sound remained, fainter now. Then silence.

He had his work cut out for him, all right. It could even be a life's work. With any luck.